BR⊗KEN GEARS

ROOK'S GAMBIT

DANA FRAEDRICH

Other Titles By Dana Fraedrich

Interior Design for Intergalactic Travelers

SKATEBOARDS, MAGIC, AND SHAMROCKS
Skateboards, Magic, and Shamrocks
Heroes, Legends, and Villains

BROKEN GEARS
Out of the Shadows (Lenore's storyline 1)
Into the Fire (Lenore's storyline 2)
Raven's Cry (standalone prequel)
Across the Ice (Lenore's storyline 3)
Falcon's Favor (standalone queer cozy mystery romance)
Death Cults and Taxes (short story collection)
Rook's Gambit (standalone heist adventure)

ESPEC BOOKS' FORGOTTEN LORE ANTHOLOGY INCLUSIONS
A Careful Application of Fish → *A Cast of Crows*
Amber Waves of Bane → *A Cry of Hounds*
Imagination Unbound → *An Assembly of Monsters*
Rules for Haunting → *A Curiosity of Cats*

This book is a work of fiction. Any references to historical events, real people, or real locales are used fictitiously. Other names, characters, places, and incidents are the product of the author's imagination, and any resemblance to actual events or locales or persons, living or dead, is entirely coincidental.

Copyright 2025 Dana Fraedrich

Maps by Hannah Pickering, Heather Boyajian, and Dana Fraedrich

Cover digital scrapbook pieces courtesy Doudou's Design

Book cover by Dana Fraedrich

Chapter heading art by Dana Fraedrich

Content Warning: This book contains death, grief, child abuse, and bullying.

ISBN: 9798987843611

WordsByDana.com

For Grandpa, the master locksmith who taught me how to pick locks as
a child.

The Continent Of
Invarnis
Duskwood
Springhaven
(Formerly Prism)
Cobalt
Bay
Dogwood
Lane
Bone
Port
Bone
Bay

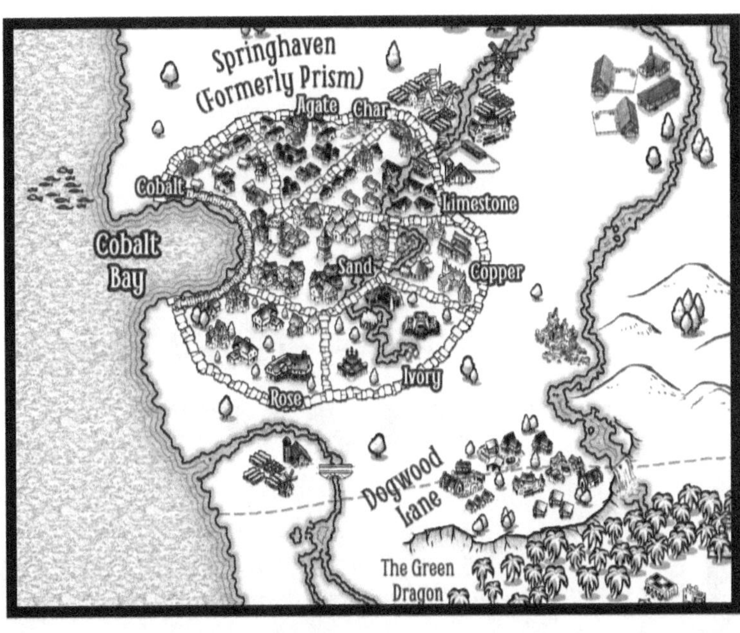

Springhaven
(Formerly Prism)
Agate
Char
Cobalt
Limestone
Cobalt
Bay
Sand
Copper
Ivory
Rose
Dogwood
Lane
The Green
Dragon

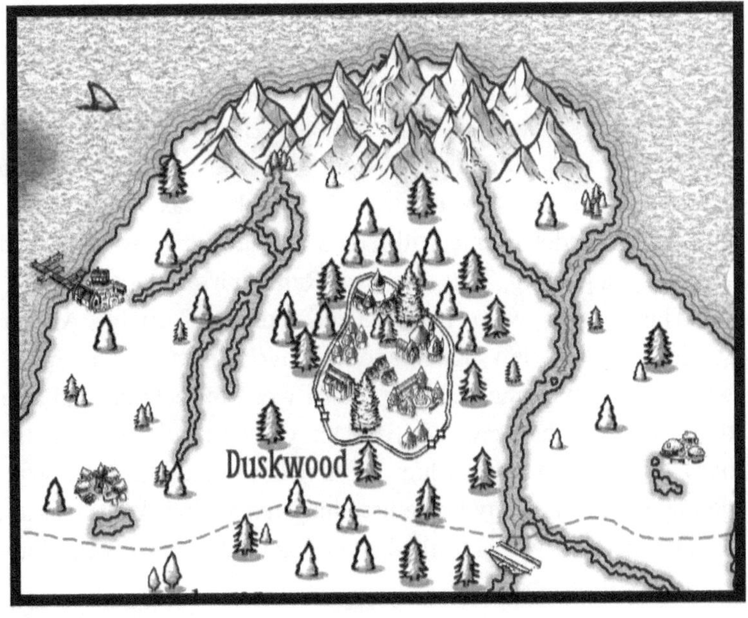

Duskwood

0
PETTY REVENGE POWER PLAY

octor Clotworthy's Finest Itching Inducer. Completely natural! One-hundred percent pure ground rose hips. No harsh chemicals...

Varick trailed off from reading. Why did it matter that a prank was all natural? Was there really such a strong demand in the joke shop industry for such things? He shrugged to himself and looked back through the large, stone entryway, back to the stables where his grandfather, Randolph, was busy petting Tallywags. Rudely-named, ill-tempered but highly bribable, and, ironically, a gelding, Tallywags was Randolph's favorite horse.

The stables were quiet at this time of night. All the stablehands had left hours ago to have dinner and attend to whatever people who actually had to work for a living did after their workday had ended. Even knowing this, Varick listened hard for anyone besides himself and his grandfather. Only the gentle noises of sleepy horse breathing resounded. Well, that and Randolph's soft words to the beloved animal, and the occasional crunch of apple slices.

"Better hurry up," Randolph cooed, letting the horse lip another piece out of him palm.

The soft words floated easily through to Varick, just inside the attached carriage house. In the stall next to Tallywags', Silken Sunflower was stirring. They should have brought more treats. She'd make a fuss if she saw her neighbor getting goodies and not her, so Varick returned his attention to the mission. He'd read the safety precautions three times already—don't breathe it in, don't let it get onto your skin or into your eyes, don't leave within reach of children. That last one made Varick grin. He was still a child, *technically*, for the next year and a halfish.

Wearing an old pair of leather gloves, he carefully unscrewed the lid of the jar and set it aside, onto the mounting step of his older brother's phaeton, a sleek, sporty little open-topped carriage. Then, covering his mouth and nose with the sleeve of his evening jacket, Varick began to sprinkle the phaeton's seat with the fine powder. It shone like dust motes in the faint light of the petrolsene lamps they'd just barely turned on, before disappearing into the plush, velvet upholstery. If anyone asked, they were here to visit Tallywags, which wasn't a lie, just not the whole truth.

That was how Varick and Randolph survived the rest of the scorpion nest that was their family. The other members of the Pendragon clan were always trying to take, take, *take*—joy, confidence, secrets, peace of mind, pride, anything they could— so Randolph had taught Varick long ago how to only give over the barest bits of information, never anything extra.

Silken Sunflower was starting to nicker at Randolph, who showed his empty hands to her.

"Varick," he called softly, a touch of beseeching in his voice.

Silken Sunflower wasn't buying it. She shook her head and stretched her nose toward Randolph's waistcoat pocket.

"I'm nearly done!" Varick whisper-called back. He'd faced

away from the phaeton before removing his face from his sleeve to answer. Maybe he was being overly cautious, but he didn't want to risk inhaling the fine powder.

While Varick sprinkled the last bit of fine, velvet seating with Doctor Clotworthy's Finest Itching Inducer, Randolph allowed Silken Sunflower to explore his pockets, which left small, golden hairs across the expertly woven fabric. She might start throwing a tantrum otherwise.

"Done!" Varick announced.

It would not teach Magnus not to leave cat poo outside the door of Varick's apartments after the housemaids had been in—though better outside his door to end up on his freshly shined shoes than under his pillow and worse, which was precisely why Varick kept his doors locked. No, Magnus could not know Varick was behind his future itching fit, so the lunkhead would learn nothing. But Varick would feel some small, twisted sense of victory while his brother harmlessly suffered. No members of staff could be blamed, so no one would be unfairly sacked—Varick had checked this with Randolph, just in case there was some risk he hadn't thought of. And though his grandfather never partook directly in Varick's petty revenges, he'd long been there as a sort of guide. You didn't hurt the innocent, no matter how badly you yourself were hurting. That was the rule. It was frustrating at times, but Varick agreed. Randolph had taught him to understand power dynamics and fairness, or rather, the *un*fairness of the world.

Tonight had not been frustrating, though. Tonight had been a complete success! After securely re-capping the bottle and carefully doffing his gloves into a small pouch he'd attached to his belt, Varick quickly but quietly scuttled back over to where Randolph was letting Silken Sunflower snuffle, rootle, and shed over his entire person for treats. A piece of dropped apple lay nearby, half-hidden under a bit of hay sticking out from the stall door. Varick wasted no time in plying the spoiled, amber mare with it. That settled her, and when Varick turned back to his grandfather, he found the man examining the damage to his attire.

"She really went for it," he said, holding up a half-detached, cracked button.

Then Randolph began to sway. He caught himself on the nearby stall bars, just as Varick had begun to reach for him. The man was chuckling before Varick could even speak.

"That wine at dinner tonight must have gone to my head," he said. "I am getting to be a lightweight these days."

Varick examined his grandfather. He was already back to looking at his clothes, albeit with one hand still gripping the bars of Silken Sunflower's stall.

"You sure you're alright?" he asked.

"Of course, of course." Randolph gestured toward the pouch at Varick's hip, and it's itchy contents. "Just make sure none of that rubs off on you or any of your other clothes. Or misery will have what it loves best."

Varick smiled. Magnus had plans to go driving tomorrow. He wouldn't shut up about it at dinner that night. Varick couldn't wait to see how his idiot brother fared by tomorrow evening.

"I'll repair your button for you," Varick volunteered as the two made their way out of the stables. "There's a new technique I just read about that I'd like to try. I can show you if you want."

"And so the pupil has become the teacher," Randolph said, his dark eyes warm and twinkling. He put a hand on Varick's shoulder and gave it a loving squeeze. "I'm proud of you."

Varick beamed, and they plodded up the path and back around to the family house together.

1

DEATH AND COAL

Varick felt no change as death slipped in. His grandfather, Randolph, might have just been sleeping. His hand, which Varick held between his own, still effused warmth as it always had in life. On the other side of the sickbed, the family doctor, a man called Gillespie, cradled the old man's wrist between his fingers. Doctor Gillespie referred to a bronze pocket watch sitting open in his other hand, though Varick already knew it wouldn't be necessary. The doctor's frown deepened. He shook his head. He fiddled with something on the side of the watch, and Varick looked away. As per custom, Doctor Gillespie stopped the watch at the time of death. In his periphery, Varick saw the doctor place the stopped timepiece on Randolph's unmoving chest—a silent statement that his job here was done.

Outside the tall, broad windows, birds flitted and frolicked in the bright autumn sunshine. A bell tinkled somewhere outside—likely a courier racing by on a velocipede. On the one hand, it didn't feel real, or perhaps that was just numbness. And on the other hand, Varick felt it very rude for the world to continue on so bloody normally when time had just stopped for Randolph. The least it could do was give them all a moment, a pause to respect the life that had just passed.

"Well, that's that then," came a voice like frosted steel. It blew cold and sharp from right behind Varick and had even less compassion than the world. He resisted the urge to flinch, the same battle he had fought daily for all his almost-fifteen years.

Chairs and fabric shifted in unison, a susurration of whispers behind his back. Now came the change.

Desperation clawed at Varick from the inside. *No,* he thought. *Please, don't leave me. Not with them.*

"Come, Varick," snapped the icy voice.

His grandmother, Patricia. Varick had never understood how Randolph could have married her. Money, position, and family expectations, of course, were the whys of it. But in all the ways she was cold and hard, Randolph had been warm and soft. Varick wanted to obey Patricia's command. He knew what would happen if he tarried. But a lump was forming in his throat, a stone so heavy it threatened to pull his head onto the side of the sickbed. Heat prickled in his eyes. Varick wanted nothing more than to lay his head down and weep.

"I said come," Patricia said. Her tone was all the warning he would get.

Legs shaking, Varick lifted himself from his chair, hauling the stone in his throat up with him. His eyes looked to his grandfather's face again. Peaceful. And then to where he clasped the man's cooling hand. He refused to lift his eyes to Doctor Gillespie. Much as Varick didn't want to see what waited behind him, he wanted even less to see pity in the doctor. Pity was useless in a house like this, now that his grandfather was gone. Varick swallowed hard. Swallowed again, trying to force everything down. He turned.

Standing behind him were the rest of his family. Not all-*all* of them. No, all that would more than take up the entire room, and there were no small rooms within the Dragon's Keep—the vast manse that housed the top echelon of the Pendragon clan. All bore dark, piercing eyes, dark hair, and—except for Patricia— various shades of copper-colored skin. Patricia's skin was fair and slightly pink, like the outside of a scallop shell, which suited the hard, cutting woman perfectly. Most, like Varick, were slender as well, like snakes. And every one of them, dressed in the finest frocks and jackets money could buy, looked at him as if he were a stain.

"I want Varick here, next to me," Randolph had croaked in his final moments. It seemed like an age ago now.

His last words had been for his youngest grandson. Not his wife or son or either of his other grandchildren.

Hate seared Varick from every direction, every gaze a focused beam of dark light wishing to skewer him. He imagined cold collected behind him with each second that Randolph's spirit no longer inhabited his body. Varick gathered the cold around himself. He wanted to appear aloof, impervious to their scathing stares. He tried to wear it like armor against them, but it only drove home the sense of loss.

"You are strong, and clever, and capable." At the end, Randolph had wheezed these words to Varick so softly that he'd had to strain not to miss anything. "You deserve love. I love you, Varick, and that's something they can never take away. Remember, for me."

His grandfather, the one who had always shielded Varick, was gone. Forever. Varick's vision blurred, and his throat tightened.

"Are you *crying*?" The question came from Varick's father, Henry. The older man said last word like it was a particularly offensive habit. How could he he be so indifferent about the death of his father?

Varick shrank in his spot. He looked down, willing the tears to dry up. A sharp rapping snagged him by the chin and yanked his head back up—years of conditioning, lest his head be yanked up for him. Patricia gripped her ivory cane in both bony hands, rings glittering from atop her satin gloves.

"Stop that right now, or I'll give you something to cry about." She narrowed one eye at him, focusing her aim.

Using his thumb and hoping to make the move look graceful, Varick wiped away his tears. He tensed every muscle, as if that would squeeze his tear ducts shut. It seemed to work, for the moment.

A giggle tittered from the other side of the room. Varick slid his eyes that direction. Behind his mother, stood his siblings, Constance and Magnus. Constance was grinning behind her hand as she whispered to Magnus. Varick couldn't hear what she was saying, nor did he want to know.

Another rap on the floor from Patricia's cane snapped Varick's attention back. When she spoke, she sounded as if they'd just wrapped up a boring meeting. "We're done here."

The family filed out by rank. First Patricia, then Varick's parents, followed by Magnus and Constance. Varick turned around one last time. Doctor Gillespie was standing a little ways off. He devoted his energy to being unobtrusive as he scribbled into a small notebook. Varick looked at his grandfather's face a moment more, but pressure rushed back into his eyes. He averted his gaze to the bronze watch still sitting on Randolph's chest. None of the rest of his family had even looked at it. Varick took it, spun, and left, knowing his old life—a better life—had died alongside his grandfather.

Randolph Pendragon
Forever in our hearts

Varick wanted to smack the urn to the ground. The words engraved on the the little plaque at its base mocked him, yet he couldn't tear his eyes away. He pulled at his collar. The stiff white fabric, starched within an inch of its life, itched as it pressed into the flesh below his jaw. His cravat was choking him. All around him, ladies dressed in black crepe and men in ebony suits talked in muted tones. They spilled out from the grand main hall into the tiled loggia and from there throughout the gardens, all sipping at gilt-edged glasses and snacking on canapés. Waiters carried the delicate treats on shining trays in a sort of somber dance through the crowd. The urn sat in pride of place in the center of the room on a stand, with cypress boughs and marigolds for decor. Top hats bobbed throughout the space as insincere condolences were shared, followed closely by gossip. None of these people cared, Varick knew. They all just wanted to know to whom Randolph had bequeathed what. Randolph'd had his fingers in more pies than a baker, and therefore had accumulated some independent wealth not tied up in the Pendragon estate. That in itself was not so strange. All the Pendragons tried to do the same—family money could only get one so far. But no one knew just how many income streams Randolph'd had, nor how deep and wide those streams flowed. Of course, the rumor mill had plenty of theories.

His own private fortune rivaled the Pendragon family's.

Everything was in gold bars, so that his wealth increased with gold values.

He had a secret vault containing all of his many riches.

And while the guests postulated and whispered and gossiped, every eye scanned for weaknesses, whether it be in dress or otherwise.

Varick gripped the stopped fob watch in his pocket. Its slight weight was a life buoy in a grey, cold sea. He rubbed his thumb along the back, feeling the inscription there he'd seen thousands of times: *Never apart.* The watch had been a gift to Randolph from his older sister, Megaera. She was Varick's great aunt, who he hardly knew at all, but, by Randolph's accounts anyway, was actually a really lovely person, and, Varick assumed, was also currently wandering around here somewhere. The inscription made him angry now. A stinking load of bull dung, that was. Randolph was gone, though Varick's brain still hadn't accepted it. Unbidden, thoughts he wanted to share with his grandfather kept popping up in his mind—random, little natterings; complaints both big and small; things he was excited about—only for the realization to wash over him once more that he'd never again get to share anything with Randolph.

An unwelcome noise finally pried Varick's gaze from the urn and its taunting words. It was the *tap-tap* of Patricia's cane on the floor. Coming closer. Varick skittered in the opposite direction from the sound. His lithe frame allowed him to slide between "mourners" like a well dressed cat. Names ticked off in his head as he passed.

Onion Breath Uncle Jason.

Cousin Mason, the brown-noser.

Other cousin Leopold, as interesting as a wet mop.

Other-other cousin Chester, the family accountant.

And Barnacle Morgan. Varick couldn't remember exactly how she was related, but he seemed to remember her being removed a time or two, whatever that meant. Varick's relations might well outnumber the stars.

The only people he didn't recognize were the mutes, professional mourners paid by the family to enlarge their black parade of supporters. As if the Pendragon clan needed any help to be numerous. They were like rabbits. Vicious, back-biting rabbits with red eyes and sharp, pointy teeth.

Varick found a spot by the wall, behind a massive plinth, half as tall as he was and topped with an equally tall vase and arrangement of funeral flowers. Varick rather liked flowers. Flowers didn't have to be anything but pretty, but the heavy redolence seeping from the vase's huge gathering of poppies drenched Varick. It coated his tongue, thick and cloying. He made a face, equal parts grateful for the obscenely large decor that hid him and embarrassed by it. The Pendragons never did anything over the top, but they continually flirted with the other side of that line.

He watched as Patricia led indolent Uncle Albert to the urn and gestured to it. She pressed a hand to her chest, but her handkerchief remained parched and unmoved from where she'd tucked it into her sleeve that morning. Varick clenched his hands into fists at his side.

If only the old toad would dry up into the husk she is, he thought.

He reached into his pocket again. Rubbing his thumb over the watch's intricate engraving called up memories of Randolph schooling Varick on his temper.

If you react, they've won. That's why they try so hard, so they can claim more victories.

Varick drew a long, slow breath through his nose the way Randolph had taught him. And again. Control ebbed back into Varick's muscles, shaky and tenuous though it was.

"Five coppers says they don't keep up the sham for a month."

Varick jumped, narrowly avoiding knocking into the vase. The small voice had floated just behind his ear, though he hadn't seen or heard anyone approach. He turned to find a boy a few years his junior, about thirteen, standing there. A skinny frame with dark skin, eyes, and hair. He was fairly innocuous looking. In fact, on first glance, Varick had thought him even younger, but that had been down to the fact that he was a tad small for his age. The lad wore the typical somber funeral attire of an upperclass young gentleman, but one look told Varick the suit was straight off the rack. No frills, no embellishments, just solid seams and good—but not exquisite—fabric. Definitely not a Pendragon. The boy clearly hadn't spent a day of his life in comportment lessons. He slouched even as he leaned against the wall. But at least he was looking solemn. *Actually* solemn, the way one is supposed to look at a funeral, unlike every single member of Varick's family.

One of the mutes then? Who had, ironically enough, just broken the cardinal rule of being a mute by speaking. Varick looked him up and down again. The respectful expression, coupled with the way he'd seen right through the charade, poked a pinhole of light into Varick's dismal mood.

"It won't even be that long," Varick replied. "They'll be phasing out of black within a week."

It would be a subtle transition. Starting with deep plums, evergreen, and indigo, they would slowly fade to amethyst, emerald, and sapphire. The upper classes had stopped observing the usual mourning dress traditions so long ago, it was now seen as its own sort of status game—how artfully could one slide across the color spectrum from mourning garb back to normal dress. The lower classes, who didn't have money to buy garments in every hue, were stuck with the traditional black until the appropriate mourning period had ended. A sudden, stark change from one to the other before the appointed time was one of the worst ways the lower classes could bring scandal upon themselves.

"Yeah. 'Spose you'd know better than me," the boy said. His gaze flitted over the assembled crowd, this time with hunger shining in them.

Varick swept his gaze over the boy again. The jacket hung oddly on him. Mutes were provided clothes by the hiring agency, so it hadn't been tailor-made especially for him like Varick's had, but that wasn't the problem. It was in the shoulders and around the torso. More lessons from Randolph surfaced. The boy barely filled the jacket because it was just his bones holding it up. Varick looked at the boy's wrists. Sure enough, scarecrow thin.

"What's your name?" Varick asked.

If you're going to ask an impertinent question, make certain to do it with respect and use the person's name, Randolph had always advised.

The boy cut his eyes to Varick, but he didn't have any of the guardedness Varick saw when he looked at himself in the mirror. "Coal. You?"

Varick hesitated before he realized he was doing it. Why should he hesitate? This boy was nothing to him, just someone who'd move out of his life by the end of this shameful charade. He mustered his best manners the way Randolph had always shown him and even summoned a smile. It was faint, but it was there.

"Varick Pendragon, pleased to meet you."

He was about to begin a new line of conversation when Coal beat him to it. "Glad to meet you too, Varick Pendragon. And now that we're properly introduced, I should say I'm sorry."

Varick's smile turned down into a confused pucker. "Sorry? Sorry for what?"

"For this." And Coal reached forward and shoved the ridiculously large vase from the plinth.

Varick watched in shock as it fell and smashed into a million pieces on the creamy marble floor. Silence sucked every ounce of air from the room. Every eye turned onto Varick. Heat tingled and climbed up his neck.

"What *have* you done?" Unsurprisingly, the question came from Patricia, still standing before Randolph's urn.

"Don't let him near Grand Daddy," added his sister

Constance from nearby. "What a tragedy if little Ricky broke him."

Varick's insides writhed. "It wasn't me!" he blurted. "It was…" He turned back, gesturing to where Coal had stood not moments before.

The boy had vanished.

Through the crowd, Varick's mother, Victoria, approached. Her height, accentuated by her coiffure, created a stately form. People parted for her as shoals of fish part for a shark. The black crepe veil draped fashionably over her hair served as the telltale dorsal fin of her approach.

"Varick," she intoned. That one word spoke volumes. Her disappointment, her anger, her expectation for him to apologize to everyone. *Now*.

The heat from Varick's neck rose into his face. He was not even supposed to blush unless it was intentional, and only ladies should make themselves blush, and only at fortuitous moments. More scorn twisted his mother's face into an even deeper frown.

Stop, Varick begged of his body. In response, he started to sweat.

"I'm sor—" His voice cracked.

Somewhere else in the room, Magnus barked out a laugh. It had been short, but he hadn't tried to hide it. His mother took a deep breath and placed slender fingers against her temple, as if she was getting a headache.

Varick wished he could sink between the marble tiles. He remained perfectly solid, however. Everyone continued to stare silently as if they had all rehearsed for just such a moment as this. The sound of someone clearing their throat—it sounded a bit like a growl and definitely like Varick's father—echoed through the room.

"I'm sorry, everyone." Varick pushed out the words as steadily as he could. "I'm… I'm very distressed. Please excuse me."

He knew he shouldn't run, shouldn't have reacted. The entire display had shown weakness from every angle. Venomous words people didn't bother to quiet slithered after him, sinking their syllabic fangs into him.

"I hear he's always acting out for attention like this. And to think the other two are so well turned out."

"He always has been the frail one in the family."

"You would think he'd behave well today of all days, after how Randolph doted on him."

As soon as he was out of eye line and earshot, Varick dashed as fast as he could up the grand staircase and as far from the others as he could.

2
CLOSETED SCHEMES

arick pushed the door to his sister's room open. It swung noiselessly on well-oiled hinges. Thick rugs swallowed any sound his tiptoeing might have made. Not that there was much danger there; he was an expert tiptoer. Though all the guests in attendance were likely running the house staff off their feet, he glanced around, ears and eyes sharp for signs of one nearby. All remained still and quiet in the long, opulent corridor, just as it had been when Varick had gone to Magnus' room just now and nicked a silver letter opener.

Varick often stole small possessions from his siblings when they'd been particularly nasty to him. He'd always leave them to be found somewhere else later, after it had been long enough to make the absence properly frustrating—somewhere incriminating if he could frame them for some other little mischief. Though never in a way that would get innocent members of staff in trouble… innocent, being the operative word. Guilty, however, was another story.

There had been that one time when Varick's father had locked him in a storage cupboard for two whole days after Varick's horse had broken a leg. Varick had jumped a hedge and hadn't realized the other side was soft from the rain. The horse had lost its footing, and Varick had barely escaped serious injury. The stable master had the animal put down that very evening, despite Varick's insistence that a new healing contraption was on the market—a spring-riddled exo-casing that would support an animal's injured leg while it recuperated. He'd read about it in a gentleman's magazine and had railed against both his father and the stable master's stubborn idea that there was "nothing to be done." He'd gone so far as to dash from the room where he'd argued with both men and headed for the stables. To do what, given that the poor animal was lame, he didn't know. But Varick had loved that horse and had suffered in the cupboard for defending it. Later, he'd stolen his father's favorite cufflinks and planted them in the room of the stable master, who'd been summarily sacked for the theft.

This was how Varick vented his rage and fought the injustices within his own life. It was all he could do. He occasionally applied his little revenge schemes to his parents, though there wasn't as much reward there. His parents weren't accountable to anyone, except perhaps Patricia in some respects, and those three were too deeply allied for Varick's thefts to have much effect.

Now, inside Constance's apartments, Varick took care to soundlessly close the main door behind him, keeping the handle turned so the latch wouldn't click. For her earlier cruel words downstairs, he'd decided to tamper in one of her jewelry cases. Earlier that week at tea, she'd mentioned a black pearl set she was excited to wear soon. Excited. Because they'd all known Randolph's death was coming. The man had deteriorated quickly in what Doctor Gillespie had described as a "cascading systems failure." Varick scowled at the memory. Yes, if he did it right, the silk cord stringing the pearls together would break soon after she donned it. At an inopportune moment, he hoped, but that bit would be out of his control.

From the entrance, it was a quick, straight zip through her sitting room, across the bedroom, and then into her dressing room.

The dressing room was rather like a giant closet with ambitions of becoming a fashion showroom. Constance had several mannequin displays for her brand new, newly updated, or just plain favorite ensembles, while all the rest waited their turn on well-spaced, circular, spinning racks—one did not risk crushing crushed velvet and other fine fabrics. How the house staff kept the exposed gear works for the racks both well-oiled and sparkling clean was impressive and mysterious. A vanity table sat off to one wall with its legs demurely concealed by a floor-length dust ruffle. Heaven forfend that anyone see a well-turned, wooden leg and be tempted into *ideas*.

Like clothing, particular pieces of jewelry were displayed in pride of place as well. Having closed the dressing room door with as much care as the others, Varick turned his gaze into his sister's private sanctum and began his sweep for the black pearl set. Not half a second into the search, however, he froze.

Coal stood at one of Constance's many jewelry cases, also frozen. His hand was closed around a topaz necklace, mid-lift from where it usually rested on a velvet pillow.

Varick's eyes bugged out of his head. "What do you think you're doing in here?"

"Nothing." Coal delivered his answer in an inconceivably innocent tone, given that he'd been caught red-handed. And he still hadn't moved.

"You can't tell me nothing." Varick gestured to the hanging topaz necklace. "You're clearly in the middle of filching my sister's jewelry."

Coal's eyes narrowed as a smirk stretched across his face. "And what are *you* doing here?"

Varick blanched and shifted his gaze, searching for an excuse. Of course, there was none to be found. Not only was it the height of unseemly for a gentleman to be in a lady's boudoir, he was deep in enemy territory.

People knew he didn't get on with his siblings. Though, like so many things, his parents had turned what would have been a mark of shame for anyone else into an advantage. Magnus and Constance were trophy children in the usual way of trophy children everywhere—high-achieving, though only in the *correct* areas, and keeping up all the right appearances. Varick, however, was the inverted version of this, an infamous problem child. He pushed back and asked why all the time. He'd been that way as long as he could remember. He didn't know why. Perhaps his parents and grandmother had missed the window to get their claws into him. They already had two children to dote on, after all, and Varick had always heard that he'd been an unhappy baby. Thus, Randolph had taken Varick under his wing early on, so perhaps that explained his "rebellious tendencies," as his parents and grandmother had put it. Or perhaps it was simply something ingrained in him from birth. Whatever the reason, his parents had made certain to bewail their difficulties with him to everyone within their illustrious circle—his meanness of spirit in the face of all they'd done for him; his delicate constitution in regards to the fish course at dinner; his inability to understand the good sense in following even the most basic rules of good behavior, which would certainly only serve to smooth his path through both life and society. And his parent's peers had eaten up their sob stories, showering Henry and Victoria with sympathy.

Varick didn't know if Coal had knowledge of this reputation, which meant he might. Embarrassment, followed closely by

anger, surged through Varick. He drew himself up and puffed out his chest the way other Pendragons did when they were insulted.

"It doesn't matter. What matters is that you, little cur, aren't where you're supposed to be. And after you framed me for breaking that vase too."

Coal threw his head back and laughed. "That was good. I nearly believed you meant it." He finally lowered his hand and replaced the necklace.

"I do mean it!" Varick snapped. "You set me up."

Coal straightened the necklace so it sat perfectly displayed. No one would have known it had nearly been pinched. "I needed people distracted. And I apologized, didn't I?"

"I should have you dragged out by your ear, arrested, and locked up in the Halls of Justice."

"Now I really don't believe you. You're not like that. And besides, how would you explain how you found me?"

Varick crossed his arms over his chest. It was true that he didn't think many people deserved the Enforcers' wrath. The Enforcers, the city's "peacekeepers," locked everyone found guilty, no matter the crime, away in the Halls of Justice. For life. No appeals, no exceptions, end of story. The Pendragons were not as zealous about turning people in as others—imprisoned people couldn't be used as effectively as non-imprisoned people. Even so, the lad hadn't been wrong on either count, and that got Varick's ire up even more. Before he could say anything else, however, he heard a door open and close in the rest of the apartments beyond. He spun and cracked opened the dressing room door.

"What is it?" Coal whispered.

"Petunia, Constance's maid," Varick whispered back. "She's likely here to prepare Constance's dinner ensemble." He turned wide eyes onto Coal. "Which means Constance will be up soon too."

At the same time, Varick and Coal pulled pocket watches from their jackets. Not thinking, Varick had grabbed his grandfather's. The motionless face stared back at him, reminding him of what he'd lost. Randolph would have known what to do.

"Your dinner chime goes off at six," Coal said. "Your sister's got just over an hour to get up here and get changed."

"She's really pushing it today," Varick muttered.

They both turned back to the crack in the door. Petunia was scurrying around the bedroom, wittering to herself as she built up the fire and refreshed the water basin in the little washroom, which stood discreetly off to the side. Varick always thought Petunia had been well-named. The petite, meek woman would eventually be crushed beneath the merciless boot of this place. In just a few years, the young woman's dark hair had gone silver around the temples. But stars, she was quick. Too quick for Varick and Coal to risk making a break for it.

"Hey, your watch is stopped. You need me to teach you how to wind it?"

Coal began to reach, but Varick snatched the watch away. "Don't touch it!" Coal gave him an openly quizzical look, and Varick lowered his eyes as he put the watch away. His gaze fell on Coal's own timepiece. It was shabby, most of the shine having been rubbed away. A large crack marred the glass face, but the tick was steady and regular. A cheap paste ruby earring hung from the chain.

Varick looked from the earring to Coal, who tucked the whole lot back into his pocket.

"We need to hide," Varick said. He looked around the room for a likely place. "Petunia will need to come in here eventually."

Only then did Varick realize how open everything was. Because, of course, this was where Constance brought her lady friends to show off. Behind the changing screen wouldn't work. Underneath the vanity was an option, but even just one of them would take up most of the available space in the kneehole.

Coal was already diving beneath one of the spinning dress racks. "In here!"

Varick made a face. He didn't love that option either, but it seemed the best one they had. Within, Coal was already settling himself against the rack's central pole. It sat neatly fitted within a wide, smooth metal base that didn't risk catching expensive fibers in sneaky splinters of wooden floorboards.

Varick crawled over to the other side, and the two listened hard for sounds of an incoming Petunia. Around them pressed thick layers of silk, taffeta, organdy, velvet, lace, and more. Ribbons and flounces, shirring and ruching all worked together to conceal the boys rather completely. Varick logged this away as one more reason to appreciate fine clothing. His eyes flicked to Coal's hand as the lad reached up to touch a spray of embroidered seed pearls. Was Coal thinking of plucking them off the dress, like tiny ivory berries?

Varick considered again the poor fit of Coal's jacket. The way it bunched around him now showed just how little there was of Coal to fill it.

When he spoke, the forest of fabric soaked up the sound of his voice, but Varick was still careful to keep his voice down. "Are you stealing because you don't have money for food?"

Coal gave Varick a sidelong look. "What do you know about buying food? Don't the servants just magic it up for you?"

Varick pressed his lips together. *Because Grandfather made sure I knew,* he thought.

He couldn't say that to this boy, this jewelry-stealing urchin. That was the sort of sentiment people could weaponize. So instead, Varick lifted his chin and looked down his nose, or as much as one could in the situation.

"You're the one who thinks he knows so much about me. You tell me."

Coal shrugged and volunteered nothing more. Varick didn't press. He found a small space to peek through, and waited. A few minutes later, Constance appeared. When she passed into Varick's slim line of vision, she was practically dancing around the space, her face aglow with delight. The disparity between her expression and onyx funeral attire made her look almost manic. She flitted into the dressing room, out of Varick's sight, but he heard the sound of her settling in at her vanity table. Thank the stars he hadn't tried to hide there.

"Petunia, quickly now," Constance said.

Varick heard her fingers snap—her gloves were already off—and he pulled a face. She *loved* snapping her fingers at people; it was his sister's way of insulting people without directly insulting them. "Lord Kippermink and his son are here. They're part of the set joining us for dinner."

At the mention of dinner, Coal's stomach grumbled next to Varick. He looked at the skinny lad again, who very deliberately did not return the look.

"They're a good family, so I need to look my best," Constance continued, as if she wasn't always informing Petunia where everyone within her acquaintance stood in society's hierarchy. "And I had such a time getting him away from that odious Eloise Lee."

"Do we think the young master Kippermink is of marriageable quality?" Petunia tried to keep her voice even, but she sounded tired.

"Perhaps. They have enough money—from banking, mind you, so nothing distasteful—but he has a very weak chin. I don't know that I could stand being married to a chin like that. In any case, I want him fawning over me by the end of the night."

Varick rolled his eyes. At sixteen, Constance was just shy of a year and a half older than him. She likely wouldn't marry for another seven or eight years. That was a few years more than other girls her age, but everyone knew his family never rushed something as crucial as marriage contracts, considering divorce was too shameful to ever consider.

Constance prattled on, all the while interspersing instructions to her maid. There were a few more young men of note joining them for dinner, all of whom she had taken time to circle around to downstairs.

"No, no, no," Constance chided. "Not that gown. It's far too austere for dinner. I need something with more panache for this evening. Let's see what else we can rustle up. Honestly, you are daft. At times like these, Mother and Father ought to dock your pay and give me the difference."

Coal and Varick looked at the gowns around them and exchanged a horrified glance. Constance was coming *over here*! Thankfully, Varick already knew the inventory of this rack well. He'd snuck in before to stain his sister's best gowns with cherry cordial and tea, but only where the stains wouldn't be seen until the gowns were removed from their usual spots. His eyes darted, running ensemble equations in his head. Color and time of day, season, necklines and frippery. He had his answer before Constance had made it halfway across the room. Varick grabbed Coal's skeletally thin wrist and dragged him across the smooth metal base to an area filled with summertime day dresses in whites, creams, and pastel shades. The two melted back into layer upon layer of linen and cotton.

"I'm thinking a black organza overskirt atop the burgundy gown. And gold accents. Ugh, I simply cannot wait until we can get back to wearing proper clothes. All these dark shades wash me out. I'm positively melancholy about it."

Varick ground his teeth. He wanted to take a pair of scissors to every single one of her garments. He nearly jumped when he felt something touch his shoulder. Years of practice stopped him, though. *Don't react. Don't give them the satisfaction,* chanted in his head like a mantra. He looked and saw Coal's hand on his shoulder. His other held a finger in front of his face, making a shush signal. Varick shrugged off Coal's hand and shot a nasty look. He'd let his emotions get the better of him… *again*. Varick had begun to breath more loudly through his nose as he'd sneered unseen at his sister. He found that his fists were clenched too, but he wasn't about to admit that Coal had been right. Coal didn't let it go, though. He patted the air in a placating gesture, then jerked a thumb toward the sound of Constance's voice and mimed having his hands cuffed.

Varick understood, and he refocused. It would be one thing for him to be found in here. But however miserable his own punishment, it wouldn't be anything compared to what would happen to Coal. Constance and Varick's parents would throw Coal to the Enforcers like a bone to hungry dogs. And Coal would then be imprisoned for the rest of his life and tortured for information about how and where to find more criminals just like him.

The sound of Constance snapping her fingers again drew their attention. "Spit-spot, Petunia." Constance's words were clipped now, a sure sign she was losing her patience. "This dress isn't going to change itself. Why are you being such a slug today?"

The meaning of the words hit Varick, and he turned his face into one of the gowns. "Don't look at my sister while she's changing!"

Constance might be a pain, but Varick wouldn't stand for anyone getting cheap peeks at her. Not that there was much chance to see anything beyond the frothy material poofing around them. Plus, there was the changing screen as well, but the reaction had been automatic.

Coal already had a hand over his eyes, though. "I'm not!" he hissed back. "I might be a *little cur*, but I'm still a gentleman."

It was the first time Varick had heard the boy sound angry. And that was understandable, because Varick had made an assumption, the sort that everyone else in his family would have made. Being poor, and a thief to boot, *obviously* meant Coal must also be only too happy to commit any and every other type of crime as well, including being a pervert.

"I'm sorry," Varick said.

From the corner of his eye, he saw Coal's brows bob in surprise above the hand covering his eyes. "It's okay. I get it. Blokes are dogs."

To Varick's surprise, as his reply came to him, his own mouth quirked up in the barest hint of a smile. It shone through in his voice, even hushed as it was. "Now that's not fair. What have dogs done to deserve that sort of slander?"

Coal let out the tiniest snort of laughter before catching himself. Thankfully, Constance's endless stream of inanities drowned out their whispers.

What seemed like ages passed. Not a minute went by wherein some type of claptrap didn't spill from Constance's mouth. She picked at Petunia, complained about the drabness of funeral attire, ranked her so-called friends' physical features.

"My *garnet* earrings, you little fool," she snipped at one point. "Those are almandine."

Petunia's voice was plaintive. "These are the only dark red ones in here, my lady. Perhaps you lent your garnets to your mother? Or perhaps a friend?"

Constance sighed, and Varick could imagine the hair flip that went with it. "Don't you think I would remember if I did? Sometimes I wonder why I keep you around." A clock in the hall chimed—a quarter of an hour until dinner. "We don't have time for you to remember where you last put them. The almandine will have to do." Her footsteps retreated from the room, and her next words sounded as if they came from the bedroom. "Let us hope for your sake they haven't permanently disappeared."

"Yes, my lady. I'm sure they'll turn up."

Both their footsteps left the dressing room, and Varick waited until he heard the distant sound of the main apartment doors close before he moved. He peeked out and around the dresses. He and Coal were alone again. And before Coal could scarper, Varick leapt out and spun the dress rack as hard as he could.

Dresses flew out from their hangers, sleeves waving exuberantly through the air, as if they just did not care. And, as expected, Coal was thoroughly ejected from the spinning metal base. He zipped out on his rump from under the dresses and made good distance across the polished floor.

A huge grin spread across his face. "That was fizzing! Do you want a go?"

Varick ignored the question and speared Coal with a glare. "Did you nick her garnets? Petunia might get the sack because of you."

Coal shoved a hand into his jacket pocket and extracted a fistful of jewelry. "Dunno. Maybe? And anyway, I bet Petunia would be happy working for anyone besides that chattering bird."

"It's a job," Varick argued. "It's how she feeds herself. You don't get to decide for her. Put the earrings back, put it all back."

Coal clutched the jewelry to his chest, squaring a challenging glare at Varick.

"Put it back *now*, Coal."

Coal pointed his chin at Varick. "Make me."

Varick let out a angsty groan. He wasn't about to lower himself to a bout of fisticuffs with this little scamp, nor did he want any of the trouble doing so would bring. And anyway, the lad's thin frame made it difficult to blame him for wanting to keep the jewels. Besides, they were nothing more than trinkets to Constance. She could buy chests of pieces just like them, each one more glittery than the last. There was still Petunia's fate to consider, though.

When no good solution presents itself, it's your job to create one. Randolph's voice rang in Varick's head.

He scanned the dressing room. If Coal returned the garnets but took something else, it was the same problem rescheduled for a later date. No solutions there, so Varick turned inward. He glanced down at his own attire.

A set of diamond cufflinks graced his sleeves. A matching cravat pin sat at his throat. The rest of his family claimed diamonds were invisible, and so Varick had received numerous diamond accessories over the years. It was absolute rot, but useful rot at the moment.

He began to detach the accessories. "Here, take these instead. They'll fetch you as much as the rest of that lot together."

Coal narrowed his eyes. He probably thought this was a trick. "Why?" was all he asked.

"Because it isn't right for Petunia to suffer because of you," Varick replied. "You're not leaving here with Constance's jewelry.

He held out his cufflinks and cravat pin to the boy. The sleeves of his jacket flopped open now, but he kept his eyes locked on Coal's. Finally, Coal relented, though his mouth was still set in a hard line.

"If these turn out to be fake, I'm coming back to give you two black eyes," Coal said.

"Then I'll enjoy never seeing you again, because they're as real as you and me."

Varick held out his other hand, palm up to receive Constance's pieces. They made the trade, neither fully letting go until they had the other half in hand. Then Varick shoved the purloined jewelry into a random drawer beneath one of the display cases.

"The maid's coming back!" Coal hissed.

Varick spun. Coal had his eye to a crack in the dressing room door. Varick had known Petunia would be back to search for the missing jewels, but he hadn't thought it would be right bloody now!

"Quick, behind the door!" Varick said.

Both boys huddled against the wall behind where the door would open. Sure enough, Petunia swung it wide a moment later, hiding them from view. She fretted to herself too quietly for Varick to make out the words, but he heard her beginning to shuffle throughout the space. He dared a peek around the door and saw her on the far side of the room, engrossed in riffling through a case near where he'd stashed the pieces. He crept out, smooth and silent as vapor, skirted around the door and back out to the sitting room. Coal was right on his heels.

"I need to get down to dinner," Varick whispered. "Can you get out on your own?"

Coal waved an easy hand at him, his usual cheerful demeanor back in place. "No sweat."

Varick made a face at the crude expression, but nodded anyway. "Good luck."

With that, he slipped into the empty corridor, followed closely by Coal. Varick saw the boy as far as the grand staircase. He wanted to make certain Coal at least made it back down into the thinning crowd below—a number of hangers-on were still milling about, likely trying to angle for a seat at the Pendragons' vast banquet table. When Coal got down the stairs, the only person who seemed to notice him was a broad-shouldered waiter, who simply nodded at the lad and offered a canapé from his nearly empty tray. Satisfied, Varick hurried to his own room to remedy the sad state of his jacket sleeves before dinner.

3
HOUSE OF PIRANHAS

The floor rushed up to meet Varick's back. He let out an unbidden grunt as his helmet smacked against the shining wooden floorboards. The button of Magnus' fencing foil stabbed Varick's padded fencing jacket hard enough to sting. And, as Varick expected, Magnus drew back and stabbed again and again.

"Dead, dead, dead," Magnus declared with each hit.

At three years his senior, Magnus was both taller and stronger than Varick. He had learned it was best to play dead until Magnus got bored. It was a shame bereaved families weren't expected to give up their everyday hobbies and lessons. And no one in the Pendragon clan would think of disrupting their own enjoyments for something so small as Randolph's death. It'd been four whole days since the funeral, after all. Varick stared up at the equally shiny, wooden, coffered ceiling. Thin pillars and claw-footed benches stretched along the sides of the long gymnasium. Mechanotherapy machines scattered about the space as silent sentinels. Their cables, which were attached to weights on many of the contraptions, wound around wheels and ended in either handles or levers, which users were expected to pull to develop their strength. Magnus always made a big show of using these whenever Constance brought her friends around. Varick diverted himself as he waited for Magnus' showboating to end by watching the glare of sunlight fade. It shone through tall arched windows. A cloud must have rolled across the sun's bright face, and the distant peal of thunder promised an autumn shower in the near future.

"Not very sportsmanlike," came a nasally voice from nearby.

That would be Master Rigby, the boys' fencing instructor. Silver-haired, hook-nosed, and sharp-eyed, the man had always reminded Varick of one of his father's gyrfalcons. Despite the man's admonishment, he made no move to intercede or punish Magnus for the blatant ungentlemanly conduct. He never did.

"It's just a good bit of fun with my little brother," Magnus replied. "You know I'd never finish like that in public."

Master Rigby sniffed disapprovingly, but only said, "Again. This time, Varick, perhaps you'll keep track of your feet."

As Varick stood, he was glad for his fencing mask. With it covering his face, he didn't have to fight the heat crawling up his neck. He'd tripped while trying to leap away from Magnus' aggressive strikes. Varick hated his fencing lessons. His sole goal during them was to simply get through with as few bruises as possible. Magnus was quite good, in their level anyway. He'd won the title of Junior Fencing Champion several years in a row. Varick wished Master Rigby would move the big lout to a more difficult league, but Magnus hadn't shown any interest. His older brother might not have been the sharpest knife in the drawer, but Magnus likely knew more advanced competitors would put him on his rear, just as he'd done to Varick so many times.

Varick, for his part, had given up trying to quit the lessons.

"Fencing is a manly sport," Henry had said. "If you don't like it, stop whining and get better."

When Master Rigby called for the boys to begin their next bout, Varick edged his way back along the fencing strip, which was outlined along the floor in paint.

"Oh, hello. It seems we've arrived late." The voice belonged to Constance.

From his periphery, Varick saw two other ladies trailing his sister, though his focus was too much on avoiding Magnus' foil to identify them. Magnus' eyes strayed to them, and Varick took advantage of the opportunity. Perhaps this time he'd get in a point against the great berk. Varick thrust, his foil aimed straight for Magnus' chest. Yes! For the first time in his life he was going to win. And in front of others even! He smiled, relishing the taste of imminent victory. Magnus' eyes flicked back to him. The taller boy's foil whipped up and parried Varick's away. Magnus' next attack flowed from his defense. And Varick's joy disintegrated within him as Magnus' foil came straight for his heart.

Varick froze when the button made contact again. As Magnus had promised their fencing teacher, now that there were other people around, he shed every aspect of childish torment. Magnus stood straight, form perfect, while Varick's arms fell to his side.

"Point," Master Rigby called.

Constance and her friends clapped politely while they walked to one of the benches. She would *never* describe herself as a sportswoman—it veered too far from the ultra-feminine, highly fashion-conscious persona Constance had curated—but she quite enjoyed sport and often watched her brothers' fencing practice. And thus, the entourages she almost always trailed, had to join her. Like his sister, Magnus would not rush into any marriage without thorough vetting and an impressive investment of time. After all, any outsiders wishing to marry into the illustrious Pendragon clan would have to prove themselves very patient indeed, even to the point of sacrificing other match opportunities.

Varick tried to block out the ladies' tittering as fencing practice continued. Again and again, he was beaten, just like always. He did his best to follow Master Rigby's instructions, but Varick was no match for Magnus' reach or strength. At last, their lesson came to an end. Like an Old World automaton, Varick bowed to his opponent, his tutor, and the ladies. He said all the right words and ticked every required box before quitting the gymnasium. As he went, he could hear Magnus asking the ladies which mechanotherapy machines they wanted to watch him use. A changing room lay beyond the gymnasium, and Varick stripped off his fencing garb there before continuing onto his room. Sweat made his clothes cling to him, and he couldn't wait to bathe. Being so young, he didn't have to have a valet and preferred it that way—one less person to fight against in this house of piranhas. Inside the solace and safety of his apartments, Varick leaned against the door and closed his eyes. Just a year and a few months to go and he'd be of age. Then he could get his own flat and escape his cretinous family. He released a sigh. But that seemed so far away.

"Bad day?"

The voice startled Varick so much he leapt off the door before his eyes had time to pop back open. When his gaze landed on the speaker, the gears in his brain ground to a halt. He must not be seeing things correctly.

It was Coal. Sitting on top of Varick's writing desk, his feet planted on the seat of its chair. He wore a suit again, but this one, unlike the provided mute's outfit, was shabby, made of a mishmash of dark-colored, cheap materials, and had been badly patched in more than a few places. Varick didn't see an overcoat anywhere, which was concerning given the crisp weather outside, but at least Coal had a decent flat cap.

"Wh-what the bloody blazes?" Varick spluttered.

"Ooh, didn't you know you high and mighty types knew those sorta words." Coal also wore an unbelievably broad grin, given the utter daring of his being here.

Varick gaped for another moment. His wits had gone running around and smashing into one another like one of those scenes in a stage farce. Only one response offered itself up in his disbelieving mind. He threw an arm toward the door and said, "Get out!"

Coal laughed, rocking back and kicking his legs. "I didn't come through the front entrance, mate."

"What are you doing here?" Varick was nearly shouting now.

Coal shushed him. "Not so loud. You wanna get me caught?"

This had to be a strange dream. Who would ever take such a risk as sneaking into the Dragon's Keep? Much less a boy with his whole life in front of him. Granted, the Pendragons didn't keep a staff of armed guards or anything around—so ungenteel— but they weren't afraid to lay hands on a body, to say nothing of commanding the staff to do the same. With all those servants walking around, how had Coal avoided being seen? Coal ignored Varick's incredulous expression and cast his gaze around the room.

"You got any other shiny bits you don't mind parting with?"

This little ragamuffin was unbelievable! "I beg your pardon?"

Coal patted his belly. "I can't remember the last time I ate so good. Even as little as my cut is, those baubles fetched a pretty price."

Guilt sliced through Varick. Just earlier that day, he'd enjoyed a sumptuous lunch with multiple courses. Even so, that was no excuse for Coal's behavior. And anyway, who was he to come here—to break in—and make Varick feel guilty? It certainly wasn't Varick's fault he'd been born into the Pendragon family. If he'd been given the choice, he'd have picked someone else. He covered his feelings in the way all Pendragons did.

Doing his best imitation of Constance, Varick stuck his nose in the air. "I'm not keeping you fed like a stray cat. What in all of Invarnis possessed you to come back here and try and leech off of me?"

The crooked smile Coal gave Varick made him think the little urchin was fighting to keep from laughing. It made Varick's haughty facade wither and die. He hated that charade, as had his grandfather, and now Varick had gone and pulled it out as easily as he would a familiar waistcoat.

"See?" Coal's expression softened. "You're not like the rest of them. I told you so back in your sister's room. And when you exchanged your jewels to keep that maid from getting in trouble, I knew I could trust you."

Varick nearly started back at the statement. *Trust?* Trust was a foreign concept in this house. He'd certainly never known it… except with Randolph. Varick shook his head. Randolph was dead now. There was no one left he could rely on. And besides, Coal was a thief. A sneaking, little scoundrel who just wanted a meal ticket. Well, to be fair, Varick was a thief too. He wanted to tell himself it was different, and it was, sort of. But also, it wasn't.

Grandfather would have given more. So much more. It was the bane of the Pendragon household how much Randolph had donated to charity. "And those horrid soup kitchens he started!" they would moan. Of course, that didn't stop the family from capitalizing on the opportunities said soup kitchens created, always making sure the newssheets knew how much they helped those poor, underserved wretches of the community.

Varick took a deep breath. He held up a finger, demanding a moment while he walked over to the window seat. His thoughts had been yanked in so many directions the last few minutes, he needed to wrangle them back together. He flopped onto the cushion, knowing his mother would have scowled if she'd been here to see it—half the reason he'd flopped in the first place. Coal, meanwhile, bobbed his head and waited. Varick rubbed his face with his hands. His clothes still felt sticky with sweat. He just wanted to wash yet another miserable day away.

"Coal," he groaned from behind his hands, "I can't keep giving you things." That was point number one. Undeniable and therefore helpful in making Varick feel like he was getting a grip on the situation. He heard Coal's intake of breath and held up his finger again. Thankfully, the boy obeyed and swallowed whatever comment he'd been about to make. "I know my family has plenty of treasures, but even if they don't notice something missing, the staff would. When I steal things, I put them back somewhere else… usually. What I'm saying is there are too many factors in play to risk it." That fact was another foothold gained for Varick. He didn't say aloud the next thought queued up in his mind.

I know you're hungry. Anyone can tell just by looking at you that you've been denied basic needs. That's why you steal, why so many steal.

"The real crime is that so many people go hungry when we've got more food than we could ever eat," Randolph had often said. If he'd had more power in the family, he could have done more, but that involved politics. Multiple Pendragons held positions in Springhaven's magistrate council, but Randolph had been too kind for the sort of cutthroat tactics needed to win in them over to his cause. Still, he had established his food banks and soup kitchens, but their funding might dry up now. The family was going to hear the reading of Randolph's will tomorrow.

Varick finally uncovered his face and looked to Coal. "I have an idea, but let me freshen up first, alright? Can I trust you not to take anything while I do?"

Coal gave him a falsely coy shrug, palms up in the air.

"Coal," Varick warned. "I can still rat you out, you know."

"But would you?" the boy teased.

Varick raised an eyebrow at him. "I don't know. Keep pushing and we'll find out."

Coal's grin slowly faded. Clearly he wasn't certain where Varick's line was either. "Fine. Go shine yourself up. I won't steal anything."

Varick hesitated. "Do you promise?"

"Cross my heart, stick a needle in my eye, all that." Now it was his turn to pause. "I cut out the middle bit. You know, with what you been through."

Varick was so surprised by that he forgot to school his expression. He hadn't expected sensitivity from this little rascal. His eyes prickled, and Varick tried to force his words out before his voice had a chance to start cracking—he didn't quite make it.

"Thank you. I won't be long." The tears pressed forward, and Varick escaped to the privacy of the bathroom.

When he reemerged in fresh clothing, having had a good cry and a nice wash, he found Coal sitting at his chess table. It was tucked near the wide, heavily curtained window. Coal had his legs tucked up against his chest as he examined the pieces—onyx and silver on one side and gold and ivory on the other. They'd have been easy to steal, but all appeared to still be in the positions Varick had left them. He had a game against himself going.

"Do you play?" he asked. He was both genuinely curious and trying to train himself out of preconceived notions. He'd slipped up in that way with Coal before, and Varick wasn't okay with that.

Coal shook his head. "Nah, but I seen others play."

Varick nodded. He had a notion to offer to teach the lad. It was what a friend would do. A friend might also have corrected the grammatical gaffe from a moment ago, but he and Coal were not friends. Coal was here because he needed something. Varick knew that should have bothered him, but instead it felt good. Everyone else in his life saw him as useless and a disappointment. If he could actually add to someone's life, well, that would be a nice thing, wouldn't it? With that thought, Varick's idea solidified in his head.

"Come over here." He beckoned toward his wardrobe, all glossy hardwood and intricate inlays. "You'll need to wear some of my old clothes."

"Why?" Coal asked.

"Because if anyone here thinks you're looking for a handout, they'll send you away. If you pose as a guest of mine, though, they won't think twice about feeding you."

Coal unfolded himself from the chair and walked over, head cocked to the side. "And I reckon you'd only have friends from other highfaluting families, yeah?"

"Of course," Varick replied automatically. He was sorting through his collection of shirts for the oldest, and therefore smallest, pieces. "My parents say it wouldn't do for a Pendragon to fraternize with commoners." What he didn't say was that he didn't have any friends in any case. Constance and Magnus had seen to that in a variety of creative ways. Siblings really were the worst. He paused, considering his statement. "Well, what they call commoners. My grandfather, though, never believed in all that bloodline rot. People are people, good and bad, whether they have money or not."

"Yeah, I heard about your granddad." Coal's voice was soft. "He's the one who set up all them free meal places and whatnot, huh?"

"He did." Varick kept his head inside the wardrobe in case tears threatened to surface again.

"He seems like a good one." An easy silence passed between

them. Then, in a subject backtrack extreme enough to give Varick whiplash, Coal said, "So around here, people who can afford food get fed and people who can't don't. Think about that for a sec."

Varick pulled his head out of the wardrobe and fixed a glare onto Coal. "I *know* how stupid it is. You don't have to tell me. I certainly don't make the rules." He thrust a small pile of clothes at Coal. "Here, change into these. They won't quite fit, but I'll peg them into shape once they're on. You can change behind the screen or in the…"

Varick had been about to offer the bathroom as well, but quick as a wink, Coal had shed his jacket and had his shirt half unbuttoned. Varick dropped the clothes onto the floor—a part of him cringed at treating such fine garments so poorly—and spun. It wasn't that other bodies made him squeamish, but he was protective of his own, as well as his privacy. And thus, not having Coal's explicit consent to see him undressed, Varick instinctively gave the lad the same consideration he himself would want.

While he waited for Coal to finish, Varick focused on a filagree and ribbon-thin glass suncatcher hanging in the window. The delicate pieces of helical glass strands threw different colors around Varick's room and had been made by a rather well known glasssmith in the Copper district. Varick and his grandfather had often visited the shop just to see what new wonders the artist had wrought. Only then did Varick realize the next time he went, it would be the first time without Randolph. He might even have to share the news of his grandfather's passing, if the glasssmith hadn't seen the newssheet obituaries.

Stars, Varick needed a distraction. He asked Coal, "Do you want me to call you Coal around others? Or would you prefer a pseudonym?"

Over the rustle of clothing, Coal asked, "What's a sue dumb inn?"

"Pseudonym," Varick corrected, sounding out the syllables. "It's a false name."

"Cor, that's a fun idea! How about something really fancy like Alistarion or something? You can look now. My bits are hidden again."

Again? Varick wondered. *Isn't he wearing underpants?*

On second thought, it was probably better not to know. He turned carefully and Coal was indeed dressed in Varick's clothes, which hung a size or two too large.

"Good. Now stand up straight with your arms at your sides. I'll fix everything so it looks nice. Or, at least… passable." He looked again at his clothes on Coal's too-skinny frame. He'd even said he'd gotten to eat well these last few days. Varick worried for just how bad Coal's situation was.

"You're the boss," Coal agreed, and he got into position.

Some tailors, Varick knew, used pins to secure fabric into place. Randolph, however, a keen sewist, had always preferred to clip his material with small, spring-loaded clothes pegs. He'd taught Varick all he knew, and Varick had the job well underway in minutes.

"You'll need to correct your speech as well," he told Coal as he worked.

"Talk more toffee-nosed you mean," Coal smirked. He then stuck his nose in the air and, in a hugely over-affected manner, said, "Pip pip, that chappie there." He pointed at an imaginary person in the distance. "What *is* he wearing? A *tuxedo*?! What does he think this is, a beach holiday? Makes a cove not even want to get wangjoogled this eve, wot?"

Varick pulled a face, which Coal couldn't see. "I honestly have no idea if you're being serious, but no one speaks like that. Just talk like I do, alright?"

"You got it," Coal replied, and Varick suddenly began to doubt his plan.

"You have to be able to pull this off," he warned. "I can't save you if they think you're not the right sort." He reached forward so that Coal could see his hands and made little finger quotes around the word, "right."

Coal nodded. "I can do it." He paused. "If Carver was here, he'd be able to mimic any type of person you wanted. He's great at voices."

"Who's Carver?" Varick asked.

"Eh, just a friend."

Well, that was a dodge if I ever saw one, Varick thought.

"I *can* do this," Coal repeated. He sounded as if he were trying to convince himself as much as Varick.

Varick made a noise of acknowledgement at that, but nothing more. A friend might say something else, something encouraging, but he was decidedly *not* looking for a friend. He was going to get Coal fed and then get him out of here. If they played their cards right, maybe Coal could finagle another meal out of the scheme later. But that was it. Really.

Coal fidgeted his hands.

"And don't fidget," Varick said.

"Sorry."

Varick clipped one last peg into place and came round to inspect his work. "Alright, that'll do. Let's go. It's getting close to afternoon tea, and the kitchen staff won't want us underfoot." Then he added sulkily, "Plus, I'll have to go join my family."

"Don't you get to decide your own schedule?" Coal asked. "Rich chappies like you always have free time in stories."

Guilt twanged in Varick as he realized he'd assumed that Coal couldn't read. No time for that now, though. "My family probably wouldn't notice if I missed a meal or two." A thought occurred to him just then. "Maybe more than that?"

He and his grandfather had often opted to eat by themselves either out at a restaurant or in the small—relatively speaking—

breakfast room. And Varick could do what he liked outside of lessons. Before, when his grandfather had not been busy with his own affairs, they'd often walk the grounds together, take in entertainments outside of the house, or sew. Now with Randolph being gone, Varick hadn't thought much about how to fill his time. It had been too painful, and, in order to distract himself, he'd spent most of it playing chess by himself in his room or mindlessly fixing simple issues with his clothing. Now that he was thinking about it, his family probably wouldn't care what he did so long as it didn't reflect badly on them.

Pensively, he added, "They'd mind if I missed lessons. They're paying a pretty penny for all my tutors, after all."

Coal seemed to be mulling over his own thoughts. "Duly noted." Then he looked brightly up at Varick. "How's that for talking right?"

Varick sighed. "Maybe just try to say as little as possible."

4

THE PORK PIE PLAY

he kitchens of the Dragon's Keep were, in a word, labyrinthine. They were located in the basement level of the great manor. In this underbelly dwelled the true work area of the house. Varick led Coal down a staircase rather smaller and far less grand than those used by the household above. As they reached the bottom, the sound of laundry being cleaned and dried drifted to meet their ears. Laundresses cackled to one another as they shared jokes and traded stories. There was a room just for ironing, and another for the house's hired floral arrangers and plant caretakers. A stone corridor took the two boys past the doors for all these, past several pantries and cold rooms, various areas for the staff to eat and sleep and pass time, and finally to the main kitchen.

Varick didn't pretend to know what went on in the smaller kitchens; he hardly understood what happened here in the main one, beyond ingredients being turned into food anyway. He scanned the room for Mrs. Thackston, the head cook. There, standing at one of the long worktables, she was busy telling off a scullery maid. Varick motioned for Coal to wait. Thank the stars, he obeyed, though that might have been down to indecision. Coal's eyes had grown to the size of saucers as his gaze flicked from a huge loaf of bread here, a giant pot of soup there, a silver dish of sauce cooling across the room.

"How many people you feeding?!" he hissed.

Varick didn't answer. In truth, he didn't know. His parents or siblings or both were always entertaining. At last, Mrs. Thackston dismissed the scullery maid, and Varick pulled Coal along behind him.

"Mrs. Thackston," Varick said crisply. "My friend and I are hungry."

That was it. That was the power of being a Pendragon. He simply had to speak a need and the people around him hopped to it. At least, that was the way it usually went.

"You and your friend can wait until teatime, Little Lord Pendragon," Mrs. Thackston's tone sounded decidedly uninterested in negotiation.

Varick's brain skidded to a halt, looked back at what had happened, and tried to figure out where things had gone wrong. Coal absolutely could *not* join them for tea, but Varick didn't want to send him away empty-handed either. Mrs. Thackston was not what Varick would describe as soft and warm, but she'd never been stingy with food. Anytime he and his grandfather had wanted a cheeky little snack, they'd come down here and... Oh.

His grandfather. That was the missing piece. Randolph had always been on friendly terms with Mrs. Thackston, and he'd always been the one to make requests for himself and Varick. Before Varick could even decide what to do next, Coal was speaking.

"And even without a how-do-you-do?" He sounded impressively like some of the more jovial lads in Varick's peer group. He bowed fluidly to Mrs. Thackston. "And how *do* you do, my good woman? Eldred Hedgewood, and I'm very pleased to make your acquaintance."

Varick had to stop himself from making a face, but disgust saturated his inner monologue. *Eldred?*

Coal held out a hand, and a whisper of a smile pulled at the corners of Mrs. Thackston's mouth. She wiped her broad hands on her apron and took Coal's proffered one.

"Susanna Thackston, charmed."

Coal jabbed a thumb in Varick's direction. "The guff you must put up with from this lot."

For just a moment, Mrs. Thackston's eyes shifted uncomfortably around the room. Coal must have noticed, because he changed tack both instantly and seamlessly.

"I'm sure they're all very good to you, don't get me wrong. When a chap's hungry, though, hoo! His manners go right out the window." Mrs. Thackston's face relaxed, and Coal went on. "My gran was a cook, bless her. Worked day and night so the family could work their way up. Didn't know her long, but what I do remember reminds me a lot of you."

Varick watched the exchange in frozen disbelief. Was this actually going to work? Mrs. Thackston might know that the Pendragon's by and large didn't approve of what they called "new money," but it was also a well known fact that he, and his grandfather before him, were the black sheep of the family.

"She sounds like a fine woman, Master Hedgewood," Mrs. Thackston said with an approving nod. She then looked to Varick with a sharper eye. "I'd like to think grief's what's made you forget your manners, Master Varick. I know Master Randolph taught you better, but I fear other influences will leave their stain, in time." She couldn't speak out directly against her employers, but Varick caught the implication behind her meaningful look. "Stick with this one. He seems solid."

Varick could practically feel the self-satisfaction radiating off of Coal.

"I apologize, Mrs. Thackston," Varick said. He wished his cheeks would stop burning. A part of him wanted to snap at her, threaten to have her sacked, but he was already ashamed with himself and knew that would only make things worse. "That was very rude of me."

"Too right," she agreed. Then she softened. "Got a plate of pork pies ready to go over there. They're for the will reading tomorrow, but we've got more than enough to spare. And take some funeral biscuits too. Got enough of those leftover to clog up all of Cobalt Bay."

In a lonely corner of the kitchen, atop a small butcher block on casters sat a tray of wrapped, lightly spiced biscuits, each embossed with a skull. Two, Varick knew, occupied each wax-sealed packet. They'd served as parting gifts for all of those who'd attended the funeral the other day.

"Thank you, Mrs. Thackston," Varick said, allowing his unadulterated gratitude to show.

She gestured with her head. "Get on with you now. You know you shouldn't be down here anyhow." One last look at Coal and she added, "Take a few extra pies. Put some meat on those bones."

Coal tipped an imaginary hat to her. "Thank you very much, ma'am."

"And don't let me hear you blabbing about this," she finished, sharpness entering her voice.

There it was. An unspoken threat hung in the air. Generosity was a dangerous weakness in the Dragon's Keep, both upstairs and down. If Varick told any of his family about this little kindness, Mrs. Thackston would likely have her wages docked. There were plenty of other people busy in the kitchen. One of them could tattle on Mrs. Thackston as well, though he knew she had all of them firmly under her floury thumb.

Varick made a decision right then and there. He bobbed a bow of thanks to the woman. His grandmother would have outright smacked him, no matter who was watching, for "lowering himself" so, and to a *servant* of all people. But Mrs. Thackston had been generous when she didn't have to. Plus, he wanted to stay on her good side. And now that his grandfather was gone, he had to take the lead on that.

The storerooms under the manor had long been favored sanctums for Varick. They were stuffed with items people rarely looked for and full of nooks and crannies to hide in, or through which to make a sneaky escape. He and Coal stretched out under a tent he'd made with an enormous tablecloth and some stacked-up chairs. After a little cajoling by Coal, Varick had decided to skip afternoon tea with the family. It hadn't been hard.

"What are you gonna do?" Coal had asked. "Show up just so they can ignore you the whole time? Or be mean to you? Skive off just this once. Show me something fun. I bet there're lots of neat places in a palace like this."

Varick had almost corrected Coal. His family had actually descended from royalty. In the Old World, before the War of Light had destroyed magic and the people had restructured the government, the Pendragons had lived in the old palace, which now served as Springhaven's Parliament building. Thus, to him, the grand house in which they currently stood was by no means a palace. But then he'd realized what a stupid thing that was to quibble over and agreed. He liked the idea of impressing Coal. Plenty of people were impressed by the Pendragon's wealth and influence, but neither of those were things Varick had earned himself or had control over. A secret hideaway he'd created was.

And besides, his family really wouldn't miss him. Even with the strangeness of knowing he'd have to kick Coal out sooner or later, this was a far more enjoyable alternative. And he knew this was likely the grief talking, but right now, Varick found he didn't care as much about consequences.

Both boys were enjoying their pork pies immensely. Coal had absconded with no less than eight of the pastries, each the size of a large man's fist. He'd already eaten half of one, though not before he'd set four aside and wrapped them up in a cloth napkin Varick was certain would never make its way back to the manor. As he ate, Coal's pleasure was shown in the way he was taking tiny bites of his pie, making it last.

"Coal," Varick ventured. "You said earlier that you only got a cut of those diamond cufflinks and cravat pin I gave you."

"Mmhmm," Coal replied, smacking his lips in delight.

"Why not all? How is it that you only get a portion of their worth?"

Coal did a jaunty little hand spin and pointed at Varick. "Give the kid a prize, he got it in one."

"But why?"

"Cause you gotta know a fence. *And* the fence has gotta wanna work with you."

"So?" Varick asked. He didn't actually know what the term "fence" meant, but he gathered from context that it was someone to whom you could sell ill-gotten goods. Or maybe a fence was a kind of shop? A crumb dropped off the pork pie he currently held and landed on his lapel. He picked it off before it could leave a grease spot.

"A lotta fences are in cahoots with the bosses."

The bosses. That rang more familiar. Any time people talked about crime in Springhaven, they talked about criminals like they were running a company, a crime company. Sure, upstanding citizens were warned to watch out for petty thieves and pickpockets. Burglars burgled houses and shops. But the invasive weeds with thick, gnarled roots buried deep in the soil of society, choking the life out of all the law-abiding plant-life around them, were the bosses. Though, crime lords was the term Varick had more often heard.

His mind immediately went to his family'a various business dealings—exclusive agreements they had with certain manufacturers, the careful balance of supply and demand, schemes to partake in the profits from other people's hard work. And the Pendragons had their fingers in many different industry pies. Not trade, of course. No, that was beneath them. But banking, land, and even a few promotional schemes wherein select family members were paid to wear a certain jeweler's wares or tailor's bespoke creations to public events as advertising. Was that how the crime lords and fences worked too? Varick shook his head. This was too big for him to wrap his mind around right now, and he refocused on Coal.

"Have you tried securing employment anywhere? Getting a proper job, I mean?"

Coal turned over to lean on his elbow. Still holding his nibbled pork pie in one hand, he shrugged."Tried loads of places, but they don't wanna hire a dirty, little thing like me. And the places that will take someone like me churn through people like sausage."

Varick had heard about the dangerous working conditions in factories. There had been various movements throughout his life to require better safety practices, but the news of those events had flitted in and out of the house and around him like moths. His grandmother and parents scorned the initiatives, saying things like, "The *real* problem is that people just don't want to work. But they want to be paid *more* anyway." Varick had, thankfully, had his grandfather there as a guiding hand. Though, Randolph's rebellions against the rest of them and their back-biting was

always quiet, never within earshot of the family.

Varick looked at the pork pie in Coal's hand. "Would you want to work in a kitchen or something?" He didn't actually know if he'd be able to convince Mrs. Thackston to take Coal on, but Varick was all too aware of the fate that awaited thieves and other criminals—a lifetime sentence in the Halls of Justice.

"Eh." Coal shrugged. "Dunno. Never had the opportunity."

Questions bubbled up in Varick's head, but before he could say more, the noise of the storeroom door opening sounded. It was followed by a couple of staff members discussing what was to come out and where it could probably be found. Quite a lot of chairs were mentioned and Varick looked to the supports for his makeshift tent.

"They're getting ready for tomorrow's will reading," he whispered to Coal. "Come on, we can get out this way without being seen."

Coal quickly but carefully wrapped the last of his treats in the napkin and used his tie to secure it to his wrist like a reticule. Varick led the way under a maze of table and chair legs, around carefully wrapped statues and other artwork, and underneath constellations of drunken chandeliers budging against one another as they hung from the ceiling. They finally reached a strange, low platform connected via various cables, pulleys, and gears to a square of wood in the ceiling.

"Get on," Varick said, leaping onto the platform.

Coal looked at it curiously. "What is it?"

Again, Varick had an opportunity to show off. After a lifetime of being, at best, a tiresome afterthought, this felt good, really good.

He smiled widely. "Wait and see."

Coal obeyed, but his eyes remained on the complex network of machinery. "Cor, Fulcrum would love this."

"Who's Fulcrum?"

"No one. Don't worry about it."

Varick smiled again. Coal's hands fidgeted. The taller lad suspected he was beginning to understand the way his small, light-fingered companion operated. He was good at pretending when he meant to, not so much when he'd slipped up.

With Coal in place, Varick said proudly, "Now, watch."

With a flourish, he pulled a lever on the side of the platform. It made a terrific *cr-chk* noise. Above, a cable dragged a counterweight from its resting place. As the weight began to sink, things all around them began to turn and move. Ropes wound around winches, gears rotated, and the platform began to rise. Slowly, but relentlessly, the two lads ascended skyward. About halfway up to the ceiling, the wooden square above them split in half and opened wide, revealing a square hole. Varick arced an arm near the top, as if presenting a miracle of technology, and Coal copied him, adding a little arm waggle for emphasis. They rose through the hole like prestidigitators doing a big reveal. The sun was just starting to set in the sky, tinging it lavender and apricot, as if to join in the spectacle. No one was around, just as Varick had suspected would be the case.

"This trapdoor isn't used much except for garden parties. They'll be using the one that's closer to the veranda."

Coal gave an approving nod, and Varick's chest bloomed with pride. He'd hoped Coal would be impressed.

The realization that this was the end of their clandestine adventure ebbed in, though it was not too sad. Bittersweet really. It's wasn't like their acquaintance could continue, after all. It'd be too difficult, what with Varick's family and Coal's situation and all. Coal seemed to read the situation and patted the pouch attached to his wrist.

"Thanks for the pork pies. These'll last me a bit."

"Thank *you*," Varick replied. "You're the one who pulled off that great acting job. I really didn't want to have to explain you to

my family over tea."

"I didn't want to have tea with your family," Coal replied. "They seem pretty awful."

And before he knew what he was doing, Varick was laughing. Laughing like he had not since before Randolph had died. "You have no idea. *Everyone* is going to be here tomorrow. It's going to be ghastly."

Coal chuckled with him until silence seeped between them.

"Well, I guess this is goodbye," Varick said. He held out his hand, "Best of luck, Coal. It's been nice knowing you. Can you find your way out alone?"

Coal smirked at him. "What do you think?"

Varick chuckled. They shook hands, and he watched as Coal disappeared into the falling dusk. Only after he'd gone did Varick realize the lad was still wearing his clothes, and he still had a set of Coal's.

5

BATTLE OF WILLS

When they were all gathered like this, the entire Pendragon clan resembled less of a family and more of an assembly of delegates. There were similarities, to be sure. Dark hair reigned most prominent, and some shared the same slender build as Varick. Rich food and indolent lifestyles changed this latter feature for many, however. Varick's own father, for instance, sported an impressive paunch. Everyone was dressed similarly to how'd they'd been during Randolph's memorial a few days ago, but they'd been trying marginally harder then to hide the avarice shining in every eye now.

The family's solicitors—a small squadron of them—were currently cloistered in the salon, which adjoined the music room. Rows and rows of chairs had been arranged here in that latter space and spilled out into the main hall beyond in order to seat everyone during the reading of Randolph's will. Varick, his grandmother, and their immediate family sat in the front row. After that, the seating arrangements got squiffy, and anyone who

had not been assigned a seat would have to duke it out in a viciously polite game of musical chairs. Some of the ladies had already feigned feeling faint and claimed spots for themselves, as well as a few "indispensable" companions. Randolph's ashes had been moved into here as well. The urn stood on display at the front of the room, as if Randolph was going to oversee his own will reading from beyond the grave. Varick felt sick as he watched person after person use "paying their respects again" as an excuse to horn their way into the heaving music room.

He looked out the tall, intricately mullioned doors that led out to the loggia from the music room. He could escape that way, but the solicitors were due out any moment now, and doing so at such a large, public event would draw his family's ire. Varick wished he could at least listen from outside the windows, which had been opened wide to allow the morning's chilly autumn breeze to circulate through the room. He didn't really care if Randolph had left him anything, Varick just wanted to hear his grandfather's wishes. Who had he snubbed in death? And to whom had he shown affection? Randolph had done his best to hold his own against the biting, clawing, machinations of his fellow Pendragons, but even so, Varick had always felt his grandfather'd been too generous with them. Every New Year celebration week showed that, as he handed out thoughtful gifts to everyone around him. Granted, being thoughtful didn't mean the recipients *liked* the gifts. They were often less flashy than was customary for the Pendragons, but that never deterred Randolph.

As he recalled this kind habit, Varick looked to the urn holding his grandfather's ashes. Tears burned in his eyes, and he looked quickly away again. This was not the place for a show of weakness like that. It was easier to push them back this time. Grief, Varick had noticed, was capricious. Sometimes it grabbed you at the most inopportune moments and refused to let go. Other times, it just tapped you on the shoulder for a quick word before leaving again.

The door to the salon clicked open. Every head turned to watch, like hungry scavengers, as the solicitors emerged. They each carried thick portfolios, and Varick wondered just how much paperwork went into death.

Most family heirlooms had not belonged to Randolph to pass down, such as the Dragon's Keep itself. That belonged to the family at large, and would pass down the line of succession for all time until there were no Pendragons left alive to inherit it. There were plenty of possessions Randolph had acquired throughout his life, though. And Varick knew his grandfather had done a bit of investing here and there, though he'd kept that close to the vest, even from Varick. And then there were the soup kitchens and food pantries Randolph had founded—the Turnip Network, as it was affectionately known. Varick suddenly wondered if his grandfather might not have opted to leave all his wealth to charity. It wouldn't surprise him, and it would *really* rub the collective Pendragon nose in its own bad doings.

Varick didn't bother to look back at the jostling noises happening behind him. They went on for several minutes, and he heard plenty of backhanded compliments being exchanged as people tried to win or lost battles for seats. Finally, however, the noise died down as each person accepted whatever seat they had acquired. Anticipation thickened in the room. It hung in the air like Auntie Latrice the Lush's choking rose perfume. Varick tensed, ready to endure any pinches or kicks from his siblings, who sat on either side of him. They often tried to make him cry out during public events like this, and he had learned to harden himself early on.

The solicitors sat at a table that had been set at the front of the room just for this occasion. They blocked Randolph's urn from view, and Varick was glad for it. He'd prefer to see his grandfather in his mind's eye during this process, as he had been in life, not as a pile of ashes inside a posh jug. The men at the head of the room thanked everyone for coming and explained how the process would work—it would be tedious and long, given all the details to be shared that day. As if scripted, it was at that moment that the house's butler, Whitby, entered, followed by a fleet of footmen. They rolled in carts topped with pitchers of water and glasses and arranged them around the room. Varick settled in for a long morning.

Three hours. They had been gathered for three hours already and were due to break for lunch soon. Varick had to admit, the solicitors had made a good effort to streamline the process—they'd indexed family members by name and cross-referenced bequeathments—but with so many assets being divvied up between so many people, it still ended up a long, dull garble of who's-getting-what-where-and-when.

Varick had yet to be included in any of the handful of mass endowments left to swaths of grandchildren, great nephews and nieces, and young cousins. They'd been small valuables mostly, which Varick didn't care about. He just hoped they wouldn't be wasted on the recipients. Varick sighed inwardly. Randolph had probably intended them as collateral for those young people, a means to pursue whatever passions they might have hidden in their hearts. Randolph was always trying to do things like that. He'd hear of some eleven-year old third cousin half removed or whatever who was interested in caterpillars, and he'd send the youngster a book, a magnifying glass, and a terrarium with a letter to let him know how they got on with "the crawly little fellows." They never did.

Randolph's falconry birds, hunting dogs, and horses were divided up and left to various family members. Varick was pleased to have gotten Tallywags, especially since Varick's father had forbade him from having any more horses after the locked-for-two-days-in-a-cupboard incident. Varick nearly burst out laughing when the reading solicitor's face turned beet-red as he made the pronouncement.

Similar to Varick's secret thefts, Randolph had enjoyed hosting little rebellions to get under their family members' thin skins. Buying Tallywags had been one such move. The horse had been given the rude name by its rough-tongued former owner, who'd received a sharp kick to the nether regions from the animal just a few hours after it had been born. Randolph had laughed at the name, and had great fun explaining the meaning of the term to Varick. He'd refused to change it, much to the entire family's chagrin, and Varick was all too pleased to carry on that proud tradition.

On the list went. All of Randolph's clothing was donated to charity, and many of his philanthropic responsibilities—chair of this or treasurer of that—passed onto family members who needed the publicity enough to make it an incentive for them to carry on what Randolph had started. And, in a shrewd posthumous maneuver by Randolph, all those endowments related to charitable causes would be announced in tomorrow's newssheets. All had been arranged; the recipients simply needed to pick up where he'd left off. Varick was surprised, however, when the solicitors announced that he would head up the Turnip Network when he came of age. Until then, Randolph's wife, Patricia, would do so. Varick snuck a peek at his grandmother. Those food pantries and soup kitchens had been Randolph's pride and joy, and he'd taken Varick to see them on numerous occasions. His grandmother, however, was another story. She'd always hated them, and her watery eyes narrowed at the news. Varick, however, was keen on the idea. He had no idea what he wanted to do, well, not for a living, but for his life. One could do a lot worse than providing food security. Already, Varick was asking himself questions like, "Is there a way to make food reach people, instead of people having to come to the food?" and "How can I make sure no one is getting missed?" Just a year and a bit until he could take control from Patricia, assuming she didn't torch the places to the ground first.

Finally, they came to the matter of money. Varick stopped listening. It would get split up according to some system of Randolph's devising, and Varick settled in for a long, boring list of numbers and names. He slouched as he settled. A moment later, something sharp poked his thigh. He sat straight up again while his eyes snapped down to the offending spot. There, he saw Constance pressing the point of her embroidery scissors, which she kept on her chatelaine at all times, into his leg. The scissors left a hole in the fine fabric, and Varick felt his hackles rise. He liked his clothes in order. It was one of the only things he had control over, and Constance simpered at him as she twisted the scissors, making the hole larger. Not only was she messing with Varick's apparel, but it would be yet another thing about which his family would judge him. Before he could reach for the scissors, though, she shoved them back into their little silver sheath with a click.

"Sit up straight, little brother," she hissed at him. "Posture shows pride."

Varick wasn't stupid enough to start a quarrel here. Constance would play the innocent victim, and everyone would believe her. Besides, he wasn't about to disrespect their grandfather in that way.

"Varick Pendragon."

His head snapped up to look at the solicitors. All of them looked at him as if he'd done something wrong. He hadn't said anything! Constance was the one talking, though she wasn't the only one now.

"I beg your pardon?" she said next to him. All smugness had fallen from her expression.

Around them, murmurs grew like a babbling brook.

"I'd like you to read that again, please," Patricia said.

Yes, Varick thought. *What did I just miss?*

The head solicitor cleared his throat and looked back to the paper in his hand. "I leave all monetary accumulation to my grandson, Varick Pendragon."

"Monetary accumulation?" Magnus said. "Does that mean all his money?"

No surprise the colossal dolt didn't understand. But Varick couldn't believe what he'd heard. Surely there had to be some mistake. From the corner of his eye, he saw his mother whack Magnus across the hand with her fan.

"Don't be so gauche," she scolded her eldest.

Magnus sulked and rubbed the place where her fan had left an angry red mark.

The head solicitor inclined his head. "In this context, young master Pendragon, yes, monetary accumulation means liquid assets, or in common parlance, all of Randolph Pendragon's money."

The babbling brook around Varick rose to river rapids. People started talking to him, placing their hands on his shoulders and asking him things. It took all of Varick's willpower not to shove them off and march from the room. He stared forward, in the direction of the urn again. He wished he could ask Randolph why. Because his grandfather had just made Varick a target.

6

POWERFUL GAMS

What a nightmare the afternoon became. The shocking proclamation had ended the will reading, with tea and light refreshments following. After Varick had hastily signed some final paperwork put forward by the solicitors, a wave of new horrors came calling. Everyone suddenly wanted a piece of him, and they lined up to pick at Varick the same way they picked through the cucumber sandwiches and scone varieties. Family members who'd never deigned to speak to him came out of the woodwork, each with lavish praise and a sudden interest in his future.

Onion Breath Uncle Jason cornered Varick, and began proselytizing about the surefire returns to be made by investing in messenger pigeons. "They're jolly smart!" He said this while showering Varick in cake crumbs. Uncle Jason did not believe that talking and chewing should be separate activities. "They can find their way home from hundreds of miles away. And the market is rife with opportunity. Why pay a courier when you can just send a pigeon?"

Later, Chester, the family accountant, caught Varick by the elbow and began to drawl about the various accounts Randolph'd had and Varick's need to sit down with him and go over them. "You'll want to set aside an entire day, in order for me to properly educate you on your new fiduciary responsibilities."

Management of a charitable organization was one thing. You had to be of age to take on a role like that, just as you had to be of age to sign for a mortgage or rent a flat. Money, however, was just… money. Anyone could have it. But what did that mean for investments? Investments, with dividends and strategies and whatnot, that seemed like something one had to be of age for too, but Varick wasn't really certain. Why hadn't Randolph warned him this was coming?

As soon as he'd been able to escape the throng of snacking relatives, Varick had legged it over to the southern garden in order to hide behind some of the fulsome plant life found there. The southern garden was actually a sunken, hexagonal room with a pointed glass ceiling that sat catty-corner to the music room, where the will reading had taken place. It was called the southern garden because it boasted a miniature jungle of plants, all of which had been imported at great expense from Bone Port on the southernmost tip of Invarnis. It contained potted palms and citrus trees, colorful ginger plants, orchids, and cascades of bromeliads in huge terrariums, some of which were larger than a full-grown man.

As Varick hurried down the steps into the indoor garden and behind a stand of several palms, he was surprised to find none other than Randolph's sister, giver of engraved fob watches. Constance always called her GAMS, for Great Auntie Megaera— spinster. Because Megaera actually was a spinster and Constance was the embodiment of salt in your tea. Auntie Megaera was currently sitting on a carved stone bench next to the tall, curving palm trees, gazing up at them. Around their crowns drooped bunches of dates, nearly ready for collecting. The plants here served as a way to offset the cost of importing rare treats such as these, and as a way to impress guests. Varick was just about to turn and retreat, hoping his great aunt hadn't noticed him, when she lowered her head and pinned him in place with her clear, hazel eyes.

Megaera shared many of the same features as the rest of his immediate family, though she was a shade darker than he and her once-umber hair had lightened to a snowy white. She had it pulled back into a loose, practical knot at the nape of her neck, and her long fingers were set with nothing more than a single, elegantly designed moonstone ring. The most curious thing about Great Auntie Megaera, though, Varick noticed, was her dress.

Randolph'd had a great appreciation for clothing and fashion. And so, at Randolph's knee, Varick had learned to read people's clothing as he would a book. Great Auntie Megaera's dress was, in many ways, just like those worn by the other women gathered in the Dragon's Keep that day—cuirass bodice with a high collar and fitted sleeves, the fabric of her skirt draped and pinned rather skillfully over her bustle, creating a glorious waterfall effect. The strange thing about her ensemble, though, were her buttons. The smoky grey pearls—or possibly just glass made to look like pearls—ran up her front. Buttons, like so many other things in their ridiculous society, made a statement. Buttons up the back, as with every garment Constance, Patricia, and Victoria owned, meant that you could afford a lady's maid to help you dress. Buttons on the front meant you had to lower yourself to attending to your own attire. Nevermind that, should a lady have other ladies in the house to assist, the need for staff could be easily circumvented. Varick had also heard of some cleverly designed dresses on the market that had false buttons on the back and hidden hook and loop closures on the front.

Being a member of the Pendragon clan, Great Auntie Megaera was certainly in a position to be able to afford a lady's maid, so why on earth would she be wearing a dress that screamed she couldn't? Especially *here* of all places.

"Come, child, sit with me." She patted the place next to her on stone bench.

Varick might have bristled at being called "child," but Great Auntie Megaera was old enough that most everyone was a child to her. The average life expectancy in Springhaven was about sixty, but there were always outliers. Varick was convinced spite was what kept both Auntie Megaera and Patricia alive. Megaera was Randolph's senior by several years, and everyone knew she hated Patricia as much as Patricia hated her.

Auntie Megaera was clearly not asking, and Varick silently obeyed. She looked back up to the dates and spoke.

"Do you know, when I was a young lass, I used to scuttle up these trees and collect the fruits in a little pouch hanging from my waist. Well, not *these* trees. This was when I was living in Bone Port. Beautiful place, but hot as a kettle's arse."

Varick burst out laughing. He hadn't seen it coming, just as he had not expected to hear such language from what might have been the matriarch of the Pendragon clan, had circumstances been different. The fact that she was both female and unmarried had been the reason everything had passed to Randolph, despite Megaera being older. A moment later, Varick caught himself and swallowed the laughter, covering his mouth in shock. Megaera lowered her eyes to meet his wide-eyed expression of horror.

"They've really gotten to you, haven't they?" she asked in a sympathetic tone.

Varick swallowed hard, not knowing what to say. He'd never really sat down and talked like this with Great Auntie Megaera. That was mostly down to her having lived for years in various places around the continent of Invarnis, and the fact that having her visit anytime besides during the enormous all-family get-togethers always resulted in a huge quarrel between Randolph and Patricia, which Patricia had often won. When she hadn't, she perched nearby like a kingfisher, striking down any private conversations Great Auntie Megaera might try to have with one of the children. Constance and Magnus had swallowed the poison Patricia spewed against Megaera from an early age. Despite not believing any of the nasty things Patricia and other people in the family said about the spinster aunt, Varick didn't know her, not really, and therefore didn't know if he could trust her.

Megaera smiled sadly when he remained quiet. She looked away, pondering the humid contents of a nearby bromeliad terrarium. It stood on fat, curling little feet and rose as tall as Varick. Sprays of bright orange, red, and deep green dotted over a fuzzy canvas of green moss.

"Randolph and I corresponded frequently," she said. "Did you know that?"

"Yes, ma'am," Varick replied. Randolph had often kept Varick apprised of Megaera's adventures, whether it was taking in the view of waterfalls within the Green Dragon—the jungle to the south—or bear hunting in Duskwood to the north. It had been like listening to someone relay what had happened in a novel, however, since Great Auntie Megaera was more a legend to Varick than a real person.

"I know you haven't been permitted to know me well, except through Randolph's letters, so this probably sounds as condescending as every other bit of unsolicited advice you've gotten since the solicitors dropped all that money onto your head." She turned to look at him again. "*Live*, Varick. You have such opportunities before you. Travel, eat, take lovers."

At this last suggestion, Varick blushed from his sternum all the way up to the tips of his ears. Megaera chuckled, a raspy, crackling sound, but full of joy.

"Very well," she conceded, "perhaps you're a bit young for paramours." Her shoulders twitched in a genteel sort of shrug. "Or perhaps not. I was barely older than you when I… well, I learned early on that I didn't want to be tied down to one person forever. Perhaps you'll feel the same, perhaps not. Whatever you do, though, I heartily recommend you choose yourself first. I did, and look at me."

Megaera held her head high and spread her arms wide before her. She was withered as a dry leaf, but Varick could see a vivacity in her he hadn't ever seen in any other Pendragon.

"Randolph did the same, but in his own way," she reflected. "He was always reserved, even as a child."

Memories of their times together flooded into Varick's mind. More than he could track at once. An entire lifetime of love and support, all gone now.

"I miss him." The words dropped from Varick's mouth without him meaning for them to. With them came the emotion he so often had to hide.

Megaera's eyes shone with tears. "I know, child. I do too. He was the best of us, I think." She hesitated a moment. "Would you like a hug? It's alright if you'd rather not."

The freedom she granted him with those six little words made his emotions surge. Only Randolph had ever given him that same freedom, to express or not express himself in whatever way he saw fit.

"No," Varick replied, allowing a tear to roll down his cheek. "But thank you."

He didn't want to explain that, most of the time, when one of his family touched him, it came in the form of pain. And he saw in Megaera's gentle expression that he didn't need to. She simply nodded, and that was that.

She turned back to the bromeliad terrarium. "You really should travel, though. It's an invigorating experience. I think you'd like Duskwood. It's clear and sharp, much like you."

Varick felt neither of those things. He felt muddled and soft, vulnerable, all the time.

"And with that clod of a brother of yours being the oldest, you needn't worry about the expectations of being a firstborn," she went on.

"My grandson will make his own decisions, thank you."

Varick and Auntie Megaera looked up to see Patricia standing atop one of the short stairways that led down into the southern garden. Plush rugs had muffled the telltale sound of her walking stick on the floor. Her eyes scraped over the sight of Megaera's buttons, which shone in the lamplight as if they were mocking Patricia.

Varick suddenly realized that Megaera very well might have chosen the outfit *because* it would make them judge her. A silent, rebellious statement, just like the sort of things Randolph used to do.

Like an empress, Patricia descended the few stairs and prowled slowly over with a menacing *tap-tap* on the tiled, marble floor of the sunken garden. Varick stood without thinking. Other times, when he'd not done so fast enough, Patricia had rapped him across the shins as punishment. Megaera, however, kept her seat and smiled like a panther at her sister-in-law.

"Of course," she said. "That's just what I was telling the boy, that he should do what he wants with his inheritance."

Varick had to fight not to flinch as Patricia placed a hand on his shoulder, and he felt claws there.

"Yes," Patricia countered. "And he will have firm hands to guide him."

Megaera's eyes remained cool while she bared her teeth. "I'm certain you're going to try your best." To Varick, she gave a gentle nod. "It's truly been a pleasure catching up with you, Varick. I hope we'll get to do it again soon."

With that, she turned her face from Patricia in a silent dismissal. Varick's eyes went wide in surprise and was grateful Patricia could not see. No one treated Patricia Pendragon like that, especially in her own home. No one, apparently, except Great Auntie Megaera.

The cold autumnal air nipped at Varick's nose. They were just barely into the season, so daytime was still perfectly pleasant, but night held a distinct chill. As he sat on the dizzyingly high roof of the Dragon's Keep, the stars twinkled above him, equally cold, but he liked it that way. Indifferent though they were, the stars were also constant. Varick appreciated constancy. The roof tiles beneath his feet and behind were cold too, and that was less nice, but at least he'd brought a shawl—long ago stolen from Patricia —to keep the worst of the chill from his backside.

A lot of toadies had finagled invitations to stay for dinner. That wasn't exactly strange, as the Pendragons often had dinner guests, but rarely so many that had not been preplanned. None of Varick's immediate family seemed to quite know what to do after the day's events. They kept shooting him acid looks, but none approached him. Even Patricia had left off after separating him from Megaera earlier that day. She'd muttered something about his great aunt getting a nasty surprise when she suddenly found her pursestrings cut, but Patricia's shriveled raisin of a heart had clearly not been in the warning. Otherwise, she would have made it to Megaera's face. There was nothing worse than making a threat and then not being able to follow through. It made Varick think that he would, in fact, have to sit down with Cousin Chester about his new accounts sooner rather than later. Stars, but that was bound to be a deadly dull meeting. And he'd have to keep anyone from finding out about it. They'd want to join in and learn just how much wealth Randolph had accumulated for himself.

"Blimey, but this is a thinker. How'd you get up there anyway?"

Varick's eyebrows knitted together at the sound of the voice. He knew it, but it made no sense for it to be here. He leaned slowly to the side, looking for the source of the words, being careful not to topple over the side of the roof. It was steeply hipped, and Varick's feet planted solidly on either side of the ridge. Down, down, down the length of the roof's planes, hanging out of a window just below the bottom edge of the roof, was Coal. He was dressed in all black with not a stitch of Varick's borrowed clothing to be seen. He looked from side to side, clearly searching for where he should climb next.

"Bollocking hells!" Varick exclaimed in as quiet a voice as he could manage. Sound traveled extremely well up here in the clear air. "What do you think you're doing?"

Coal glanced at him with a broad grin. "Coming up to join you, of course."

Varick gripped his hair in his hands. Any number of responses came to him in that moment. Like the fact that Coal had no business coming to see him because *they were* not *friends*! Then again, Varick didn't actually know at what point someone crossed from being an acquaintance to an actual friend, given that he didn't have any, either because he didn't get on well with his peers or because Constance and Magnus always told hideous lies about him and tormented away any potential friends he might have made—usually the latter. He also thought to cry out, "you're going to fall!" But that seemed less than helpful, so he searched for an actually useful response.

"That finial next to you, it looks like plaster but it's actually iron. You can use it to swing around onto the bit between it and the roof."

A long silent moment passed before Coal asked, "The finny-whatty?"

Varick groaned and clenched his fists. His heart pounded, certain at any moment he was about to see this foolish little imp get himself splatted all over the ground below.

"The finial. The spikey thing sticking up next to the window!"

"Oooooh," Coal said. "I gotta remember that one."

Then, nimble as a cat—granted a cat who had to reach a bit—Coal pulled himself across the open air and was soon scampering up the roof tiles toward Varick.

"You really get around, don't you?" he said upon reaching Varick's spot. "I looked all over for you inside before going back outside and looking up here. And I wouldn't have even seen you if it weren't for your coat flapping in the breeze."

Varick far preferred to hide in the storage rooms instead of on the roof for this very reason—he was visible here. But chairs and whatnot were being re-stored down below, so this had been the next best option for escape. He didn't say any of that to Coal, though. Instead, he just leveled a glare at the boy.

Coal had taken a moment to extract a small, shabby notebook from a pocket. He was using it, and an attached miniature pencil, to write down the word, "finial," as well as its meaning. He finally looked up and met Varick's glower.

"What?"

"You went all over the inside of the house?" Varick demanded. "I assume no one saw you because you're not out on your ear, or worse, in the hands of the Enforcers, but you could have been. Why the blazes would you take such a risk?"

Coal was entirely unflapped by both the stare and the words. "I told you, I was looking for you."

"Yes, I heard that part, but why?"

The scruffy boy hesitated only a moment before replying in a softer voice. "I read the papers today. Thought you might need a bit of non-family company."

Varick groaned and laid his head on his knees, pulling up the collar of his coat to cover as much of his head as possible. He'd known it was coming, but stars, they were bloody quick about it. He'd known someone would tell the newssheets about the other dictates of the will, those Randolph had not arranged beforehand. Varick had known it wouldn't be long before all of Springhaven knew he was the sole inheritor of the former Pendragon patriarch's monetary assets. He just hadn't counted on it being so… immediate. He imagined, as if in a play, someone dashing from the room as soon as the proclamation had been made, shouting at a hansom cab to "take me to the nearest newssheet office and make it snappy," and relaying all they'd heard—with some colorful embellishment—to eager reporters hungry for a story to plaster over the front pages of the afternoon newssheet editions.

"Let me guess," Varick mumbled from inside the cave he'd made, "ladies fainted, someone screamed, and people broke out in fisticuffs over the news?"

He heard the sound of fabric shuffling, and then Coal said, "Only in the trashier rags. But they all used the same picture of you, and it's a nice looking one too."

"That's not as helpful as you might imagine."

Varick wondered how many strangers with "great ideas" and "opportunities" for him would send their cards round to the Dragon's Keep over the next few weeks. And how many would members of his family want to indulge? Not many, he knew, but a few would probably sound promising enough to have a meeting, whether Varick was there or not. And then how many more family members would hound him about the results of meetings they'd had without him even knowing it.

What made it all the worse was that Varick had no idea what

he wanted to do, both with his new wealth and his life. He certainly wasn't going to follow his father into politics—Henry had recently nabbed himself the position of Speaker of Springhaven's magistrate council. Bully for him. Instead, Varick rather enjoyed maths and his business theory lessons. He'd always imagined he'd land on an answer eventually, but now, adrift as he was and with the winds of consequence howling on the horizon, he had a very bad feeling he was going to be pushed far too quickly in one direction or another.

"I should just take my aunt's advice and move," he grumbled.

"You sixteen already?" Coal asked.

Varick sighed. "No." He couldn't do anything on his own until he came of age in a year and a bit.

A long silence ensued. Then Coal asked, "You wanna get out of here?"

Varick lifted his head and looked at the lad with a befuddled expression. "What?"

"Do you wanna go somewhere that isn't here? Get away? Not for a whole day or anything, just for a while?"

Varick noticed that Coal was fidgeting again. Was he feeling bashful about trying to further their friendship? Or whatever it was that was growing between them? That was kind of sweet actually.

"Where are we going to go?" he asked. "It's getting late. We're not adults, and the only places that would let us in are probably already closed." What he didn't say was that he also suspected that Coal didn't have any money with which to patronize an establishment, or at least not much.

Coal gave Varick a crooked grin. "There're lots of places, free ones even, if you can get there."

Varick didn't understand that. What he did understand, though, was that this boy, this strange but well-meaning boy, was offering to lead Varick out of his stupid situation for a little while and provide some kind of respite. No, Varick didn't know where they were going or what they were going to do, but it would be away from his horrible family. It suddenly hit Varick that Coal reminded him a bit of Great Auntie Megaera.

"*Live*, Varick." Her words came back to him, almost as if on the wind.

He smiled. "Yes, alright. Let's get out of here."

7
FLYING LESSONS

neaking through the dark and off the Pendragon grounds proved exhilarating. There was nothing illegal about the two being out—Springhaven did not have a curfew or anything —but two underage boys wandering alone through the city when respectable young gents should be winding down for the evening was *suspicious*. What, after all, could two unsupervised adolescents possibly be up to that wasn't, in a word, trouble? While still making their way off Pendragon family property, the boys had to avoid fallen leaves, which would crunch treacherously beneath their feet. The groundskeepers did their best to keep the crisp, colorful little blaggards raked up and bagged elsewhere for mulching, but they were no match for relentless Mother Nature. Varick made a game of tiptoeing between them like an obstacle course. He and Coal had to stick to the shadows of trees and buildings and plot a circuitous course that avoided the great, open swathes of lawn. Coal had the advantage of having done this already, but Varick steered him

toward the orchards. It was a longer route, but allowed them to grab some ripe apples and pears in case they got hungry later.

Outside of the property, a whole new world, a desolate, nighttime world, awaited Varick.

He was no fool and keenly aware of the fact that he did not possess what he'd heard referred to as "street smarts." He'd only seen this term used in novels, and no one in any of his circles had any either. Thus, Varick had never known how one came to learn such skills. Coal, however, exhibited them in spades. His body language shifted instantaneously from one environment to the next. Coal stiffened and his eyes sharpened, flicking back and forth, searching for… well, Varick was not quite certain what he was looking for.

"What should I be doing?" he whispered.

"Shh!" Coal hissed. His hand shot up in a gesture of silence so fast that Varick flinched away from it.

It was like the boy could fragment his vision, because he examined Varick with a sliver of his gaze while keeping the rest on his surroundings.

"Sorry," Coal said.

Varick swallowed hard, feeling embarrassed, but he wasn't about to address the weakness he'd just shown. "I'll just follow your lead then, shall I?"

Coal gave him a tiny but firm head nod before darting from the perfectly manicured hedges concealing them. Varick heard all too loudly of the scrape of his own shoes echoing through the still night air as they crossed from Pendragon land into the rest of Springhaven. The property rose gently behind them into a mount, the Dragon's Keep a jewel atop its pinnacle. At this time of night, anyone standing outside the tall, imposing fence, as Varick did now, could see the lights of the manse twinkling, far, far off in the distance. Here, they were near the western edge of the Ivory district, near the Rose quarter. Across the road was the edge of a public park known as the city gardens. Varick thought that might be where Coal had in mind. After all, there were probably a fair few places within the gardens' lush greenery where someone could hide without fear of discovery, but when Varick silently signaled the question to Coal, the boy only shook his head.

Instead, they made their way down the pristine streets. Trees and topiaries lined them on either side at regular intervals, and the two boys darted from one convenient shadow to another. Coal stopped often to check their surroundings. Varick did the same, though he wasn't certain what they were looking for until, without a word, Coal pulled Varick behind a bush clipped into the shape of a squirrel. Coal pressed a finger to his lips, though Varick had already learned to hold his tongue until he knew it was safe. His eyes followed the line of Coal's gaze. A broad, distant ball of light bobbed in the darkness between the street lamps. A lantern. When the lantern-holder strode into a pool of lamplight, Varick recognized the telltale blue and grey uniform of an Enforcer walking his beat.

A few of his family members had enlisted in the order, though it was often third, fourth, and so-on-born sons who'd opted for such positions. The pay was apparently not very good until one achieved placement in the higher ranks. Enforcers were the law in Springhaven, and not even Varick was certain his clout could save Coal's skin if they were caught. Coal, in his all-black garb, looked every bit a criminal at work. An Enforcer, if he assumed Varick was up to no good—and, again, what more did he need than the boys' ages and Coal's clothes to suspect such?— could march Varick home and ask his parents if they'd known he'd been out so late? And in the company of one like Coal, who looked every inch a scallywag? And if Coal, as a minor, had no home to go to, he'd be thrown into an orphanage.

The two boys crouched low behind the bush-squirrel and its broad planter, though the Enforcer was still a ways off. Varick's heart flapped in his chest like a trapped bird. This was like when he snuck about and hid at the Dragon's Keep, but the trouble would be so much worse if things went south. Varick regulated his breathing, counting silently to himself as he controlled each intake and release. Coal, he noticed, did the same, and they soon fell into rhythm together.

Finally, after what felt like hours, the Enforcer passed by the boys and their hiding spot. They waited a bit longer, just to make sure the Enforcer was well out of earshot. Varick was surprised to find himself grinning. They'd done it! It felt like he'd just won some kind of high-stakes game. After that, Varick began to pick up more of Coal's tricks. He watched the way the lad moved his feet—a controlled rolling of toe to heel. His arms lifted slightly away from his body, and he remained in a shallow crouch as they moved. When Coal turned, he used just his waist to do so. The whole thing looked silly and felt a bit unnatural, but the results could not be argued. Coal moved as noiselessly as a mouse and always had complete control of his whole self. With a little practice Varick started to as well.

Varick knew they must have been going north, because they soon reached the border of the Sand quarter, delineated by butter-yellow stone walls. The Ivory district had white, sparkling walls, like quartz. These were a throwback to the city's Old World name, Prism, which had changed after the War of Light to signify the brave new world being forged. He and Coal made far better time after this.

Sand was mostly a mostly commercial district comprised of shops of every shape and size. Like living things, over the years, buildings had grown and consumed one another, been split up and shrunk, added onto in all sorts of configurations. The evolution had created countless little nooks and crannies, alleys and shortcuts. Coal led the way up stairways, over bits of wall, and along balconies and terraces. Eventually, they made it to a rooftop, and Coal stopped, turning to Varick with a big grin. The rooftop didn't look like anything special. It was flat, like several others nearby, and clearly some birds or other small animals had made their homes up here, but that was the extent of interesting features.

"What…" Varick began, speaking again in careful, hushed tones.

Before he could finish, Coal spun and took off at breakneck speed, straight for the narrow gap between this building and the next. Varick didn't even have time to shout as he watched Coal make a beeline for certain death. Then, at the last moment, Coal pushed off the roof, sailed through the air, and landed soft-kneed with both feet on the next rooftop over. He ended the move with a somersault and bounced back up victoriously while Varick gaped. It'd looked for all the world like Coal had flown, if only momentarily. The boy beckoned for Varick to follow.

Varick's mind raced. The gap wasn't all that wide. He *could* fall, but he'd have to make a right meal of it to do so, altogether forget to jump at the last moment or something. Which meant, realistically, he'd make it without a hitch.

And then he'd be able to do it again. And *again.*

The city of Springhaven opened up to Varick in an entirely new way. He knew he ought to care for his own welfare more, that this was probably grief blunting his decision-making skills, but he didn't care about that right now.

"*Live,* Varick." Great Auntie Megaera's words came to his mind again.

A ferocious, challenging grin spread across Varick's face. He took off. The rough surface of the roof whisked by him. The edge came up fast. And then, with a great leap, he was airborne. He was flying across the space, crisp autumn wind flapping through his clothes and beneath his outstretched arms.

This. Was. *Exemplary!*

Then the next roof came rushing up to meet him. How was he meant to land? How had Coal done it? He'd made it look easy. Soft knees, that was the ticket, and then bounce. He wouldn't really have to somersault, surely. That was just something Coal had done for chuckles. Varick positioned his legs, ready for the impact.

Solid rooftop caught him with far less forgiveness than expected. When Varick touched down, the bones in his feet vibrated, and he stumbled. Inertia was still very much in play, and he pitched forward. Thankfully, he had the wherewithal to catch himself, but he rolled hard to the side, and his rump took the brunt of things. Varick shut his teeth around the groan of pain that crawled up his throat, just barely muffling the sound.

"There's a better way to do that," came Coal's quiet voice.

He extended an arm, but Varick waved him away, grumbling. Coal was already giving his lesson at a rapid-fire pace.

"To land when you're roof-running, do it on the balls of your feet and keep your spine straight. Think of it like there's a spring under your heels; they shouldn't touch until you're stable. And use your arms for balance, like this." He held his arms out in front of him. "If you need to fall, fall forward. You can catch yourself with your hands, sort of like you did, but use the movement to push yourself where you want to go, or, if you're going really fast, curve into a roll." Coal then propelled himself forward, catching himself on his hands, and transitioning into a roll, being sure to tuck his head before springing back up at the end of the rotation. Easy, yeah?"

Varick looked at him with an expression of indignant disbelief.

"Now you try," Coal urged.

Varick didn't want to try anything at the moment, except for a few extra pillows while settling into his favorite chair to recover, but he'd come all this way already. And he had to admit, what Coal had just done looked spectacular.

"Show me once more. *Slowly* this time."

Coal obeyed, talking through the different moves his body made, and then backed up to give Varick some space. Varick mimed the moves at first, talking through them. And then, with a deep breath and a prayer that he wasn't about to injure himself further, he pushed off and allowed himself to topple forward.

The result was sloppy, and Varick by no means sprang right back up the way Coal had, but he completed the rotation. Sadly, however, a knee of his trousers did not. The rough roof—floor, he supposed it could be called—caught the fibers of the fabric and refused to let go. There was a soft ripping sound, and Varick felt coolness and then warmth against his knee.

"Bollocks," he sighed. The blow was softened by the facts that Constance had already marred these trousers with her scissors earlier that day and, more importantly, he'd done it! He'd achieved the impressive roll maneuver.

"Don't go trying that with a jump until you're better at it." Coal paused, considering. "A *lot* better. I don't need you smashing in your own head in on my conscience. Got it?"

"I understand," Varick agreed. He already planned on practicing in the gymnasium.

"Righty-o. Let's keep going!"

Coal continued to lead them across the rooftops, clearly familiar with the route. They didn't actually need to leap across too many more gaps, but those they did Varick cleared with far more grace. He was nothing like as agile as Coal, but at least he didn't injure himself again. He stumbled a few times, though, and nearly fell only once. That was because the landing site had been slanted, and Varick's feet went out from under him on the gabled roof. As gravity grasped onto his sliding form, so did Coal, catching the taller lad around the wrist. A quick apology rushed out.

"Sorry about the grabbing, mate."

Uncomfortable though he was with the contact, Varick smiled. Coal had caught him without a moment's hesitation. He didn't know if Coal risked getting pulled down too, but Coal clearly didn't care.

"Thanks… mate." The word rolled awkwardly off of Varick's tongue. It was not part of his usual vernacular, but it felt right to say.

At last, several stories up, they came to a rooftop with a flat area in the center of four cross-hipped roofs. It was a bit like being in the bottom of an enormous bowl. Huge chimney stacks stuck up at regular intervals all around the flat area, which seemed strange to Varick.

"Where are we?" he asked. The world looked so different from high up.

"Hotel," Coal said.

Ah, that made sense. Varick had never stayed in a hotel before—he'd never even left Springhaven, not unless you counted being out in Cobalt Bay on a steamship cruise—but he understood the principle. He suspected the chimney stacks connected to all the fireplaces in all the rooms beneath their feet.

"This way." Coal trotted along the roof ridges with the ease of a mountain goat.

It did not escape Varick's notice that his new friend had stopped watching his volume. And given the noise flowing out of the windows below them, he wasn't surprised. It sounded like a party was happening below, the sort where libations had been flowing for a while. The hotel probably had a gaming room or event space of some kind down there. There was the sound of music as well, which only added to the cacophony. Varick was well aware that his clothes had already suffered from their escapades. Between bushes and rooftops, he was twigged and dirtied, and his ripped trousers also now sported some light blood staining where he'd skinned his knee. But this adventure had been his choice, and he didn't regret it. He'd never had fun quite like this. Besides the sheer adventure of it, with Coal, he didn't have to watch himself, constantly calculating if he'd get in trouble for saying this or doing that. When he made a mistake, Coal took time to teach him and even catch him when he fell. It felt… like a sort of safety.

So Varick followed the lad to a dormer window. It was open a crack, and Coal slipped inside.

"Thank you, Carver," Varick heard him whisper as he negotiated his way inside—not quite as effortlessly as Coal had made it look, but still with a respectable amount of stealth and skill.

The name pinged something in Varick's brain. He'd heard it before, but that thought was quickly buried by new ones piling up. Where were they? The room they'd entered looked like nothing more than miscellaneous storage. Bolts of fabric and neat piles of tablecloths and napkins in every color were arranged neatly on shelves throughout the room. Why were they here? Coal was already heading for a door at the opposite end of the room.

"Coal, what are we doing here?" Varick asked.

The music was much louder now. It sounded like it was coming from just on the other side of the door, so he wasn't worried about being heard.

"We're not stealing anything," Coal assured him, giving Varick a bright smile.

Varick had not actually made that assumption, though now that Coal had gone straight there, in conjunction with the smile, Varick's sense of suspicion popped its head to the top of his mind. It was the same as if someone had cheerily volunteered that, apropos of not much else, their cousin didn't start fires. One might automatically wonder if, in fact, the aforementioned cousin might not have a bit of a pyromania habit.

Varick narrowed his eyes, but he was smirking. "That wasn't technically my question."

"Just wanted to put your mind at ease," Coal replied.

He opened the door, and music washed inside the little room. On said door, Varick saw a sign that read, DECORATION STORAGE. Beyond, he could see a walkway and a railing. They must be on a sort of gallery level. Across a vast, well-lit space, hung what he suspected was the twin of their side of the gallery, hung with lights and paintings, though Varick couldn't make out the subject matter from here. He followed Coal's lead, who'd begun edging outside of the room.

So far the boy hadn't steered him wrong, and he had said they weren't here to steal anything. Coal had said he'd wanted to put Varick's mind at ease. Perhaps he'd thought stealing had been Varick's first thought, given how they'd met. Varick decided to trust Coal. He wanted the boy to see that he, Varick, did not always think the worst of him. And besides, if the rest of this evening was anything to go by, whatever Coal had planned, it was probably fun.

Out on the gallery, pressed against the wall, Varick finally discovered the reason for all the jolly noise: a casino night.

8

ALL FUN AND GAMES

own below, tables for whist and poker, hazard and other dice games, and roulette ranged throughout the room. Waiters circled with trays of drinks, and eminently dressed men and women wearing masks played, bet, drank, danced, and chattered. Varick rolled his eyes. The social gymnastics of participating in a fabulous night of gambling and cavorting, yet disguising oneself because of the possible social scandal was almost too absurd to be believed. Having fun wasn't a bad thing! Society was stupid. Upperclass society, doubly so.

"You know what?" he muttered to Coal. "Steal from these numpties. I don't mind. They deserve it."

"Yeah?" Coal asked.

"Nevermind this stupid…" he motioned at the crowd below. "performance." He could recognize a couple of people in the crowd just by their build or hairstyle. All from his parents' circle, all just as shallow and mean. Some of the masks didn't even cover the whole face. Some of these preening peacocks didn't

really want to hide their identity, they just wanted to pretend and play this idiot game. He went on. "They only see all the ways their money can serve *them*."

Coal canted his head. "Is it the gambling? You think that part's not okay? Or do you feel like they shouldn't get to have fun until they've saved the world? Can people not do both, have fun and help people?"

"Of course they can. My grandad did it all the time! He supported artists and small business owners and held fundraising galas for the Turnip Network." Varick sighed, thinking harder about the question. It was a good one Coal had posed, and certainly one Varick felt he needed to know how to answer, given his own privilege. "How the rich are or are not taxed aside—and that's a big aside—if we're just considering people's personal choices, I think you can do both if you *think* about things and make thoughtful choices." He motioned again at the crowd. "They don't do that."

"Ah," Coal said thoughtfully.

He didn't say more, and Varick suddenly felt that he'd revealed too much of his inner self.

"Sorry, I didn't mean to…"

He wasn't quite sure how to articulate what he felt he'd done, wasn't certain what was safe to share now, but Coal was giving him one of those unabashedly happy expressions.

"This is nice," he said. "I like it, the two of us, spending time, sharing. Getting into the real meat of what makes life even more lifey!"

Varick couldn't help but chuckle. The reaction had been a really pleasant surprise, and he felt more of that same feeling of safety again.

"Good talk," Coal chirped. "Now, focus up! How do you feel about creating a diversion?"

Varick pulled a face. "People down there know me. I'd need

a disguise first."

"Yup. Good thinking. Follow me."

With that, Coal headed down the gallery and into a discreet men's room, Varick right behind.

"Sometimes you get lucky." Coal pushed open the door, looked around the space, and then, "Aha!"

On a counter near the sinks lay a discarded mask. White, decorated with black swirls, a comically long nose, and a spray of black feathers.

Coal lifted it up and, against the background noise of someone being sick in one of the stalls, whispered, "Today is our lucky day." He then got a whiff of the mask gagged, and jerked his face away, eyes wide and looking as if he were contemplating death. "Okay, it's less lucky for you. Sorry."

Varick gave it a delicate sniff and coughed. The bloody thing reeked of booze! Had the man gone swimming in the stuff?

"So me creating a distraction will help you with… something?" Varick asked. He was looking at the mask with deep distrust. Could you get drunk off of just fumes if they were strong enough?

"Right," Coal said. The sounds of misery escalated momentarily. Coal gave whoever it was a sympathetic grimace. "There's a job I have to do, and I'd like your help with it. Please?"

The please got Varick. No one ever *asked* him for things, much less politely. Coal had been kind, and Varick wanted to help him.

"Alright. Give me a couple of minutes."

Both looked at the reeking mask again, and Coal saluted Varick like a soldier going off on a dangerous mission. Varick tied on the mask and took a moment to get acclimated to his toxic new environment. Then, when he felt confident that he wasn't going to pass out or anything, Varick headed out.

The plan was not complicated, helped immensely by alcohol and the fact that Varick knew a good handful of the players down below. He just needed to make sure no one recognized him. The mask covered his upper face, its long nose going fully over Varick's, but it left his chin and mouth exposed, which made the mystery of why it smelled so bad even more mind-boggling. Varick had considered going back to the decoration room and trying to fashion a fake goatee or some such out of a bit of tablecloth or napkin, but he didn't have scissors or a way to adhere it, and he didn't want to leave any trace of their being here. So he'd have to lean on good old ego and speed.

Varick grabbed a glass of dark, amber liquid from one of the passing waiters and pretended to sip as he made his way toward his target: one Mister Abbott Hurst.

Abbott Hurst was the sort of man who wore a suit like he was trying to bend it to his will and described himself as, "refreshingly honest." That, in this case, being a confusion of the words, "unmitigatedly rude." And this evening, he could also be described as five cups deep and guilty of verbally abusing dice for not conceding to his demands, being that they were dice and all.

Varick waited until the tirade of Abbott's latest loss had ebbed and the next player was trying their luck. Then, he went in for the strike.

"Bad luck, Bottie," he said, making his voice deeper and a touch more affected. Varick's father and their various cronies always called the man by this nickname. Anyone who called him Abbott or Mister Hurst was either a rival or an underling.

"It's these sodding dice," Abbott replied, not quite shouting but very definitely slurring. Then something seemed to occur to him. "I don't know who you mean by this Bottie business, though. You must have me confused with someone else."

Yes, because everyone's wearing a dead hedgehog as a beard these days, Varick thought, though he made sure not to eye up the telltale facial hair as he mimed another sip.

Out loud, he said, "I thought you should know, Lord Quincy's over there saying some… well, rather unsavory things about you. By name. And pointing." Varick gestured back the way he'd come, drawing Abbott's gaze away from himself.

Lord Quincy had been laughably easy to spot too. Who wore a signet ring to what was supposed to be a clandestine event?! Especially one edged in sparkly, distinctive rubies?

"Is he now?" Abbott asked.

Varick then watched as the big man lumbered over to Lord Quincy, who wasn't a small man himself, and began to accost him, verbally at first, then with a light shove or two. This earned a big shove in return, which sent Abbott stumbling back into a nearby table, scattering coins and bank notes across the floor. While a bellowing Abbott Hurst moved to give as good as he got, other players scurried to grab up the spilled money, whether their own or someone else's, it was impossible to tell. Another table was tipped over in the growing fray, and Varick was impressed with himself as he saw the ripples of his little ploy spreading throughout the room.

He caught sight of Coal skittering by in the background, carrying a briefcase. A broad-shouldered, somewhat familiar waiter, meanwhile, nipped into the cloakroom, and Varick decided now would be a good time to disappear. He followed Coal through a doorway under the gallery. It was nothing more than another storage room. This one, however, was for furniture and other large things that would be a nuisance to haul up and down the stairs. Coal already had the briefcase open on a handy spare table and several folders extracted from it. Varick spied the letters P.L.A.C. stamped across them all, each one followed by a different abbreviation, like M.T., A.R., and V.V.. Coal had documents from the one bearing the suffix A.R. out and was carefully laying blank sheets of paper atop them.

"Great job out there," he said, while Varick puzzled at what he was doing. "Did you see the lady trying to be sneaky and stuffing bank notes into her evening gloves? Cracking stuff."

Varick didn't answer. One of the pages Coal had removed from its folder looked like schematics for an airship. Why would he need any of this?

A moment later, the boy produced a small bottle of liquid from his pocket, along with a tightly folded cloth. The slightly sweet smell of some kind of spirits hit the air when he opened the bottle—much nicer than the miasma soaking into Varick's pores inside his mask, though that bar was pretty low. Coal used the cloth to apply a thin layer of the liquid all down the blank papers before giving them a flip and pressing them flat against the original documents.

"What are you doing?" Varick asked.

"Research."

Varick opened his mouth again, but found he wasn't certain what he was going to say. He didn't understand what Coal had meant by his answer, but also… did he much care? He'd said he didn't mind if Coal stole from these rich knobs. Had any of that just been Varick shooting off his mouth out of anger? He ran the risk calculation in his head. Would any innocents be harmed by Coal's… research? He didn't see how. After that factor was out of the way, as Varick watched Coal work, Varick found he felt no misgivings about whatever this kind, funny boy was up to.

With a practiced deftness, Coal peeled the papers he'd applied his chemical mixture to away from the documents. A mirror image of every line of ink had transferred to the blank papers. Amazing! Before Varick knew it, Coal was packing his copies away into his jacket and the documents back into the folder from whence they came. Varick had no doubt the lad had taken special note of how they'd been ordered and was replacing them just so.

"Ready to go?" Coal asked.

Varick shrugged. "This is your operation."

"Wrong. It's *our* operation."

Varick's face hurt a little from how big he smiled at that.

The scene outside had only gotten more chaotic. Here, a violinist was holding his broken instrument in one hand and poking a shouting card dealer in the stomach with his frayed bow. There, a couple of women had each other by the hair in one hand and fistfuls of each other's jewelry in the other. Multi-membered fracases were happening all throughout the room, and every member of the serving staff seemed to have abandoned their trays and posts. In one smooth motion, Coal sent the briefcase sliding across the floor and underneath an overturned table. Once they were up the gallery stairs and outside Decoration Storage again, Varick sent his stinking mask sailing over the railing, feathers fluttering and ribbons trailing the whole way down. He was struggling to keep from laughing, giddy as he was from the success of their escapade and the satisfaction of seeing people, usually so buttoned up and crafty, having devolved into such a juvenile riot of humanity.

Back through the dormer window and up to the roof, Coal settled back against the warmth of one of the hotel's chimneys and was looking out over the city of Springhaven. He looked… pensive? He was fidgeting anyway. He should have been gazing like he owned the place, though. Varick was not so foolish as to romanticize the boy's everyday struggle for survival, but for just this moment, Varick envied him. He envied Coal's freedom, even knowing that freedom came with the danger of being caught by the Enforcers and forced into an orphanage, even knowing that Coal had to scrape and steal for basic necessities. Varick saw cage bars when he thought of his own life, a gilded cage, true, but a cage nonetheless. Coal had no gilding in his life, but he also had no cage.

Standing atop the roof's ridge, also looking out over the city, also leaning against the chimney and letting its warmth seep into his back and shoulders, a thought whispered through Varick's mind. *Do you ever think you could leave it all behind?*

"About time you showed up, Coal," came a voice from below them. "I've been waiting ages."

9

SOBER CATS IN CLOWN WEAR

Varick popped off the chimney stack like he was spring-loaded. He spun toward the voice; a man of middling height and build was sauntering toward them. He had to look up, given he was on the flat valley between the hipped roof edges. Varick wasn't always good at guessing adults' ages, but this chap looked maybe in his mid thirties. His attire, however, shouted one word and one word alone: Average.

The newcomer sported sandy hair cut in a popular style, so popular in fact that it was forgettable. His suit was fine, serviceable, nothing special. His trilby went as unadorned as one could be without looking odd, his scarf-pin so unostentatious as to not even be there, and his coat could have come from any shop either just respectable enough to live in the better part of the Sand quarter or on discount in its more upscale sister-district of Copper.

Varick wondered to himself why anyone would work so hard to appear so overwhelmingly plain. Perhaps to be invisible even

in plain sight?

"Oh, heya, Mercury," Coal said.

Coal's voice held a distinct note of discomfort, and he didn't look at Varick as he made his way down the roof to the flat portion below. Varick wasn't certain whether to flee or try the old snobby posturing technique on this so-called Mercury—he was already up high; it would be effortless to look down his nose at the man. He didn't want to show fear or leave Coal alone here. Why had the boy left the high ground when he wasn't exactly giving off an air of "this bloke is on the up-and-up." Or was it just the situation that was sticky, what with them being a couple of kids where they definitely had no business being?

Act like we belong then, Varick decided.

He narrowed his eyes and glared as he slid down the roof to join Coal. If nothing else, they were two against one. Mercury closed the distance between them. He extended a hand and spoke in a perfectly pleasant tone.

"Mister Varick Pendragon, yes? The name's Mercury. A pleasure to meet you."

Varick did not accept the hand, nor did he expect there had been any question in the man's mind as to whether he was, in fact, the presumed Varick Pendragon.

"Mercury what?" he asked in the coldest voice he could muster. The snobbery was strong with him tonight. He even managed a tinge of the same condescension his grandmother managed as easily as breathing.

Mercury gave him a smile that might have read as amusement to an untrained eye, but Varick had seen smiles like that before. There was no mirth in them, only grease. "In my business, m'lad, we don't do surnames. Only sobriquets."

Behind him, Varick heard Coal say to himself, "Sober cats? Are there drunk cats too?"

Mercury chuckled, another hollow maneuver meant to try

and ease tension. "You've met my protégé—"

"What do you want? We were trying to enjoy a nice evening, and here you come waltzing in without even a proper introduction." Varick cut in so fast it was as if his words were a knife slicing between Mercury's sentences.

"A nice evening breaking and entering?" Mercury countered.

Stars, that carefully controlled voice of his was so annoying. It was like when Constance spun her sharp little verbal barbs, the ones that appeared innocuous on the surface, but each one left a cut. "Don't you look *so tired*, Delphinia. You ought to get better sleep." "Chastity, what an *interesting* name." "Hasn't Rhonda made such a *brave* choice with that dress?" And then if anyone dared complain, she'd affect injured innocence and insist only the best of intentions. Varick assumed Mercury played similar games.

"We haven't broken anything," Varick countered.

"Trespassing then. You and Coal are enjoying a rapscallion's night on the town when well-behaved nippers would be asleep in their beds by now." Varick opened his mouth to object, but Mercury raised a quelling hand and spoke before Varick could even get a word out. "You asked what I wanted, and I'm telling you. So listen." Varick's jaw tightened. Mercury was doing that thing now where he slowed down his speech, as if Varick teetered on the verge of a tantrum. "I want to present you with an opportunity."

Varick felt the blood drain from his face, maybe even from his whole body. He felt cold and empty suddenly. Coal showing up at the Dragon's Keep, luring Varick away, getting him to create a distraction so that Coal could make copies of those documents, which Coal was, at this very moment, coming forward and silently handing over to Mercury. He didn't meet Varick's eye as he took up station next to the man. Of bloody course. Everyone just wanted to use him.

Mercury tucked the papers into his jacket. "I can tell by your

face that you're already skeptical, and I don't blame you. Your grandad, may he rest in peace, leaves you a giant wad of cash and suddenly everyone knows what's best for you. And miraculously, what's best for you just happens to serve their interests. Have I got anything wrong so far?"

Varick's words were clipped when he replied. He didn't even have to feign resentment this time. "Spot on, which is why I suspect whatever you have to *offer*—" He fairly spat the word. "—will be as unappealing as the rest."

"It'll help your friend Coal's… situation," Mercury said.

Varick bristled. "He isn't my friend, clearly."

Coal stubbed a toe into the rooftop, hanging his head. Varick wanted to tell him he was right to feel ashamed. Also that he could stop pretending he cared. Also that he was no different than everyone else in Varick's life. And so many other things. Varick wanted to hurt Coal the way he was hurting now, but he couldn't decide what might cut the deepest, and Mercury kept talking as if Varick had not spoken.

"Your grandad was a generous man, Mister Pendragon. Did a lot for charity, didn't he? And I suspect, what with him having left the entirety of his liquid assets to you, that he raised you up at his side, yes? He believed in you. Don't you want to help others just as he did?"

A lump as hot as magma burned in Varick's throat. It heated up his face and scorched down to his heart. He felt Randolph's watch hanging heavily in his pocket.

"You're nothing but a cheap swindler," he snarled. "Trying to use my grandfather's death to manipulate me." He looked to Coal. "And you're no better."

If Coal had a response, Varick didn't hear. Blood rushed in his ears, as loud as crashing waves. He turned on his heel and walked off. Trudging over the hipped parts of the roof would not be an epic spectacle of an exit, but he didn't care. As he focused on his footing, Mercury approached again, but he gave Varick space.

Looking up at the retreating lad, he said evenly, "Cheap I am not, nor am I a swindler. The investment is legit, and it's a big one, big enough to set Coal and a handful of others like him up for life. It's not much. You wouldn't be ending poverty or anything, but you'd be able to say you helped a few out of destitution. Think about it."

Varick tried to ignore Mercury as he climbed, but the words sailed up to his ears and wormed their way inside anyway.

♜

Varick slunk around yet another corner, sticking close to the buildings. Nothing was familiar, but he was fairly certain he was going the right way. At least he was still in the Sand quarter. Its yellow walls glowed faintly in the light of the half moon. He couldn't remember the way he and Coal had come, and the rooftops offered no signs as to how to get back to the Ivory district. Not knowing what else to do, he'd climbed down, which he'd immediately regretted. All those stairs and alleys and cut-throughs created a labyrinth. All Varick could do was follow a single direction—he'd hit different colored walls eventually. And then, he'd hopefully be able to figure out where he was. The roads here had evolved with the rest of the Sand quarter, though, and they often shifted or curved suddenly, or in one case so far, simply ended.

Varick was nearly to the point of being willing to hire a hansom cab, not that he'd seen many about at this hour. The only reason he wasn't there yet was because the driver might recognize him from the newssheets. And if they did, they might talk to hungry reporters willing to pay for gossip on one of Springhaven's richest young gentlemen. The last thing he wanted

was his family knowing he'd been out. There was no way to explain that he'd wanted to get away because he hated all of them and had just wanted a bit of time wherein he didn't feel trapped inside his own life. At best, they'd mock him. At worst, he'd end up thrashed and locked in a cupboard again, or worse.

His not-at-all-straight-but-it-was-the-best-he-could-do path wound into yet another alley. Varick followed it, only to find a dead end. The alley simply ended in a skinny vertex between wall and building. Varick ground out a sigh of frustration. He wished he'd never trusted Coal and just stayed on his own roof. Varick turned to retrace his steps, only to find his path blocked by two figures.

Both wore suits of mismatched colors and had darkened around their eyes with kohl or something similar. They also both looked a fair bit older than Varick, one being slender and tall, the other round and even taller. Varick swallowed hard and went to tip his hat to the duo before remembering he'd left it back at the Dragon's Keep.

"Evening," he said, trying to tamp down on his toffee-nosed accent. He even attempted to drop his G's, though he wasn't quite able to let them go. He kept his voice down in an attempt at peacekeeping. "I seem to have gotten a little turned around. I'll just be going... then." He'd been about to say, "shall I" before realizing at the last minute that would be a dead giveaway.

The round one pressed a fist into his other hand, cracking his knuckles. He too checked his volume. "Not without paying the toll, you don't."

Varick mentally prepared to part with all the money in his pockets—just a couple of gold, but it was more than a week's pay for a lot people. "Of course. How much?"

The skinny one cocked his head to the side and raked his eyes up and down Varick's clothes. "With nice threads like that, I reckon you can afford fifteen."

"Fifteen… silver?" Varick asked hopefully.

"Nah, gold," the round one said.

A bead of sweat rolled down Varick's brow. "I don't have that much on me." He pulled out what he did have and quickly counted six gold coins and two silver. He allowed his voice to ring louder now—better to be heard by a passing Enforcer at this point than risk suffering at the hands of these two. "This is everything, and you're welcome to it with no trouble if you'll just let me pass."

The skinny one threw back his head and laughed. He snatched the coins from Varick's outstretched hand, counted and pocketed them, and pulled a stout, curved knife from his belt.

"We'll take the rest in fingers," he said. "What do you think, Gill? Two should make up the difference, yeah?"

"Three," came Gill's response, with sickening enthusiasm. "But as we're all gentlemen here, let him pick which three."

"Now see here!" Varick was practically shouting now. "There's no call fo—"

The skinny thug came rushing at Varick. Just as he did, a small figure, dark as the shadows, darted diagonally down between them, striking the incoming attacker's arm. It bounded off the side of the building and came back from the other direction. The skinny one jumped back after the first strike, then stabbed at the figure, but his knife found only air. The shadow bounded off the opposite wall too and bounced as soon as its feet hit the pavement. It jabbed at the skinny one's leg this time, making him retreat further with a colorful swear.

Varick's mouth hung open. It had all happened so fast! Only now did he realize the small, leaping figure was none other than Coal. The boy's face was twisted into an evil grin, dark eyes glinting in the moonlight. The boy stood, but his feet remained positioned to spring.

"Piss off, Parker," Coal ordered. He'd changed his usually

chirpy voice to a grating vocal fry. "Or maybe I should tell Bizzy you're hunting on his turf."

Gill drew level with his comrade and loomed over Coal and Varick. "You know what we do to tattletales, runt?"

Unbelievably, Coal's grin grew. "You cut out their tongues. 'Cept we both know you won't do that. We're with Mercury, and you won't break the peace without Hue's permission."

"Forget them, Gill," Parker hissed next to him. "We got the scab's money."

A darker spot was spreading beneath where the goon pressed his hand against his arm, where Coal had hit him the first time. Varick's eyes flicked down, and sure enough, he spied the glint of a small, short, triangular blade, no longer than the width of Varick's hand.

Gill looked over to his partner and growled. "Fine." He pointed a sausage-like finger at the boys. "Watch your backs, you little cockroaches. If we catch you again, you won't live long enough to cry over what we're gonna do to you."

With that, the two thugs made their way back down the alley, Parker limping and leaving a small trail of blood behind him. As soon as they were gone, Coal spun around to face Varick, his expression as cheerful as ever.

"Whew! That was a close one," he said, keeping his voice down. "I wouldn't have known who they worked for if it hadn't been for their clothes." He looked back in the direction they'd gone. "Looks like clown wear to me, but to each their own, I guess."

Varick did not reply and only scowled down at the boy. Inside of him, a war raged. On the one hand, he was infinitely grateful to Coal for saving his skin… and his fingers. On the other, there was still his betrayal. Coal finally looked up at his face, and his smile faltered.

"You're still mad at me, huh?" he said.

"Of course, I am," Varick snapped. "Why wouldn't I be? You set me up so yet another person can try to use me to their own ends. *You* used me to your own ends."

Coal held out his hands. "Okay, yes, I did, but you'd get a piece of the score. Mercury didn't even get a chance to tell you about that part."

"Don't act like *I* did something wrong," Varick snarled. "I don't owe him anything, just like I don't owe *you* anything."

With that, Varick began to stride out of the alley.

"Varick, don't!" Coal whisper-shouted after him. " You're going the wrong way."

Varick stopped. Now *that* probably was true, but then which bloody way was he supposed to go? He balled his fists at his sides, trying to collect himself and figure out what to do.

"I can take you home," Coal offered in a small voice. Varick could tell by the sound that the smaller lad had come closer, though he hadn't heard any signs of approach.

"Yes, I think you should. You owe me that much at least."

There was a pause, and Varick peeked back to see Coal fidgeting. He waited.

Finally, words burst from Coal in a rush like steam from a pipe. "Okay, but I *did* save you too."

Varick spun on him. "It's because of you I'm even in this mess!"

"Shhhhh!" Coal hissed, making a placating gesture. "Fair enough. Call it even then, yeah?"

Varick growled to himself. "Just get me home."

Coal bobbed a nod and looked back at the building. "You're good at climbing. Let's go this way."

With that, Coal ran for a drainpipe and scuttled up it as easy as anything. Varick growled again and stalked after him.

10

A Dog and Pony Show

Coal got Varick home without incident. It was quiet and tense the entire way. At least it was after Coal had started to try and apologize. Or maybe to explain himself. Varick didn't let him get far enough to find out which.

"There's nothing you can say that makes tonight okay." Coal tried once more, and Varick had snapped, "No!" so loud it echoed.

Once they were back on Pendragon grounds, Varick told him to go away and never come back. It was deep into the wee hours of night by now, well past midnight. Varick snuck around to the door of the main kitchen, which, in his experience, was always unlocked thanks to all the activity coming and going through there. When he tried the handle, though, it remained firmly unmoved. Varick's heart sank. He was going to have to stay out here the rest of the night, and it had gotten properly chilly. He slumped back against the doorframe and closed his eyes. Stars, he felt exhausted.

"Locked out, huh?"

The familiar voice whispered right next to Varick, and he just about leapt out of his skin. It was by luck alone that he managed to swallow his startled yelp. The night's events had made him as jumpy as a rabbit in a wolf den.

"Coal!" he grumbled. "You're like a bad penny, always turning up. Do you know that?"

Coal's bright grin shone in the darkness. Ignoring the question, he said, "Watch this."

He then extracted a small, rolled-up packet of thin, metal rods. Some were squiggly, while others had tiny picks or hooks at the end. Coal extracted two of the rods and set to work on the lock. Varick suddenly understood how the boy had managed to get around the house.

"You're a *proper* thief, aren't you? Experienced."

"Aw, cheers, chum." Coal beamed at the unintended praise. "But really I'm still in training."

"Did Mercury teach you how to do this?"

"Naw. Not much of a teacher, Mercury. He doesn't have much interest in that sorta thing. You gotta have something to offer for him to let you into his crew."

Varick's eyebrows flattened into an angry line. "Like money."

"Not gonna lie, he was gonna ask you to be a backer for this job, but he likes what I told him about your stealth skills too."

The sound of the bolt rolling out of its slot was the most glorious noise Varick had ever heard. He slipped inside with one last backwards glance at Coal.

"We're *not* even, and we're not friends. Don't let me catch you around here again, Coal. Am I understood?"

The boy's eyebrows creased a little, but he managed to hold up a sad smile. "It's been really nice knowing you, Varick."

With that, he pulled the door shut in his own face. Varick

eased the bolt home again and crept through silent corridors and up the stairs. When he finally made it back to his own apartments, he found a note sitting on the small, enameled tray near the door to his rooms. A purple wax seal, his mother's own special motif of daffodils, glared up at him. This was normal practice within the house, and it was one of the few things he appreciated in his family's habits. Notes gave him time and space to not only to formulate safe responses but also prepare himself for whatever fresh hell those notes heralded. Varick sliced the missive open with his abalone-handled letter knife. He daren't get caught out not knowing something she'd deigned to send him a message about.

We have been asked to play in the Saffron Club's croquet tournament tomorrow, as the Jones household has all come down with colds. You will be ready to leave by 11 o'clock.

Varick sighed and looked at the mantel clock. It was just coming up to a quarter past three. He took only as much time as strictly necessary to change into his nightclothes, hide his spoiled clothing, and crawl into bed. It was going to be a very long day tomorrow.

♜

The vast green of the croquet course played off the deep wine color of Constance's be-ruffled day dress. Randolph had only been gone a little over a week now. Varick had been right when he'd told Coal how short-lived their all black attire would last. The fact that she wore a band of black crepe, as did they all, around her arm was little consolation.

It had turned out that only two of the Pendragon clan were needed to play in today's event. The rest were along for reasons

Varick neither knew nor rated high enough to be told. Constance and Patricia had both put on grand displays of courage in stepping up to represent their family in the tourney, with the eldest son and mother of the Evergreen family playing opposite. The two ladies, terrible cheats and thick as thieves, had grasped each other by the hands and made proclamations that a bit of activity would surely lift their spirits after their "ineffable loss." Other well-to-do families were in attendance as well, all enjoying the autumn sunshine and myriad refreshments on offer. Varick, who'd only gotten a scant few hours of sleep, was slightly mollified at seeing Lord Quincy and a few others in attendance sporting black eyes or other various dishevelments. Of course, the reasons given for such ranged everywhere between sonambulatory nighttime indigestion and being whacked in the face by a shying horse. Magnus had wandered off to go enjoy some billiards, while Varick had been "encouraged" to go enjoy some time with his playmates.

That he hadn't had "playmates" since the age of seven and that he rarely enjoyed the company of his parents' friends' children mattered not a whit to anyone, but he stalked off toward a knot of older children and younger adolescents anyway.

The young people were gathered around one Falcon Smoke —a year Varick's junior and hailing from a family all weirdly obsessed with birds. The throng was not surprising considering the young man in question had brought an actual *pony* to the croquet tournament. Could he be any more of a show-off? He didn't flaunt his unsolicited show-and-tell offering, though, like Constance and Magnus would have. He didn't even baby it like so many women watching the match did with their tiny, spoiled, smush-faced lapdogs. Falcon seemed genuinely overjoyed with the animal and acted as if everyone else would clearly feel the same. Varick felt bad for the footman standing by with a shovel and ready to clean up the animal's leavings as soon as they hit the

carefully maintained grass.

Varick hovered at the edge of the little group, listening to the questions some of the younger ones demanded of Falcon.

"Does he eat a lot?"

"How fast does he go?"

"Does he pull a cart?"

"Can I ride him?"

To this last one, everyone latched on as if all of them didn't have equines of their own. It reminded Varick that he hadn't visited Tallywags since Randolph had passed. In truth, Varick had been a little scared to. He had a strong notion that seeing Tallywags would only make him cry. But the animal deserved better, and Varick a mental note to do so soon.

"He's pretty," came a soft voice off to Varick's side.

From behind a pair of round sun-spectacles with smoke-darkened glass, Varick side-eyed a young man standing next to him, perhaps a year or two his senior. The lad, slightly familiar, was bronze-skinned and tall with well-built shoulders. Varick wondered if perhaps his family had recently been invited to join the club. That sort of thing happened occasionally, a family gained enough wealth and prestige through business or art or scientific discovery, but it required sterling references and multiple nominations by existing members in good standing. He also wondered if the lad might be a junior pugilist, what with those impressive arms.

The young gentleman gave Varick a shy smile and asked, "Do you like horses?"

What. Rotten. Luck.

He was new and looking to make friends. He'd probably suspected Varick of being an equally shy soul and thus had dared to push out the social boat. It's wasn't that Varick was against making new acquaintances. It was just that someone always spoiled it for him, and he had long ago wearied of that particular strain of disappointment and heartache. Memories of last night and Coal's betrayal came forward to rub salt in that particular wound.

Varick leveled his voice to the brink of disinterest as he replied, "I suppose so. I have one anyway."

The shy smile grew. The chap ventured to put out his hand. "Archibald. Archibald Sweeney, but you can call me Archie."

Varick gave the most perfunctory of smiles in return and shook Archie's hand. "Varick Pendragon."

"It's nice to meet you, Varick Pendragon."

In the background, Falcon was helping a small girl onto the pony's back. The pony stood patiently until Falcon took its reins and began to slowly walk it around a circuitous path. It barely blinked as some of the younger children squealed as if they'd taken off at breakneck speed. The gathered sprog all oohed and aahed and clamored for the next ride.

In the manner of awkward individuals everywhere desperately trying to make smalltalk, Archie grabbed a hold of the subject at hand and drove it forward. "What's your horse's name then?"

Varick's eyebrows lifted, and a real chuckle slipped past his careful defenses. In a low voice, he admitted, "It's very rude. My grandfather named him." A sudden pang of sadness shot through Varick's heart. "My… late grandfather."

Archie's head tipped, and he gave Varick an empathetic grimace. "I'm sorry for your loss. My grandad's dead too. He died last year." He hesitated a moment before adding cautiously, "It's a strange thing, isn't it? How they can make such a profound impact on your life and then they're just… gone."

Varick nodded, not trusting himself to speak for a moment. He distracted himself with the thought that Archie really must be from an upwardly-moving family—the pit of vipers that was Springhaven's upper crust hadn't poisoned and hardened him yet.

Archie gave him a small, encouraging smile. "So what's this rude name your granddad gave your horse?"

Varick returned the smile, a rare gift, and glanced around to ensure no one else was within earshot. "Tallywags."

Archie burst out laughing, a clear, joyous noise, and a few of the gathered young people turned their heads. None approached, though, many still jockeying for a turn on the pony.

"A word of advice, Archie." Varick kept his voice low like before and his tone pleasant. "Don't trust the people here. A bunch of backbiting jackals, the lot of them."

Archie's brows crimped with concern. "No offense, but doesn't that mean I shouldn't trust you either?"

Varick's smile soured into a sardonic curve. Archie was clearly a sharp lad. Varick gave a smooth little shrug, "It does. And I wouldn't blame you if you didn't. It's just that you're clearly new around here and you seem really nice. You should know what you're getting into."

As if to illustrate his point, a commotion started in the queue, if the messy clump of the most eager youngsters could be called such. A boy about Varick's age was pushing back a slightly smaller, younger member of the throng. Varick knew them both —the former a little snot by the name of Eamon Lee and the latter a morose boy called Harry Evergreen. Eamon was pushing the unfortunately monikered Harry back, who was almost in tears and trying to shove his way past the taller Eamon.

"I was next, fair and square," he whined.

"My family has more money than yours, so get back in your proper place," Eamon sniffed.

Some of the other children laughed, others simply watched. The little girl from before, whose turn with the pony had ended, was calling Eamon a bully. None of the adults, sitting a little ways off in their chairs and sipping drinks, had even looked toward the group. Heat churned in Varick's belly. Any sense of self-preservation fled as anger and grief melded inside of him to cook up a muddling stew of emotions. Scenes from the last fortnight flashed in Varick's mind—Randolph's falling ill and then passing, getting blindsided by the inheritance, Coal's false friendship. Varick marched over to the Lee boy, pulled back a fist, and punched him square in the nose. Eamon went stumbling back under the blow, blood erupting from his nostrils and despoiling his crisp, white shirt.

"You're a spoiled little ratbag!" Varick snarled. More words that he'd swallowed down over the years came clawing up his throat without a thought. "You think you deserve to be treated like a prince just because an accident of birth landed you in a rich family."

Someone was tugging at his arm. "Varick, stop!"

Varick's head snapped toward the voice, toward the hand around his arm. It was Archie. Varick glowered as hatefully as he could over his sun-spectacles. How dare he defend a little brat like Eamon Lee?

"He's a soggy pile of chicken grot, I get it," Archie soothed, "but people are *looking*."

Varick glanced back. The adults were finally taking notice. Some of the gathered children had run over to tattle on him. The hot anger in Varick's belly cooled to a cold lump of stone as his father turned to listen in on the nearby reports.

"Bugger me," Varick muttered.

11

Two Steps Forward, One Step Back

"Come on!" Archie urged.

He tugged Varick's arm again. Varick followed, not knowing where they were headed but wanting to forestall whatever punishment awaited him. They ran around the perimeter of the building and, once they were out of sight, darted for some shrubbery that ringed the club. A line of windows opened wide to the sweet, autumn air, and the boys risked a careful peek inside. Both were just tall enough to see over the sill.

"It's the ballroom," Varick said.

"And it's empty," Archie added. "I can give you a boost."

Before Varick could insist he was a perfectly capable climber, Archie grabbed Varick around the knees and launched him up and through the open window. Varick grunted quite an ungentlemanly word as he landed unceremoniously on his rear, which still sported deep bruising from last night's shenanigans. Archie followed right behind, smoothly vaulting himself over the windowsill on one beefy arm, legs bent and feet well clear of the frame. He landed with a thump next to Varick's discarded-marionette-esque form. Archie then grasped Varick's arm and bodily pulled him onto his feet. Without thinking, Varick snatched his arm away.

"Will you stop touching me!" he growled, barely remembering to keep his voice down.

Archie put his hands up. "Apologies, mate. Didn't know that was a sore spot for you."

Varick froze, checking that his senses hadn't been addled when he'd hit the ground. "Wait… what?"

"No touching. I got it," Archie clarified.

Varick blinked at him. "What happened to your voice?"

He hadn't been imagining it. From the word "sorry," Archie's voice had gotten deeper, stronger. Not drastically so, but enough that even the unobservant would take note.

"Bit of an affectation, I admit," Archie said. "Didn't want to scare you off."

"Scare me off?" Varick demanded. "What the blazes are you talking about?"

Archie took a deep breath. "My real name is Carver. I'm a friend of Coal's."

Varick's whole expression transformed into a series of incredulous V's. "Oh, you have got to be joking. Is no one in this city capable of being honest with me?"

"On my grandfather's spirit, you'll have only truth from me from now on."

Varick scowled and looked Carver, formerly Archie, over again. As before, something niggled in the recesses of his brain. "Do I know you from somewhere?"

"Maybe." Carver mimed holding a tray. "Ring any bells?"

Puzzle pieces clicked together for Varick. "You're a waiter," he accused. "You were there, at the funeral. And last night too."

Carver gave a humble little shrug. "I'm whatever a situation might need, within reason. That turns out to be a waiter more often than you might think."

Varick couldn't deny he was impressed, which was annoying because that made it harder to be upset. So he circled back to a subject still giving his anger plenty of fuel.

"So you work with Coal, stealing things?"

"That is correct, though I don't have anything like Coal's skills. I'm usually the guy who just cases a place or leaves a convenient window open."

That's right. Coal had thanked someone called Carver last night when they'd snuck inside the hotel.

"He's really upset, Varick." Carver went on. "He feels terrible about the setup, but he didn't know what else to do. We need a backer and you're harder to corner than a cat in a round room."

"He could have sent me a note," Varick threw back. "Or that Mercury fellow could have."

Carver gave him a dubious look. "And what would we say?" His tone turned sarcastic. "Hello there, you don't know me nor any of my associates, but would you like to participate in a lucrative but somewhat clandestine operation? Please respond back at your earliest convenience by leaving your reply under the mossy rocks near the ornamental carp pond."

Varick scowled. "You forgot to include 'illegal' in your description." He wasn't actually certain that was the case, but with everything he'd seen, he was fairly sure he wasn't far off.

"Besides," Carver pressed on, "I can guarantee any note we sent to you wouldn't have made it."

Varick was about to demand what that meant when the sound

of a set of ballroom doors being unlocked resounded from the other end of the room. Like a rabbit to its warren, Carver dove behind the long, heavy curtain beside the window frame. Varick followed automatically. The consequences of his actions could wait, and they'd keep like a booze-soaked fruitcake.

The space behind the curtains provided a little leeway to move without rustling the heavy fabric. Carver, who seemed to remember what the lad had said about not touching him again, shifted slightly away from Varick. It was a small gesture, but took some careful effort inside their hiding spot, and Varick felt a appreciation settle over him. To have this boundary respected, especially in this tricky spot, said a lot about Carver. When was the last time his own family had respected his boundaries?

The door opened, and someone, a member of the Saffron Club's staff by the sound of it, began providing a tour of the space. Varick and Carver hid, remaining still and learning all about the amenities available to anyone wishing to engage the ballroom for an event. At one point, while the tour guide elucidated his guests about the age and worth of the chandeliers, Carver caught Varick's eye. With only his face, Carver performed a mimicry of the guests' responses.

"Over a hundred years? Well, I'll be." Carver's face went farcically amazed in response to this.

"Hm, not that impressive considering chandeliers are harder to loot, wouldn't you say?" Varick joined in and, to this, he pulled a sneering face so extreme he looked like a horse caught mid-sneeze.

"It's so much silver, though." Carver's nose pinched as if he'd just stepped in a pile of dog turds.

"Platinum, not silver," the tour guide said. "I assure you." As one, Varick and Carver shared a smug "that's them told" look.

On the game went, with several pauses to stave off laughter until finally the tour moved on almost ten minutes later. The boys

waited until they heard the door close and lock again before emerging from their drapery hideout.

"Well, that was fun," Carver said, looking pleased. "Where were we?"

"Illegal activities." Varick replied flatly.

Carver flicked his index finger in the air. "Ah, yes. Well, to that point, it's not *exactly* illegal."

"How is it not *exactly* illegal?"

"The item in play doesn't technically belong to anyone, except whoever stole it last." Varick cocked a skeptical eyebrow, and Carver returned a helpless shrug. "Look, Varick, you're not actually on board, so I'm not at liberty to disclose certain details."

Varick sighed. Even just listening to this was a terrible idea. Accomplices to crime were as severely punished as the actual crime-committers themselves. But he couldn't deny he'd had more fun with these jolly miscreants in just a few days than he had in a long time with anyone, besides his grandfather. And even that hadn't been quite the same. Plus, the mystery of what this "job" he'd been hearing about was an enticing one.

"So what was last night? Why did Coal trick me into helping him? Is it so you all have dirt on me, so you can blackmail me into helping you?"

Varick did not even know this suspicion had been lurking inside of him until now. He felt the beginnings of a cold sweat break out over his skin, but Carver was already waving the idea away.

"No, Mercury doesn't know anything about that, and Coal's not gonna tell him. Neither am I. He just thought you needed a bit of fun." A pause. "So? Did you?"

"Did I need fun?" Varick asked. He wasn't certain what to make of a question like that just now.

"Did you *have* fun?" Carver clarified.

Varick grumbled inwardly. Blast it all, yes, he had. He'd had the time of his life. Even now, after everything, thinking of how the casino night had imploded in on itself gave Varick a toasty warm feeling of satisfaction. That had been *his idea* that had set things off. Last night, Varick had won. He'd toppled the powerful. Who was to say he couldn't do it again? He didn't want to admit any of this to Carver, though. He could still be lying, even if the beloved, dead grandfather on whose spirit he'd sworn to tell the truth was real. But to what end? Varick still held a lot of cards. Money and family reputation did a lot for one's credibility, especially against admitted thieves, who he could always report and deny any involvement with.

"Mercury only wants to use me for my money," Varick muttered. "I don't mind telling you, the joke's on him. I don't even know how much I have. I haven't sat down with my accountant yet."

Carver gave a noncommittal wag of his head. "Well, you should probably do that, no matter what."

"Of course, and I will… just as soon as I figure out how to schedule it without any of the rest of my rotten family knowing. They'll connive their way into the meeting and stars know what else." That pinged something in Varick's brain, something Carver had said before they'd jumped behind the curtain. "What did you mean any note you'd send to me wouldn't make it?"

"So glad you asked."

Carver reached into his inside jacket pocket and withdrew a creamy, tri-folded sheet of paper. It was a pricey sort of paper people like the Pendragons used for everyday things like list-making and letters. Varick didn't recognize the wax seal on it—a beech tree—but Cousin Chester's name, written in a tidy hand, and his own as the intended recipient practically leapt off the page. He snatched the letter from Carver's hand.

"What are you doing with my mail?" Varick snapped.

"Rescuing it from your parents' clutches."

Carver didn't sound smug as he said it, which surprised Varick. He was too busy opening his purloined mail to react, though.

To: Mister Varick Pendragon, the letter began.
From: The office of Chester Pendragon, Esquire.

As much as I appreciate how much you value your parents' guidance, the letter you asked them to send to me in response to my previous communique re: the arrangement of your grandfather's monetary assets bequeathed to you in his last will and testament, will not suffice. You, as the sole account holder...

"Wait, letter *I* asked them to send?" Varick said aloud. "And what previous communique?" The penny dropped. Carver had said this letter, this *second* letter, had been rescued from his parents' clutches. Varick had known his family would set meetings without him or his knowledge, but he hadn't actually considered that they'd tamper with his mail. His ears grew hot with fear. Nothing was beyond them, and now with all the money he'd come into...

"So how did you get this?" he asked, his voice soft and angry.

"Coal," Carver said. "He's been watching the house, saw your father pop this near the window this morning. He just had to wait for a few minutes with no one in the room."

Carver rubbed his chin thoughtfully, and Varick noticed just the barest scatterings of facial hair there—wispy promises of a beardy future dotting his bronze skin. He rubbed his own smooth face. He wasn't exactly looking forward to the day he'd have to start shaving, but it'd be nice to be able to say he had to.

"Far be it from me to insult anyone else's family," Carver

mused, "but from what you and Coal have told me, they're all pretty slippery, yeah?"

"You forgot grasping and vicious," Varick replied.

Carver nodded, and it was only then that Varick realized he'd been expecting Carver to question him, to tell Varick how he probably had it wrong about his own family. The simple acceptance wooshed through Varick like a cool breeze on a brutally hot day.

Carver only asked, "Do you want help?"

"Help with what?" He couldn't imagine Carver or Coal, and certainly not Mercury, actually *helping* him with anything. Not without paying a price anyway.

"Setting up a meeting with your accountant without your family knowing?" The way Carver said it, he made it sound like it'd be the work of a mere moment. When Varick only stared at him in befuddlement, Carver explained. "We can intercept your mail, or better yet, act as go-betweens on your behalf. That way, we won't stir up suspicion over lost messages. We can even act as your..." Carver considered his words. "Well, probably not a valet. Only Mercury looks old enough, I think."

"I don't trust him," Varick put in. "I don't even really trust you or Coal, but Mercury stinks of an agenda."

Carver's head bobbed in agreement. "He's wily, but he took all of us in off the street and gave us a place, so long as we earn our keep anyway."

"How generous," Varick drawled. He almost added, "I don't care," but that wasn't quite true. He was glad of it, for Coal and Carver's sakes. Instead, he said, "It doesn't change the fact that I don't like him."

Carver shrugged. "Fair enough. Coal or I can pose as..." He waved a hand. "Some kind of low level staff to accompany you."

Varick examined Carver again. He was at least a head taller than Varick, and with those shoulders, he could pass for older than he was. It was just that his face that might give him away.

"If we put a beard on you, you'd look older," Varick said. "You could be my secretary." He examined Carver's checkered day suit and gave an approving nod. "That outfit will work. You'll have to come by the Dragon's Keep to get my reply. It'll have to bear my official seal, otherwise people won't believe it came from me."

"Coal's a much better sneak than I am," Carver reminded him.

"I don't want to see Coal." Varick's tone brooked no argument.

"Understood. Meet me somewhere easy to hide then? Around midnight tonight?"

"The stables." Varick grinned. "Look for Tallywags."

A warm, answering smile crept up Carver's face. "Are we doing this then?"

"I'm not agreeing to anything," Varick said. "I don't even know what my situation is yet, so I don't know if I could be your…" He thought back to the term that Carver and Coal had both used. "Your backer. But if you want anything from me, you have to help me *first*."

In truth, Varick knew he shouldn't even be considering this, but Mercury's words from last night echoed in his mind: *The investment is legit, and it's a big one, big enough to set Coal and a handful of others like him up for life. It's not much. You wouldn't be ending poverty or anything, but you'd be able to say you helped a few out of destitution.*

Randolph had always helped people, and he'd been clever about it. He'd always managed to strike a balance between shrewdness and generosity. "Give them an opportunity to impress you," he'd liked to say when he'd taken a chance on someone. Begrudgingly, Varick had to admit what Carver had said about why they'd approached Varick as they had made sense too. What options had they had besides subterfuge? And now that he knew his parents had tampered with his mail, he found needed help too. Maybe, just maybe, there existed a chance he and Mercury's crew really could help each other. Varick was furious with Coal, yes, but he didn't want the boy to starve. And Carver had said the thing they'd be stealing was meant to be stolen, so was it really even theft? Varick would be savvy like his grandfather. He could do it. He'd achieved a great victory just last night after all. He'd take this one step at a time, starting with Carver. Nice and easy and safe. Yes, that would work.

Carver extended his hand. "Thank you for the opportunity, Varick Pendragon."

Varick smiled and shook. "I hope to be impressed."

For the first time in a long time, he felt optimistic. That is, until he remembered punching Eamon Lee, and that he still had to face his family.

12
COVERT ACTIVITIES

The slap came swiftly and with no small amount of rage behind it. Varick had been expecting it and rolled with the impact. Fire exploded over his cheek, but he resisted the urge to rub it. His mother had found him first, after he'd unhappily trudged out of the ballroom to face the music. Victoria had been crossing the Saffron Club's long, octagonal front hall just then, which waited just beyond the ballroom doors.

"You wretched little cur!" she snarled in a low voice. "You humiliated us in front of everyone! You will apologize to Eamon, you will apologize to his parents, you will apologize to us, and you will do it *now*."

Varick said nothing. Any argument or attempt to justify his actions would only result in being hit again. She was so furious, he thought she might anyway. No one was in the hall at the moment, though that hardly mattered in this case. He'd struck one of his peers without apparent provocation. Plenty of people would say he deserved such punishment. Thus, he plodded along obediently, his mother ushering him across the hall to the tearoom. The Lee family was sitting at a table with tea and other refreshments, the young Eamon with a couple of wads of cotton wool shoved up his nostrils.

Varick's words were automatic—a rote apology citing his offense, some empty epithets about how ashamed he was, and a wish he didn't really mean that Eamon could forgive him. He didn't give two coppers about the boy's opinion of him. Eamon Lee was a rotten little brat. He always had been and he always would be.

Eamon's replies were just as meaningless. He said, "I forgive you, Varick," though, with his clogged nose, it sounded like, "I forgib you, Barick."

With the socially expected tick-boxes checked, Victoria then herded Varick back out to the front hall and down the stairs of the Saffron Club's covered front portico. Outside, the Pendragon family coach waited, all gilt curves and oiled mahogany. Varick spied Constance's far-too excited face peek out the window and then turn to chitter at someone else. After he'd climbed in and seated himself next to his grandmother, Patricia started in on him.

"We were about to leave without you. You're very lucky you weren't left to walk home."

Varick didn't say that he would have been fine getting home on his own. It was broad daylight out, and they hadn't even left the Ivory district. Instead, he just repeated his meaningless apologies to the family.

Their driver urged the horses forward, and the coach pulled away from the Saffron Club. Henry chewed the inside of his cheek as he sat across the coach from Varick. He could practically feel the anger radiating from his father.

"A good mugging might do the pup some good," Henry said. "It'd be no less than he deserves, ungrateful as he is."

"I can reenact one," Magnus volunteered with a nasty smile.

"If you think it'd be educational for the little weevil."

"Don't be stupid," Henry snapped, turning his ire onto his eldest. "It's beneath you."

Magnus muttered an apology and promptly shut up after that.

Constance, who'd always been cleverer than their older brother—not a difficult feat, to be fair—used the opportunity to try and pile on Varick's trouble. "Do you think Ricky's disgraceful display will hurt our standing with the Lee family? You have some dealings with them, don't you, Father?"

Varick bristled at the horrible nickname, but he only clenched his palms, careful not to let his frustration show to the family. He'd once upon a time, back when he'd still thought there might be a shred of good in any of them, told Constance that he didn't like the name. She'd simply laughed at him and repeated it in a singsong voice until he'd left the room.

Henry harrumphed in his seat. "No. A scuffle between tykes isn't enough to hurt the mutual benefit we share."

"Besides," Victoria piped up, "I understand from Erin Lee that they've been having some trouble with Eamon. She admits he's badly cosseted, and he resents having his indulgences limited."

"A firm hand would sort that right out," Henry grumbled.

The conversation turned toward Constance and Patricia's croquet match. They'd won, and Varick knew they'd cheated somehow, though they'd never admit to such a thing. He kept one ear out in case he needed to respond—he wanted to avoid any more trouble today if he could—but the other part of his mind turned to the upcoming ploy to meet with Cousin Chester in secret.

That night, as agreed, Varick nipped off to the stables just before midnight. They were less a single building and more of a U-shaped complex, with areas for the horses, their tack, feed, and equipment. And then there was the section for the various Pendragon coaches and cabs and everything that went along with keeping them maintained. There was the main family coach, of course, large enough to comfortably accommodate all six of them, and an identical backup, just in case something ever went wrong with the main one. The family owned a couple of phaetons as well for when they wanted to be seen. As they only held up to two people—and that was assuming at least one of them was a gent, given the allowances that had to be made for the volume of a lady's skirts—Patricia, Victoria and Henry, Constance, and Magnus each had one. That last one's itching inducer treatment had worked well, and Varick planned to deploy another round soon. He had neither wanted such a flashy vehicle, nor had he been deemed deserving. A brougham, however. Now *that* was his dream carriage. Nice and enclosed, so that no one could see him or bother him.

As Varick crept through the chilly night, listening to the gentle sound of sleeping horses, he was surprised to find Tallywags was not in his usual stall. Even his nameplate had been removed, and for a terror-drenched moment, Varick wondered if someone—Patricia or perhaps Henry—had called for the animal to be put down. His heart pounded as he stalked along the aisle of stalls, eyes scanning for the familiar old nameplate. He passed Thunderstride and Silken Sunflower, Springtime Cardigan Heart, Ambertress, Golden Hour's Heavenly Glory, and the many more plainly-named horses used to pull everyday carts and carriages, like Bob the Fourth, and those which had been purchased in matching sets, such as Bold Dandy and Gold Mandy, but no Tallywags.

Please, please don't have killed my horse, Varick mentally begged of no one in particular. He should have come down

sooner. He shouldn't have been such a bloody coward and—
Ohthankthestarsthereheis!

Tallywags had been moved all the way to the end of the aisle, and Varick suddenly realized why. One of his family's constant complaints, after Randolph's contemptible refusal to rename the bally creature, was his insistence on keeping Tallywags—and his humiliating nameplate—near the stable entrance for the "entire world" to see their shame. Varick and Randolph had often laughed at the family's dramatic use of the term, "entire world," given what a small fraction of Springhaven's population ever received the honor of an invite to the Dragon's Keep.

At least the uppity equine was not alone, not at the moment anyway. Carver stood at the stall door rubbing Tallywags' dark neck. He turned well before Varick reached him, and gave a silent nod of greeting. Varick nodded back.

"Did you give him a treat?" he asked quietly once he was close enough to Carver and Tallywags.

Carver smiled. "Yeah, apples."

"Smart. Bribery's the only thing that works on him."

Tallywags was a sight to behold. He was of fairly average size at fifteen hands, but his coat was a beautiful blue roan with black points and a black mane and tail. Thanks to the tireless efforts of the younger stable lads—to whom the task of brushing the temperamental animal fell, and who were also not above bribery—Tallywags' coat shone like liquid metal even now under the faint glow of the low petrolsene lights.

Also a sight to behold was Carver's face, though Varick couldn't quite puzzle out why. It looked darker somehow, but unevenly so.

He gestured at the strange new shadows on Carver's face. "What's... going on... here?"

"I made myself a beard," Carver explained. "Coal said it looks like a nest of dead ants. I wanted to get your thoughts before I went around saying I worked for you."

"Right," Varick said, fearing the worst. "Let's go up to the loft. We can light a lamp up there, and I can get a better look."

They were soon above Tallywags' stall, in a little tucked-away space just under the angled roof. In the golden light of an oil lamp, now that Varick could see properly, he couldn't for the life of him figure out how Carver had done what he'd done.

He had sideburns now, but they looked like they were in the process of slowly eating his head. His false beard was uneven as well, both in coverage and thickness.

"What happened?" Varick asked in a whisper.

"I know it looks bad, okay?" Carver replied. "When I realized I'd messed up, Coal tried to help me fix it, and the more he helped, the more it grew."

Varick paused before saying, "It doesn't look bad."

Carver gave him a confused look, and Varick went on.

"It looks horrendous. It looks as though you're suffering from some sort of virulent hair disease. You *cannot* go around looking like that."

"I don't know what else to do," Carver said.

Varick shook his head. "Absolutely not." He thought to himself and then asked, "Is it alright if I touch you? On your face?"

"Yeah," Carver said. "That's fine."

Varick grabbed a bit of the hair in between his fingers and pulled. It remained firmly in place.

"It's attached," he said stupidly.

Carver gave him an obvious look. "Yeah, with glue. How else was it gonna stay? Willpower?"

Varick pondered for another moment before saying, "This is going to hurt. Is that still fine?"

"Do what you have to do."

Varick yanked as hard as he could. The false hair came away

in a clump, and Varick dearly hoped those bits attached at the end were dried glue and not skin. Carver hissed a creative swear, wincing.

"Steel yourself," Varick warned. "There's more where that came from."

Carver let out a low grumble, but stayed still while Varick went about strategically ripping off bits of his disguise. In a few minutes, he'd finished, and, with a hand, Varick fanned cool air the angry red splotches on Carver's face.

"There we go. All better."

At least, he certainly hoped it would be all better by tomorrow. Now it looked like Carver might be suffering from a rash, though that was easier to explain away than the hair-creature with a hunger for human faces from a few minutes ago.

In regards to tomorrow, Varick removed a letter from his pocket. The gold-flecked, glossy black wax of his seal—a lavender sprig—shone in the low light. He handed it over to Carver for delivery.

"Remember, my family can't find out about this meeting," Varick warned. He rather felt Carver didn't need the reminder, but he was working with Mercury, who Varick didn't trust as far as he could throw the man, and Coal, who'd betrayed him once already.

Carver nodded, looking over the letter. "Lavender?" he asked, taking in the seal.

Varick rolled his eyes. "I know it's supposed to represent distrust, but it's pretty. And I like the way it smells. Isn't that enough for a flower without tacking on some spurious meaning?"

His family had ridiculed the choice when Varick had it registered with Springhaven's Directory of Official Insignias. Granted, the black wax with gold flecks had been a piss-take, being as ostentatious as possible just to get under their skin, but Varick felt his point still stood.

"Fair enough," Carver said.

And once again, Varick felt none of the judgement he'd expected.

13
MONEY, IT'S A CRIME

It really had been as easy as all that. After Varick gave Carver the letter for Cousin Chester, which had helpfully included some suggested dates and times for a meeting, Chester had sent back a reply the very same day with his selection. Then, Varick just had to get through the next few days without his family being any the wiser. He worried Chester would blab, and Varick kept an ear out for evidence of this. He dearly wished the Dragon's Keep had secret passages to hide in and spy from, like grand manors in books always had. Sadly, however, despite spending a good deal of his life looking Varick had never found a trick wall sconce or secret bookcase doorway. There were dumbwaiters and laundry chutes and staff corridors, but all of those risked easy discovery. Thus, in order to effectively surveil his family, Varick had no choice but to—*shudder*—spend time with them, or at least in their vicinity.

One advantage of being thought of as an odious little tick was that people tended to want as little to do with you as possible. Except when people wanted something *from* you, of course. For Magnus and Constance, this usually meant using Varick for entertainment. In those situations, he had plenty of hiding places to retreat to. And anyway, it was Victoria, Henry, and Patricia he thought most likely to get wind of his plans.

Varick wasn't able to join in for much, as Henry was often busy with his duties overseeing the various Pendragon interests—mostly tenant farmers working the orchards and other productive parts of the Dragon's Keep lands, with more on the outskirts of Springhaven that produced dairy products and meat. He also had a number of business investments, from which he drew dividends.

Patricia and Victoria, too, were often busy as the patronesses of several artistic and intellectual institutions, and a handful of workhouses. The latter were laughably described as charitable establishments. Varick knew they couldn't be when the two women worked so hard to promote them, trotting them out any time they wanted to add a little shine to their reputation.

The only time Varick was really able to hang about was during meals, when his father was reading, his mother painting, or his grandmother practicing or performing in the music room. They were all surprisingly nonplussed by his unusual presence, which was suspicious. Or perhaps Varick was simply getting better at being invisible. In any case, he heard nothing from any corner of the Dragon's Keep to indicate that Chester had let news of their meeting slip.

The morning of that momentous appointment, the wind blew brisk and sharp. A rainstorm that night before had brought colder temperatures, and Varick liked it. He felt it made him sharper too, and gave him a good excuse to pull the collar of his coat up around his face. He knew it was paranoid to suspect his movements were being tracked, but this was too important not to take a bit of extra care.

Getting away had been a cinch. He'd started by taking a turn about the vast gardens and kept taking turns until he'd made it down to the ornamental carp pond, before making a beeline for the nearest exit. It'd been a short cab ride after that from the Ivory district to the Copper quarter where Cousin Chester worked.

Varick had expected a bank, some towering edifice of marble and ironwork. Chester was an accountant, after all, and banks were where money lived. The tall, slender brick building Varick had arrived at instead was surprisingly unassuming. Only the placard outside confirmed he'd come to the right place:

PENDRAGON, UMPLEBY, AND JOHNSON
FIDUCIARY ADVISORS AND PROBATE SOLICITORS

Inside, however, was more what Varick had expected. A reverent hush permeated the lobby. This sanctuary of dark, highly polished wood, dedicated to the care and keeping of money and other assets, was no place for foolishness. Carver was already there, waiting for Varick on a long sofa of deep green brocade. He'd offered to come and take notes, as any good secretary would. Varick had nearly refused, but changed his mind at the last second, though he wasn't ready to admit why, even to himself. True, that meant Carver would hear all the grisly specifics of what Randolph had left behind, but everyone who'd bothered to read the newssheets already knew Varick was the proud owner of a shiny, new collection of money.

They shook hands in greeting, and Varick fought not to cringe at the state of Carver's fake beard. He couldn't tell if it had suffered those few days since Varick had seen him last or if Carver'd had to reapply it. There was nothing to be done about it now, though, and Carver fell into step behind Varick. He was now really rather pleased that he'd agreed to let Carver come along.

The lobby wasn't large, but at a grand, intricately carved desk sat a very serious man with a very serious face and very serious spectacles. It all made Varick feel small, like a child playing at grown-up things he didn't understand. He didn't even know what the word probate meant, for goodness sake, so it was nice to have Carver with him as an entourage, if a single person could be called such.

As the bespectacled gent greeted him and asked his business, Varick was still trying to figure out the best way to handle, well, everything. Not having an answer or any time left to decide, he fell back onto the only option he knew.

"We're here to meet with Chester Pendragon. We're expected," Varick replied loftily. And he immediately hated himself for it. Stars, he sounded like such a knob. This wasn't who he wanted to be, but he didn't know how else to behave and still wrest respect from people.

If Varick's rudeness offended the man, it didn't show. The poor chap probably dealt with human paper cuts like him all day. Instead, the man stood and gestured toward a door set into the back of the lobby.

"Of course, if you'll follow me."

Along the way, they passed several more doors, all shut, with nameplates indicating whose office it was or what use the room served. Chester's waited down at the far end of the corridor, just around a corner. The receptionist opened it and motioned Varick into Chester's own little waiting area.

"Tea will be along shortly," the man said, before leaving as smoothly as he'd come.

Varick, still not knowing how to act, squelched a smile. Tea sounded amazing right about now, but he daren't drop his snobby act. Not now that he'd established it, and not when it was all he had.

"Mister Pendragon, Mister Sweeney," Chester's secretary

greeted with a nod. He was a willowy man with wavy, medium-dark hair and a meticulously trimmed beard that probably made Carver's want to crawl off his face and throw itself onto the nearest roaring fireplace. "Mister Pendragon will be with you both in a moment."

Varick had been a little surprised that Carver had reused his Archibald Sweeney alter-ego, but figured the lad knew his clandestine business best. Meanwhile, the secretary pressed a button on his desk, which Varick knew must be connected to a system of thin cables and pulls, which would snake its way into Chester's private office area and ring a chime within. Sure enough, a few seconds later, a soft pinging could just be heard through the wainscoted wall. Chester appeared soon after with a facsimile of a smile on his face. It was not that Chester's smile was insincere. It was more as if he'd never learned how to do one properly and had left off trying to improve years ago.

He greeted Varick and Carver with handshakes and then gestured through the doorway. "Please, come into my inner sanctum." He gave a self-indulgent little laugh that sounded like a horse's whinny. A subdued whinny, but a whinny nonetheless.

Was this Cousin Chester trying to be winsome? He then offered the two chaps seats, not before the ornate office desk, but rather at a corner table with accompanying tufted leather chairs. When the tea arrived, it would be quite the comfortable little spot, and that was when alarms went off in Varick's head. He didn't *want* to be comfortable here, and certainly not when his cousin and their myriad insufferable family members all knew about the pile of cash Randolph had left to him. How big a pile, well, Varick would soon find out.

Thank every star in the sky Chester didn't try to make smalltalk on top of this poorly deployed charm offensive. He opened a folder thick with paperwork and stuck to the facts.

"Now, Varick, in regards to your parents having access to

your account—"

"Absolutely not. And not my grandmother or siblings either." Both Varick's tone and stony expression said he would not argue, nor would he explain himself further, and that was that.

"Certainly, not to worry. That is also the way Randolph preferred things." Chester made a note on a page attached to the inside front cover of the file.

Varick may have perhaps misjudged Chester a touch. Randolph had trusted him, which said a lot.

"I didn't realize you'd taken on a secretary," Chester said. "How long has that been the case?"

Or perhaps not. *You mean you didn't hear about it through the Pendragon grapevine,* Varick thought.

What he actually said was, "I only recently took him on."

A pleasant ding resonated from a small set of doors in the wall. Chester walked over, slid them into wall pockets on either side, and from a tray suspended on cable, lifted a fully-stocked tea service out of his private dumbwaiter.

"That's awfully handy, isn't it?" Carver asked.

Varick had to agree. He had a sudden fantasy of having meals delivered straight to his apartments.

"The latest design," Chester drawled. "Only the best for the best."

He gave Varick that same awkward smile again, and Varick summoned up the coldest glare he could manage.

As Chester began to serve the tea, he spoke as if the glare had not happened. And as if Carver were not sitting right there. "Well, Cousin, a word of advice. Make sure you vet Mister Sweeney well if you haven't already."

Varick shot a glance to Carver, whose expression remained calm and even, despite the disrespect. He decided to follow Carver's lead and play things cool. "Why do you say that?"

"Well, besides the fact that his face looks like it lost a fight

with a push mower—"

Steady on! Varick's inner monologue interrupted. *It's not that bad. And what do you even know about push mowers, you over-boiled parsnip?*

"—anyone who suddenly wants to be in your good graces should not be trusted."

Ah, now this was familiar territory. But, possibly for the first time in his entire life, Varick had the upper hand. A mirthless grin settled on his face as he sipped his tea.

"Let me be very clear, Chester," he began icily.

Now it was Carver's turn to follow Varick's lead. He tipped his head and matched Varick's tone. "Crystal clear."

The support made Varick feel instantly more confident. "I haven't mentioned hiring Mister Sweeney to anyone because I don't want people to know."

"No one," Carver put in.

"I am not a popular member of our family, as you well know, and I don't wish to give anyone ammunition against me."

Carver shook his head, sporting a look of deep disappointment. "Mm-mmm."

"That includes people they can try to use against me." He turned to Carver, "No offense meant, old man. I know you're loyal." That wasn't really true, but Varick dearly wanted to rub Chester's upturned nose in his own mess.

Carver tipped an invisible version of the bowler hat he'd doffed at the door.

Back to Chester, Varick went on, "If I get the merest hint of loose lips on your part, I will happily take my custom and all my money elsewhere. I have oodles of options, after all."

"*Oodles,*" Carver warned.

Varick was having a grand time with his own performance, but beneath that, he worried. Was he enjoying the same sort of games the rest of his family did? He was doing it in a sort of self-defense, though, and to a lesser degree, in defense of Carver as well. He thought back to his and Coal's conversation from a few days ago. As with money, could he have it both ways? Have fun wielding these tricks and do good at the same time? Varick sipped his tea again and let the words settle over Cousin Chester. Randolph had trusted this man. Now it was time to see how the accountant reacted to be challenged.

Chester spread his hands before him and gave as good as he got, in his own poindexterish sort of way. "Of course. You'll notice no one else in the family heard of this meeting. Because both my secretary and I are nothing but professional. I want your business, Varick, so we can both prosper for many years to come, which means anything we discuss stays within this room."

Varick trusted that sort of brutal honesty more than anything else Chester might have said. Randolph had used Chester's services for years, so there must be some integrity to be found here.

"That being said," Chester went on, "it is my duty as a professional to remind you that we will be discussing some very sensitive matters here today. Are you certain you'd like Mister Sweeney privy to them?"

This might be a bad idea, Varick knew. Yes, the broad strokes of Randolph's bequeathal were known, but at the end of today, Carver would know how it all broke down. There was still a difficult issue that barbed painfully inside of Varick, however, and he allowed Carver to stay. Varick had already decided if there were any passcodes or combinations to be discussed, anything that granted access to or use of assets, only he should be acquainted with those. That would at least provide a sturdy layer of protection in case Carver turned on him too. He explained as much to Chester, all except that last part. Chester nodded in understanding.

"Easily done. Now, let us begin with the simplest

accounts…"

There began a lengthy outlining of what Randolph had left behind. Cousin Chester was comprehensive, making sure Varick knew how long each account had been active, how much interest they were expected to earn per quarter and had done historically, and dozens of other bits of minutiae. There were several safety deposit boxes, of which Varick noticed Chester did not state the identification numbers for, though he was handed an itemized list of the contents for each, as well as what each piece was worth. And, yes, it was all available to Varick *now*. No need to wait until he was of age to access it.

"Randolph was very specific about that," Chester said. "I did not ask why, that's not my business. I will advise, however, that you consider carefully the many jobs your money can perform. Spending it is the least of these. Wise, lifelong investments are always, well, wise."

Carver, meanwhile, took notes at lightning speed. And as the mountain of accumulated wealth grew, Varick felt a strange new sensation: potential.

He could do anything with his life, once he was of age, of course. He could invest in exciting new technologies. He could travel, as Great Auntie Megaera had. He might even be able to feed the whole of Springhaven, at least for a bit anyway. More maths was needed for that. A lot more if he tried to make it sustainable. And he could certainly, if he really wanted to, back Mercury's job, whatever it was.

14
CHESS MOVES

At the end of the meeting, Varick and Carver shook hands with Chester and thanked him for his time. Varick said he'd be in touch, needing to mull over all the new information and not wanting to betray anything. They also thanked Chester's secretary for the offer to lead them out, but said they could find their own way—it was a mostly straight path, after all, with only a single turn.

It proved to be an unwittingly strategic move. As Varick and Carver walked back down the hall and toward the turning, the sound of a familiar voice caught in Varick's ears.

"And the poor lad won't need to hear of this until it's done?" Patricia's voice bounced down the narrow corridor like a rubber ball. "The prospect would only put more strain on him."

Varick stopped dead in his tracks and threw out a quick gesture for Carver to do the same. Carver froze, eyes and ears sharp. Varick thought fast. He knew his grandmother's voice, but he needed to see her too, and who she was talking to. He pulled out his grandfather's pocket watch, with it's shining bronze face, and angled it so he could see around the corner. It reflected Patricia's rigid form in a familiar midnight blue visiting dress. She was shaking hands with a man he couldn't recognize from the tiny reflection.

"That's correct," the man assured her. "We don't need to do anything that will put undue stress on the young man."

Varick's stomach turned. There were countless young men they could be discussing, but he had a bad feeling this was not about some minor cousin or distant nephew.

"Thank you, Mister Umpleby," Patricia said.

The man led her down the hall, back toward the building's reception area. Carver started to move, but Varick shook his head. They waited, and as as Varick suspected, the man—Mister Umbleby, apparently—returned a minute later. Varick had guessed correctly that he'd only been escorting Patricia out. No mere secretary guides for her, only the best. He watched as Mister Umpleby disappeared into an office midway down the corridor and waited to hear the click of the latch.

"Alright, let's go, quick!" Varick whispered.

They strode with purpose the rest of the way to the reception area and out the door, making a quick check that Patricia was not right outside alighting into a coach or anything.

Varick stared at the chess board, but his mind wasn't really on the game. After he and Carver had put a few blocks between them and Cousin Chester's office building, Varick had ducked into a little alley. A big-top circus of worries and feelings had begun to unfurl inside his head, and he needed a retreat.

"What now?" Carver had asked. He'd also handed over the notes he'd taken during the meeting, simple as that.

Varick had stared at the papers for a moment, waiting for some trick, but none came. Carver had played the role of secretary perfectly. Well, Varick had said he'd hoped to be impressed, and he was. So was Carver expecting some kind of verdict? If he was, he didn't press, and Varick wasn't ready. He couldn't focus as possibilities trapezed around his skull, while elephant-sized concerns paraded below them.

"Would you like to get some lunch?" Varick had asked. "On me."

Carver shrugged while sporting a bemused smile. "Sure."

They hadn't talked much over the meal, secured at an upscale but casual bistro—translation: somewhere no self-respecting Pendragon would patronize. And the lunch offer had extended to one for Carver to come back to the Dragon's Keep for a game of chess. They set up in an out-of-the-way storage area near the stables, which housed overflow supplies, out-of-fashion horse tack, and other forgotten equestrian gear. Somewhere in their sparse conversation over lunch, it had come out that Carver had learned to play chess from his grandfather, though Varick had found he didn't have the energy to inquire further.

He was trying to sort all the thoughts and feelings buzzing inside of him. After the initial excitement of discovering that Randolph had left him enough money to do literally anything he wanted, a deep but subtle sadness had settled over him too, a gauzy veil over the excitement that did not silence it, only somewhat muffled it. All that wealth also represented the finality of his grandfather's absence. Then there was whatever Patricia had been speaking to Mister Umpleby about. It *could* have been about someone else. After all, she tried to have as little to do with Varick as possible. But the uncertainty clawed at him. And then there was this job of Mercury's. The man had said it would improve Coal's situation. Varick looked sideways at Carver, who was considering his next move. He suspected the job would also help his new fake assistant.

Carver took a pawn with a knight. He was being awfully good about putting up with Varick's strange mood. He hadn't even asked why Varick was being… well, he didn't like to use the word clingy, but even he had to admit he'd worked hard to not be alone right now. He thought back to when he'd agreed to let Carver join him today, when he'd been facing the prospect of finally learning what Randolph had bequeathed to him. Varick recognized what he was feeling now was similar to then. He'd felt afraid and vulnerable and hadn't wanted to be alone. But why Carver? Perhaps because he'd been available and Varick had been in an advantageous position. He didn't like that idea much more than he liked to admit his vulnerability. The latter was bad enough, but the former felt like he'd used Carver. Varick didn't want to use people like his family always did. Or perhaps it had been because Carver too had lost his grandfather. The prospect of having someone there with him who knew what it was like, as Varick had faced yet another reminder of his loss, that was a comfort… assuming Carver had been telling the truth.

Varick moved one of his rooks into a strategic position. They were his favorite, and he considered them to be the best pieces on the board. They even gave the king extra power through the castling move.

"So you said your grandfather taught you to play?" he asked, apropos of nothing.

Carver nodded. "He started when I was little. We'd play in the evenings, after he'd come home from work and made us dinner. We both got better once I was old enough to start doing the cooking. It gave him more time and saved his energy."

Carver moved his queen, which Varick maneuvered to block, sacrificing another pawn.

"What did he do?" Varick asked.

"He was a solicitor. Workers' rights and labor laws sort of

stuff." As he spoke, Carver thumbed a plain little tiepin that held his ascot neatly in place.

"Ah," Varick said. "But he passed about a year ago, right?"

"Yeah." Carver paused their play. After a long moment, he asked, "Do you want to talk? About your grandad, I mean?"

Varick blinked fast, just in case his eyes decided to do something stupid like well up with tears. For once, the sucker punch of grief he'd been expecting didn't come. It'd be nice if there was some way to avoid all this uncertainty and just get it all out of his system at once.

"No?" he said in response to Carver's question. "Yes? I don't know."

Carver tipped his head to the side. "I'm here if you want to talk. Or if you don't."

"I don't know why it's so hard." Varick flapped a helpless hand as he made this confession. "My grandfather was old."

Really old, in fact. Randolph had been an outlier of age, like Megaera and Patricia were, though having money to pay for doctors was surely a factor there. He might have even been a great-grandfather if he and Patricia or Varick's parents had gotten together earlier.

Varick went on, "I always knew he might go at any time, but when it actually happened…"

He waited again for the emotional blow, but still none came. Stupid, capricious grief.

"Yeah," Carver agreed. "It's a bloody bugger of a thing."

Varick sighed. It was nice to hear someone say it, though no one in his circle would have used such coarse language to do so. Everyone had sent condolences and thoughts and all that other rot. Varick had not known until now that he'd wanted someone to, instead of sugarcoating things, call out what a sodding misery it was. His chest ached, missing Randolph. There was so much happening, and the one person Varick could have relied on for guidance was gone. What was the right way to handle... everything?

Start with people, Randolph had often said. *Other people have struggles, just like you do, but most of them don't have the funds to solve what money can.*

"I'm sorry," Varick said suddenly. "I've been really selfish today. And you've been far more patient than I deserve."

"I could just be trying to get on your good side so that you agree to back Mercury's job," Carver said.

Varick raised an eyebrow. "Is that what you're trying to do?"

"No. Grief is hard. I didn't have anyone when my grandad went." Carver paused again. "He always wanted me to live my life, whatever that looks like, but to live it kindly."

Varick said nothing for a while as the words settled over their little hideaway. He made another play on the board, as did Carver.

"I think our grandfathers would have gotten along," Varick said at last.

Carver nodded, and Varick spied the bob of his throat as he swallowed down some emotion. He considered simply giving Carver some distance and playing on, but then remembered the kindness that had been extended to him.

"I'm not good at feelings," Varick said. "But if you want to talk, I'm here too."

Carver chuckled. "First rate sales pitch you've got there."

Varick chuckled too.

"I don't know what there is to say," Carver said with a shrug. "I just really miss him."

"Yes," Varick replied. "I know what you mean."

They gave some time and space to their feelings, playing in silence with long spaces in between moves and neither one hurrying the other to take their turn. Only later, after conversation had begun to pick up again, Varick asked a question that had been brewing in him since that morning.

"What else can you tell me about this job of Mercury's?" he asked.

Carver looked up from where he'd just moved a pointy-hatted scholar. He locked eyes with Varick. "I told you, I've said all I'm allowed to about it. You'll have to meet with Mercury if you want to know more."

Varick grumbled to himself, but not too seriously. He'd expected this might be the answer.

"It's just a meeting," Carver said. "You'll eat, you'll talk, job done."

Varick let his head fall back and sighed dramatically. "Fine. I'll meet with the smarmy git, but I want it somewhere public, where he can't try to pull anything."

Carver gave him a shrug and said, "Okay, if that's how you want it. Want me to set it up like before, so your family won't know?"

"Please," Varick said. It wasn't the smartest move, he knew, to go meet a stranger somewhere without anyone knowing where or who, but his family knowing was an even worse option. He dithered over one more item before deciding it too was a better option. "And can you do something else while you're at it, please?"

"What is it?"

"Can you tell Coal I want to talk to him?"

15

Bad Eggs, Jarred Ducks, and Dead Pendragons

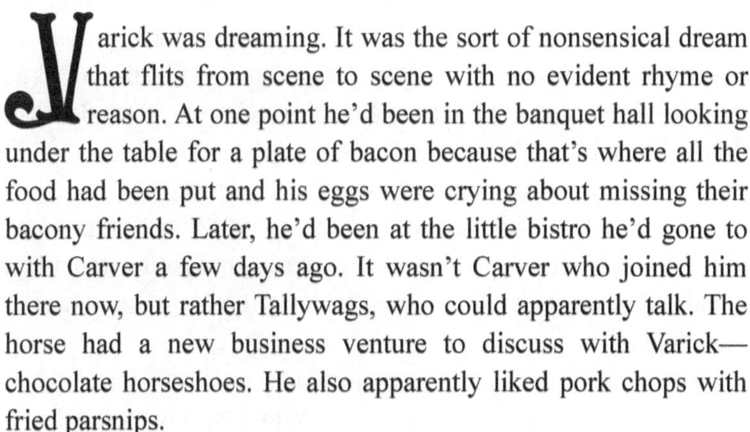

Varick was dreaming. It was the sort of nonsensical dream that flits from scene to scene with no evident rhyme or reason. At one point he'd been in the banquet hall looking under the table for a plate of bacon because that's where all the food had been put and his eggs were crying about missing their bacony friends. Later, he'd been at the little bistro he'd gone to with Carver a few days ago. It wasn't Carver who joined him there now, but rather Tallywags, who could apparently talk. The horse had a new business venture to discuss with Varick—chocolate horseshoes. He also apparently liked pork chops with fried parsnips.

"Wake up!" Tallywags was whispering to Varick.

In his dream, the horse suddenly leapt across the table and sat on Varick's chest. He didn't remember falling from his chair, and he knew he should be crushed beneath the horse's weight. Yet Tallywags only weighed enough to cause some slight discomfort, not death.

"Varick!" Tallywags said. Why was he whispering? And why did he suddenly sound like…

The dream dissolved and Varick found himself staring up into Coal's exuberant face.

"Wheh?" Varick muttered, still drunk with sleep. He grunted a few more nonsensical noises before collecting enough of his wits to groan, "Get. Off."

"Oh! Right!" Coal exclaimed, but still quietly. "Sorry. I forgot about the whole no-touching thing. I'm just so excited that you don't hate me!"

His face beamed in the light of the gibbous moon streaming in through the windows. Varick liked to sleep lightly. When he was much younger, Constance had snuck in once and painted a clownish mask onto his face and then claimed that he'd played with her cosmetics and gone to bed with them on, staining his bedclothes. His father had called him "unmanly" and sentenced him to only cold baths for a fortnight after that. Magnus had liked the joke so much that he'd tried to repeat it, but the great dolt had gotten himself caught and Constance only agreed not to tattle on him if he gave her his next two month's allowance.

Varick sat up and rubbed his face. "I don't hate you. And I don't hate touching. I just don't like unnecessary touching. Handshakes make sense, but you don't need to sit on my chest to wake me up."

Coal was busy doing a jerky little dance. It had started when Varick had said he didn't hate him. While Varick yawned and stretched, his sleepy limbs popping, Coal responded to his explanation in a sort of singsong way, still dancing.

"Got it. No nonsensical touching."

"What are you doing here, Coal?" Varick grumbled.

Coal ended his dance with a flourish of fluttering fingers. "You said you wanted to talk."

"Now?" There was a distinctive whine in Varick's voice. "It's the middle of the night."

"Easiest time to sneak in," Coal said. "Not as fun, though. There's basically no challenge."

"My windows are locked." He pointed to illustrate which ones he meant.

"And?" Coal looked genuinely curious as to what his point was. Fair enough, the latch was likely less complicated than the kitchen door had been.

Varick sighed and flopped back onto the bed. "You are killing me."

"Fulcrum says that to me sometimes," Coal said. "Can I sit on your bed?"

"Please do not." It came out more petulantly than Varick had meant for it to, but he was too cranky to care much at the moment. "Who's Fulcrum? You've mentioned… him? Her? Them? Before."

Undeterred, Coal bounded into a recamier, which resided at the end of the bed and thus was not technically part of it. "Fulcrum's my brother." Then, before Varick could respond, Coal went on, speaking quickly. "So is this about the job? Is that why you wanted to talk to me? Carver said you want a meeting."

"Stars, Coal, I've only been awake for two minutes. Calm down."

Coal's mouth snapped shut, but the energy seemed to transfer to his eyes. They widened and he stared at Varick, still and unblinking.

Varick seeped out from under the covers, away from the stare, grabbed a dressing gown, and wrapped himself in it. Under normal circumstances, a servant would creep in here just before dawn and build up the fire in the fireplace, ensuring it was nice and toasty for when Varick rose. As it was, a bed of glowing embers was all that remained. Varick also donned a pair of rabbit fur slippers and a cap before realizing Coal's only outerwear was the ill-fitting jacket he currently wore, the same he'd been wearing the day they gone roof-running, as Coal had called it.

"Are you warm enough?" Varick gestured to the fireplace. "It's better over here. I have your other clothes too. And blankets too."

He laid a single piece of firewood onto the embers and poked things a bit with the poker. He didn't really know what he was doing and was certain it showed. Thus, he didn't put up a fight when Coal took over and soon had proper flames licking at the log. The smaller lad then held his hands close to the newborn heat.

"What happened to the suit I gave you?" Varick asked, handing over the small pile of clothes Coal had left. He'd hidden them, not wanting to see them or for one of the house staff to take them, thinking they were rags or something. They were not Varick's to do with what he liked after all.

"I gave it to Fulcrum. It fits him a sight better than it did me."

Varick nodded and curled up in an armchair that flanked the fireplace. He found it ironic that so much seating littered his apartments when he almost never had guests to fill it. Though Coal was so thin, he'd have to get really creative to fill most seats. At that, another thought occurred to Varick.

"Does Mercury feed you?"

"Nah, he's not our dad or anything," Coal explained, "but he lets us sleep at his place for a cut of what we make for ourselves. Way better than outside."

Varick had *thoughts* about that, but now was not the time. "You know there are soup kitchens where you can get food, yes? I happen to own some. Well, I will when I come of age."

Guilt thrummed dully inside of him. He hadn't done anything

in regards to the Turnip Network since the will reading, at which time he'd just signed his name on a bunch of long, legal forms to say he'd heard all the information presented and understood. He may not have management of the places yet, but the least he could do was check in the way Randolph used to.

Coal shrugged. "Yeah, but there are always those workhouse people around. It's enough to put one right off their pudding."

"What workhouse people?" Varick asked. His grandfather had never allowed solicitation of any kind in his soup kitchens or food pantries. He'd believed that people should be able to get food without being disturbed. "Not at the Turnip Network sites."

Coal turned to look at him. "Yes at the Turnip Network sites. They're the worst now. Really pushy bad eggs coming in, trying to make folks these sign legal contracts, promising beds and food, but you're better off on the streets. They pack too many people into these big rooms for sleeping and eating, and if they get sick, *they're* the one having to pay for a doctor, which they can't afford on such bad wages. People don't know what they're signing, and then they're bound by law to work off their contract. Carver explains it better, but that's the gist of it." Coal shook his finger and donned an officious tone. "You're not only hurting yourself, but the city as well. Consider what you could contribute once you have new skills and experience under your belt. Factories need experienced workers, and it's all free to you! Don't be such an ingrate."

Varick had heard about workhouses, of course. The Pendragon clan at large was in favor of them, many members touting them as charitable organizations that offered a panacea for society's ills. Randolph had been on the opposite side and had taught Varick much the same as what Coal described. In addition, a handful of Springhaven's laws prohibited assistance to the able-bodied poor if they refused work when it was offered, which had been some of the impetus for Randolph founding the Turnip

Network.

Varick nodded. "People have to do really heavy labor at the workhouses, don't they?"

Coal had huddled closer to the fire. "Yeah. Breaking rocks for gravel, picking oakum, the sort of stuff you'd have to pay people a bunch of money to do voluntarily."

That lined up with what Randolph had taught Varick too. And something Coal had said, like a lighthouse in a storm, flashed through the mire. "Did you say they're the worst *now*? As in, recently?"

"Oh, they'd always try and hang around outside, but the folks working the kitchens would run them off. One time, I watched this big woman—like a walking steamship, she was!—march out and threaten a whole group of them with a pair of rolling pins. That was a great day." Coal grinned at the memory, but it faded too soon. "Last couple of weeks, though, no one's been stopping them. The workhouse people just hang around *inside*, sifting through everyone who comes in. Last I went, I saw this bloke get right in a lady's face. Called her all kinds of names, and the people serving meals just stood and watched. They looked right piqued, but didn't do anything to stop it. I haven't gone back since."

Varick had no idea how many soup kitchens Springhaven had, but he made a mental note to move looking in on the Turnip Network up the priority list. He'd make sure these "bad eggs," as Coal called them, were barred from his establishments. For now, though, he focused on why he'd contacted Coal in the first place.

"Thank you for bringing this to my attention. As far as why I wanted to talk to you, I need to break in somewhere. Carver says you're a better sneak than he is."

Coal preened with pride. "I am. What's the target?"

"An office building—"

"Boring," Coal broke in. "I can do that in my sleep."

"Well, that's what needs doing." Varick had a hard time keeping himself from pulling a face at Coal. Was this what a normal sibling relationship was like? Varick suddenly felt he understood Fulcrum a bit, despite never having met Coal's aforementioned brother. "I think my grandmother is… doing something. I need to get into her solicitor's office and find out what. Or at least, find out if it has to do with me."

Coal asked a few more pertinent questions—what area of the city, layout, building height, brick or stone, exits, any security precautions that Varick was aware of? Varick described the offices of Pendragon, Umpleby, and Johnson and said he hadn't seen any security measures in place. Then again, he hadn't really been looking for them either.

At that, Coal rolled his eyes. "Typical. Let's get going then."

"What? Now?" Varick asked.

"Yeah, why not? The sooner the better, right?"

"Well… Ah… But…" Varick sighed, collecting himself. " Don't we need, I don't know, a *plan*?"

Coal gave him a cocky little shrug. "I've got a plan."

♖

Well over an hour later, as the wee hours of the morning drew into their weest, Varick wondered if he might still be dreaming. They'd traveled via rooftop as much as possible, and he'd been glad to get some more practice roof-running. Varick loved the feel of the wind as he leapt across gaps between detached buildings, and the sense of achievement that came with climbing up and down whatever was handy. Coal had kept an eye on the position of the moon, avoiding its silvery wash as much as possible. Now, Varick was crouching behind the lee side of a cupola that topped Cousin Chester's office building while Coal went to work on one of the cupola's windows. The smaller lad sang a silly little song to himself as he worked, so soft that only Varick could hear. It provided an incongruous musical backdrop to the splendor laid out before them.

The Springhaven skyline was a sight to behold, doubly so under a blanket of silver moonlight. With the office building being so tall and Copper being the East-most district of the city, when Varick faced West, he could see all the way out to Cobalt Bay on the opposite side of the city. Along the way, he noticed more cupolas like the one he hid next to now, as well as dormers, spires, and small turrets.

"Why do you suppose we have these?" Varick asked idly. When Coal looked down at him, Varick indicated the cupola Coal was currently engaged in breaking into.

"For cooling," Coal said simply.

"What, really? It's not just decorative?"

"Yeah." Coal wiggled one of his slenderest lock picking tools this way and that, and then pushed the window inward. "Warm air moves upward, and opening these—" He waggled the now-open window back and forth. "—creates an escape for it. That creates a cycle from open windows down below, which creates a cooling draft."

Varick gave Coal an impressed head bobble. "And today I learned…" He climbed inside the cupola after Coal and asked, "Do you want to be an engineer or something when you're older?"

"Architect," Coal said. "Newer structures have entire ventilation systems built right into the walls. You can even rig them with shutters to keep in heat from the boilers and warm an entire building when it's cold out."

A thought occurred to Varick, but he had the good grace to keep it to himself. Coal would likely never achieve his dream of being an architect. He was fairly certain the lad didn't attend school. Even if his criminality wasn't known and he'd therefore avoided a spot on the Enforcers' *Wanted* list, the fact that he was an orphan and homeless meant that a different sort of prison loomed. Until they came of age, known orphans were forced to live in orphanages, which were often overcrowded, understaffed, and under-resourced.

Thankfully, their task prevented the lads from dwelling on the subject. Once they were inside the building, by silent agreement, they both went quiet. The small landing inside the cupola was littered with ash, and Varick deduced that the employees of Pendragon, Umpleby, and Johnson used this area to take sneaky smoke breaks. A small, filigreed pipe tamper tucked into the corner of the windowsill confirmed Varick's suspicions. Coal pocketed it without a word. A skinny set of stairs led down from the cupola, widening as they reached the working floors of the building. Under Varick's guidance, they'd soon arrived and had broken into Mister Umpleby's office.

"So what are we looking for?" Coal asked, looking around the tidy office.

The layout was the same as Cousin Chester's, but the upholstery and other textiles differed. A large set of windows graced one wall, but the curtains were shut against the moonlight, so Varick and Coal were forced to use small candles that Coal kept on him for light.

"Anything that says my name," Varick explained.

He started with the desk, and an image-still atop it displayed a couple. The man, Varick realized, had been at the will reading. Varick reeled his mind back, trying desperately to remember anything specific Mister Umpleby had said. It was all a blur. There had been something like six or seven different solicitors at the will reading, and they'd become interchangeable to Varick throughout the process.

"I found files," Coal announced. He stood before a cabinet comprised of lots of slim, locked drawers, which pulled out into individual clipboards with filing loops attached the far end. Coal had already freed the file bearing the label, "Pa - Pf."

"Is there a lock you can't pick?" Varick asked.

"Oh, sure. These are all just really simple." He paused, cocking a mischievous grin. "Most locks are, though, so I haven't yet found one I can't beat."

He traded Varick the file for his candle.

"Then why haven't you gotten rich stealing from a bunch of families like mine? Or a bank?"

"That's different. Getting in is the hard part. Everyone was occupied at your granddad's funeral, so I could creep around pretty easy and pretend to be one of those hired mutes, but it's not usually like that. If I get caught, there aren't a lot of cover stories that'll get me off the hook, and those big houses are usually crawling with servants. There might be dogs around, who can rat you out, or worse. And security systems are getting better. I just heard about one, basic spring-loaded alarm with optional clockwork delay, *but* the shutoff key has magnets *inside of it*, so you can't easily make a copy. Plus, you gotta know *all* those factors going in." Coal shook his head. "And you can forget about banks. Cracking a vault is a whole different jar of ducks."

Varick had only been half listening as he flipped through the pages on the clipboard. There were so many bloody Pendragons to sift through! But Coal's last words caught his attention.

"Jar of ducks? Don't you mean kettle of fish?"

Coal looked at Varick as if he were mad. "Who's boiling up a kettle of fish tea?"

"Who's jarring up a bunch of ducks?" Varick countered.

"Hmm." Coal considered for a moment. "Pot of jam?"

"Pot of jam," agreed Varick.

At last, Varick found a set of forms with his grandmother's name on it. And then another. And another. One especially long collection of papers turned out to be her will, which Varick couldn't help but have a peek at. Unsurprisingly, Constance was favored throughout the document. Varick's father—Patricia's son—as well, of course, but Varick couldn't help but wonder if the favoritism toward Constance might poison Henry against her. For a moment, Varick felt very Pendragony indeed as he considered how he might play the two off of each other with this information, but Coal interrupted his thoughts.

"Is that it?" the boy asked.

"No," Varick replied.

He tried not to grumble the word, but having fallen prey to the same sort of game the rest of his family played, even if only momentarily so, made Varick feel weak and stupid. And when he thought of his grandfather, ashamed as well. He began flipping pages with renewed vigor. At last, his eyes fell on his own signature in amongst his grandmother's section of paperwork. It was faint, as was his grandmother's printed name at the top of of the document. In fact, all the writing on the form was, even the typewritten text. And why was the paper pink? All the rest of the forms in the file were white, though all were thin and had a strange, powdery sort of texture. A small legend at the bottom of the sheet answered his question.

White - Office | Yellow - Client | Pink - Filing

Carbon paper. Varick was vaguely aware of its existence and use, but had never had cause to use it himself. He squinted and brought his face close to the paper, trying to read the document, but the typewriter's text had struggled to make it all the way to this third sheet, and he couldn't make out what the paper said.

"Coal, that thing you did, back at the casino night, with the liquid and the papers," Varick began.

"Research." So Coal was maintaining that line. Alright.

"Sure, *research.*" Varick's tone dripped with sarcasm. "Can you do that with this?"

Coal brought his face close in the same way Varick had, being careful to hold his two candles away from his head and the paper, so as to avoid lighting it or his own hair on fire. "I mean, I *could*, but it would be even worse than this. Fulcrum's done a bunch of tests. He says every copy of a copy is a worse copy. And carbon paper ink apparently does worse job than ink-ink. Sorry."

"Hrmm, thanks anyway."

Varick looked through more of the files, but this was the only one bearing his signature and Patricia's name by themselves. It could just be about the soup kitchens, of course. It probably was. He sighed and rubbed his face. The scant bit of sleep he'd gotten was beginning to catch up with him. Maybe he was just being paranoid about this entire thing, but he couldn't shake his misgivings.

"This doesn't belong here," he muttered.

Coal nodded. "Maybe the Office copy is up in filing? Maybe they got switched?"

That seemed unlikely to Varick. After all, this sheet was a completely different color than the rest. How could someone miss that? But it was worth checking out. Thus, they replaced the file. Coal made sure everything was locked up again, and they were soon making their way back through the building once more, looking for where Filing copies were kept.

It took over an hour and a half of searching. The office building was well organized, certainly, but it was also quite tall and full of rooms. Only on a second sweep did they discover that some of those rooms contained other rooms, which had not been mentioned on the doorplates. The file room hid within the basement, which turned out to be a labyrinth of dim passages, a large boiler room, storage rooms, and some other maintenance-type areas neither of them knew the purpose of. The file room was a vast, tiled area with floor-to-ceiling drawers and an equally tall ladder that rolled along a track. Again, thanks to good labeling practices, Varick and Coal found the racks containing the Pendragon files without trouble. The issue now was wading through all the dead Pendragons who'd come before. When Varick realized this, he let his head fall back and groaned.

"Why does my stupid family have to be so stupidly big?"

Coal worked on the hanging folders containing V-names while Varick took the P's, just in case. When Varick found nothing amongst all three Patricia Pendragons of history, he began to look through the all the rest of the P's. Maybe it had been mis-filed. At least he could ignore all the pink pages. Or rather Varick tried to, as he finger-walked his way through Paige, Pascal, Patience, Peter, Poppy, Preston, Prunella, and even a Purity, at which Varick made a face. He still held hope that some clear, shining evidence of sneaky-doings by his grandmother would suddenly appear. But there was nothing. The filing racks weren't even enclosed on the bottom, so there was nowhere for things to have accidentally slipped down to and gotten lost. He and Coal even went through the *Pendragon, General Family* files. There, they found the various forms multiple members of Varick's family had signed to acknowledge their various bequeathments, which were neatly listed next to each name, but nothing concerning just him and his grandmother.

"Your grandma was just here a few days ago, yeah?" Coal asked.

"Yes," Varick replied as he tiredly flipped through pages he'd already looked through.

"So if there was an issue with the files, wouldn't she have found out when she was here?"

Varick shrugged. "I don't know. Maybe something happened between then and now? Or maybe she was in here *because* something had gone missing? She didn't sound upset, though. She sounded…" Varick tried to cast his mind back to a few days ago, when he and Carver had overheard the conversation. "Pretty satisfied. Fake concerned too, which is what has me worried."

Their conversation was interrupted by the sound of a door opening and shutting somewhere in the warren-like basement. Without a word, both boys pulled out their pocket watches and checked the time.

"Just after sunup," Coal whispered.

Varick wasn't surprised that Coal knew when daylight was scheduled to show its face. It was still awfully early in the morning, but just as scullery maids and cooks started before dawn most days, perhaps some folks here needed to get an early start on their work too. The boys took great care to close the filing racks quietly, which suddenly seemed to rattle with every little movement. They checked around every corner as they made their way back up the stairs, and thankfully only saw a cleaner trundling around the place as they went. By the time Varick and Coal made it back up to the cupola, the sun had flushed the sky with soft pinks and oranges, which bled into the retreating indigo. Coal took them back by the streets instead of the roofs, letting Varick bounce ideas off him for what his grandmother might have been talking about with Mister Umpleby.

Boarding school was an option. There were a few really expensive ones up north. And, to be honest, that idea appealed to Varick. He'd love nothing more than a reason to get away from his rotten family, which was why he suspected that wasn't the case. Of course, something to do with the Turnip Network was still the likeliest explanation. Perhaps Patricia was trying to wrest control of it from Varick through legal means? Or could she be after the liquid assets Randolph had left to Varick. But how did she expect to pull that off? The will had been perfectly clear about Randolph's last wishes in that area. By the time they'd made it back to the Dragon's Keep, Varick was no closer to an answer.

He thanked Coal for his help, not thinking about why he'd felt owed it at the start of the night. Coal smiled and saluted, promising to see Varick soon. Oh yes, because Varick had agreed to meet with Mercury.

16

DEAL MAKERS AND BREAKERS

Varick looked at himself in the intricately framed mirror and tried to imagine himself sitting at a table on the roof of the Raven's Tower. He'd dressed in a suit of black, of course—he was still in mourning—and had ornamented it with somber silver cufflinks. He'd opted for a tie over a more casual cravat, wanting to show how serious he was.

Varick had never really been in a business meeting before. As much time as he and Randolph had spent together, he'd never been privy to the man's business dealings, though Varick knew plenty of theory from his lessons on the subject. He had not even been invited to sit and wait in a reception area while Randolph went into an office and did whatever he needed to do, thus why he'd never been to Chester's office before. Looking back, Varick wondered if his grandfather had felt a measure of distrust there, worried that Varick might fall prey to the family's machinations despite either of their best efforts.

Varick had gone over his list of requirements and deal-breakers with himself so many times he'd dreamed about them the night before. There were a lot of unknown factors around Mercury's job, but what Varick did know was that he needed hard boundaries for how far he was willing to go.

The meeting was set for early evening. As long as Varick was sneaky, getting out without being seen would be no problem. The time allowed him to ride Tallywags there too, instead of galavanting across rooftops or taking a cab, which was more subject to traffic delays.

To be on time, aim to be early, his grandfather had always advised. *Aim to be on time, and you'll be late.*

The advice served Varick well, as even with the greater maneuverability of Tallywags, once Varick reached the Sand district, the streets became choked with pedestrians, other people on horseback, hansom cabs and growlers, and velocipedists—these last ones were mainly couriers on missions. Varick watched as one got caught in an especially thick knot of travelers and pulled off to the side. The courier, bearing the emblem of his employer's company, squeezed a small lever on the underside of his velocipede and gave it a fierce yank. The contraption collapsed along two hinge-points at the front and back wheels and folded into an almost square shape. The courier swung it around to a set of hooks attached to the parcel pack on his back and took off down a side alley.

Varick himself was a fine horseman, and Tallywags wasn't shy about nipping other horses to get them out of his way, though Varick had to rein in his attempts to do the same to humans in their path. Thus, with eight minutes to spare, they arrived at the Raven's Tower—or rather, just Raven's Tower, according to the painted wooden sign hanging outside. Why did everyone, himself included, add the "the"? No time to think about that now. Varick tied Tallywags to the hitching post outside, confident that, should anyone try to steal the beautiful animal, the horse would employ his own anti-theft measures.

The Tower was a tall, skinny building set right on the border between the Sand and Cobalt quarters. It rose far higher into the air than any of the surrounding buildings and was clearly an Old World survivor of the War of Light. Buildings weren't made with huge, heavy blocks of stone like that anymore. Modern builders preferring either red brick or white plaster with exposed beams of dark wood.

A young man about Varick's age waited just inside the front door, ready to take coats from patrons. Knowing that no one in Mercury's crew used their real names, Varick felt it was best to follow suit. He didn't introduce himself and instead just said he was here for a meeting. Coal had sent another note the other day with little more than where and when the meeting would take place, though he had added a line at the bottom which Varick had appreciated.

Don't worry. Miss Cali won't let anything hinky go down on her turf.

The young man looked Varick up and down, from his silk top hat to his silver cufflinks and freshly shined shoes.

"You're Coal's friend?" He sounded as if he didn't believe it.

Truthfully, Varick wasn't certain he was ready to use such a word to describe what he and Coal were. The memory of how he'd had set Varick up that first night they'd gone roof-running still stung, but Coal's easy willingness to break them into Pendragon, Umpleby, and Johnson had gone a long way toward repairing the relationship.

Varick aimed for a perfectly even tone as he replied, "Close enough."

He'd thought hard about how he wanted to come across in what he was quickly coming to think of as his business persona. Inscrutable had been the word that had come to mind. He liked

that, and it had become his watchword as he'd mentally reviewed possible scenarios and outcomes for tonight.

The cloakroom boy looked him over again. The skeptical look remained—Wait, did he assume Varick was a bad choice of friend for Coal?!—but he gave Varick a rote smile and offered to take his coat and hat, which Varick declined since their meeting was set for the rooftop. The boy then directed Varick to make his way up the staircase, which curved along the circular walls of the Tower.

"When you hit the outside, you're there," he finished.

"Thank you," Varick said automatically. Something his grandfather had always done when visiting cafes and shops and whatnot came to him then. Varick extended his hand and asked, "What's your name?"

This did not help the remaining mistrust in the boy's expression, and Varick wondered if he would have refused to answer if he wasn't working. "Spencer." He shook Varick's hand a little firmer than was strictly necessary. "I know it probably sounds pretty plain to someone like you, but while you're here, try the bread and herb butter. It's a special offering we only have once in a while." Spencer said this like some sort of dare.

Varick accepted the challenge, pouring exaggerated politeness over his words. "I will, thank you so much."

Then he began the long trek up the stairs. Along the way, he passed a few landings with closed doors and signs that read, EMPLOYEES ONLY. Another floor led off to a set of privies, and one opened up into what was clearly the main bar space. At this point, Varick was tempted to press himself against the wall and try to be unnoticeable. Adults, both men and women, sat at the bar and tables with drinks in hand, ordering meals, talking about their workdays, flirting, and whatever else people in mixed company got up to. Someone was bound to notice him, any second now, point, and cry out, "Hey! What's a fancy-dressed kid doing here?"

No, he chided himself. *No one knows I'm only fourteen. I'm a professional, here to conduct business.* A professional what, he didn't know, but the pep talk made him feel better.

As Varick scanned the room, a young woman only a few years his senior spotted him from behind the bar. She had long, wildly curly, ebony hair currently held back in braided sort of half up-do. Her skin was darker than Varick's, and her every move exuded confidence. Clearly she was a woman in complete control of herself, and she was headed straight for him.

"Hello," she said in a warm tone. "Can I help you?" The question did not condescend, but beyond that, Varick couldn't tell whether or not this woman suspected that he didn't belong.

Pulling out his own inscrutable tone, as he'd done with Spencer downstairs, he said, "I'm here for a meeting."

He held her gaze, serious but cool. When she smiled, he was pleased to see it was with more of that sincere warmth.

"Yes, Coal's friend. Welcome. I'm Calandra, proprietress of this establishment. He told me to look out for you."

Varick extended his hand and gifted her a smile he'd practiced in the mirror for hours. "Miss Cali, Coal called you. A pleasure. Which name do you prefer?"

Calandra's smile grew. "You may call me Miss Cali," and it sounded like a badge of approval. "Follow me."

She gestured him up the rest of the stairway and out a door at the top. On the circular, stone rooftop, Mercury sat at a table with a couple of braziers blazing nearby. The top of the Tower was flat and, judging by the various patches of discoloration and scratches on the wide flagstones, this area was often used for entertaining. Coal and Carver were there at the table too, but Varick's eyes pinned to their... keeper? Boss? Guardian? Mercury smiled mildly when he saw Varick, and then pointedly looked at his fob watch.

"Two minutes late," he said, clucking his tongue. "I hope this doesn't signify a bad habit."

He chuckled to himself while Varick walked over, forcing himself not to bristle.

To Calandra, Mercury oozed, "Thank you again for letting us use this space, Cali. And for the fires. Such ambiance, such hospitality."

She gave him a smile that was not nearly so warm as it had been for Varick. "It's Calandra, thank you."

Inside Varick's head, a tiny version of himself did a jubilant little dance like Coal had done in his bedroom the other night. *Prat,* he thought smugly at Mercury.

Calandra looked to the assemblage at large. "Can I get anyone anything? We have mulled cider as a seasonal special."

As she went through the night's other offerings, Varick could not help but notice she didn't mention any alcohol. Were minors even technically allowed here?

"I heard about some bread and herb butter available tonight," he said at the end of Calandra's spiel.

She smiled at him. "There certainly is. It's sort of a secret menu item. A friend of mine makes the bread; it's very good. We usually serve it as an accompaniment to the soup, but I can bring some out for you."

Coal was bouncing in his seat, but was keeping uncharacteristically quiet. Probably an order from Mercury.

"We can do better than bread and butter, I think," Mercury said. Was he trying to affect some kind of snobbery? Did he think that was the way to impress Varick? Short sighted. Calandra didn't seem like the sort of person you wanted to be on the wrong side of.

Before he could go on, Varick put in, "*I'd* like some." He was also *not* going to fail Spencer's bread-based challenge because of this git. To Calandra he added, "Please. And a round of mulled ciders for everyone who wants one, on me."

Coal's face practically exploded into a beaming smile. Carver too looked pleased, though far less effusively. Mercury ordered a steak and kidney pie, while Varick ended up getting the soup, a hearty squash and sausage combination. Carver and Coal ordered a plate of rarebit to share. The food and drinks were brought out —Calandra claimed there'd been a mistake in the kitchen and they'd made two full rarebit orders instead of one to share. Oopsie, what's a proprietress to do? Happy accident for Coal and Carver, they each got their own. Varick played along with what was clearly a kindly sham, and Calandra promised to come back and check on them in a bit. With her departure, they got down to business.

"Alright," Mercury began. "So you want in on our little caper, do you, mate?"

Varick raised an eyebrow at him. "One, don't call me that. We are not friends. Two, you're the one who needs me. I'm doing you a favor by being here."

"Of course." Mercury began tucking into his pie. "What would you like to be called?"

Varick had thought a lot about this too. The idea of a nickname appealed, and he wanted something intimidating, something impressive. He was ready. In a low, serious voice, he said, "Knifestorm."

Coal, who was drinking his mug of cider with both hands wrapped around it, choked a little. Carver, paused, and was clearly trying hard *not* to look at Varick. Mercury had no such scruples. He threw back his head and laughed a proper guffawing belly laugh.

Varick's face burned. What? What was so wrong with that? Knifestorm was a scary name!

When Mercury had collected himself, he waved a hand. "No, m'lad. That's not the sort of monicker one takes on in this business. You'll want something a bit… more subtle. Something you can deliver on."

Varick had the distinct impression Mercury had softened his words at the last minute

The man went on. "Keep brainstorming. We'll just use the names we all know for now."

Varick was secretly grateful for the reprieve. He had no idea what name he should choose instead. Maybe he'd get Coal or Carver to help him later.

"As for this favor you're doing for us," Mercury said, "you're right. My apologies. You just seem to have taken a shine to these two." He jerked a thumb at Carver and Coal. "And why shouldn't you? They're good little sports."

Coal and Carver both gave quick smiles, but they still said nothing.

"What do you know so far?" Mercury asked.

Varick sat up straighter and began slathering some of the herbed butter over a slice of warm, brown bread. "I know that you need a backer for this job of yours, which seems to be just another way to say money. I also know that the thing you're going after has been stolen before. Did it legally belong to someone in the past?"

Mercury nodded approvingly. "You actually ask good questions."

He gave a quick look around them to see if anyone was eavesdropping, then flicked his head at Coal and Carver. The two hopped up to skirt the perimeter of the Tower, looking over the sides to ensure no one was listening from there.

"All clear," Carver reported after a few minutes.

Mercury thanked them and leaned forward, his steak and kidney pie temporarily forgotten in the drama of the moment. In a soft voice, he said, "To answer your question, no. It's called the Nightfall Crown."

17

KINGS AS THIEVES, THIEVES AS KINGS

arick blinked at him. "A crown? An actual crown."

"It's really pretty!" Coal burst out beside him. He was half-standing up in his seat. "Wait until you see it! It's the shiniest thing I've ever seen in my life, and I've only seen the image-still."

Carver placed a stilling hand on Coal's arm, and the boy sat back down properly.

Mercury chuckled. "All in good time, my boy." He turned back to Varick. "The crown was commissioned by a thief called Vapor somewhere in the neighborhood of seventy or so years ago. The story goes that he was bored and wanted to see if anyone could steal it from him without him knowing. What made it interesting is that the crown is made of glass. Some gemstones too, of course, but the glass makes it tricky. Vapor put out the challenge: Break the crown, and you lose. Kill anyone, you lose. Get caught, and you lose. Present it to him whole without him knowing it was you who took it, and you win. You even got to keep the crown."

"I assume someone managed it?" Varick said.

"Spot on. Vapor kept it locked up, of course. Couldn't make it too easy. One morning, a visitor comes to Vapor's place, a real upstart. Went by Pan. Pan walked in carrying the crown on a pillow of golden silk—he had a flair for the dramatic. True to his word, Vapor congratulated him and let him keep the crown as a reward."

Mercury was a good storyteller, and he clearly enjoyed this one. Something tugged at Varick, though. "But the Nightfall Crown still exists today? After all this time? That means that Pan didn't sell the gemstones off or anything."

Mercury pointed at him. "Precisely. Pan kept the challenge going. It's passed from thief to thief over the years."

"But why?" Varick's brows cinched together. "What's the point? Just so you can say you did it?"

Mercury sat back in his chair and resumed his steak and kidney pie. "Something you've gotta understand about our world, young one. Reputation is everything. Just the power of your name can keep people off your back. Having stolen the Nightfall Crown opens doors for you. It lets people know you've got chops."

Varick nodded. He could see the logic behind that. Something was still bugging him, but he set it aside for now. "You said this job would help your crew's situation. How? If the Nightfall Crown only grants clout, what does that actually do for you all?" He looked around at the entire table.

"Carver," Mercury said, "would you like to tell him?"

Carver's voice was serious and soft as he said, "We're not just gonna steal the crown."

"But it's okay, because the stealees are loaded," Coal hurried to add. "You said you didn't mind stealing from rich people."

Varick's eyes narrowed, but he didn't outright scowl. He didn't love that Coal had outed his personal philosophies to Mercury, but he didn't expect there was much Mercury could do about it. Varick's family may regard him as they would a slug, but if a no-name random stranger showed up at the manor and said Varick was fine turning a blind eye to the robbing of people who could afford to be robbed, they'd have more concerns about how the visitor got through the front gates than anything else.

He kept his eyes on Coal. "Go on."

Coal looked to Mercury, who gave him a nod. "We're gonna pull the heist on an *airship*." He breathed the word reverently, as if it was the same as riding a long-dead, Old World dragon or something.

Mercury pulled a trifold pamphlet from inside his jacket and slid it across the table to Varick. "This one."

Varick read the cover.

Angrec's Respite
A Prism Line Air Cruise property

The latest in modern airship innovation!
Come recuperate yourself with our state-of-the-art facilities,
Springhaven's finest dining, entertainment halls, and more!
Only available to 200 of Invarnis' finest citizens. Secure your spot
today!

Beneath the words was an ink drawing of a huge airship. The gondola looked as large as the Springhaven museum, which was probably necessary, given all those modern innovations, entertainment halls, and other facilities. The envelope resembled a marlin with its long, sharply tapered nose, though Varick couldn't help but wonder if perhaps it was meant to resemble its namesake flower.

Invarnis' former monarchy abolished itself about a hundred years ago at the beginning of the Dawn Age, when the government, calendar, everything had been overhauled. Therefore, it was generally considered déclassé to refer to anything as "royal," but people still found a way around it, like with the *Angrec's Respite*. The angrec orchid symbolized royalty, a sort of secret code to indicate only the wealthy need inquire. Varick rolled his eyes at the wordplay. When he read further down, however, even having seeing through the subtle language of the ship's name, his jaw dropped.

"They want *how much* for a ticket?!" he exclaimed. "For a three-night cruise? That's highway robbery."

"Skyway robbery?" Coal offered.

Mercury's chuckle was mirthless this time. "Makes you wonder who the real criminals are, knowing to what better use that money could go. And now you see why we need a backer."

"You want four tickets?" Varick gawped.

"No, but thank you for the offer."

Varick was about to protest, joke or not, that he most certainly had not been offering, but Mercury was already moving on.

"If you read further, you'll see domestic help travels at a far more reasonable price."

"Reasonable," Varick scoffed. Then he looked up at Mercury, to Coal and Carver. "You want to pose as my attendants?"

"You're quicker than you look," Mercury said. He snaked an arm across to Carver's plate and nicked a morsel of rarebit off of it. He gestured with the stolen bite before popping it into his mouth. "There're two others in our crew, so that'd be five in all, plus your ticket, of course. The current owner of the crown will be a guest as well, and she's no fool. She's not about to leave it at home, all alone and unattended."

Varick sat back in his chair. He had not expected anything like this. A bank robbery perhaps, or a break-in to a vast manse similar to his own home. The rest of the pieces fell into place. In addition to the crown, Mercury and his team were going to steal from the ultra-wealthy aboard the airship. No doubt all those peacocks packed into one place would be overflowing with jewels. Varick said nothing as he began to read through the pamphlet more closely. The others at the table gave him space, idly chatting as they sat and ate and waited. Calandra returned at one point, and Varick ordered more cider without even thinking about it.

He'd seen this airship before, at the casino night. On the schematics and other documents Coal had made copies of. P.L.A.C. - A.R.. Prism Line Air Cruises - *Angrec's Respite*. So Varick had been involved with the job before he'd even known there was a job. But Carver had said he and Coal hadn't told Mercury about that night and weren't going to. Varick certainly wasn't about to volunteer that information either. He felt a small sense of triumph at that, like they'd chosen him over Mercury.

The voyage set off in a few month's time, just after Varick's fifteenth birthday. Part of the fee covered travel visas out of Springhaven, a night in a luxe hotel in Duskwood, and a first class train ride back to the city. The writer of the brochure apologized in advance that all travelers who didn't already have clearance to travel outside of Springhaven would have to complete application and interview processes with the Enforcer order to acquire the necessary travel documents. Both the apology and the warning was warranted. The amount of red tape required to travel outside the city was worse than… well, Varick didn't actually know what was worse. He just knew it was a constant complaint of his family. Not even they'd sprung for a holiday outside of the city, saying they'd rather stay home than jump through all those administrative hoops.

"You'd think a family as prestigious as ours would be given some credit," his mother often said.

Translation, Varick always thought in response, *you resent not being immediately given whatever you want.*

"Invasive is what it is," his father complained. "Wanting to know about our activities and associates. Requiring *references.*"

"And you have to go to *them* for an in-person interview," Patricia had piled on. "Don't they know how busy people are?"

Randolph, on the other hand, had always described their choices as cutting off their noses to spite their face. He'd wanted to take Varick traveling, but Victoria and Henry had never allowed it. A waste of time and money, and then they'd start in on their complaints again. Now that Randolph was gone, though, and Varick controlled his own finances, he wondered how much sway he might have with them. Stars, he might have to promise some favors. But if he could pull it off, he'd get to fly! To see Duskwood and get away, at least for a little while.

Varick looked up from the brochure. Realization had just whacked him over the head with a billy club. "You're going to use the trip as a way to get out. To leave Springhaven." He looked around the table. "All of you?"

Coal nodded, looking a little ashamed.

Carver held up his hands. "Haven't quite decided yet, but it's nice to have the option."

"No," Mercury replied, shaking his head. "I'm coming back. Gonna be the new king of thieves with that crown."

Clearly, Mercury didn't care for all things royal being out of fashion.

Varick rolled the idea over in his head. This was phenomenally stupid. Why would he risk… what? What was he risking? Let's say he did agree to back Mercury's plan. If things went south, he could always claim that he'd been tricked. Oh, what horrible pack of conmen he'd been bumfuzzled by!

He looked at Coal and Carver, though. He didn't want them getting locked away for life on his account, but they were already in. And he had a feeling Mercury was going to make this happen come hell or high water. He shot a look at the man as he thought. Mercury, who'd finished his steak and kidney pie and had moved onto a plum crumble for dessert, caught the look.

"I know what you're thinking," he began.

"I assure you, you do not," Varick snapped. Blazes, how he hated it when people did that.

Mercury held up his hands. "Very well then, *in case* you think I'm just some grasping, conniving rogue, allow me to defend myself. I was not born with innate charm, like some, and we live in a hard world. I'm just trying to make the best of things, and help out those I can along the way."

He motioned at Coal and Carver, who were also enjoying their own plates of plum crumble, which Coal had immediately taken to call plumble. Mercury had been the one to offer to buy the desserts. Perhaps Varick was being too hard on the man. He knew he had a deep distrust of parental-type figures, and with good reason, but he also knew varied blends of both decent and dishonest people existed in all walks of life. His grandfather had been kind. Great Auntie Megaera was too. Varick thought back to his conversation with her on the day of the will reading. She'd encouraged him to go live for himself, to travel.

He blinked, thinking. After a moment, he said simply, "I'm not old enough to travel unattended."

"Isn't that why you have attendants?" Coal asked.

"No, not like that." The wheels in Varick's head had picked up speed and were whirring with activity now. "And I have some notes on those parts too, but give me a moment."

There were rules about unaccompanied minors and travel. The *Angrec's Respite* brochure even said—albeit in tiny print along the bottom on the very back flap—that all staff must be of age and all guests under the age of sixteen must be accompanied by a guardian.

Mercury scratched his cheek thoughtfully. "I hadn't considered that."

Why the blazes not? Varick wondered. *Especially if your plan hinges on me joining you?*

"I supposed we could forge some of your papers," Mercury went on. "Or I could pose as a new teacher for you and your brother and convince him to go as an educational endeavor."

"No," Varick retorted. "Those are bad plans." The fact that Mercury had overlooked his age didn't make Varick feel particularly confident. But as he saw gaps in the ideas, he also saw how to fill them. He ticked off the various possibilities on his fingers. "One, I would rather permanently don a beehive as a fencing mask than be under my idiot brother's care, who, by the way, has as much interest in broadening his mind as a clump of pondweed. Two, I'm too well known for forged papers to work." At a simpering look from Mercury, he added, "I'm not boasting; that's just a fact. When the newssheets reported on my grandfather's will reading, they included a feature on me. Forgeries aren't an option. And while no one else in my household will want to go on this trip either, believe me, we don't want any of them with us anyway. But I bet my aunt would go."

"Your aunt?" Carver asked. "Is she…" He gave Varick a meaningful look, zeroing in where Victoria had slapped him that day at the Saffron Club. "Like the rest of your family?"

Varick shook his head. "No, she's…" He thought about the fact that he didn't really know her, but Randolph had always talked about her, relaying what she'd said in her latest letter. He thought about how kind and open she'd been at the will reading. "I think she might actually be pretty great."

I guess we'll find out, he added mentally.

Mercury leaned back in his seat and folded his arms over his chest. "I don't like it. Bringing a woman along mangles the rest of the plan. We can't wait on a lady. She'd have to bring her own staff." He waved his hands. "No. It doesn't work."

"It works better than your convoluted ideas," Varick insisted. He could feel his temper rising, but he tamped it down, focusing on the deal-breakers he'd set for himself earlier. He remembered the buttons on Great Auntie Megaera's dress the day of the will reading, the buttons that went up the front of her bodice. "Listen, I know what I'm talking about. It'll be fine." He stabbed a finger into the cruise brochure like a dagger. "I know how this world works, so you need to listen to me. By taking my money, you're taking me on as an equal partner too. That's the deal. You let me handle my aunt, alright?" He fixed Mercury with a hard stare. "Or maybe you start from scratch and figure out a different way to get your hands on the Nightfall Crown."

Now it was time for Mercury to think. He rubbed a hand over his jaw, his light eyes locked with Varick's dark ones. Inside, a little part of Varick hoped he might call the whole thing off. If things went south, his crew would spend the rest of their lives in the Halls of Justice. But a much larger part of him yearned for the challenge and adventure such a job promised. To break free of his family, even for just a few days. To see and explore beyond the walls of Springhaven. And to help give Coal and Carver get a fresh start at life. Varick didn't like the idea of losing these kind lads almost as soon as he'd met them. It made his heart ache in an all too familiar way, but to say, "No, you can't try for a better life because I'll miss you"? Absolutely not. That was selfish, pure and simple. Coal and Carver deserved better.

Finally, Mercury cocked a half-smile and asked, "So that means you're in?"

Varick took a deep breath, mustering his courage to take the leap. "So long as my terms are met, I'm in."

18

CODS, WASPS, AND HORSES

Mercury gave a pleased sort of chortle and reached across the table. "We have an accord then."

As Varick shook Mercury's hand, Coal punched the air and threw his arms around Carver in a tight hug before breaking off again and starting up another one of those funny little shuffling dances. Varick couldn't help but wonder if this was some sort of replacement behavior for the touching. If so, the consideration gave him a warm, fuzzy feeling inside. Carver, meanwhile, smiled broadly and leaned back in his chair, arms crossed over his chest in a pose of relaxed satisfaction.

"Oh! Didn't you say you had notes about our parts?" Coal asked. "Lay 'em on us." Before Varick could answer, he added, "I'm willing to play starring roles, perform lady parts, and do accents."

Varick opened and closed his mouth a few times, unsure how to respond. "Don't worry about that. The issue is with the number of people. I don't need five attendants."

Mercury waved a hand. "Yes, yes, we know. You're not like those other rich rotters."

"No." This time, Varick allowed his annoyance to show. "Five is excessive for *anyone* in this situation. I could get away with three at most—valet, secretary, and footman. And the footman is pushing it."

Carver tipped his head to the side. "Could you maybe be an eccentric?"

"I could, but it'd still attract a lot of attention, attention you don't want, I'm sure."

Coal gasped and slapped his palms down on the table. "I know! We could hide in your luggage. I bet you could fit two of me in a steamer trunk."

"You would suffocate," Carver informed him matter-of-factly.

"No!" Coal insisted. He gesticulated wildly as he spoke. " You drill holes—wait for it—in the *bottom*! That way, no one can see them."

"The bottom?" Varick chimed in. "Upon which the trunk sits, flat against the floor?"

Coal fwumped back into his chair. "Hmm. I see what you mean."

"Something along those lines may not be a bad idea, though," Mercury said. "Let's put a pin in that, especially since that'd make it less people to buy tickets for."

Fewer, Varick mentally corrected, but he was not enough of a pedant to actually say it out loud.

From there, the meeting wound down. There were plans to go over, and Mercury told Varick that he'd need to meet the rest of the team. In a few days, Coal would handle showing Varick the way to The Riffraff Inn, as Mercury referred to the place his crew laid their heads. That would be their base of operations going forward. Varick still didn't like the idea of going anywhere

Mercury could potentially trap him, but he had a plan for that. As they shook hands again right before breaking up for the night, Varick asked one last question.

"Aren't you at all worried I'm going to take this information straight to the Enforcers? I could turn all of you in."

Mercury's answering smile looked like it was trying to be empathetic. "You could, but I think we both know you won't."

He glanced back to his two young protégés, and Varick knew that Mercury didn't just think he was right. He knew it.

♜

Coal did a lot of coming and going over the next few days. Firstly, Varick needed to send a letter to Great Auntie Megaera and float the idea of the airship cruise to her. To keep his family from intercepting any messages from her, Coal arranged the comings and goings of these correspondences, which Varick began paying him for as he would any courier. The message part was easy enough.

Dear Auntie Megaera,

I'd dearly love to get away from my rotten family. How about an overpriced holiday through the clouds together to assuage our shared heartache? Alas, I am naught but a child, and if you say no, I shall be bereft of such an experience, because heaven knows I'd rather be hung up by my toes over a lake of piranhas than take a trip with any of the rest of these walking cods. I look forward to your reply. Best wishes and good health.

Your delightful great-nephew,
Varick

Or rather, that's what Varick would have liked to write. He was sincere, however, over how she was coping with the loss of her brother. It seemed a bit gauche to send a letter that both mentioned her grief and called the other members of their family a collection of male genitalia—or maybe it would have made her day. He honestly didn't know either way, a travesty Varick meant to correct in short order.

Varick soon learned his continued worries in regards to meddling from his family were entirely justified, for Great Auntie Megaera's first reply mentioned previous letters.

What previous letters?!

The paper in Varick's hand shook as he read:

My dear Varick,

I was honestly both surprised and delighted to hear from you. I'd rather suspected your family of keeping my correspondences from you. Perhaps you did receive those other two letters and simply haven't had time to reply. I rather hope it's the latter, and if so, I'd love to hear what mischief you've been getting up to.

The last sentence momentarily shook Varick out of his rage.

How does she know? he wondered to himself, just before remembering that Great Auntie Megaera was old and that was the way the elderly often spoke about striplings like himself... often followed by complaining about them, despite the fact that the elderly were once young themselves, getting into all manner of their own mischief.

He skimmed over several more lines of niceties, as well as a paragraph about missing her brother's letters. She added that receiving Varick's letter had, "added sunshine to my day." The thought warmed his heart, but at the same time made him even angrier. Sweet old Great Auntie Megaera, grieving her brother, and Varick's vile family members pawing through his mail and stealing what little opportunity for cheer he might give her.

Finally, after a lengthy cataloging of her own adventures—a

gallery opening from an up-and-coming artist, an exclusive tasting at one of Springhaven's premiere restaurants, a venture into crossbreeding roses—she got to Varick's suggestion of the cruise.

This Angrec's Respite *holiday you mentioned sounds like quite the diversion indeed. I'd love to go, but I'm afraid I'm not certain what my future financial situation will be. Your grandmother, from what I gather, has been inquiring about cutting me off from family funds. My financial advisors don't think she has a leg to stand on, but she might try to drain me through rounds and rounds of legal tomfoolery. Please accept my sincerest apologies. A trip with you sounds ever so lovely.*

And, Patricia, if you're reading this because you have been obstructing communication between Varick and me, I'd say you're a wrung out wasp, but that'd be an insult to those industrious men and women who actually know the meaning of hard work.

Varick blinked and looked to Coal, who'd made himself comfortable in front of the fire with a book and a package of biscuits. Varick had begun squirreling away shelf-stable goodies in his room for Coal's frequent visits.

"Coal, do you know what a wasp is?" Varick asked. He could still feel his rage, waiting right behind his curiosity.

"It'sa nasty bug. Stings you," the boy replied absently.

"Yes, but as a term of abuse. Slang, I suppose. Do you know it in that context?"

"Ooooh," Coal said. "Painted lady or rent boy who's got a disease. Their sting is in the way you get infected with it."

Varick smiled an evil smile then, letting his anger flow. He crushed the letter in his hand. Back before he'd learned from Carver that they'd been tampering with his post, he'd gone so far as to ask both his parents and Patricia if any mail had come for him. Not only had they lied right to his face, but he'd endured insults along with the lies.

"How do you usually receive mail?" his mother had sniped. "If something had arrived for you, one of the staff would have delivered it to your room. You know this. Now stop wasting my time with your witless inquiries."

Back then, Varick had begun to wonder if he was being paranoid. He wasn't, he knew now, and he scolded himself for doubting his instincts.

Thank the stars for Coal. Varick's next letter offered to pay for Megaera's ticket. He wrote that it was important to him for them to make up for lost time. He might have felt guilty about such a maneuver, except that he meant every word. Plus, of course, all the other benefits that would come with her agreement.

In the meantime, just as he'd known would happen, "opportunities" came calling to him from various family members, little by little, sniffing around with ideas and requests and invitations to luncheons and dinners. He distrusted the lot of them, given that what he received likely came filtered through his parents' and grandmother's scrutiny. Right off the bat, he ignored the ones from distant cousins and the like, people who'd barely acknowledged his existence before and cared not a jot until he'd had something to offer them. His closer relations also only concerned themselves with what he could do for them, but they tended to eschew letters and go through his immediate family members first.

"My brother has contacted me," Varick's father said to him one night over dinner. "He has an interesting business venture idea." Henry's brother happened to be the infamous Onion Breath Uncle Jason.

"Oh?" Varick replied mildly. "Is this about the pigeons? Are

you going to invest in him then?"

Henry then gave Varick a song and dance that could have, maybe, almost, if one only caught about every third word, been described as fatherly about how, now that Varick was getting older, perhaps it was time he started exploring opportunities the business world had to offer. Varick was fairly convinced his father just wanted raw-onion-eating Jason off his back and was trying to schluff the man onto Varick.

Patricia had also called Varick to her sitting room to inform him of a letter she'd just had from "my dear friend, Lord Quincy." Varick's grandfather had once told him that Patricia had long been having an affair with Lord Quincy. Anger bubbled in Varick at the mention of the name. Lord Quincy, also of the casino night shenanigans, already a politician, apparently had aspirations to become a railroad tycoon as well, but the same red tape that plagued the Pendragons' holiday possibilities was also slowing Quincy's progress. He needed money to hire crusaders— people who made it their business to influence how members of the magistrate council wrote legislation and voted.

Magnus, sharp as a bowling ball, had simply come to Varick and said, "We should bet on boxing matches."

"Oooh, Ricky." This purring prelude to a request from Constance came at him a few days after he'd sent his offer to Great Auntie Megaera. "That lovely chap, Galineer, you remember? The one with a fancy for breeding those pretty cobs with the long feathering on the legs. He's looking to start his own stud line."

Varick very nearly ignored his sister on principle, but Constance had a penchant for making deals. She'd approached him while he'd been exercising in the gymnasium, so it was only the two of them at the moment.

"That's very industrious of him."

Varick kept his tone bland, pretending to focus on his

workout. He was doing cable pulls in order to improve his upper body strength. He'd tried doing the pull-up bars earlier, but even a single pull-up proved much harder than he'd anticipated.

Constance came around to lean against the wall to which the cable, pulley, and weight system attached. She affected a casual posture, but Varick could see her angling.

"He's very sweet, you know," she went on. "Most men who like animals are. You can always tell a person's character by how they treat their animals."

Varick made a noncommittal noise at that. He didn't believe that was strictly true. Constance, for instance, enjoyed the company of dogs, but not even she was permitted to have one. Too smelly, too messy, too hairy, said Patricia, and Henry, her son, had been brought up to believe the same. It was the only thing their grandmother had ever denied Constance, so she doted on her horses instead. In fact, Varick couldn't be sure if his sister was actually interested in this Galineer chap at all, or if she was simply interested in his admittedly beautiful steeds.

Constance sighed. "It's such a shame, really. He's developed such a fine breed, but it's been difficult getting people to invest in him."

Translation, Varick thought to himself, *his rich mommy and daddy don't want him building a name on equine copulation.*

Or, as Coal might call it, interhorse.

"What does that require then?" Varick asked, injecting just the tiniest note of interest into his voice now.

Constance pushed up from the wall. "Oh, it's ever such a clever plan. He wants to hold a horse trials event, wherein several of the competitors will be on his best animals. That way, everyone can see what versatile creatures they are. Galineer, being the show-runner, will get to promote his stud services right there in front of the perfect audience." She flipped back the curls of her updo. "The show was my suggestion."

And no doubt Galineer would thank her with the gift of a prize example of the breed. Even so, Varick didn't bother to smother the impressed bob of his eyebrows. It actually was a rather good scheme. If it wasn't seen as beneath their high rank, Constance could dominate any segment of trade she chose.

He knew the answer before he asked the question, but if he was going to entertain this idea, he was going to make her work for it. "Why are you telling me about this?" He grunted a little, moving into a new set of repetitions on the machine.

Constance widened her eyes and puckered her lips in a flawless imitation of innocence. "I thought you might be interested in investing. You being a fellow horse enthusiast, after all."

Ah, so that was her ploy. In the way Randolph had left Tallywags to Varick, she'd seen a workaround for their father's ban on Varick purchasing any horses for himself. Varick's enjoyment of riding had been no secret, and Constance must have surmised that she could tempt him with an avenue to acquire more animals. Prize steeds from Galineer for the both of them then.

Varick put on a bit of a show contemplating the idea while he finished this round of pulls. Finally, he slowly released the cables, allowing them to retract onto their winches and lower the attached weights to the ground.

"What's in it for me?" Again, he already knew the answer.

Constance gifted him a winning smile. "Galineer has agreed to give you one of his horses, so long as he retains exclusive breeding rights." She pulled a pout. "Father's edict about you buying one really has gone on a terribly long time, hasn't it?"

Did this sort of charade really work on other people? It must. Constance had no end of admirers. All the money her family came with had to play a part, of course, and none of them probably knew the full extent of what she was *really* like.

Varick considered his answer carefully, weighing his estimation of Constance's powers of persuasion.

"I would actually want something else."

19

HORNETS FOR BREAKFAST

She batted her eyelashes and kept her tone light as she replied, "Oh?"

Varick hesitated, but only a moment. His family would have to find out about the cruise sooner or later, wouldn't they?

"There's a trip I want to take," he said. He gambled on a lie then, remembering what Megaera had said about Patricia in her last letter. "I'm trying to get Auntie Megaera to go with me, but she doesn't really want to."

Constance made a face. "That grumpy old hag? Why?"

He gave a shrug and dodged. "I suppose it won't be so bad. You know that I don't always get on well with Mother and Father. And it's an airship cruise. They won't endure the rigamarole for getting out of the city. I'm not old enough to go by myself, and Auntie Megaera already has her travel permits. It's *really* expensive on top of that, but it'll be fun to do something I've never done before."

Constance still looked disgusted. "But with *GAMS*?"

Varick had heard Constance use the name before. It was an insult based on the initials for Great Auntie Megaera—spinster. He ignored the jab and started dabbing his sweaty face with a flannel he'd set nearby for just such a job.

"If it gets really bad, I'm sure there are places on board I can escape to."

Constance began to saunter about the room, her forefinger tapping her cheek in thought. "So in exchange for funding Galineer's horse trials event, you want me to… what? Try and convince the old bag to go with you?"

Varick waved a hand at her. "I'm working on that. I think I've almost gotten her worn down, too. What I'd like from you is to convince Mother and Father to let me go."

"I don't have any more sway over them than you do." Constance crossed her arms over her chest.

Horse feathers! Varick's inner voice screamed.

Instead he gave her a knowing little look. "You and Grandmother share a special bond, though."

Like rotting detritus and bottom feeders, he added mentally.

"If you can convince her it's a good idea," Varick went on, "then I'm certain she can convince Mother and Father."

Constance pursed her lips and considered. "That's really all you want?"

Bugger, Varick thought. He'd seemingly low-balled himself. But he could use that to his advantage.

He faked a bashful grimace. "I wouldn't mind a horse as well, but I didn't want to appear too greedy."

Constance gave him one of her manufactured tittering laughs. "How very shrewd of you, little brother. I'll see what I can do."

He mustered another smile, but it was weak. Blazes, he couldn't tell her to prioritize the trip without giving the game away.

From there they negotiated. Varick made it clear that he

didn't want to be involved in the planning or execution of the horse trials. He didn't even want to be cited as the financier, nor did he want her coming back with a higher number down the road. He wanted a firm figure before he gave anyone a copper. Constance's opinion of him wasn't so low that any of this surprised her. She insisted, however, that Varick put a little money down on the front end. "A good faith payment," she called it. He'd wanted to withhold all funds until she'd done her part, but Constance didn't trust him to uphold his end of the bargain either. Thus, they decided to take turns. First a small portion of the backing from Varick, and then Constance would have to deliver results from her end before Galineer got the rest. Having shaken hands on the plan, Constance swept out of the room in a swirl of silk and lace, off to begin her arrangements. And Varick had his own to attend to.

During one of Coal's many visits, Varick set a date and time for when he was to go meet the rest of Mercury's team. It took some finagling on Coal's part because Varick had specifically asked to go when Mercury would be engaged elsewhere—no opportunities for capture and ransom notes or anything like that. Coal had already began to use Varick's room as a sort of rest stop between either doing tasks for Varick or whatever else it was he did during the day. It was never discussed; the boy simply started showing up and passing time there. If he stayed the night, he slept on the recamier at the end of Varick's bed. Varick wordlessly started leaving a blanket and a hot water bottle there, and Coal was always gone well before the house staff arrived in the morning to build up the fire.

At last, the day came. Varick dressed well again, though his outfit today was more social call and less business meeting—a cravat instead of a tie paired with a black and grey plaid waistcoat. It was just barely midday now, and again, he was able to ride Tallywags out to the meeting spot. For ease, Coal had told Varick to come to the Raven's Tower again.

When Varick arrived, Coal was standing out front of the Tower. He was busy munching on a piece of bread that looked suspiciously like the brown loaf they had been served during the meeting with Mercury.

"Cali had some day-olds!" Coal announced through a mouthful of crumbs. He lifted what had once been simple, burlap sack for carrying grain, but had been cut and converted to a large shoulder bag. "Want some?"

Varick very nearly said yes—it had been delicious—but he remembered the grand array of breakfast items he'd had available to him that morning, the way he'd filled up on fried potatoes and eggs and ham and tea and crumpets, knowing he had a full day ahead of him.

"I'm alright," he replied. "You enjoy."

"Roger that," Coal said, before devouring another mouthful. "Leave the horse. Let's go."

"Leave the…" Varick looked at the hitching post and up at Tallywags.

The horse looked back down at him with the same expression he always did, an expression uncannily like a cat's—expectant but ready to be unimpressed.

"But where are we going?" Varick asked.

"It's not too far, but some of the way is just easier on foot."

With that assurance, and knowing Tallywags both could and would make anyone who tried stealing him regret it, Varick tied up the horse and followed Coal along the border wall between Sand and Cobalt. They took alleys and backroads this time instead of rooftops, and Varick suddenly felt very silly being dressed as nicely as he was, scurrying around corners and over fences. Thank goodness he'd been working on his physique. It took more than a bit of extra effort to avoid mussing his clothes on a few parts of their route, and Varick could feel the newly developed wiriness of his muscles working.

The buildings around them began to grow more rundown, and Varick understood why when they reached Viola Meadow.

Varick had never actually heard of the place, but signs with pointing hands painted onto the sides of buildings had told him it was this way. The size of those painted signs had indicated it was rather an important area. When they arrived, however, Varick wasn't quite certain what he was looking at.

Viola Meadow was a large, strange, triangular-ish space where the Cobalt, Sand, Limestone, and Agate districts all met. The purple color of the walls told Varick they were technically in the Agate quarter, the poorest section of the city, and this meeting of so many different crossroads had resulted in a sort of open-air bazaar.

Booths and tables and even small huts had been erected, and people were hawking… well, what *weren't* they hawking? A cart rolled by, bearing the words "Seamot D. Sausages" in faded red letters on the side. A set of tables nearby looked more menagerie than shop, as small cages hung from tall arches of bent and lashed willow branches. The cages contained colorful birds, slender cat-weasel looking creatures with striped tails, giant hairy spiders, grey puffs of fur with large ears and long tails, and several varieties of lizard. Across the way, a small hut housed handmade pottery glazed in every color of the rainbow. Everywhere Varick looked was an artisan or street food vendor or merchant selling things he'd never seen the likes of.

The air bubbled with melded conversations. Sweet and spicy and sharp scents danced past one another. At either end of the strange space, large gateways to the Cobalt and Limestone quarters stood, gaping wide in their respective blue and green.

Over Varick and Coal's head arched the boundary between Sand and Agate, yellow on one side, purple on the other. Varick wondered how anyone navigated a place like this.

"You wanna look around?" Coal asked beside him.

Varick did, but not right now. He had business to attend to today, though that needn't stop him from asking questions. Just how to do so tactfully?

"We're in the Agate district now, yes?" He knew that; he just needed a lead-in to where he was headed.

"Yup." Coal bounced beside him as he walked. The boy clearly thrived in this sort of hustle and bustle.

"I thought Agate was…" Varick's words trailed off as he searched for a polite term.

"A slum?" Coal supplied.

"I wasn't going to… I mean… *I* didn't…" He realized there was no way around it. "Yes, that."

"Watch your pockets," Coal said.

Varick instantly looked around, searching for… what? Somewhere wearing a bandit mask, clearly looking for someone to pickpocket? He shoved his hands in his pockets, feeling first for his grandfather's watch—still there—and next for the rest of his possessions.

"Is that sort of thing a big problem around here?" he asked.

"Not really," Coal replied casually. "You just look like an easy mark."

"I do not!" Varick insisted. He then realized he actually had no idea what might or might not identify an easy mark.

Coal was already talking again, though, as they reached the midpoint of Viola Meadow. "Agate is a slum. If you mean the *actual* definition of the word."

"Meaning?" Varick asked.

He turned his head to watch a food vendor stabbing small cubes of meat and vegetables, according to his customers' orders, onto long, wooden skewers. Holding at least ten at a time, the man held the skewers over an open flame, slowly turning the food without any protection at all as the flames licked dangerously close to his skin.

"Meaning," Coal replied, sounding like he was reciting from a book, "a dirty, overcrowded area where poor people live." He looked back to Varick. "You hear a word enough about the place you live, you get curious what it means."

Varick nodded. He didn't know what to say to that.

"Heya!" Coal suddenly called.

He waved too, and Varick looked in that direction to see Carver chatting with a woman next to the doorway of a… oh. The building bore a wooden sign that read, THE TREACLE BARREL. It had the appearance of an ordinary public house, but the women and lads standing on the second and third floor balconies silently denoted the alternative services offered therein. Pavement nymphs, Varick had heard them artfully described, as well as painted ladies, rent boys, and soiled doves. Like the women on the balconies, the woman with whom Carver had been chatting appeared perfectly respectable—hair pinned up, hat in place, gloves donned—save for her décolletage, which was prominently displayed. Likewise, the chaps had their neckties undone, allowing them to hang loose and salaciously around their necks, the top few buttons of their shirts unbuttoned, while their shirtsleeves were rolled up to expose their forearms.

When Coal called, Carver looked and waved back, motioning that he'd join them in a moment. When he did, Varick looked at him, then back to the woman, but he didn't ask questions. Carver's business was just that, *Carver's* business. Coal, however, was of another mind.

"Was that Posy? Have you all gained any traction?"

"A little," Carver replied cheerfully. "There's gonna be a rally tomorrow night to gather more members." He looked down at

Varick and explained, "I'm helping the city's doxies to unionize."

Prostitution itself was not exactly illegal in Springhaven, but public indecency came with some pretty hefty fines, and practitioners of the amorous arts, being comprehensively viewed with an unfavorable eye, weren't afforded such privileges as the benefit of the doubt. This was wholly hypocritical, given that people from all levels of society made use of the so-called, "rough trade services."

Carver's broad shoulders made easy work of making way through the crowd. Today, he wore a plain, woolen waistcoat, a bowler hat, and a coat that fit his shoulders but was too large everywhere else. Varick also clocked the neck kerchief at his throat, pinned with the same, plain tiepin as he'd paired with the much nicer suit he'd worn when posing as Varick's secretary.

"I didn't know you were coming to see us today," Carver said. "That is why you're here, right? Or did you just need to get out for a while?"

Varick looked for a gibe in those words. Some crack about his being sheltered or coming down off his throne to see them, but there was none. Carver's face, as always, was open and sincere.

"I'm meeting the team," Varick said.

"But before that," Coal put in, "a quick stop for some peace of mind."

They reached the end of Viola Meadow, which emptied out into Agate proper. Here, the cobbled roads had been maintained, but the buildings—anything that was private property—looked hard-used. Street signs had been reinforced with metal frames and many of the shop windows had bars on them. The utter lack of greenery stuck out to Varick. In the Ivory quarter, trees and plants in huge stone planters lined the roads. Flowers hung in baskets from the lampposts there, and the glittering quartz walls multiplied the light. Here, smoke from nearby factories had darkened the walls to a grimy plum.

Despite the desolate feeling of the place, pockets of brightness stood out. On one corner, someone had used found objects to create a sculpture gallery on their tiny patch of front lawn. Over there, a small allotment had been turned into a community garden. A sign stood outside the fence, inviting people to take what they needed. Below it hung a box and a request for seeds for future plantings.

At last, they made their way down a skinny, winding alley. Coal stopped them at the mouth of it and gave a florid wave of his hand.

"Tadaa!"

Varick looked around but didn't understand. The alley opened to a dingy but otherwise ordinary looking street. Mostly people on foot, but a few hansom cabs, growlers, and people on horseback passed in an easy stream along the cobblestone road. On the other side squatted a cooperage. It was a long, low building with broad, open doorways all along its front and barrels of all sizes on display. Groups of men on break or making deals used them as chairs and tables. The smell of heated metal and burning wood stung Varick's nose.

"Look there," Coal said, pointing.

Varick obeyed, following the line of Coal's arm. It took a second, given how the flow of traffic obstructed his view. At last, though, Varick clocked him: Mercury.

The man stood just inside the cooperage, laughing and shaking hands with another gent. He was shorter than Mercury but had arms like train engines. He also had the look of someone who ate fistfuls of hornets as a show of dominance. In front of them clustered a collection of large barrels marked with the words "Airsick Sherry" across them.

"You said you didn't want Mercury around," Coal explained. "So I tailed him earlier, made sure he went where he said."

"And what exactly did he say?" Varick asked. "And how did you ask? Will Mercury be suspicious?"

"Oh, I didn't actually *ask* him where he was going. I looked in his diary."

Varick canted his head and, with piqued interest, said, "Say more."

"Mercury always carries it in his jacket," Carver explained.

"Which he left unattended the other day, and I seized the moment." Coal gave a modest shrug, but he was grinning.

Carver put a hand on the side of his face and said in a playful stage whisper, "Not the first time it's happened."

Varick nodded and looked back to Mercury. "What else is on his agenda for today?"

"This is *Business Meeting, Guthrie Cooperage, Agate*," Coal recited from memory. "Next, is *Drudgery, Center Street Apothecary, Sand*. He'll be there until evening."

"Who's the mean-looking chap he's talking to?" Varick asked.

Coal and Carver exchange clueless looks and shrugged.

"Probably just be some ol' bloke," Coal said. "Come on, you've got a crew to meet!"

Once they'd retraced their steps and started covering new ground again, Varick noticed the walls getting even darker than the smoke-stained ones from before. Large splotches of black, where magic had marred the once-glorious walls, spread like an infection. The scars were getting larger as they walked. Back before the War of Light, the Agate district had been the jewel of Springhaven, or Prism, as it had been called then. It had been a center of arts and entertainment, where anyone who was anyone went to see and be seen. The part the war had destroyed, nothing more than a burnt out husk in some places, was an area now known as Char.

"We're not..." Varick's voice cracked. He cleared his throat

and tried again. "We're not headed into Char, are we?"

"We sure are." Coal answered the question like Varick was winning in a guessing game.

"Why?" Varick demanded. "Isn't it—" He stopped himself before he could say it, snapping his mouth shut on the word.

"Haunted?" Carver and Coal offered together. They both looked far too amused.

Carver gave Varick an easy head bob. "That's what the people here *want* others to think."

"It's really fun," Coal explained. "If people start sniffing around, especially people looking to build or... reviffy... reveeree... What's that word, Carver?"

"Revivify," Carver supplied.

"Yeah, revivify the area. If people come in looking to do that, some of the local bosses will arrange spook shindies. There's an understanding there that they gotta work together when it benefits everyone. Sometimes, we'll hide and wail and throw stuff. But others, when we really wanna scare the pants off people, we'll dress in costumes and get up to all sorts. You gotta be careful, though. Can't get caught or made; it'd ruin the whole game."

"It's not a game to the crime lords," Carver said warningly. He looked to Varick. "But he's right, it is a good time for all. Well, everyone except the developers."

Varick smiled sardonically. He could just imagine Coal really getting into an assignment like that. Then again, he'd seen how ruthless business people could be when they saw an opportunity to make money.

"What happens if they persist? I imagine not everyone gives up that easily."

"In that case," Carver explained, "either the crime lords themselves or one of their best sneaks pays a visit to the developer's house and gives them a good haunting there. A lot of times, a threatening message written in chicken blood on the wall will do the trick."

Varick laughed. His mind was already turning over ideas to torment his family in the guise of a vengeful spirit. He wished he'd come upon this idea years ago.

At last, they arrived at a low, boxy building. Varick couldn't be sure what it had been in its past life, as the post where a sign had once hung stood rotted and splintered. The building stood alone on the block, surrounded by rubble blackened by long-dead magic. Even weeds seemingly refused to grow over what remained. The windows, most of which were broken, had been boarded over.

Coal and Carver led Varick around to the far side of the building, where a skinny path through the rubble lay hidden until they were practically on top of it. A thick, metal door met them at the end of the path. This was it, he realized. He was about to meet the rest of the team. Varick straightened his waistcoat and hat before realizing his clothing choices might do the opposite of make a good impression.

20

THE RIFFRAFF INN

Carver knocked a tune against the door, clearly a code of some sort. A small window slid open, and a mouth containing a missing tooth appeared.

"Password," the mouth growled.

"If a dove comes to the city to live," Carver whispered, "does that make it pigeon?"

The doorkeeper said nothing, just slid the little window closed. A moment later, the sound of gears turning and bolts shooting back could be heard, and the door swung back on well-oiled hinges.

"Thanks, Marlowe," Carver said as the three slipped inside. "How's the headache?"

The space they walked into was vast and mostly empty, lit low with petrolsene lamps. An impressive collection of cracked and broken mirror pieces helped to reflect and diffuse the available light. One floor took up the entire building, save for a curtained-off loft area halfway up the far wall. Some scattered oddments huddled beneath it.

"Better," Marlowe said, answering Carver's question. "Did the steam thing you said."

"Glad to hear it. My grandfather swore by that remedy."

Carver smiled and reached up to pat Marlowe on the back as he spoke. Carver was tall, but Marlowe, standing several heads taller than Carver even, was a giant. He sported a healthy set of muttonchops and had a head of thick, curly, strawberry blond hair. He looked a good few years older than Varick and like the sort of chap who'd break your face just for looking directly at him. A varied collection of scars peppered the young man's hands and arms. A few marked his face as well, including one that seemed to have left a permanent slit in one of his eyebrows.

Carver then turned to include Varick in the conversation and said as smoothly as any gent in Varick's circle—and with a thousand percent more sincerity—"Marlowe, I'm very pleased to introduce to you our backer."

Varick noticed that Carver had not given an actual name for him, an unforgivable faux pas in polite society. But they were not in so-called polite society, and Varick was learning the rules of this world quickly. He extended a hand, as did Marlowe, and watched as his was swallowed in the young man's grip.

"You can call me V," he said. "Pleased to meet you, Marlowe."

Varick had thought hard about the decision after the disastrous debut of his Knifestorm monicker. He'd gone for simplicity this time. After all, while his real identity wasn't exactly a secret, a layer of obfuscation was still a good idea. He had no aspirations for this side of society. He was here to do a job, a job that would help his newfound associates, and nothing more. And he certainly didn't want to be known for it.

The big lad nodded and grunted, "Same."

"Come on!" Coal said, hopping around the space. "You gotta

meet Fulcrum too."

Varick examined The Riffraff Inn, as Mercury had called it, more closely, while Coal trotted over to a ladder that led up to the loft above. Along the space beneath the loft, some bricks had been loosely stacked to form a low wall, and pallets laid on the floor, each in their own little segment of the area. Other bits and bobs clustered in tidy groupings on the floor or atop makeshift shelves on the wall. As Varick drew closer, a table made of more bricks and a couple of wooden planks could just be seen on the other side of the half-wall.

"How do you have lighting?" Varick asked. "Surely, someone somewhere can see that petrolsene flows out to here."

"The bosses keep the bigwigs at the petrolsene company paid off," Coal explained. "They don't ask questions and just gotta keep others from doing the same."

Varick was fairly certain he had some distant family members involved in energy supply—at a high level, of course—and wondered if some of them were beneficiaries of this arrangement.

Coal took the ladder up to the loft with the speed and agility of a squirrel.

"Fulcrum!" Coal called as soon as he alighted at the top. He swept the curtains aside with a flourish.

Varick observed that they were comprised of everything from tattered sails to actual curtains, stained and filched from who knew where. They hung from bits of cobbled-together metal pipe and wooden poles hung in a similarly higgledy-piggledy way from the ceiling.

"Lemme stop you right there," came a strident voice from within.

Varick stopped on the ladder as commanded, but Coal gestured him on, despite the edict.

"The backer is here. He calls himself V," the voice went on.

Varick tentatively followed Coal into the loft. Against the

nearest wall, another lad—Fulcrum, presumably—hunched over a worktable. He appeared maybe somewhere about Carver's age, possibly having gained his majority or just shy of it, and had an array of screws, nuts, bolts, leather and metal bits, and other small, sundry spare parts spread before him on the desk. His dark hair was grown long, possibly just past his shoulders but tied back at the crown of his head. Part of one side was bald and scarred in places, the rest in that area clipped close to the head, presumably to help it appear not quite so patchy. He wore a grimy shirt, dark trousers, and a dark waistcoat he'd left unbuttoned. Varick spied a cheap paste ruby earring hanging from a ring of tools attached to Fulcrum's belt, a match for the one he'd seen hanging from Coal's fob watch chain the day they'd first met.

"You've brought him up here to meet me." Fulcrum finally raised his head. Over one eye, he wore a set of telescoping lenses that made him look like a cartoonish mad scientist. "Hello, V. I'm Fulcrum, Coal's half-brother. Tolerable to meet you. Is that all you needed?"

Varick's mouth opened and closed a few times, unsure how to take this brusque greeting. Finally, he simply asked, "Yes?"

"You're a *full* brother in my heart," Coal said. He went and hugged Fulcrum around the shoulders.

Fulcrum had already returned to his work and ignored Coal. Fulcrum's skin was dark too, but closer to Varick's own warm coppery tone, not as dark as Coal's cool onyx. They shared the same eyes, though, sharp and bright.

"So…" Varick began, "that's everyone then?"

"Yup!" Coal replied. "The whole, top-notch team."

"Drink us in," Fulcrum chipped in from the side in a flat tone.

"What do you all do?" Varick asked, looking around.

The loft was nearly as empty as the downstairs. A medium-

sized safe sat in one corner, while a couple of empty crates turned onto their sides gathered with some mismatched chairs at the back of the office. And that was it.

"What does Mercury do?" Varick added.

"He mostly keeps to himself," Coal replied.

"Sometimes finds jobs for us," Marlowe added.

Carver motioned Varick over to the crates and chairs. "He's pretty picky, always weighing the size of the reward. He likes cloakroom jobs best, but only if they pay big. We're usually left to our own devices."

Varick sat down in one of the chairs. The varnish was peeling off of it, but not as badly, he noticed, as the one Carver had chosen for himself. Coal and Marlowe followed. A deck of cards sat atop one of the crates, and the smallest and largest of their party started up a game of Speed. The regular sound of cards being played and occasionally slapped provided a background tattoo to the conversation.

"When you say, 'cloakroom job," Varick asked, "do you literally mean robbing a cloakroom?" He remembered spotting Carver disappearing into one at the casino night once the chaos had kicked off.

"Sometimes," Carver said. "A cloakroom job can be any heist where there're a lot of valuable items in a confined space and not a lot of oversight. That's the plan for the *Angrec's Respite.*"

"Show him the picture!" Coal insisted. He slapped down on his and Marlowe's shared crate and yanked away the pile of cards a split second before Marlowe got it.

Marlowe, in turn, pronounced a swear Varick had never heard before. Coal added the new cards to his pile.

Carver pulled the closest crate toward himself, and Varick watched with interest as he pulled at a groove on the bottom panel, revealing a shallow, hidden drawer. Within laid a collection of papers, blueprints, doodles, notes, and more. Varick recognized the mirror-image pages Coal had created during that same casino-night-mayhem.

"Should you be showing him those?" came Fulcrum's voice from his worktable. "V hasn't actually invested anything yet, if I recall."

"And what do you bring to the table, Fulcrum?" Varick snapped. He hadn't meant to; it'd just come out. Fulcrum reminded him uncannily of some of the little tattletales he knew from his social circles.

Before Fulcrum could answer, Coal said, "He's a great tinkerer. He can rig together all sorts of stuff." Coal swept one hand toward the curtain system. "He made all this!"

Slap! Marlowe's hand crashed down on nothing again, missing Coal's other by no more than an eyelash's breadth.

"Oh? What else have you made?" Varick wheedled.

"I made that false bottom in the crate." Fulcrum still did not leave his worktable as he spoke. "And a knife that can be hidden in the toe of a shoe."

Varick allowed himself to be slightly impressed. "Alright, that's pretty good."

"It's a lot harder than just handing over a wad of cash," Fulcrum snipped.

"I have other skills too," Varick shot back.

"Having money isn't a skill."

"He's really good at sneaking," Coal offered. "And climbing."

"How are you at acting?" Carver asked.

"And fighting?" Marlowe added.

Varick looked around him, scowling. How had this turned on him?

"We're just asking," Carver soothed. "The more we can all do, the better off we'll all be."

"He's a pretty okay actor," Coal said. He looked at Varick, pausing his game with Marlowe. "Carver's teaching me. He's our grifter. And Marlowe, our hitter, taught me some stuff too."

Varick still bristled, but he put his annoyance to the side for now. Pointing to Coal, he said, "And you are the…"

"Thief," Coal proclaimed.

"But you're all thieves."

Carver chuckled. "Yeah, it's kind of one of those word games. You know, how every rectangle is a square, but not every square is a rectangle."

"Right." Varick nodded. "And Fulcrum is the tinkerer. So what's Mercury's role?"

Carver was sifting through the collection of papers collected from the crate. "Planner."

"He prefers mastermind," Fulcrum said.

Of course he does, Varick thought.

Carver put two sheets on top of the crate. One was an image-still of what Varick assumed was the Nightfall Crown, but, like all image-stills, sepia tones comprised the entire picture. The other sheet looked like hand drawn schematic with small, neat, block-lettered labels. Instead of an exploded machine, however, most of the paper was taken up by a colorful artist's rendering of the Nightfall Crown.

Thin, woven gold wires formed the framework for the crown, threaded with thousands upon thousands of tiny filigree loops of smoked glass, creating a shimmering, multifaceted plane that reflected light from every angle. The flash of dancing sparkles had even been caught in the image-still. The front of the crown rose up on either side in in an ascending wave of sunbursts, each one set with a star field of small aquamarines, sapphires, and tourmalines. At the apex of each sunburst sat increasingly larger fire opals, while smaller rubies, garnets, topazes, and citrines sat scattered below them like courtiers to kings and queens. The labels denoted the dimensions, types of gemstones, and other materials of the crown.

Despite himself, Varick whistled. The Pendragons had plenty of pretty treasures, but nothing like this. When his ancestors abdicated the throne, most of their jewels had been used to fund the country's recreation, though a few choice pieces had suspiciously managed to remain in the family. Just thinking about the challenge of it made him excited.

"So what's the actual plan for getting it?" he asked. "I know it'll happen while we're all on the airship, and from what Mercury said, it sounds like a couple of you will swipe it and as many other goodies as you can at the same time."

Carver smiled. "I'm so glad you asked."

From the pile, he produced the side elevation schematic of the *Angrec's Respite* that Coal had copied. He also offered a piece of broken mirror, given everything on Coal's versions was backwards. The airship's gondola resembled a steam-powered riverboat in basic concept, with tier upon tier of decks. The biggest difference, however, besides the greater number of decks on the airship, was, where the wraparound walkways on an ordinary steamboat were open to the air, those on the *Angrec's Respite* were walled off with glass panes that angled out and up to the deck above it. Each subsequent deck increased in circumference as one ascended, making the gondola resemble a flower bud. The design provided nearly three-hundred-and-sixty degrees of airborne, bird's-eye view sightseeing.

"Down here in the bowels of the ship are the storage areas, including the ship's vault, where all the safety deposit boxes live." Carver pointed as he spoke. "During the third night—that's the last night of the cruise—we're going to hit them, focusing on the Nightfall Crown first."

"How do you know it's going to be down there?" Varick asked.

"We don't," Fulcrum said, "technically."

"It makes the most sense," Carver said. "If Spindle—that's the current owner—keeps it in her stateroom, getting in and stealing it would actually be much easier."

"A baby could break into a stateroom," Coal said.

Varick actually chuckled at that, and Carver smiled.

"We're going to need to figure out which safety deposit box belongs to Spindle, but they're not assigned until a guest is on board and actually goes to store valuables in them, so no way around that."

"Can we plant someone in the office?" Varick asked. "Pose as one of the staff? Or bribe them?"

"Bribery would be easiest," Marlowe said. He squared a look at Varick. "But who's gonna do it? You? People know your face."

Varick was a little surprised. Marlowe hadn't struck him as someone who'd be terribly into reading, especially newssheets. And that, he realized with a creeping feeling of shame, was a judgmental assumption on his part, which made him a grade-A ass.

Carver was shaking his head. "Bribery doesn't seem likely. Mercury inquired about positions when he first started planning for this job. They require references, *lots* of them. They only hire people who don't know any other direction but up-and-up. Potential hires have to go through an interrogation with the Enforcers, like anyone applying for travel visas, but the Enforcers can also go to applicants' homes if they think there's reason to be suspicious and search for any evidence of criminality or connections."

"Is that legal?" Varick asked.

"It's unprecedented," Carver said. "There's never been a need for anyone to consider whether or not it should be. But applicants grant their consent to the possibility of a search in order to be considered for a position on board."

"Alright, so bribery's out," Varick agreed.

Carver nodded. "And as for posing as a vault employee, it's only two managers and a tight rota of specialty security personnel."

"But we get to be cleaners," Fulcrum said, a distinct note of sarcastic joy in his voice. "Since apparently, only a few of us get to come as your servants."

"Um, *staff*," Varick corrected, though he wasn't certain that helped his case.

"We get to be repairpeople too," Coal added, who was actually happy about the fact.

"And cooks," Marlowe said. He slapped down a hand and managed to grab a pile of cards while Coal was distracted by his excitement.

"All those have lots of employees and rotation between trips," Carver said.

"How do you know all this?" Varick asked.

Carver's mouth quirked up into a rascally little smirk.

"Posy helped," Coal laughed.

Varick remembered the woman Carver had been speaking with in front of The Treacle Barrel, who he was helping to form a union for Springhaven's doxies.

"One of her ladies has gotten very cozy with someone who happens to work at Prism Line's headquarters," Carver explained.

Varick stood and began to pace, the gears of his mind picking up speed. "Right, so a couple of you will be getting around the airship disguised as workers. And we won't be able to find out which safety deposit box to hit until we're on board. Because if this Spindle is smart, which we assume she is since she stole the crown before, she won't keep it in her room. I'm guessing that means there's no chance of her leaving the crown at home either?"

The rest of the crew shook their heads.

"Everyone in this world knows Spindle stole it," Fulcrum said, referring to Springhaven's criminal underworld. "The owner before her, Lethe, spread the word himself twenty years ago when she cut his petrolsene lines, caused a blackout, and swiped it. The tradition behind it is almost sacrosanct. She's not going to leave it where it can be easily snatched. She's going to make it a challenge, just like everyone before her."

Varick looked around at the team. "Sacrosanct, really? Do we believe this?"

Everyone shrugged, and Varick noticed the mood in the room had shifted. He narrowed his eyes, trying to read the group's body language.

"Do you all not care about the crown part? Is it just about the other jewels for you, or…" A horrible thought occurred to him then, and as much as he disliked Mercury, he deeply hoped he was wrong. "Do you all have a choice here? If you refuse to help with the job, will Mercury kick you out?"

21
THE SOPORIFIC SPONGE STRATAGEM

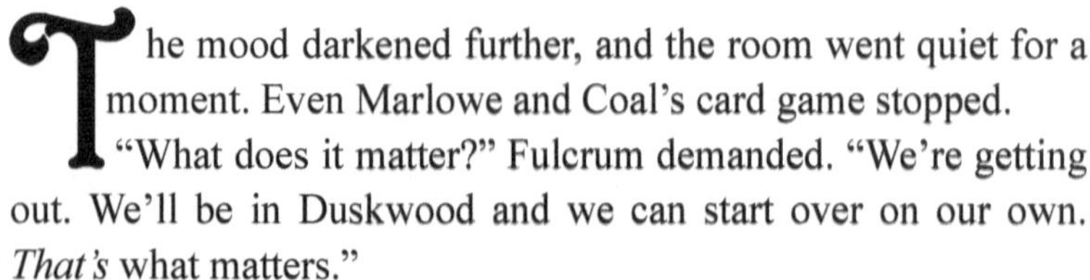

The mood darkened further, and the room went quiet for a moment. Even Marlowe and Coal's card game stopped.

"What does it matter?" Fulcrum demanded. "We're getting out. We'll be in Duskwood and we can start over on our own. *That's* what matters."

Heat rose in Varick's throat. Mercury was using them, all of them, for his own shot at criminal glory. He'd said he was going to come back as the new king of thieves. Varick could read between the lines. This job could be so much simpler if the Nightfall Crown weren't a factor. They all knew it, but Mercury wasn't settling for that. It put the focus on all the wrong things and, on top of that, made the whole situation riskier. He considered Fulcrum's angry words just now and wondered what Mercury would do if he didn't get the crown, if he had threatened outing them as orphans or even turning them into the Enforcers. What other opportunities might he have passed up because the job didn't come with accolades? Because it wasn't an immediate get-rich-quick scheme?

Varick took in the collection of talent around him. This was a good crew. They were wasted on Mercury. And nothing Varick could say would help either. There was little he could do for them while they remained at risk of the Enforcers. They were trapped, and this job was their ticket out.

"I see," he said at last, releasing a deep sigh. It drove his anger back down, for the moment anyway. "Well, best make sure we all have what we need to succeed then, right?" He turned back to Carver.

"How are we actually getting in night of the heist?"

The rest of the crew exchanged looks.

"Mercury said he doesn't need to know that part." Fulcrum shot a pointed look at Varick. "Because you won't be there."

"But he didn't say V wasn't *allowed* to know," Coal put in.

Carver gave Fulcrum a conciliatory smile. "Your little brother's got a point."

Fulcrum crossed his arms over his chest and harrumphed.

"Coal and Fulcrum are going to have to make a copy of the vault door's key," Carver said. "You and I are on intel duty for that. All the lockboxes will have keys as well, so we need to find out how that system works. Presumably, there will be two keys for each box—a guard key and the client key. But we suspect the vault will have backup client keys somewhere."

"Can you imagine?" Coal asked. He then slipped into his extreme toffee-nosed act. "Well, *I* don't know where I put the bally key! I have *people* for that, but they're all back at home. I am severely understaffed here and positively quanked by this ordeal. I need a glass of bubbly to settle my poor nerves."

This time, Varick caught the barest whisper of a smile on

Fulcrum's face, but it lasted only a second.

"All that to say," Carver chuckled, "the more information we can gather, the better. We should at least have the guard key, of which there should only be one. If worst comes to worst, though, Coal can manually pick the locks, but it'll use more time."

"I'll bring something to store in a safety deposit box." Varick released some of his residual anger into a nasty smile. "And I'll be a royal pain about it too."

"That shouldn't be difficult for you," Fulcrum muttered.

"Is there something you'd like to talk about, Fulcrum?" Varick snapped.

The lad shook his head as he screwed something to something else at the desk. "Nope."

Varick took a deep, calming breath. "Go on, Carver."

"Marlowe will pose as kitchen staff and get chummy with the vault's security detail. He's on getting to know their work schedules. All of us are responsible for taking notes throughout the first two days: Who's there, when, and where they're patrolling. When the time comes, Marlowe will do what he does."

Marlowe cracked his knuckles demonstrably and grinned. "Punch them hard enough, they'll go right down."

"Can't we just, I don't know," Varick said, "sneak up behind them and knock them out with a cloth soaked in… whatever chemical it is that makes people pass out?"

Fulcrum looked at Varick as if he was some kind of simpleton. "That's not a real thing. The effect isn't instantaneous. It takes time."

"It's in books," Varick objected. "All over the place."

"If that were possible," Fulcrum drawled, "people could be kidnapping each other left, right, and center. But we can buy more time by draping a cloth soaked in ether over their faces. A soporific sponge, I think it's called."

Varick still didn't like it. The security guards were just doing their job. And he didn't feel confident that Marlowe, or indeed anyone, could actually punch someone with enough surgical precision to both knock them out and avoid causing head trauma.

"There has to be a better way. I don't know what it is yet, but…" At seeing both Marlowe and Fulcrum give him displeased looks, Varick pivoted. "We'll keep the punching in our back pocket, alright? And the soporific sponge thing as well. Don't fret, we're still going to need plenty of brains and brawn, even if we don't use those options."

The two hardly looked mollified, but didn't object further. Varick couldn't be certain, but he wondered if it was because they knew, without him and his money, the job couldn't happen. The power imbalance of it made him no different than Mercury, and that made Varick feel very slimy indeed. A part of him didn't want to say the words, to appear soft to the team, several of whom he barely knew, but he couldn't stand being put the same light as Mercury.

"I'm here to stay, whether we agree on methods or not. I won't take my ball and go home if I don't get my way, in case that's what you're all thinking."

Marlowe and Fulcrum's expressions remained inscrutable, but Coal and Carver looked pleased.

"After that it's practically done," Carver said. He seemed to want to move the conversation away from awkward subjects. "Coal gets us in with the key, and we grab what we can. A couple of hours should give us plenty of time, so that'll affect how we decide to handle the guards. We'll stash the goods in a borrowed housekeeping cart, leave everything as we found it, and make our way back up to your stateroom to store our loot. The A.R.—"

"Arrrrr," Coal put in, doing his best impression of a pirate, which was not terribly good at all.

"—disembarks the next day at the passengers' leisure, but we

plan on leaving good and early, before anyone can discover what's happened. The goal is that we're gone before banking hours begin. That is to say, when the vault opens to passengers for the day."

Varick nodded, mentally logging and cataloging the information. "How are our extra people getting off board? And for that matter, on? I assume it'll be easier to steal work uniforms once we're all there rather than going through that insane hiring process."

"Lotta that depends on you," Marlowe grunted, slapping down more cards. He and Coal had resumed their game.

"Who're you gonna have as your helpers?" Coal asked.

"Who makes the most sense?" Carver amended.

Varick sat back down in his seat and thought. "We've already established you, Carver, as my secretary, so I don't think that should change. Not that I expect Cousin Chester or anyone else from the bank to be on the ship, but being my secretary will give you a good deal of freedom." He looked at Marlowe and Fulcrum, or rather, he looked at Fulcrum's back, and sighed. "I think Mercury will have to be my valet. He's the only one who looks like he has the experience."

What he really meant was, *Coal looks too young, Marlowe looks too tough, and either Fulcrum or I will end up throwing the other off the airship*, but "experience" was faster.

"I don't really want a footman. It doesn't make sense. The ship's stewards will do a lot of the same work." Varick's family had taken steamship trips before, but those could only go around Cobalt Bay.

Carver nodded. "Leaving shouldn't be difficult, from what I've gathered."

That lined up with Varick's experience. During those Cobalt Bay steamship cruises, each member of his family'd had to show their identification papers to get on board, but only his father or

Randolph had to be present at checkout for their entire party to disembark at the end.

"So that leaves the problem of Marlowe, Coal, and Fulcrum getting on board to solve."

Varick thought back to Coal's ill-conceived idea to sneak on inside a steamer trunk. Carver and Marlowe, meanwhile, discussed what would be needed for Marlowe to possibly pose as a porter. That was the only staff position they'd not nailed down yet, as porters were often employed by the docks, not the airship itself, and none of them knew how Duskwood's docking stations worked.

"Steamer trunks would be easiest," Varick remarked after a few minutes. "An excess of luggage wouldn't be so very odd. Is there something we can do to ensure no one suffocates inside of one?"

"Fulcrum?" Carver said.

"How should I know?" he asked. At least Varick wasn't the only one he got testy with.

Carver's tone was soothing. "You're the smartest one here. You seemed the likeliest to know."

"Mercury suggested rugs," Coal said.

He now held most of the deck, and managed to slap and pull the thin pile of cards before Marlowe, even while turning to look away.

"Are you cheating?" Marlowe asked.

Coal looked affronted. "I would *never*. Not against you anyway."

"I'm not bringing rugs," Varick said.

"Why not?" Fulcrum asked.

"No one brings their own rugs on holiday. I'll look mental."

Fulcrum made a gesture that said he didn't think that would be so bad, but his heart didn't look in it. He must have known as well as Varick that it was a flimsy idea. He looked up at their backer, brows cinched in thought.

"Why don't steamer trunks have wheels?"

Varick held up his hands. "I have no idea. I know some makers starting giving them domed lids to keep other trunks from being stacked on top. My family went for them like cats to fish."

The two lads exchanged a look, and for the first time, understanding passed between them.

"I don't know how I can get some here," Varick said.

"And I don't think I can sneak into your house," Fulcrum replied. "That's Coal's talent."

"We'll figure something out," Varick said. "And wheels still aren't a bad idea either, if we can pull it off."

From there, the group discussed their unsolved problems some more. In addition to what they'd already mentioned, Varick didn't want the Nightfall Crown getting stored with the rest of the loot. He didn't trust Mercury not to make off with the lot of it. He suspected the rest of the team would argue if he said that, though. Mercury was a louse, to be sure, but from what he'd seen, the crew seemed to trust their boss… to an extent, even if they didn't like whatever ultimatum he'd given them.

Instead, Varick suggested, "You know the old adage, don't put all your eggs in one basket? Well, maybe your plunder shouldn't all go into the same cart. What if you get stopped, or caught?"

"What do you suggest?" Carver asked.

"Pockets aren't enough," Marlowe added.

"I know," Varick said. He'd already been thinking of pockets and clothing. Menswear didn't have a lot of extra space, but womenswear… "How do we feel about wearing dresses?"

The group exchanged a variety of looks.

"Bad for fighting," Marlowe said. "Hard to move and too much to grab."

"I already said I'm willing to play lady parts," Coal put in.

Carver said, "If it works for the job."

When Varick looked at Fulcrum, the tinkerer simply pulled the tie from his hair and let his dark locks fall in a cascade of thick waves over the scarred side of his head. With a bit of makeup, jewelry, and the right augmentation to the dress, Fulcrum could easily pass for a handsome woman. His dark eyes dared Varick to make some sideways crack. Varick only smirked and pointed at the tinkerer.

"You've got the role."

"Awww," Coal said in disappointment.

22
BIRTHDAY GIFTS

Over the next few weeks, Varick split his time between his normal life—lessons, meals, and generally trying to avoid his family members—and what he had begun to think of as his other life. Constance, shockingly, held up her end of their bargain. Varick had wondered if she might lose interest in Galineer, and thereby the ploy, and he'd have wasted his deposit on the horse trials scheme. About a week after their negotiation, however, Patricia summoned Varick to her sitting room. There, he found her and Constance enjoying some tea and light refreshments together. He noted the salmon and dill finger sandwiches particularly—they were a favorite of Patricia's and had been employed by Constance, no doubt.

"Varick," Patricia said without preamble. "Your dear sister tells me you wish to go on a trip with you Great Aunt Megaera."

Varick swallowed a gag at the mention of "dear sister" and assumed his most deferential tone. "Yes, Grandmother, that is correct."

"And the reason for the trip?" Patricia asked.

"New experiences broaden the mind. I'd like to see more of the world, and it'd be good to explore business ventures in that industry."

"Ricky, do you fancy yourself a future airship pilot?" Constance tittered. She batted her eyelashes over her teacup.

What the blazes was she doing?! She was supposed to be helping him. Perhaps she really had lost interest in Galineer's pretty cobs and was finding fun in this new torment. Nevertheless, Varick smiled smoothly at her.

"Nothing like that," he assured them. Airship piloting, even for a luxury air cruise line, fell into a category similar to trade. "But, if this trip goes well, I might look at investing."

Patricia nibbled demurely at one of the salmon and dill sandwiches. "Luxury travel is an area in which the Pendragons don't currently have any influence. It's certainly something to consider." She looked sharply at him. "I don't believe you've approached your parents about this, is that correct?"

"Yes, Grandmother."

"And how long will you be gone?"

"Five nights. Three on the cruise, one overnight in Duskwood, and one to get back on the train."

Varick's heart pounded in his chest. Was this actually going to happen? It hadn't felt real without knowing if he'd have permission. There'd been discussion of forging a guardianship release form, but that left the issue of Varick disappearing for nearly a week and the subsequent hullabaloo of all that. The forgery would be discovered in the end.

"And who will be paying for this little sojourn of yours?" Patricia asked.

Varick didn't blink. With Constance, he'd left this detail vague. He summoned every ounce of guile he possessed and said with impressive confidence, "Great Aunt Megaera."

Patricia sipped her tea. "Interesting."

Then no one said anything for a long moment. Varick wasn't certain what might tip the scales in his favor. Constance, however, apparently had an idea, and he wasn't certain it was a good one.

"Perhaps it's not a good idea. Little Ricky here was telling me it's *very* expensive. And Great Auntie Megaera can be so unpleasant."

An arch of her perfectly maintained eyebrows was all that Patricia betrayed. Her voice was even as ever when she replied. "What will you do if you do not go on this trip, Varick?"

He tried to look innocent, widening his eyes in the same way Constance did. "I suppose I'll have to explore other opportunities here."

"Indeed," Patricia replied. She lifted another tiny finger sandwich and inspected it for blemishes. At last, she pronounced, "I believe this will be a good opportunity for you, Varick. Don't worry about your parents. I'll speak with them; they too will see the benefits of this excursion."

Varick's face fought him as he squelched the full-on grin that threatened to appear.

"Thank you, Grandmother," he just managed to say in a level tone. "I'll be happy to handle all the arrangements and correspondences. You won't need to do anything."

"See that you do," Patricia drawled. "The less anyone is exposed to that perpetual gadabout, the better."

She waved him away like a fly, and he bowed smoothly to both ladies. He'd never been so pleased to be dismissed.

The timing couldn't have been more perfect. Coal brought Megaera's response to Varick's room the very next day. Great Auntie Megaera proved the tougher nut to crack. She hemmed and hawed about Varick "wasting money on an old biddy like me." Not only that, but she never traveled without one of her dogs, and it would be an extra expense. She wasn't saying no, though, and Varick jotted off a quick line in reply.

Bring your delightful dog. And if it helps, do this for me as an early birthday gift.

He didn't actually think her dog would be delightful. In Varick's experience, companion animals of the ludicrously wealthy were often rotten little ankle-biters. Its presence in this not-so-little ploy, however, concerned him not at all. If the little cur started to cause a problem, he'd simply shove it into a cupboard for a while.

It wasn't another day before Great Auntie Megaera wrote back that, as his aunt, it was her duty to spoil him for his birthday and therefore, she would go. This time, when Coal did his happy dance, Varick joined him.

Varick also spent much of his time during these weeks visiting the crew at the so-called Riffraff Inn. After seeing Coal lock pick the doors of the Dragon's Keep, Varick had wanted to learn. It seemed quite the handy skill. Coal, in turn, wanted to learn chess, which Varick was all too happy to teach him. Carver took it upon himself to coach Varick in acting and accents, though Varick hadn't been interested in the latter.

"A good accent sells a part as well as clothing," Carver had counseled. "Sometimes better, since clothes can be bought or stolen."

"Or made," Varick had countered.

And that was how Varick also began to teach Carver how to sew. A few sewing and chess primers went a long way too, for when Varick wasn't there. And Coal, lacking access to such a book for lock picking, wrote one himself, using the fine paper he nicked from his new friend's writing desk. While Coal's metaphors in the little, folded volume were difficult to follow—

imagine you're putting on a puppet show, but none of the puppets have strings—the hand-drawn illustrations had been meticulously detailed and labeled. After seeing Coal's talent with paper and ink, Varick put in a special request with him on the sly.

And, being curious about the most taciturn member of their party, and perhaps feeling a little bored with his usual activities, Varick one day went to look over Fulcrum's shoulder.

"Whatcha working on?" He was practicing one the the new manners of speech Carver had taught him. Something nondescript middle class, though Varick's enunciation was still too precise to make it convincing.

"Sharpening knives," Fulcrum muttered. "Just plain old throwing knives."

"There's a specific type of knife for throwing?" Varick asked, genuinely interested. The flat blades with rounded handle ends looked unlike any knife he'd seen before.

To answer his question, Fulcrum picked up one of the blades he'd been honing and tossed it toward the back wall of the office. It stuck with a hearty *thwang* sound. Varick's jaw dropped. Fulcrum had made it look effortless.

"You could hide one of those inside a sleeve," Varick said. "Well, not those. They're too big, but a smaller version. Could you make me some? And teach me how to throw them?"

The buying, selling, and ownership of all manner of weapons were highly controlled, to say nothing of ranged weapons, with their longer reach. Even Varick knew simply buying knives like Fulcrum's would be no easy feat. He thought back to the ill-fated night he'd run into Gill and Parker, the two thugs Coal had fought off for him. While Varick didn't intend to get lost in the middle of the night again, he liked the idea of being able to defend himself if it came to it. And Fulcrum's demonstration seemed effective indeed.

"What are you gonna do in exchange for me?" Fulcrum

asked, his voice flat.

Get you a haircut? Varick thought to himself, glancing at the messy bun into which Fulcrum's long hair was currently corralled. It was beyond unfashionable for a gent like him. But those glorious locks had also gotten Fulcrum the part of secondary storage compartment in the form of his Dress of Many Pockets, as Varick had begun to refer to that piece of the plan.

Instead of some snappy comeback, however, what he said was, "What do you want?"

"Eggs," Fulcrum said without missing a beat.

Varick did, though. He stared at the lad, blinking. "You want… eggs?"

"Yeah. Eggs are the chatelaines of the food world. You know how many things you can do with eggs? Mostly I want to use them to create beauty treatments to sell. You can make a mint with good beauty products. But you can also use them to make glue or a makeshift plaster, or clean leather. The shells are high in calcium, if you don't mind the crunch, and make a good abrasive. You can even grow new chickens from them."

Varick blinked at him some more. "That's all you want?"

"I'll need materials too. Something I can melt down easily. Pewter will probably be the easiest for you to get your hands on. And I need clay for a mold too. They won't hold an edge for long, though. Pewter is a pretty soft metal."

"That's not very encouraging. Are there any other options?"

Fulcrum considered. "Bone, maybe? Flint?" When Varick gave him a narrow look, he gestured around him. "Do you see a smithy here? I can only work with what I have. So do we have a deal or not?"

"Very well," Varick agreed. "I'll bring you the materials."

"And don't forget my eggs."

That part turned out to be more difficult than Varick had initially imagined. Rather than tromp through the chicken yard at the Dragon's Keep, he opted to steal one or two at a time from the larder. Not enough for anyone to really notice. He managed to break in with his newly-learned lock picking skills. Thank the stars dogs were banned in the house, or the task would have been much harder, though a cat or two was permitted downstairs as a form of pest control. And the cats didn't care one way or the other about Varick's existence. Getting the eggs safely across town, however, resulted in messy pockets and then messy saddlebags. Varick only succeeded after sewing special pocketed pillows in which to transport his fragile currency.

Marlowe, apparently feeling left out—or maybe Fulcrum had put him up to it—approached Varick one day, pointed at him with a thick finger, and declared, "You're gonna learn to fight. Proper like. Up close."

"I know how to fence," Varick said, not sure how else to respond.

Marlowe spat on the ground. "Pah! Fencing is like fighting with toothpicks. If you're gonna stab someone, do it with feeling."

Varick didn't necessarily want to stab anyone, with or without feeling. What he *did* want, however, was to knock Magnus down a peg or two in their fencing lessons. Perhaps Marlowe's techniques could equip him to do that… somehow.

Days later, after Marlowe had summarily wiped the floor with Varick for the fourth time, Coal approached him.

"You know what your problem is?" he asked.

"That Marlowe was full-grown by the age of ten and is twice my size," Varick muttered. He was dusting off his clothes, though he didn't know why. Marlowe had said they'd go again when Varick'd had a rest.

"No," Coal informed him. "You're too polite."

"That's what I keep telling him!" Marlowe cried. The big lad was stretching his stocky limbs inside the sparring ring they'd

drawn onto the floor.

"No!" Varick shot back. "You just keep shouting, 'Wrong!' and then tripping me."

"Because you're doing it wrong!" Marlowe said.

"But that doesn't tell me *how*!"

"Look," Coal said, bringing the focus back to him. "You keep going into that ring like Marlowe's gonna follow some kinda gentleman's code for fighting. This isn't chess. You can't just pick a move from a list. You've got to be oppy… oppen… Fulcrum!"

"Opportunistic," called his brother from his workstation.

"That's it," Coal said. "You gotta be opportunistic."

Varick held out his hands. "Can you elaborate?"

"Here, watch me have a go," Coal said.

Watching Marlowe pound his small friend into a pulp seemed an extremely unpleasant activity, but there was no stopping it. Before Varick could say a word, Coal was already zipping toward the ring. Marlowe cracked his neck threateningly before squaring up. The exercise quickly turned from nerve-wracking to inconceivable. If Marlowe was a bear, all lumbering heft and strength, Coal was a hummingbird. He leapt and danced and even once slid between the much bigger chap's legs to punch him in the back of the knees. It wasn't long before Varick could see a viable strategy here. Coal just had to wear Marlowe out, wait until he got sloppy and then go for a soft spot. It'd be much faster if Coal used weapons, like he'd done when he'd been fighting Parker. His short push dagger had not been immediately lethal, but enough of those small stab wounds and weakness from blood loss would end a fight sooner than anything else. Varick called for a halt to the match.

"I see what you mean now," he said. "Don't wear Marlowe out too much. I should have another proper go at him while he's still fresh."

Coal practically skipped out of the sparring ring. He'd barely broken a sweat. Meanwhile, Marlowe drank in deep breaths, and his shirt had darkened with perspiration in a way it never had for Varick.

"How do you do it?" Varick asked Coal. "How do you decide what to attack? When to dodge?"

"You just gotta take it all in, moment by moment," Coal explained. "Where are his arms? What's exposed. How long til that foot reaches you? What's around to pick up and use? Don't forget your knees and elbows. And you gotta know how fast you are too."

Varick nodded. "Alright, I can do that."

Two minutes later, he was lying on his back and staring up at Marlowe's grinning face in the sparring circle. But that was one minute better than he'd done yet. And he'd even managed to get in a hit on Marlowe! The bigger gent was rubbing his shoulder where Varick had elbowed him, buying him that one extra minute just as Marlowe had been about to trap him in a hold.

"Be sure to practice those moves," Marlowe said, offering Varick a helping hand up. "You'll get faster when you do them a lot."

Varick was getting faster on the rooftops too. He and Coal would run roof-running drills during the night, progressing through leaping distances and wall-scaling difficulties. Things got really exciting when Coal decided he was ready for what he called building bounding. It was the sort of thing Varick had seen him do that night, bouncing diagonally down between building walls just before Varick had nearly lost some of his digits to those two thugs. Thankfully, they started learning by bounding *up* some walls first, just so Varick could get a feel for the motion without falling to his death. It was these sort of considerations that made Coal such a good teacher. And Varick had to admit, he felt supremely impressive doing it, after about a million stumbles and falls, of course. He was grateful to more than one washing line that had provided something for Varick to grab onto when he'd inhabited that strange place between being terrible at the activity and just approaching decent.

Mercury was not present for these visits, as Varick only went over when the man was scheduled to be out. And he apparently didn't frequent the place much anyway, only when he came over to stash some ill-gotten goods in the safe that occupied the corner of the loft, or work on the *Angrec's Respite* plan. He communicated with Varick when necessary, via notes sent through Coal. Mercury had eventually approved the Dress-of-Many-Pockets addition to the heist plan, but only after initially sneering at the idea and then Varick writing back to argue that it was also a better hiding spot for the Nightfall Crown. Mercury only agreed to a dress for Fulcrum, though.

"I don't want this turning into a farce because you all want to play dress-up," he'd said in neat handwriting on the paper.

A few weeks after Varick and the rest of the crew had fallen into a routine together, their backer arrived to find the door ajar and building empty of comrades. The petrolsene lights were still on, but they'd been turned even lower than usual.

"Hello?" Varick called into the cavernous space.

Had something happened? He backed toward the door. Was The Riffraff Inn no longer safe?

"Don't leave!" came Coal's voice from the little alcove beneath the loft.

Some whispering ensued from that area, and Varick stepped forward again. Coal hadn't sounded worried, but what the blazes was going on? The whispering died down, and beyond the edge of the half-wall of stacked bricks, Varick just made out the edge of Marlowe's big frame as he squatted behind the structure. When Varick drew close, Coal, Carver, Marlowe, and Fulcrum all leapt up from behind the wall.

"Surprise!" they all shouted, in a disjointed assortment of excitement levels and timing.

Fulcrum looked as if Coal had dragged him along, which he probably had. But to his credit, the surly lad had vaguely waved his arms when he'd drawled, "Surprise."

The actual surprise part of the party had been rather spoiled by Coal's call and seeing Marlowe. That is, until Carver brought forth a cake, an actual layer cake, decorated with snowy white frosting and rosettes.

"What…" Varick began.

"It's your birthday soon, right?" Coal asked. "You said the cruise was after it."

"Yes." Varick was still trying to collect his wits. He stared at the cake as Carver set it down. "It's next week actually."

"Perfect," Coal said. He turned to the others. "This still counts, right?"

"Seems fine to me," Carver replied.

Marlowe nodded, while Fulcrum said, "There aren't any rules to count for."

"And this cake is for me?" Varick asked. He still couldn't quite believe what was happening.

"Of course," Coal chirped.

Varick looked closer at the confection. "Did you steal this?"

"Don't worry about it," Coal replied.

"It says, 'Happy birthday, David.'"

"It's chocolate!" Coal was grinning like a cat who not only swallowed the canary, but also sat before a jury of fellow cats.

Varick smiled and then began to laugh, a proper belly laugh, and the crew shared a happy afternoon of cake and stories.

23

Harpies and Bureaucrats

Completing the travel paperwork for the cruise turned out to be an expert balance of bootlicking and bureaucracy. Prism Line Air Cruises had a handful of days set aside to work in cooperation with the Enforcers to conduct interviews for those travelers who did not yet have visas. Varick, being a minor, had to be accompanied by whomever was to be his guardian during the voyage. Thus, he'd set up a day to spend with Great Auntie Megaera so that she could sit in with him during his processing.

He'd taken a cab to meet her first thing in the morning at the Halls of Justice, the heart of the Enforcer order's operations.

The immense building rose up at least a dozen floors, all white marble streaked with black and grey. It had been built at the beginning of the Dawn Age and was supposedly magic-proof. Though with magic having been eradicated during the War of Light, how anyone was supposed to be able to tell the magic-proof-ness was working was beyond Varick. All Springhaven's prisoners were housed somewhere in the vast building, and the cruise brochure had taken great pains to assure travelers that the visa interviews would take place in the administrative section of the building, many floors and locked doors away from the prison sector.

Great Auntie Megaera arrived right on time with a tiny mop of a dog in her arms. The little creature had long, russet-colored fur with black tips; a squashed-in nose; and dark, mournful eyes that made it appear as if it might start crying at any moment.

"Who's this then?" Varick asked, indicating the dog.

"One of my precious babies." Great Auntie Megaera nuzzled against the animal's head. "This is Lionheart."

"Adorable." It was not exactly a lie. There was a strange sort of cuteness about the creature, and he was pleased that he'd been correct. Lionheart looked exactly the right size to shove in a stateroom cupboard should he start to be a nuisance.

"He's one of seven," Megaera said.

Varick's eyebrows lifted. "You must really like dogs."

Megaera adjusted her bag and the dog. "They are my life. Shall we?"

Like a perfect gentleman, Varick offered his arm and they made for the front entrance of the building. The layout was strange, given that the Halls of Justice also served as a prison. Couriers and Enforcers walked in and out through the front doors, and Varick spotted a few more well-dressed ladies and gents like Megaera and him, but that was it. Nothing at the front indicted the building's darker purpose. Prisoners were not permitted visitors, being confined to their cells for the entirety of their life sentence, and it wasn't likely that the Enforcers would trot new inmates in through the front. Varick assumed there was a back door where that happened, away from the good people of Springhaven. He wondered if those rare few who turned themselves in for purging—torture, to cleanse one of their criminality and repay their debt to society—ranked high enough as redeemed citizens for glittering, quartz front gates.

Representatives from Prism Line Air Cruises waited along the entrance path, ready and eager to escort the would-be travelers to where they needed to go, which turned out to be a small, drab waiting room. They were offered refreshments from a shining silver tray the folks at Prism Line had clearly brought in themselves.

"This is very nice," Megaera remarked to Varick as they waited. "When I got my first visa, I was left to my own devices. I got lost and walked right into a meeting of high-ranking Enforcers."

"Did you get in trouble?" Varick asked.

Megaera laughed. "No. I'll be honest, I played up the silly little lady act a bit. I think they figured if I'd really been up to no good, I wouldn't have done something so foolish."

Varick smiled. "How old were you?"

"Nineteen." Megaera said the number fondly, and her eyes got a faraway, reminiscent look in them.

"And you were all by yourself?"

Even just the mere thought was scandalous. Ladies of quality certainly did *not* take holidays alone.

"No. My dear friend, Florence Kirby, went with me. She wasn't considered a Pendragon sort of person. That might have been why I attached myself to her at first, which was not really fair to her, but we became great friends. She's passed on now, but she was my companion for many years."

Varick's eyes flicked to the few other toffs in the room. "Companion" was often a codeword for lover, especially amongst the upper class, who were not exactly against such same-sex relations, just so long as they kept it secret and fulfilled their primary responsibility—spawning more little upper class sprog. If anyone had overheard, they were pretending to not have. And anyway, Great Auntie Megaera didn't seem fussed.

"Oh, no need to look like that," Megaera tutted. "Florence and I were not romantically entangled, though I cannot honestly say the same about a few other women of my acquaintance." Megaera looked wistful again, and a small smile played at her lips. "Florence was never interested in anyone that way, and we supported each other's happiness. She reminded me quite a lot of my brother, you know?"

"Oh?"

Megaera made a little noise of acknowledgement. "He never said as much to me, but after he'd announced his engagement, I asked him why he'd agreed to marry that harpy. Do you know what he said to me?"

"What?"

"'It's my responsibility, Gira.' That was his nickname for me. I think he believed he could guide the path of future Pendragons if he contributed to the family line. Your grandmother, of course, poisoned them all, as I knew she would. Like a corpse in a pool, her taint spreads and infects everything." She looked at Varick. "Except you."

Varick blinked at her. "Huh?"

"Your grandfather was so very proud of you. With every new interest you took up, he wondered what you might do with it, how each unique aspect of what makes you you would influence the man you'd become. He'd go on and on his letters, wondering if you'd develop a keen, strategic mind from your chess lessons, or if you'd explore music more."

Varick worked to force the lump in his throat back down. His eyes were stinging treacherously. Deflection, he decided, was the best defense against showing up to his visa interview a blubbering mess. "Eh, some of my hobbies were picked for me. I'll be glad when I can be done with fencing, the same way I was when Grandmother stopped making me do voice and music lessons. I wish I'd been able to develop my horsemanship skills more, though."

"Your grandfather told me about that too. A nasty bit of unfairness that was. But now you have Tallywags."

Varick smirked at the rude name.

"It's not too late," Megaera went on. "You can pick it up again if you want. Just so long as you're happy. That's all your grandfather wanted for you, and it's all I want for you too."

Varick wondered what Randolph would have thought of the new skills he was learning, the lock picking, fighting, knife throwing, and acting. That last one had the most non-criminal applications, and Varick immediately thought about the outrage his family would feel if he dared to tread the boards. But Randolph, he would have asked which way to buy front row tickets to Varick's first play. Tears threatened to well up in his eyes again, and Varick returned the subject to Megaera's own travels as a distraction, as well as what they were both most excited for on this trip.

The interview eventually commenced, carried out by an Enforcer with a face like a sun-ravaged melon—Third Montes, as he introduced himself. Within minutes, Varick was convinced the man had been born lacking the muscles necessary to smile, but Varick was nevertheless polite and succinct in his answers. A representative from Prism Line Air Cruises was in attendance as well. He didn't say much during the question and answer session. It was possible he had been disallowed from interfering there, but he nodded and gesticulated a lot as if he was silently taking part in the conversation, trying to bolster Varick's spirits through what must be an arduous process for a gentle born prince such as himself.

Third Montes never asked anything like, "Have you ever committed a crime?" What would Varick do if he had? Confess here and now as if he'd always meant to but, dear oh dear, it had slipped his mind. Third Montes, however, did ask if Varick planned on committing any crimes.

"Of course not," Varick replied easily, and the Prism Line representative nodded enthusiastically, with an expression like he doubted Varick was even functionally capable of doing anything illegal. Had that question, ever in the history of humanity, tricked anyone into revealing their plan to do dastardliness?

Varick skated through the other questions, too.

"Are you currently in contact with anyone you either know to be a criminal or suspect of being one?"

"No, not at all."

"Have you seen anything suspicious recently that you may have forgotten or failed to report to the Enforcer order?"

"Oh no, if I had, I would've made that my first priority."

"If you were to witness a crime or even a conversation about what could potentially be criminal activity, would you report it to the Enforcer order?"

"Absolutely. Without delay."

After that came the letters of recommendation. Three of them, which all had to come from non-family members. Varick had enlisted his former chess instructor, Scholar Drury, a small, dull, heavily-spectacled mole of a man. He'd been a good teacher, though, and dour as he was, he respected Varick's appreciation of the game. He'd also gotten a letter from Master Rigby—there, Varick had been grateful the letter only pertained to his character and not his perceived skills in fencing—and Mrs. Thackston, the cook. Varick had spent time since his grandfather's death occasionally visiting the kitchens and making nice with the woman. After all, if he was going to be nicking food from her larder, he wanted to be on her good side in case he ever got caught.

What Varick had not realized was that the letters would be read aloud during his interview. Scholar Drury's was as dry as hardtack left in a desert—even the Prism Line man got bored and distracted in the middle of reading it. Mrs. Thackson's, in contrast was, well, not generous, but tacitly kind, even approaching sweet in a few places. Then came Master Rigby's. Varick didn't understand why it appeared so short. That is, until the Prism Line representative began reading.

"'Mister Varick Pendragon is of no danger to the safety of this city because he's too dull to enact any real mischief.'" The man broke off. "Oh dear." He looked to Third Montes and said more brightly, "But did you hear that? Not capable of mischief." Back to Varick, he said consolingly, "Almost done. 'Mister Pendragon can undoubtedly only be improved by travel and the subsequent broadening of his mind. Just do not let him near any important airship equipment.'"

The man from Prism Line Air Cruises did not make eye contact with Varick as he handed over the letters. Anger and humiliation roiled in Varick, and he tensed every muscle to remain composed. Thankfully, Third Montes seemed satisfied—perhaps there was some shared understanding between miserable old bastards—and he stamped a seal of approval onto fresh, new travel visa papers for Varick. Varick thanked the men, ticked all the boxes that social niceties required, and said nothing more as he and Auntie Megaera were escorted back to the front entrance. When they were finally out of earshot, Megaera came to his defense.

"What an absolute ratbag!" The heat in her tone surprised Varick enough to make him forget his own anger for a moment. "I'm so sorry you had to endure that, Varick. That horrid man had no right to embarrass you like that. I imagine he's compensating for some shortcoming of his own, making himself feel better by picking on a child." She shook her head. "Oh, very nice. What big man indeed."

Megaera's vehemence warmed Varick from the inside.

"Magnus probably egged him on."

"Well, your brother, pardon me for saying so, is an utter fathead. Here, hold Lionheart. It'll make you feel better."

Without any sort of ceremony, Megaera plopped the little dog, who'd spent the entire interview asleep in Megaera's lap, into Varick's arms. Lionheart gave him a lick on the hand, and Varick returned a perfunctory cuddle before setting the little creature down to find a spot to relieve himself. His great aunt's directive might have had more to do with her no longer being in a fit state to carry her precious little charge, given how she was gesticulating.

"Come on," she commanded. "Let's go have some lunch. My treat."

Varick knew better than to argue and hailed a cab for them. He let her angry tirade fall around him like soft feathers. Her defense of him was a balm over wounds that had been never been allowed to heal. By the time they'd reached their destination, Megaera had gone from righteous indignation to compassionate care of his own injured sensibilities, which Varick felt less comfortable with. That threatened to open up floodgates he wanted kept firmly closed, thank you very much.

Megaera requested a private, little lounge area, which were available to those restaurant patrons who preferred to dine in privacy. And it was there, as soon as they were alone, that she broke down into tears. Shocked, Varick realized she'd been holding back too, waiting until they had privacy before letting her emotions really show. He didn't know how to comfort her, but sat by and listened as she vented her own sadness. Some of it was grief, of course, missing her brother. Some of it was her own pain from growing up a black sheep in such a vicious family. And some of it was empathy, for she saw Varick in the same position she and Randolph had been in.

"I'm sorry, dear." Megaera dabbed at her eyes with a

handkerchief. "I shouldn't be burdening you with this. Children shouldn't have to…"

She broke off again, and that was what got him. No, child—absolutely, unequivocally—should have to endure what they had. And while Varick wouldn't in a million years readily admit to being a *child*—he was fifteen now!—he had endured, just as she had, all throughout their lives. Now, Varick finally allowed himself to cry too, to release all that he'd held in, not just that day, but since Randolph had died and there was no one left who seemed to understand. Until now. Together, Varick and Megaera, grieved and shared, and he was pleasantly surprised to find he felt lighter for it.

24
THE PRICE OF A FREE PAYCHECK

Travel visas, check. Permission to go with Great Auntie Megaera, check. It had become real for Varick. Mercury's heist job was happening, and Varick was getting away! Excitement welled up in him as he imagined how it would feel to float miles and miles away from his family.

Varick's mind was already on the *Angrec's Respite*. It embarked in just over two weeks! His training, as he thought of it, was going well too. He'd started landing more hits on Marlowe, and was staying in the sparring ring with him longer and longer. Marlowe had even graduated him to working with wooden daggers. They hurt a lot more and left deeper bruises than the pulled punches Marlowe delivered. All the more reason for Varick to improve.

Fulcrum had made good on his promise, too, and created for Varick some rudimentary throwing knives. Getting the material for them had been as simple as Varick purchasing various bits of pewter tableware, which Fulcrum had melted down and poured into clay molds. He'd also taught Varick how to sharpen the edges, which, as Fulcrum had said, was needed more often than a blade made of much harder steel. Varick had worked to build his skills with the knives and had moved onto using moving targets for practice. Fulcrum had built a sort of conveyor belt, which Coal loved operating. A rope could be pulled one way or the other to draw the belt clockwise or counterclockwise. To the belt, Fulcrum had mounted poles, filched from stars knew where. Atop the poles were rough sacks filled with straw and whatever other light detritus they'd been able to dig up. Varick had Carver practice his stitches on the bags.

"I don't want to see any sloppy seams," Varick had told him with a smile.

Varick had found he liked teaching, though that was probably helped by the fact that Carver was as keen a student as he.

"You know," Varick said to Fulcrum one day. "You could offer lessons with this thing."

Varick was currently practicing his knife throwing while Coal frenetically yanked the belt ropes one direction and then another. It created a fair mimicry of a dodging person.

Varick went on. "Charge people a couple of coppers for a session of basic skills. Then increase the price for more advanced techniques." Varick's thrown blade landed in the side of one of the dummies. He'd been aiming for dead center, but not bad given the unpredictability of Coal's movements.

"That's a good idea," Fulcrum said. He stood by, working to install a small knife into the sole of one of Varick's evening shoes. "How much do you reckon you owe me in back payments then?"

Varick's next blade went wide as he snapped his head around to look at the lanky lad. "Excuse me?"

"What?" Fulcrum asked flatly. "Worried you can't afford it?"

"I'm bringing you *eggs*." Varick said the word like they were rare treasures.

A slow, hard smirk curled its way up Fulcrum's face.

Varick's eyes narrowed as he tried to wrap his brain around what had just happened. "Are you winding me up?"

The smirk turned into a grin. In the background, Coal's jaw dropped, and he gasped dramatically.

"It's happening," he exclaimed in wobbling tones of awe and expectation.

"What's happening?" Varick asked.

"The magic of friendship," Coal whisper-shrieked in delight.

"I wouldn't go that far," Varick said, at the same moment Fulcrum drawled, "Too much."

Carver and Marlowe, who'd been doing their own activities, came strolling over. Coal skipped over to join them and held his arms wide as if presenting a speech before a crowd of thousands.

"Congratulations, V! You have proven talented, trustworthy, and…" The boy took a quick glance at his wrist, and Varick spied very small writing in some kind of shorthand there. "Tentacles?"

"Tenacious," Carver whispered.

"Oh yeah! Talented, trustworthy, and tenacious! We invite you to become an official member of the crew. Do you accept this great honor?"

"Uh," Varick replied.

He could just hear his old elocution instructor telling him off for such a "dunderheaded answer," as she would have said, in her precise, clipped tones. He wasn't in that situation anymore, though. He wasn't in the company of the sort of people that judged him for every little slight and misstep, much less tried to use those to their own ends. The crew embraced each other's differences and worked together to fill in for one another's shortcomings. The thought made Varick smile, though only a little. Something about what Coal had said confused him.

"What does that mean exactly?" he asked. "Becoming an

official member? I thought I already was."

"See, I knew that wasn't the right wording," Coal said. He rubbed at the notes on his wrist, smearing the ink. "Mercury really should have given us more feedback. I would have had more to work with for my speech."

"Mercury?" Varick asked. "What does Mercury have to do with this?"

"Camaraderie," Fulcrum replied blandly.

"He said he's impressed with the effort you've made to fit in," Marlowe said. "Being a real team player."

Carver added, "And he knows you aren't his biggest fan, so he asked us to present you with a little gift when we felt the time was right."

Through some impressive sleight of hand, Coal produced, seemingly from thin air, a small, wooden airship. It was a badly painted, the gondola was crooked, nothing more than a bit of tat really, but the sentiment was… well, Varick wasn't quite certain how to feel. He'd been bound and determined not to trust Mercury. His consideration for Varick's feelings was a rather pleasant surprise, though. And he certainly couldn't be accused of trying to buy Varick off with something so cheap. The little airship had no other value than sentimental, which, Varick could not help but admit was—grumble grumble—really quite sweet. Alright, he supposed perhaps Mercury wasn't *quite* so bad as he'd initially thought.

"He also agrees with you that we need a better idea for taking out the vault guards." Fulcrum said these words like they left a bad taste in his mouth, which made Varick smirk.

"Laudanum!" Coal announced without preamble.

Interesting. Varick had heard of the opium-derived drug, of course, but had not thought of using it as a full-blown tranquilizer. Given its addictive nature, opium—which his parents referred to as, "the drug of slovenliness"—and all various tinctures thereof, were categorized as controlled substances.

"I've seen it work," Coal went on. "One syringe and they fold like they've got no bones."

Fulcrum explained, "Once they're incapacitated, we're going to apply the soporific sponges to make sure they stay that way."

That did sound more reliable than Marlowe's hit-them-so-they-pass-out plan. Varick nodded his approval and looked at the little wooden airship again, then at the crew around him, feeling warmth bloom in his chest.

♜

Varick faced off against Magnus, fencing foil at the ready. He could feel Master Rigby's eyes on him. The fencing instructor's letter of reference played on a loop in Varick's head. He knew he wasn't focused the way he should be, but from the moment Varick'd slapped eyes on the man that morning, when he'd come out of the changing rooms in his fencing gear, the hateful recitation had started and would not stop for anything.

"He'd had a choice," Great Auntie Megaera had said, during their time in that private, little lounge. "He'd had a choice to do a kind thing, for a child no less, and he chose to be cruel."

Those words had sat inside of Varick, making a home. What made it even worse was that Varick *had* been improving. He'd taken Marlowe's advice and had begun practicing his fencing maneuvers along with his other blows, creating routines for them until his muscles knew the movements better than his brain. And with the way Varick had been working to increase his strength and speed in the gymnasium, he'd begun making Magnus earn his wins. Varick had only ever landed points against Magnus once in a blue moon. Now, when he really tried, Varick verged on beating his older brother. But no, Master Rigby couldn't even let him have that. More and more, often when Varick had the upper hand, the fencing instructor interrupted their bouts to criticize his younger pupil, usually for falling out of form. Granted, Varick had also begun to get creative during their matches, but he was still within the regulations. Magnus was an easy paycheck. That's all there was to it, and Varick was nothing more than collateral damage as the price for that ease.

Today, not only was Varick angry, but he was tired too. He'd been up late making alterations to one of his evening jackets. He wanted nothing more than this lesson over with and a nice nap. He and Magnus both saluted to one another as a new bout began. Varick went through the motions, counting down the minutes. When Magnus invariably beat him, Varick just stood there with Magnus' point in his chest padding.

"What a little bore you are," Magnus grunted.

"So go have lessons with someone who'll actually challenge you," Varick said.

"No," Magnus said. Varick could practically hear an unkind smile drawing across his face behind the fencing mask. "Winning's too fun."

Varick stared at his clot of an older brother. Master Rigby's letter was still providing a background tune to their session.

Opportunistic. That was what Coal had said Varick needed to be. An idea struck him. Varick could use this whole festering situation to his advantage.

"Master Rigby," he began, "wouldn't Magnus do better against more advanced opponents? He's got no room to improve with me."

Master Rigby looked from one Pendragon son to the other. Magnus' body had gone stiff, most likely with anger.

"I think not, young Varick," Master Rigby said dismissively.

"It's just that Magnus is an *adult*. So wouldn't it be better for him to get experience with other adult opponents?" Varick pressed. "I wouldn't want it to appear you'd gone soft as a teacher."

With that, Varick snapped his mouth shut. He let the implication slither through the air. Yes, Magnus was an easy paycheck, but what was that compared to reputation? Reputation secured more paychecks.

Varick walked back to starting position. He could practically feel the rage rolling off his brother as they faced one another again. It provided yet another benefit Varick hadn't even considered. Magnus' anger made him sloppy. His lunges lacked their usual control. Varick's parries and subsequent ripostes got dangerously close to scoring a point. Why hadn't Varick thought to make Magnus angry years ago? But he already knew the answer. For years, Varick had simply been enduring. He'd enact secret, petty revenges later, which no one knew about. This was a new tactic, a more direct one, and he found he *liked it*. He even grinned, not that Magnus could see it through their fencing masks, as he enacted a beat against his older brother's foil—a quick, sharp tap generally used to either provoke an attack or initiate one. The former occurred, and Magnus charged in a wild fleche. The running attack was just what Varick had hoped for. He feinted left, then went right, and landed a point in Magnus' side.

"Very good, Varick," Master Rigby said, though his voice lacked anything even remotely like praise.

Varick waited, but nothing more was said. Of course. Practice only got testier after that as the brothers took out their frustration on each other. Varick landed a few more points, though, and Magnus' performance deteriorated with each hit. Then, for once, Master Rigby let Varick finish winning a bout. Inside his head, Varick whooped and punched the air and did Coal's little happy dance. Outside, he extended a hand to shake with Magnus. His older brother slapped it away.

"I expected better from you, Magnus," came Master Rigby's

cutting words. He raked his eyes over the two younger gents and finally ended their session.

Magnus stormed off to the changing rooms, and Varick decided to give it some time before he followed. He sipped water, judging how long it'd take his brother to leave. When he at last went in to strip off his fencing gear, Varick was still feeling perversely pleased. It was only after he'd finished changing and donned his jacket again, however, that pleasure turned to dread in his stomach. His grandfather's pocket watch, always close at hand, was gone.

25
THE NOOSE OF COMPLACENCY

Panic whirled in Varick's head, making his thoughts feel muzzy and scattered. He'd checked and rechecked his pocket and searched the entire area around where he'd left his jacket during fencing practice. Nothing. Maybe he'd left it in his room? Unlikely. Varick *always* kept it on him, but he checked anyway. "Checking" quickly became turning over every inch of his apartments.

It was nowhere.

Varick rubbed his face, trying to drive back the tears burning behind his eyes. Where could it *be*?! Without it, he felt like he'd lost a piece of his grandfather's memory. A tap at Varick's window pulled his swirling thoughts back to the surface of here and now.

Coal, he immediately thought. But Coal didn't knock. Coal just showed up like a cat that'd adopted you.

Varick went over to the window just as a pebble hit the glass. Below, sticking out on the vast, rolling lawn like a sore thumb,

stood Magnus. He scowled up at his younger brother and threw another pebble.

"I can already see you!" Varick said, gesticulating at his brother. "Idiot."

Magnus jerked a thumb over his shoulder, indicating that he wanted Varick to follow him across the lawn. To where beyond that, Varick hadn't the foggiest. He motioned that he had no intention of doing any such thing, and he was just about to walk away from the window when Magnus reached into his pocket and extracted a pocket watch.

Randolph's pocket watch.

Varick would have known it anywhere. His gaze seared down at Magnus. The ratbag had stolen it from Varick's jacket. Magnus jerked the thumb again, and Varick hurried out of his room. He'd been tempted to go out the window and scale down the building, just to show Magnus what he was capable of, but it was broad daylight and he didn't want to risk being seen by anyone else. Plus, Magnus would probably tattle on him. Just as Varick reached the vast lawn, his older brother took off toward the tree line. Varick was fast, but so was Magnus, who had the advantage of longer legs and a head start. Varick didn't think; he just chased. He would get Randolph's watch back and make Magnus pay.

Varick had very nearly caught up when Magnus led their chase down to the ornamental carp pond. It sat next to the wide, graveled walking path that wended its way throughout the entire estate—a kind of bloviating walking tour. The large, slender fish in the pond puttered through the cold water, barely moving their fins. Their orange, gold, black, and white scales glinted in the dappled sunlight streaming through the trees. Large, smooth boulders ringed most of the pond, save for a section where the gravel path branched and spread out into a sloping bank that led straight into the pond.

"You clod," Varick snapped. "What the blazes do you think you're doing? Anyone could have seen you standing there. And then what? Grandmother or one of our parents might have taken Grandfather's watch off you. Is that what you want?"

Varick already knew the answer. Of course not. That's what Varick was afraid of. Magnus wanted to torment him. But words were spilling out of Varick without him even having to summon them.

"Little prick," Magnus shot back. "What if Rigby moves me to a different lesson group with harder opponents?"

A dim awareness flashed in Varick's mind that this could mean he might be free of the insufferable fencing sessions, but he was too focused to pay it any heed.

"Oh, boo hoo," Varick sneered. "Then I won't be there for you to trounce. Poor you."

"Don't be such a crybaby."

"I'm not a crybaby! I'm sick of you and everyone else always having a go at me. Now give me back the watch." Varick stuck out his hand.

Magnus, in turn, fixed him with a cold, empty-eyed look. He glanced at something behind Varick, as if someone were coming down from the house. Varick's eyes followed.

And in that split second, Magnus said, "Go get it."

In his periphery, Varick saw Magnus' arm fling out, toward the pond. He turned back just in time to see the small plume of water fountain up as Randolph's fob watch went *plonk*. Varick ran. The pond was only about waist deep, and he headed straight for the spot where the watch had gone in. Tears flowed down his face; he hadn't realized he'd started crying. As soon as his shoes touched the pebbly bottom, small puffs of sediment rose up and started muddying the water. Varick thrust his arms in, soaking himself up to the chest and shoulders. Panicked carp swam by, and more than once, Varick mistook a flash of scales for the watch. As their movements added to the confusion, Varick ended up groping blindly and praying that the watch would find its way into his hands.

"Stupid Varick."

The words pierced Varick's brain with a decidedly malicious ring. He looked up, bedraggled and soiled and trailing pond grass. Magnus stood with one foot hiked up onto the closest of the boulders surrounding the pond. Atop the boulder sat Randolph's watch.

Right next to Magnus' shoe.

The cold water shot straight into Varick's bones, into his heart. He'd underestimated his older brother. He'd tricked Varick and thrown something else while Varick's gaze had been averted.

"Magnus, please," Varick begged. He didn't care that Magnus could see he was crying. Varick was afraid to move, afraid of what his brother would do. He opened his mouth to start negotiating. What wouldn't he offer to save Randolph's much-beloved watch?

But Magnus didn't even give Varick the chance. A smile made of knives spread across Magnus' face. He lifted his foot slowly as Varick began moving, hindered by the water around him.

"Magnus, don't!" Varick yelped.

And Magnus brought his foot down as hard as he could on top of the watch. Glass crunched sickeningly. A few tiny gears exploded out from beneath Magnus' fine leather shoe. The bronze casing bent beneath the force of the blow. Magnus didn't lift his foot. Instead, he ground the broken watch beneath him, keeping his eyes on Varick.

Varick's thoughts froze as the horrible scene played out before him. Shock clouded his brain like a fog. This couldn't be happening. Like an Old World automaton, he trudged the rest of the way out of the pond, never taking his eyes off the spot where his brother's shoe pressed.

"Let that be a lesson, you little pest," Magnus was saying. "Don't cross me."

Varick didn't reply, only took another step forward. And then another. His breathing grew quiet and measured.

With a voice made of steel, "Move," was all Varick said.

Magnus waggled the one leg he held aloft on the rock like a flag of victory. "Make me."

Varick's fist snapped out as quick as a viper, striking Magnus hard in the ribs. Droplets of water flew from his soaked shirtsleeves, outlining the point of connection. Magnus let out a garbled noise of pain and stumbled back. He looked at Varick with naked shock. Never before had the little snot dared to come at him directly. Varick's hands were already flying for another blow. He caught his older brother in the throat this time. As Magnus coughed and retreated a few more steps, Varick turned and made for the watch.

More gears littered the boulder on which it sat, along with tiny fragments of broken glass. They glittered perversely in the yellow sunshine. The hands bent at crude angles now. Varick didn't know what to do. Could such damage be fixed? He didn't even know if he should touch the sad, broken treasure. What if he jostled more important pieces from where they belonged? Suddenly, a hand was there. It swept the whole mess into the pond. Like a recurring nightmare vision, Randolph's watch sailed into the pond for real this time.

Magnus' fist connected with Varick's jaw before he could make sense of what had just happened. Pain exploded all along the side of his face. Varick stumbled and lost his footing. He landed hard onto the graveled bank.

"Don't get up," Magnus growled above him. He sounded a little winded, probably from the knock to his throat. "Unless you want more of the same?"

Varick pushed the wet hair from his face and looked up to see Magnus looming over him. Cold from his soaked clothes seeped under Varick's skin. He could feel shivers coming on. And along with them, clarity. He could stay here, wait for Magnus to get bored and leave him be. That'd been what Varick had always done. He breathed in deep through his nose. That would be the easiest option, but it wasn't what he wanted to do. For years, he'd wanted to take Magnus down. It was no better than the great brute deserved. Behind him, Varick heard the sound of water lapping at the pond's edge, ripples from the drowned pocket watch. He fixed Magnus with a hard look. His older brother, in turn, spit on the ground next to Varick. Things seemed to slow down for Varick then. The seconds stretched themselves out, and Varick took in his surroundings. Well, would you look at that. Magnus' knees were right here and unprotected. And he had told Varick not to get up.

From where he sat, Varick kicked, shooting his leg out like a battering ram. This time when he heard a sickening crunch, it was that of bone and cartilage.

Magnus dropped like a stone to the ground, howling and holding his knee. It had bent all kinds of wrong beneath the force of the blow. Varick stood, and as he looked down at his older brother, writhing and screaming in pain, he was suddenly very aware of just how much Magnus was at his mercy now. That same frigid clarity still filled Varick's mind, freezing his emotions and crystalizing facts.

He could hurt his brother in so many ways. A simple strike to the groin. One good wallop could break a few fingers. He could kick Magnus' ribs in, maybe even puncture his lungs. Varick could break every bone in his face and stomp his skull into the dirt. Varick did not want to kill his older brother. But he could. Because what Varick did want was to hurt Magnus. Again and again. For every moment of mistreatment Varick had endured.

No one was around to stop him. Ability, opportunity, and desire. Varick had it all, so why not?

Because I also have a choice, he thought. *And I will not be like them. I will* not *choose cruelty.*

Varick backed away; there were more important things to focus on. Perhaps this was the key—admitting to yourself the true capacity you had within you, both good and evil, marking the heartless choices at hand, and doing the opposite rather than settling into complacency. Yes, that was it. Complacency was the noose you hung yourself with.

Varick was just heading for the pond again, wondering if there might still be hope for finding Randolph's watch, when the first shouts of alarm went up.

Bugger me, Varick thought.

Figures were approaching from further up the path. He couldn't recognize any of them from this distance, but it didn't matter. Magnus' agonized cries had alerted them to a problem, and Varick was about to be in some very serious trouble indeed. He did the only smart thing he could think of in that moment and took off.

With every stride, he felt the distance grow between himself and Randolph's lost watch.

26

FRIENDS IN LOW PLACES

The storage room was blissfully quiet. Varick's chair-and-sheet tent had been disassembled when so many seats had been needed for the will reading. He wanted cover, though, and needed warmth, lest he catch cold from being soaked in such cold weather. Thus, he'd divested a few larger, stored pieces of their white cloth coverings and wrapped himself in the sheets until he looked like a giant meringue. Then, he found a hidden spot beneath a large table. Wrapped in his somewhat dusty but warm coverings, tucked into his safe space, he'd allowed himself to cry freely. Varick cried for his grandfather, for the loss of his beloved watch, and for himself. Back at the pond, something had changed in Varick. And it made him feel as though he'd lost yet another piece of his grandfather, because the boy he'd been before, the boy Randolph had known when he'd been alive, was gone now.

He'd been there a few hours, cried out and exhausted but unable to sleep on the hard wooden floor, when he first heard the noise. It *shushed* gently, as soft as a cat stalking through a pillow factory. Varick wouldn't have heard it at all if it hadn't been so completely silent there in the storage room. Another noise followed, like the stalking cat's determined but far less nimble badger friend doing its best to follow in the cat's footsteps.

Varick looked up from where he lay on the floor. He suspected he knew what was coming and, though he wished to make himself more presentable, he found he couldn't muster the energy to do anything more than sit up in his meringue coating and wait. Unsurprisingly, a few minutes later, the edge of the sheet covering the table under which Varick hid lifted. Coal's face appeared, peering under it. He gave a sympathetic little half-smile, then turned back to someone and spoke softly.

"Found him."

Varick was a little surprised to see Carver there as well. He must have been the second sound Varick had heard, and a distant part of Varick's mind acknowledged that Carver might have taken a big risk in being here. The two entered the little hideaway, but neither ventured any further than just inside the cover.

"Rough day?" Carver asked gently.

Varick nodded, but didn't say anything. What could he say? He'd ruined everything. How was he meant to tell his friends that?

Coal looked like he wanted to scoot closer, but didn't. "I came to deliver a message from your aunt. When I saw everyone running around like chickens with their heads cut off, I knew something was up. I gathered that your brother's leg is messed up and no one could find you. I didn't know if there'd be trouble, if whoever roughed up your brother had gotten to you, so I went away and got Carver, in case I needed some backup."

"I did it," Varick admitted.

"Did what?" Coal asked.

"I attacked Magnus. I'm pretty sure I broke his leg... or his

knee. I don't know."

Carver's tone turned serious. "I know I wasn't there, but I bet he did something, didn't he?"

Something Randolph had always said to Varick came rushing back to him: *Violence is never the answer.* Tears sprang to Varick's eyes again. How disappointed would his grandfather be in him if he were here now? What would he think if he'd known how badly Varick had wanted to hurt Magnus? Varick couldn't even imagine.

"I shouldn't have done it." Varick's voice cracked as he spoke. "I was playing right into his hands."

"So he did do something?" Carver said, soft but firm. He wasn't asking for details, but open if Varick wanted to share.

"He smashed it," Varick said. He began to cry properly again. "My grandfather's watch. He smashed it and flung it in the water and it's all I had left."

Varick hated himself even more as he said the words. Because he did have other things left. He had Tallywags, but the horse would eventually die. There were image-stills, but none of just the two of them and none of them looking happy. And oh yes, there was all that money, which wasn't just a life raft in this greedy world, but a state-of-the-art steamship. But it wasn't the same. None of it meant the same as the watch had, and he didn't know how to make anyone understand that.

Coal's face pinched. He touched the paste ruby earring hanging from his watch chain. Carver, too, tentatively grasped his little tiepin.

"That wasn't okay," Coal said.

Carver shook his head. "Seems like your brother might have had it coming. If you don't mind me saying so." Carver delivered this last sentence in the flat voice of someone who knew that was the sort of thing they *should* say, but didn't actually mean a word of it.

"Violence shouldn't be the answer," Varick said, though his voice was soft with lack of conviction.

A long silence ensued. Coal and Carver lived in a world that often brought them violence, but so did Varick. In his case, though, it came from those who should have provided safety and love, and yet…

"I think the difference," Carver said at last, "is looking for other options and choosing them as often as you can. Sometimes, though, it comes down to you or them."

"Them or a person you love, too," Coal added.

Carver nodded sagely, and thoughtful silence fell between the three again. Varick's tears eventually petered out, but the consequences of his actions, the secret he was keeping from his friends, gnawed at him. The plan was dead. His parents would never let him go on the cruise now.

"What are you gonna do?" Coal asked after a while.

"Coal," Carver chided. "Now's not the time."

It was not an unfair question, but Varick swallowed down the truth. Shame heated inside him. He couldn't bring himself to say he wouldn't be going on the *Angrec's Respite* trip. He had no idea what story Magnus had spun for Henry and Victoria, but Varick knew his older brother would have made himself out to be an innocent victim. Varick wanted to sink further inside his sheets and never come out. But his friends. What would happen to them now?

Varick forced his exhausted, grief-addled brain to think, slow though it was. His deposits had already been made, so maybe Carver, still posing as his secretary, could go in his place. Great Auntie Megaera would be so disappointed, but she wouldn't waste the non-refundable booking fee. At least she'd still get to go. Maybe not all hope was lost. At least, for the crew's sake, Varick had to think of something.

27

HUNGER GAMES

After seeing Coal and Carver off, Varick snuck back up to main levels of the house. It was only by chance that he happened to cross paths with Magnus along the way. Evening had just fallen, and Magnus was busy reclining on a sofa in the long gallery that stretched between the library and the main hall. Around him, on various console tables, floated the flotsam and jetsam of soup and crackers, cakes and tea, and all the other accoutrement of a convalescent being waited on hand and foot. His leg stretched out before him on a pile of cushions, cinched up in a brace—a complex contraption of leather straps, buckles, and metal splints.

"Hey, maggot!"

Magnus' rough call came as Varick entered the house through the loggia doors and tried to slip unseen through the hall and around to the grand staircase to make his way upstairs.

Varick didn't stop, though every muscle in his body had to fight to make it happen. He knew things would go easier if he gave in, but Varick's rage came rushing back and refused to answer to the abusive name.

"Hey!" Magnus called again. "Look at me when I'm talking to you, Varick!"

Finally, Varick slowed and turned toward his brother. His voice came out low and angry when he responded. "Oh, were you speaking to me? You see, I can't tell when you don't use my actual name."

Magnus, always so quick on the uptake, snarled, "Who else would I be calling maggot?"

"Knowing you," Varick drawled, "lots of people, given your limited creativity."

"You're going to regret that." Magnus went to push himself off the sofa, but his bound leg slowed him down, and he failed his first attempt. And then the second too. His cheeks reddened, and he jabbed a finger at the floor in front of him. "Come here!"

Varick did not respond, just stared at Magnus, one disdainful eyebrow lifted.

The angry flush on Magnus' face spread up to his forehead. "What, now that I'm crippled you think you're better than me? You wouldn't be so brave if I wasn't stuck in this bloody thing!"

Varick was cognizant that he should feel remorse for what he'd done. He still felt badly for the trouble his decisions would cause his friends—the consequences of which he was still figuring out how to mitigate—and he hated all the things he imagined his grandfather would have said about his behavior. Those thoughts mingled in the back of Varick's mind like a gaggle of judgmental onlookers, all whispering nasty comments about him. He knew the right thing to do was to apologize. Violence, after all, he really did believe should be avoided whenever possible, just like he'd said to Carver and Coal. But Varick couldn't summon a single ounce of contrition for his brother. He wasn't sorry for bringing such an utter bully low,

especially given that Magnus had not been transformed even a jot by the experience. Perhaps there was a lesson in there somewhere about how this was precisely why violence was not the answer, because it didn't change anything, only escalated things. But Varick was not interested in lessons just now. Instead, he stalked forward and spoke at last.

"I'm going to say this slowly so that you're sure to understand. First of all, you're not crippled, you're injured. Anyone who knows better isn't going to feel sorry for you. They're going to realize what a dolt you are. And not just a dolt, but a willful one, given how you've had the best education money can buy. Secondly, don't ever forget, *I'm* the one who put you in that thing." He reached the spot Magnus had indicated. Varick's anger filled him up, making him feel huge as it radiated out of him. "I put you in it while you stood over me in peak fighting form. And if I did it once, I can do it again. Do *not* put me in a position to make me think I need to, because if you do, I'll do worse."

Magnus did not look afraid. He still looked furious. A vein was sticking out from his neck, but he didn't clap back the way he would have before today. Varick knew he'd never actually get Magnus to admit he'd been beat. That would be rolling over and showing his belly. His silence, though, spoke volumes.

Varick was not proud as he strode off, nor was he so daft as to think this wouldn't make it back to his parents, but a cold weight filled him. He felt hardened by it, and perhaps this was what it was like to wear armor.

♜

Varick's punishment was not nearly so bad as it could have been. Or rather, it would have been much worse if not for his recent clandestine activities and the skills he'd gained from them. Right off the bat, as entirely expected, Varick was told he was no longer permitted to go on the airship cruise with Great Auntie Megaera. Patricia had been in attendance and asked if her sister-in-law would be refunded the costs of the trip.

"Yes," Varick said automatically.

It was a last-ditch effort. He knew his grandmother hoped this excursion threatened to bankrupt Megaera, or at least severely wound her finances. If she saw that chance flitting away, perhaps she'd argue on Varick's behalf.

"That can't be true," his mother shot back. "The boy obviously has no idea what he's talking about. Trip deposits are always non-refundable. It's how they ensure their bookings remain booked."

Dear heaven above, must a Pendragon always be one-upping someone else? Always be showing off how smart or rich or cultured they are? Patricia seemed satisfied with that, and Varick sagged internally. Even if she wasn't certain, a simple bit of looking into the matter would reveal that the booking deposits were indeed non-refundable. Varick tried to defend himself.

"Does anyone want to know *why* Magnus and I were fighting in the first place?"

Of course not. No one was even remotely interested in their reasons. It helped a little that Varick's parents were nearly as disappointed in Magnus for allowing "such a scrawny little pup" to best him. Varick had apparently done a number on Magnus' knee, and the cretin would have to wear the brace contraption for at least a couple of months. And yes, as suspected, Varick's threat to pummel Magnus again if he crossed his younger brother made it back to the boys' parents too. To this, however, Varick's father was, well, not in Varick's corner, but at least against Magnus.

"If you let him get the better of you again, I'll have to consider renaming you Mag-pus. Honestly, the little whelp is half your size. It'd be beneath you to take him on in a fight even now, but to let him sucker punch you…" Henry shook his head, unable to finish.

The follow-up to this little family meeting was no better. Not bad really, just bloody inconvenient. Victoria gathered the entire kitchen staff together and trotted Varick in front of them to announce that he'd earned himself a hunger stint. He would be present at all meals, but no one was to serve him anything.

"Varick requires a reminder of just how fortunate he is to be a part of this family," Victoria announced to the assembled kitchen and serving staff. "For four days, he will watch the rest of us enjoy the gifts bestowed by the Pendragon name. If he asks any of you for food, you're to tell either myself or Lord Pendragon immediately. Water is all he is permitted. And if anyone is caught sneaking him food, your employment will be instantly terminated *without* a letter of recommendation. And believe you me, you will not be able to find work anywhere in Springhaven when we tell all our friends what an insubordinate little leech you are."

Victoria also assigned a schedule of footmen to follow Varick around the house during the day and even out into the city to ensure he didn't go out to eat anywhere. At night, one was assigned to guard the corridor just outside his door to ensure he didn't sneak down to the larder or anything. That last piece worried Varick a little. Had someone figured out what he'd gotten up to with his egg-stealing? No, they couldn't have. If they had, one, he'd have heard about it. And two, they would have assigned someone to guard inside his room too. More specifically, the window he used to sneak in and out.

As it was, Varick took to nipping out late at night and finding what street food vendors he could. Clubs were open, but he was still underage and therefore not allowed in alone. And any Ivory district restaurants ran the risk of hosting someone from his parents' circles. If one of those puffed-up peacocks saw him dining alone, word could get back to his parents. Thankfully, the

Sand quarter, bustling center of commerce that it was, hosted plenty of late-night cafes and rolling eateries. Plus, there was still the stash of food that Varick had put aside for Coal, so he was able to nosh on that during the day. When Varick grew bored, he considered practicing those acting skills Carver had taught him— looking morose around the house, or even applying a little makeup to make his face look drawn. But if living in the Dragon's Keep had taught him anything, it was that his family members needed at all times to be either avoided or emotionally managed, lest they decide to give him some new dose of misery. So he settled for quieter entertainments, like reading or puzzles.

Varick was fully aware how cruel the punishment actually was. Had he not had food stashed away already, his days really would have been awful, even painful. And doubly so if he'd not been able to sneak off at night, gorge himself, and bring more back with him. Starvation was an unnecessary cruelty no one deserved. And having done bugger all with the soup kitchens his grandfather had left to him, he decided after his sentence had ended, to go and see the situation there for himself.

28
POORLY BEHAVED

arick's lips twisted as he gazed at the building. A wooden sign hung above the door:

THE RESTFUL TURNIP
FOOD PANTRY AND SOUP KITCHEN

Painted onto the sign was a fat, white turnip complete with purple top and a green, leafy stalk. The sign had faded a bit since the last time Randolph had brought Varick here, the main hub of the Turnip Network. He really should have come here sooner. He'd had time, sort of. Rather, he should have *made* the time, somewhere between sneaking off and learning how to be a criminal. He'd told Coal *weeks ago* that he'd look in on things here. Fat lot of good he'd done for his grandfather's legacy.

Varick shook himself. Yes, he was a rich, privileged little rotter, no question. Now, enough wallowing. He was here and he meant to make… something right. That was rather the problem, though. He didn't know what had changed beyond workhouse recruiters being allowed to run roughshod over the place. At least that was how Coal had made it sound. Currently, though, things looked quiet. It was mid-morning, too early for a lunchtime rush, but a steady trickle of people filtered in and out and out of the building.

Unlike Randolph's business dealings, he'd brought Varick here numerous times to check in on things. There were other locations, but this was the home base for the entire Turnip Network. Varick wracked his brains for everything his grandfather had told him about running the place. He came up with next to nothing. Oh, he'd heard how important it was, how many people a month they served, how many pounds of food they distributed into the community. And that was all grand, but what about how the place functioned?

A wave of anger suddenly swelled through Varick. He tightened his fists against the heat building in his eyes. Why hadn't his grandfather let him into the nitty-gritty details about how his beloved food pantries worked? He'd wanted the lad to take them over—which he'd also never told Varick—so why not be a bit more helpful about the whole thing? Perhaps he thought he'd have more time. Maybe Varick had said or done something to make Randolph think Varick wasn't interested but hadn't gotten a chance to change that part of his will. Varick bit his lip and took a few deep breaths. That helped drive the approaching tears back. Randolph had declined so quickly at the end. He'd been fine one day, and then suddenly he wasn't. It was no good thinking of that now, though. It helped nothing to spend time and energy on what might or should have happened. Instead, Varick took a few more deep breaths and shifted his focus to what he did know.

Every time Randolph and Varick had visited—sometimes by appointment and others as a surprise—everyone had acted just

so. All the staff recognized Randolph onsite, and they'd all smiled and waved at seeing him. A woman called Hannah had been in charge, though she'd not always been here at the main hub. She oversaw all the Turnip Network locations. But whoever had taken Randolph through their most recent initiatives and numbers during each visit, everyone was always pleased as punch to show off all the good they were doing, how tidy the paperwork was kept. Thus, Varick had donned a disguise today. He wanted to see how people treated him when they thought he was nothing more than a dirty little street urchin.

Varick had purchased some secondhand clothes from a charity shop and dirtied them with ash from his fireplace and soil from the gardens. He smeared his face and hands with burnt wood, obscuring his features, and he hunched as he approached the building, making himself smaller, and kept his eyes down.

The building itself was nothing special. A rectangular slab of of wood and bricks located in the Agate quarter. The heavy, tiered, iron planters attached on either side of the door sat empty. There'd been cheerful bunches of flowers in them the last time Varick had been here, which had been one of the surprise visits.

Varick trudged up to the door, where a few other people were queued up. He looked down the line. It was so quiet. Was that odd? He thought back to his previous visits. Yes, it was. The last time he'd been here, the air had been full of the low murmur of people chatting. Not raucous, but comfortable. Everyone here today had their heads down.

The procession moved along slowly. Varick noticed a big man with a chiseled jaw standing at the far end of the room. He didn't do anything besides stand there, but his crossed arms and bushy eyebrows practically shouted for everyone to stay in line, *or else*. A couple of folks, mostly women but a few men too, worked nearby, either cooking, serving, or replacing the large, shallow, metal dishes gently heating over some kind of flaming fuel that gave off no smoke, but filled the air with a tangy, sticky, burning chemical sort of smell. That must be new too. Varick couldn't remember ever smelling that sort of scent before. It was the kind that got into one's nose hairs and hung on for hours.

And the people in long, drab capes and flat caps were certainly new as well. They circulated around the place like predatory fish, eyeing up people in the line and then approaching after they'd tucked into their meal. The caped people, both men and women, sported green cloth badges on their uniforms, though Varick couldn't make out the stitched words on them. They wielded pamphlets like cleavers, flapping them at their unfortunate victims, urging those people, who were just trying to get a sodding meal, to take one. When the flyers were rejected, the caped person, would draw close to their victim and whisper something. Varick couldn't hear this either, but the nasty expression on a few of their faces told him it was nothing good.

When Varick reached the long set of tables where plates and bowls were set onto trays and filled, he noticed too that the portions had shrunk considerably. But there! A middle-aged, dark-haired woman was serving on the line. It was Hannah! Her eyes were red, and Varick wondered if it was because of the burning chemical fuel. She wasn't smiling, though her face was gentle. Hannah had smiled at Randolph. She'd seemed genuinely happy then, and her eyes had not been red. Varick summoned the soft, somewhat raspy voice he'd prepared for his part today.

"Hello, Hannah, how you keeping?"

Hannah looked up from the wide dish of hard, thin rolls she served from and searched Varick's face. He prayed she wouldn't recognize him. He'd learned from Carver that a bit of dirt, a bent posture, and different clothes made a world of difference, but Hannah had always been the attentive sort. Her eyes lingered on his face for an uncomfortably long time, before she blinked and had to rub at her eyes with her arm. No spark of recognition had lit in her.

"I'm alright," she said, going back to her sad rolls. "You?"

"Still kicking." Varick gave a coarse little laugh. "Been a while since I been here. Seems different."

Hannah stiffened. "Yeah. For a few months now," was the only explanation she gave.

A few months. As in, since Patricia took over. Varick's insides curled like thorny brambles. What was his grandmother playing at? He wanted to ask more, but what could he ask without either outing himself or putting Hannah in a compromising position? Mister Granite Chin was standing nearby, well within earshot. He didn't wear the cape, but his broad chest sported the same badge Varick had seen on the others. The name Milgewort Workhouse encircled an emblem of clasped hands before a small, yellow flower. Besides, "under new management" likely accounted for the changes anyway.

"You got a problem?"

The words came from the chiseled jaw man. Varick was staring at his badge as he thought. He considered poking this particular bear just a little, curious as to what might happen. But Hannah seemed like a good person, which meant the sort who might intervene on his behalf. So he lowered his eyes and thanked Hannah for the food. She was looking at him again, and Varick turned away, toward the next helper, an older man with thinning, steel-grey hair. He handed Varick his completed meal with a weak smile. Stars, why weren't kind people like this running everything? Oh yes, greed, that was why.

Varick found himself a seat somewhat away from anyone else and lifted a spoonful of some kind of savory porridge to his mouth. The small pieces of meat within it were grey and mostly cartilage, or if he was very lucky, fat. The boiled vegetables, which bore suspicious dark spots, sagged soggy and flaccid next to that. The grain had a strange sort of taste about it. Varick couldn't tell if it was from the chemical fumes or if it had gone rancid. And he was fairly certain this meal had never seen a speck of salt. He remembered the food from before, when he'd been with Randolph. It too had been simple fare, but well-prepared, unspoiled, and wholesome. Not three minutes into his meager portions, Varick's meal was interrupted by one of the prowling caped figures. With the space next to Varick being open, the prowler, a man with an openly smiling face, plopped right down next to him, far closer than necessary.

"Good morning, m'lad," the man said. He spoke in not quite a whisper, low enough to be heard by Varick but not by anyone else. It was unsettling, which Varick was certain was the point. "And how are we doing today?"

He snuck a glance at the badge pinned to the man's cape. Milgewort Workhouse again. So presumably all the bad eggs Coal had talked about hailed from there. It wasn't a Pendragon-supported facility as far as Varick knew, and he debated how to respond. Everyone else seemed determined not to speak with the recruiters. Whatever was happening here, people had to have told others how to handle the situation. Or, more specifically, how *not* to handle it. One look back at the stony chin and its attached hulk of a man and Varick suspected he knew good and well what happened to troublemakers. He said nothing and waited. As expected—and dreaded—the caped man scooched closer.

"You wouldn't be here, you know, if you worked harder," the man said. His face was so close, Varick could feel his breath on his cheek. It smelled of boiled cabbage and peppermint tobacco. "You're a pathetic drain on society. You could be better, though. Do your part." The man slipped one of the brochures into the space between Varick's head and the tray. "Don't you want to take control of your life? Lift yourself up to a better place?"

Varick spied the words, *Room and board provided*, on the sheet proffered beneath his face. Under that was a weekly wage schedule, which was, to put it mildly, laughable.

"You see here, you get an increase after only two years on your contract." The man said this with the enthusiasm of someone giving away a once-in-a-lifetime, all-expenses-paid trip, while continuing to blatantly ignore all concept of personal space and social boundaries, because people who couldn't afford to feed themselves also didn't deserve the dignity of such luxuries, or so Varick assumed the recruiters' logic went. The aforementioned wafer thin increase was equally laughable.

Varick decided to try something. Holding his spoon aloft in mid-journey to his mouth, he lifted his eyes to meet the man's. His whole persona changed in that moment. Their two faces were so close, their noses nearly touched, and Varick allowed his gaze to bore into the recruiter's.

"And what happens if I don't want to sign up, hm? What are you going to do?"

The slightly rancid gruel dripped from Varick's spoon onto the pamphlet with a soft slapping noise. The man from Milgewort Workhouse drew back for a moment, unbalanced. Varick's stare continued to sear.

A smile spread across the man's face. As if he hadn't heard Varick's question, he said, "You must not understand the opportunity on offer here. Poor education will do that. Well, what if I told you I'm authorized to offer you a bonus if you sign on with us here and now? Half a percent of a year's wages today, in your pocket."

Varick did some quick math. At that rate, he figured someone would have enough to get by comfortably for a week, so long as nothing went wrong. He thought about the punishing work required at the workhouses, and how they didn't pay medical bills. Varick looked back to the gent in the corner. His eyes were fixed on Varick with brows drawn so closely together, it looked like a giant caterpillar had made a home on the man's face.

"Think of it," the recruiter was saying. "All that money, from a *year*. An entire year! But you have to sign on *right now*." It did not escape Varick how the man did not state the half a percent part again. "All for you, or perhaps your family. All you have to do is sign one little contract right here, right now." He pushed the gruel-plopped brochure further under Varick's face. "My shift's over soon, though. You're running out of time."

Varick was beginning to form a picture of the scheme at play here. The sentient eyebrows and rock-chin in the corner stepped in if people showed even the least sign of defending themselves against the caped harassers, who sold a bad deal dressed up like a rare opportunity. Varick would love to have a look at the books and see who was benefitting from all this and how. Meanwhile, the workhouse recruiters got to be as aggressive and disrespectful as possible, presumably so long as they never laid hands on someone first. He couldn't help but level a glare at the obnoxious little parasite sitting next to him.

"Is there a problem here?"

The big man from the corner seemed to have transported himself right next to them. Varick had to hand it to the man; moving that silently in a body that large was no mean feat. He was sure Marlowe would love to learn how. As it was, though, he was cornered. One wrong move, and either of the Milgewort people might take it into their heads that Varick had been about to try something. He hadn't wanted to pull out this particular exit strategy, but it seemed the only way to deescalate the situation.

Varick let his eyes go vacant and his face slack. Then he lifted his head and stared at the ceiling. A fool's sunshine grin spread across his face.

"Have you ever seasoned your food with the stuff they use for cleaning latrines? It's got a real zesty kick to it." Varick then laughed in a way that sounded like he'd indeed explored the recreational use of far too many chemical agents.

The recruiter and the big man exchanged a look. The recruiter's smile came back with force, and he offered the soiled paper again.

"I think you're just the sort we're looking for. What do you say?"

Varick began warbling at the rafters until the recruiter decided he was well and truly off with the clouds and moved onto less distractible prey. It took far too long a time.

♜

Patricia Pendragon was sitting in the salon when Varick approached her about the soup kitchens. It was the last thing he wanted to do, but his other methods had failed him. He'd written to Cousin Chester via Coal about the administration of the Turnip Network. Sadly, when the reply came, it provided no help. That whole business, for lack of a better word, was apparently beyond Chester's purview. He'd asked if Varick wanted him to look into the matter further, which Varick read as code for, "Do you want people knowing you're trying to find this out? Because if I ask around, they will." Varick had dashed off a quick refusal and thanked Chester for his discretion. Thank goodness the man had more to gain keeping Varick as a client than betraying him. Varick had also tried going through his grandmother's personal effects while she was out one day. She slept poorly—or so she liked to moan about when it benefitted her—and he hadn't wanted to risk getting caught creeping around at night. But as Coal had once warned him was a problem, between servants coming in to freshen that or deliver this during the day, Varick hadn't made it far.

Again, Varick cursed whatever the reason had been for him not having learned more about the Turnip Network while his grandfather had been alive. Randolph hadn't kept a secretary. He hadn't used a valet either, not trusting the family not to buy off any gent serving in such a close role. There was no one left behind who Varick could ask without raising suspicion, and he wanted to control the way Patricia found out he'd been snooping.

Thus, he was here, seeking her out in the salon to ask directly. Patricia was reclining on sofa and reading a book about musical history when Varick approached. He waited, standing directly in her line of sight for several minutes, only to be ignored, before speaking.

"Grandmother," he began tentatively.

"Scales, Varick." She did not quite snap the words, but it was a close thing.

Varick schooled his expression, wanting to scowl and complain, but he knew that would only waste time. Patricia made sure to tell everyone she met what a great appreciator of music she was. She'd insisted all three children were taught to play a variety of instruments as well as to sing. He cleared his throat and went through his musical scales just as he'd done thousands of times when he was younger.

Patricia nodded. "Good." It was not praise. Patricia would likely rather eat cockroaches than freely give Varick any kind of affirmation. "I'm pleased to see you do not need remedial lessons. I won't have one of my grandchildren embarrassing me come New Year's by singing off-key."

"Of course, Grandmother," Varick said. He paused, but she still did not look away from her book. "I have a question, please." There'd be a lecture if he didn't smother his speech with manners.

"Go on then," she replied.

"Thank you. I was wondering about the Turnip Network that Grandfather left in our care."

Patricia's perfectly manicured ash-grey eyebrow arched at that, but she neither looked away from her book nor did she interrupt.

"I've… noticed that there are some rather unpleasant people frequenting the place. People from workhouses trying to convince some of the diners to come work."

Finally, Patricia put down her book and fixed Varick with an acid stare.

"What do you mean you've noticed?"

"I went to one," Varick said, proud of himself for how self-assured he sounded. He certainly didn't feel it. "To acquaint myself with the responsibility Grandfather entrusted to me."

Patricia gave a dismissive huff. "I do not generally concern myself with what you get up to, Varick, mainly because I find it both banal and disappointing. I must insist, however, that you avoid those wretched handout factories. There's no telling what vermin you'll unwittingly bring back with you.

"Furthermore, given that the magistrate council has mandated that the able-bodied poor are ineligible for assistance if they do not accept work when it is offered, it really is quite generous for the workhouses to go out recruiting. People know the law, they know where to go if they are in need, and yet they refuse. Can you imagine what it takes to convince someone to work who has no desire to do for themselves? Who's figured out that they can simply leech off food pantries and soup kitchens? And so, if workhouse recruiters are unpleasant, it is because they must be, for the ingrates' own good."

Varick stood silently while Patricia went on her diatribe. The sofa on which she sat might as well have been a throne. When she was finished, he kept his voice even, though it was a struggle.

"I don't believe that people don't want to work. The conditions of the workhouses are deplorable." True, he hadn't seen them for himself and only had Randolph's and Coal's word for it, but that was more than good enough for Varick. "And I saw someone get right in a woman's face and insult her horribly."

That was a lie, of course, but it was Coal's truth, so it served him here. "It's no charity to use people like beasts of burden until they're broken and then throw them away. They aren't compensated fairly for their labor, and the living conditions aren't suitable for animals, much less people."

Patricia heaved a sigh of the greatly beleaguered. She stood and closed her book, patting it thoughtfully against her hand. "Varick, you are by far the most gullible of the family. You get that from Randolph; he always was far too trusting."

Not that trusting, Varick thought angrily. *He had you and all the rest pegged as the snakes you are.*

Instead, he said, "I don't want those workhouse recruiters in my Turnip Network. I want people to be able to come and eat in peace, just like Grandfather did."

Patricia's eyes narrowed. "That is not your decision, Varick. Until you come of age, I am the overseer of that rotten money pit Randolph burdened our family with."

"And you cannot make decisions without me!" Varick burst out. "Grandfather intended—"

Patricia struck out with her book faster than Varick could react. The spine caught him in the ribs. She always aimed for spots the bruises wouldn't show. The volume she held was a smallish one, but Patricia wielded it like a baton in a firm grip. Varick's muscles clenched as pain thrummed along his side. He allowed himself to stumble back, having learned long ago it was better to let distance fall between him and whoever was taking out their anger on him. Silence fell around them. When Patricia spoke again, her voice was a sharp hiss.

"If I had my way, I would shut down every one of those odious little cesspits, but Randolph worked his schemes well. I cannot because the papers will paint us as uncharitable, as if my years as a patroness of the arts mean nothing. You, however, will stay away from them. There is no need for you to concern yourself with them until you turn sixteen, and if I hear of you going to visit them again, you will be very sorry indeed. Am I understood?"

Varick's jaw clenched in pain as he gave a little nod.

"I said, am I understood, young man?" Patricia's voice edged with a warning.

"Yes, Grandmother," Varick ground out. "I understand."

"Very well," said said, resuming her seat. "Now get out of my sight."

29

WHERE'S THERE'S SMOKE...

arick reclined on a nearby roof, staring up at the stars. He'd returned to the Turnip Network's main hub not long after the disastrous talk with his grandmother and camped out on a nearby rooftop, thinking on the experience. She was absolutely hiding something. She had to be responsible for the Milgewort people being there, but he now knew they weren't directly associated with the Pendragons. On his way here, he'd swung by that particular workhouse. At the front gates, a large plaque listed the place's various benefactors. No Pendragon was listed, nor were any of Patricia's family on the other side. Family trees were easy to come by, and Varick had made a list of her non-Pendragon relations. And no one he knew of bothered to donate somewhere unless it was publicized. After all, why bother being generous if people don't see you doing it? He was less certain about her friends and other non-familial acquaintances, though. Patricia made sure to move in a lot of powerful circles. It was possible she was trading favors with someone affiliated with

Milgewort that Varick didn't know of.

He sighed up at the stars and counted off problems to be solved on his fingers.

One, why all the strange alterations to the Turnip Network? What did his grandmother stand to gain? And how to fix them when he still had almost a year before gaining his majority? Willful mismanagement could shutter the place before he even had an opportunity to get in there.

Two, figure out how to get his friends onto the *Angrec's Respite* without him, now that his parents had forbade him from going. Perhaps he could write to Great Auntie Megaera.

Dear Auntie Megaera,

Please take these steamer trunks with you. They're precious to me and need a good airing out and definitely aren't full of people.

No, that was about as likely as a blizzard in a coal furnace. And it didn't even address the issue about Carver and Mercury needing him aboard to play their parts.

And three, he still needed to both find the right sort of steamer trunks—those with the curved lids—and figure out how to get them altered for breathing, as well as where to have them delivered, without arousing suspicion.

A door shutting sounded below, and Varick rolled over on his rooftop to peer over the edge. Hannah from The Restful Turnip was locking up for the night. Varick watched her go and then, when he was certain the coast was clear, he scuttled down to ground level again and sidled up to the door. Security here was about as tight as a hot blancmange, and thus Varick was inside and creeping through the dark space within minutes.

From his previous visits, he knew where to go to find the paperwork—there was a backroom behind where Mister Granite

Jaw had been standing—though an oil lamp was harder to locate. Petrolsene lighting was available, of course. That was standard, but Varick didn't know the system well enough to know how or even if he could turn just one lamp on low. He'd had the foresight to bring matches at least, but he didn't want to waste them all looking for a lamp to light. He found the tins of chemical fuel first and decided to use one of those instead. When he opened it, it gave off that same scent as before, only this time it was not diluted from spreading throughout the air, but fresh and compressed. The harsh, chemically smell burst out of the can so strongly Varick thought his eyelashes would wither up and fall off. He pressed a sleeve against his face, eyes burning, and lit the goopy substance inside.

With somewhat better lighting now, he was able to recognize things from his previous visits. Not that it was hard. The back office was small, but tidy. A typical secretary desk, all closed up at the moment, sat next to a couple of supply closets. A coat rack stood in the corner, and that was it. Varick started with the desk. Again, it was a matter of minutes before he had the lock undone and was carefully riffling through the items there. The lit tin of fuel burned slowly and malodorously next to him, atop the desk. He was pleased to see that, despite the changes, Hannah still ran a tight ship.

Inside the desk, an ordinary collection of office supplies populated the various cubbies, slots, and drawers. A collection of bills yet to be marked, Varick noticed, sat piled by a *Paid* rubber stamp and its pad of red ink. He flicked through them. Varick didn't have a lot of experience with bills, but he'd seen a few examples during his business lessons—basic business accounting was a necessary skill, but anything more complex, his teacher, Scholar Tewksbury had said, should be handled by an expert accountant.

"Always pay your accountants well," Scholar Tewksbury had

advised. "They, more than anyone else you employ, know their worth. Right down to the penny."

Thus, Varick knew a bill's basic outline, even if he was unfamiliar with the industry, whatever industry charity fell under anyway. The first bill in the stack was for petrolsene and came from the Springhaven Energy Authority—S.E.A. for short. He actually knew a bit about this body, as it was the delight of many Pendragons to complain about the fact that their fine city-state kept energy, and water for that matter, under the purview of the government instead of allowing it to be privatized. And, as with so many who had no idea how things ran beneath the surface, my oh my, what *splendid* ideas each one had for how to run things better. To these conversations, Varick's grandfather would always reply, without fail, "Ah well, worse things happen at sea." No one ever laughed.

Varick honored the memory with a bittersweet grimace. He didn't have the same appreciation for puns that Randolph had, but it had always made the old man so happy. He sighed and moved onto the next bill in the pile. This one was for food. As was the next one. And the next. Varick set the bills aside for a moment and started going through the drawers. Inside the deepest one, at the bottom, he found an expanding file organizer and a couple of large ledgers, each dated with a different set of years, save for one. It hadn't yet been labeled. Probably for next year, Varick guessed. He started with the file organizer, which was tightly compressed at the moment. That made sense, given that it had been stored, but how to undo it? Varick examined the various springs and catches that comprised the gadget. He had no talent for such complexities and therefore started pulling things at random. Surely if he unlatched enough doodads, it'd open up for him.

But not before catching his finger in a hinge as the blasted thing snapped back during this blind exploration.

Varick swallowed a cry and muttered a string of swears under his breath as he scrambled to undo whatever he had just done. He didn't even know how he'd managed it, but after a few frantic adjustments he freed his throbbing finger from the contraption. He shook the badly abused digit, as if the pain was something he could easily flick off. He certainly wanted to. No blood, thankfully, just a horrible ache that radiated from his fingernail.

He took a deep breath, trying to stop hating his choices quite so vehemently and proceeded more carefully. At last, the sodding tension in the sodding organizer released and he was able to start extracting papers. This too, unsurprisingly, was well organized. It wasn't long before Varick found more food bills in their own sections, sorted by vendors. All of these had been paid, so stated by the large red *Paid* stamp imprinted onto each bill, each with a date and a receipt number that had been written in by hand. Varick soon realized that the older bills had all been promptly paid, usually inside of a week. The unpaid ones still sitting on the desk were nearly three weeks old now. An unmistakable trend appeared before Varick's eyes. The issues started just after his grandfather had died. A few of the most recent bills hadn't been paid until well after they were due.

Varick's mind returned to his earlier thoughts. Patricia was probably trying to choke the life out of the Turnip Network. He moved onto the ledger for this year. His eyes boggled when they fell onto a page at random. What gibberish was this? The columns were full of numbers, but they were all positive. That couldn't be right. The words credit and debit were listed at the top, but it looked like everything had been written double. He couldn't begin to make heads or tails of the categories either. Some made sense, like *Supplies*, but what were *Liability Offsets* and *Equity Payments* in this context? Varick began to pace as he flipped through the book, but couldn't find anything to explain the vague descriptions. Flipping back to earlier in the year, however, he didn't see those two categories listed. They only started after his grandfather died. So Patricia *was* doing something funny with the Turnip Network's money! He began flipping through the other ledgers, flinging them hither and yon as his frustration grew. If he could figure out what those categories meant, he could… what? Stop his grandmother from whatever she was doing? Was she skimming off the top somehow? If so, was that fraud or just plain old legal greed? He didn't know, alright, but he'd be better prepared to consider the question anyway.

He tossed ledger after ledger aside, but of course information from the past couldn't help him. His grandfather had been in charge then; Patricia hadn't had her claws in this place yet. They piled precariously all across and atop the desk. One, however, failed to open. Maybe Varick had suddenly forgotten how to open a book? He tried again, but the ledger stayed firmly shut. He looked more closely at it. It was the unlabeled one, the one that looked like an extra for next year. The deckled page edges felt real, though, as Varick ran his thumb over them. And then he realized it was because they were real. Someone had made this from an actual ledger. Clever. And they'd hidden it in plain sight. What better way to ensure it didn't arouse suspicion? It even had a little ribbon bookmark running through it. But why make it in the first place? Varick began playing with the ledger, turning it over in his hands, but carefully. His still-throbbing finger remembered what had happened to it not so long ago.

At one point, he gave the bookmark a tug, and the book replied with a little *click*. The covers separated, just a fraction, and Varick opened the ledger to reveal a cut-out within the pages. Inside rested a varied collection of papers, along with a very small book. He leaned back against the desk and opened the little book. It was written in some kind of code. He stared at the small, tightly written symbols, trying to puzzle out their secrets.

Meanwhile, his nose tried to tell his brain something. He sifted through the hidden documents, but wasn't surprised when he couldn't find a key for the code. A code was no good when you told people how to crack it. His brain continued to ignore his nose.

Varick examined the topmost paper. He guessed it was a letter from the way it was folded. And then he stopped short when he saw the seal—a thistle. That was his grandmother's symbol. He was just about to open it when his nose insisted that it really did have a rather important message for his brain. The brain finally listened.

Something smelled different now. It smelled like smoke. Varick shut the book in his hands, turned back around toward the desk, and saw flames licking greedily at a corner of one of the other ledgers he'd tossed aside. The sodding thing had landed to overhang his flaming tin of chemicals! Clutching the faux record book protectively to his chest, with his free hand, Varick snatched the ledger that had caught from atop its pile. And with the introduction of oxygen, the one beneath it, which also turned out to be on fire, flared gleefully. The one in Varick's hand sported a flame to rival the best pitch torches as it ate up the paper and glue of the book. He spied more flames flicking out from the other books in the sloppy stack.

Panic settled in.

He dropped the one in his hand back into its spot and made a grab for the tin of gelid fuel. The metal had grown hot near the flames. It bit into his fingers, and Varick instantly dropped it. The tin hit the desk, bounced to the wooden floor, and rolled on its side, splattering fuel along the way and spreading the fire with it.

"Bollocking hells!" Varick swore. He flung the false ledger to the relative safety of a darkened corner of the room.

What did he have? His gaze swept desperately across the room for something he could use. An awful bloody lot of paper!

That was all there was to hand.

Water, he thought. *I need water!* He ran from the little office.

This was a soup kitchen after all. The kitchen was mostly dark, but a couple of windows actually graced one of the walls in here. A petrolsene lamp outside threw just enough light through those windows to barely limn the outlines of the kitchen. A large pot stooped on a worktable. Varick ran to it and spied the telltale sheen of liquid inside. He grabbed it and lurched—the thing was far heavier than he expected. Still, he hobbled it back to the office. The flames had spread, but so long as he put them out, everything would be fine. The big pot in his hands gave him confidence. This much water would surely drown every bit of them. He hurled it, and watched with satisfaction as a great amorphous glob of water arced into the air, spattering yellow drops as it went.

Wait. Why was it yellow?

Varick had half a second to steep in a deep, aching sense of dread before the liquid landed and summarily exploded into flame.

"What are you doing?!" screeched a voice.

Varick then realized the screech came from him. He'd directed his question at whatever had been in the pot that was supposed to be water. He was so disappointed in it for not living up to its aqueous potential. The flames, now much, *much* bigger and beginning to, if he could use the word, *engulf* the room, only stared back at him while they continued their not-so-slow devourment of the office.

"Oh, shhh…" Varick groaned. He could not even finish the swear, as he was already switching gears to the next best option: escape.

As he spun to retreat from the enterprising inferno, he spied the faux ledger he'd tossed away. The corner it laid in was no longer dark. He grabbed it and then sprinted back the way he'd come.

30

FIRE FIGHTING

arick's feet moved him without him thinking about it. Only one thought filled his head: He'd destroyed it, his grandfather's legacy. He shouted "fire" into the night until he saw lights come on in a few of the nearby buildings. Then, hidden, he stuck around long enough to see people start a bucket chain. Someone must have alerted the fire brigade too, as they eventually arrived on their horse-drawn fire engine. The contraption they brought with them was not very large, just a simple hand-operated pump and attached linen and leather hose, but the brass tank of water behind it had to weigh at least a couple hundred pounds. The firefighters redirected those operating the bucket chain to keep the water tank full.

Not long after, Varick left the scene, just as the flames were beginning to gobble away at The Restful Turnip's dining room. Later—he didn't know how long it had been—he found himself at the door of The Riffraff Inn. Only then did he begin to come back to his senses. He fairly attacked the door, pounding it with the side of his fist. He was vaguely aware that his other arm was busy holding something. Time was an amorphous blob. He banged until someone opened the door. It took Varick a moment to recognize Mercury's face; he'd never seen the man here.

"V?" he asked, rubbing his face tiredly. "What the blazes are you doing here?"

Just behind him, Varick could see Marlowe standing at the ready. Further back, the faces of Coal, Carver, and Fulcrum peeked through whatever spaces they could around the two larger forms.

"I mucked everything up." The words fell from Varick's mouth without him meaning for them to. His mind wasn't working properly. Had he inhaled too much smoke? Is this what happened when you had more smoke in your body than air? Did it break your brain?

Mercury blinked at him. He managed to say the word, "What," before Varick barreled forward like a terrified bull in a pottery shop.

"The fire, I did it. And if Agate burns down, that's my fault too. I don't know if the fire brigade can contain it. I don't know what my family will do if they find out it was me. They already forbade me from going on the cruise, but with this…" His eyes were wild as he looked up at Mercury. "I think they might lock me inside the house forever."

Mercury held out his hands. "Okay, okay, let's start by breathing."

He ushered Varick further inside, looking this way and that for prying eyes and ears before shutting the door behind them.

Varick tried to do as he was told, tried to focus on breathing. He kept his eyes on Mercury; he couldn't bring himself to look at his friends, whose opportunities to get free of the city he'd destroyed as thoroughly as he had The Restful Turnip. Breathing was happening, but Varick's brain still whirred faster than he could keep up.

Mercury had Varick sit at the little ramshackle table. Carver brought over a copper cup, and Mercury tipped a finger's worth of brown liquid into it.

"Breathe," Mercury said again. "And drink, slowly."

A warm, sugary scent with just a hint of burnt rubber met Varick's nose when he lifted the cup to his lips. He barely tasted the liquid, but the ritual of sipping and breathing began to bring him back around to himself.

"There now," Mercury said, when Varick looked less like an overstretched crossbow string. "One thing at a time. What's on fire?"

Varick took a deep breath. "One of the soup kitchens, one of the Turnip Network's. My grandfather's."

"Is that all," Mercury asked.

Varick nodded. "At least when I left, but I don't know if it's spread."

Mercury looked at Coal. "Go check it out. Marlowe, go with him in case there's trouble. Then come straight back here."

Varick heard their quick assents and then the sound of the door opening and closing again. He still couldn't look at any of them.

"Now," Mercury said gently, "did anyone see you?"

Varick shook his head. "I picked the lock on the door. I was alone, and no one was around when I ran out."

Please don't ask me how it happened, he added mentally. Varick may care little for Mercury's opinion of him, but he didn't want to have to reveal to anyone what an utter nitwit he'd been.

Thank heaven, Mercury didn't. Instead, he said, "So no one saw you go in or come out. Then how might your family find out you were there?"

Varick's heart slowed as his overclocked brain began to consider the question. They... probably wouldn't? The realization brushed over him like a cool breeze. They'd likely never suspect that he'd take himself to the Agate quarter, much less at night. They believed the place was nothing but thugs and opium addicts. They talked like any respectable citizen who dared to step foot in the impoverished area was immediately murdered and robbed, or robbed and then murdered. And if Varick showed up not-murdered, then they'd have no reason to think he'd been there.

"I don't know," Varick replied at last.

"But do you think there's actually a chance?" Mercury prodded.

Varick thought on it a little more. It made less and less sense the more he considered the question, not least of all because he'd made no secret of being in support of the place. Why would he want to set fire to it?

"Uh, no," he admitted. "I guess not."

He looked down again and finally saw the false ledger he'd brought with him. His nearly empty cup rested atop it. He wanted to ask about it, to see if any of his friends had any thoughts on the code, but now didn't seem like the time.

Mercury was giving him an encouraging smile. "Grand. Now, what's this about being forbade from the cruise?"

Varick stared down into his cup. He hadn't meant to reveal that part. He hadn't meant for so much to happen. He sighed, not knowing what else to do.

"After I injured my brother—"

"It was fully justified," Carver put in from the side.

"—they said I can't go," Varick finished.

Mercury was quiet a moment, and Varick wished the floor would just open up and eat him.

"There was a lot of paperwork involved," Mercury mused. "Did you sign anything to say you were no longer going? Fill out any forms?"

Varick shook his head. "No."

"And your aunt hasn't mentioned anything either?" Mercury asked.

Varick shook his head again.

"Did you parents say they'd contact Prism Line Properties on your behalf?"

Varick saw where this was going, and it made the wheels in his head turn again. They all just expected their word to be obeyed. Automatically. But Varick had said he'd handle all the arrangements. His family had been left out of the process completely, so how would they even know who to contact to have Varick kicked off the airship's roster? They might have sent a member of staff to find out, but Varick deeply suspected none of them had thought that far. He said as much to Mercury, who nodded thoughtfully.

"Carver, first thing in the morning, pose as V's secretary and go ensure everything is in order for Mister Pendragon's trip. Tell them you want to make sure there's nothing else they need for your employer to have a hassle-free holiday."

"Will do," Carver said.

"But I'm still not allowed to go," Varick said. "They'll notice if I'm gone for a week. And on that subject, how *did* you and Carver get past the staff interviews? Everyone knows Enforcers can't be bought."

Mercury, whose travel papers read Mister Montgomery Preece, smiled slyly at that. "Your false nose isn't the one you need to keep clean. The Enforcers are only a problem if they know your real identity."

"Right." Varick sighed. "Well, the only people who know my face are those with access to newssheets, so…" He left the salty comment hanging in the air.

"It's not a crime to disobey your parents," Mercury said. "You can pull out if you want, but Coal and Fulcrum were really looking forward to getting out. Fulcrum's got a whole plan for the two of them, a real fresh start. And that money would set Marlowe and Carver up real nice, whatever they decide to do."

Varick's stomach felt heavy as iron. This had been the taunt living in the back of his mind since he'd hidden out in the storage room the day of the carp pond incident. But he didn't see how he could go. Disobedience earned punishment. Even if his family somehow didn't find out he'd skipped off to have a holiday he'd been explicitly told he wasn't allowed to take, it went without saying that disappearing for a week wasn't allowed. He wasn't permitted that sort of freedom. He knew it and they knew he knew it. And they wouldn't stand to be disobeyed.

Mercury's voice hardened when he spoke again. "If you're gonna abandon the job, then you gotta tell us now. So that we can make other plans."

"How are you going to do it without me?" Varick blurted. He hadn't meant to sound so petulant. He tried explaining himself. "You're coming on as my staff." Hm, he wasn't certain that sounded any better.

Mercury spread his hands before him. "We'll have to figure something out. Maybe you slept in and missed the airship."

"But you're meant to be my valet. It'd be *your* job to get me up and out the door on time." He really didn't mean to sound so nasty, but he was angry and tired and sad and tired and worried and hungry. And, oh yes, *tired*. What time was it anyway? He reached into his pocket only to realize he had no pocket watch on him.

Fulcrum must have noticed the move, because he said from behind Varick, "Nearly two." Despite the help, his tone did not sound charitable.

Blazes, Varick had forgotten the sullen young man was there. He'd heard every word of how Varick had smashed their plans to bits by doing the same to Magnus' knee. And how he wasn't willing to risk stepping outside his little bubble of safety for them. Him, who'd been handed everything just by being born. Mercury said they'd figure something out, but would they really? The entire plan hinged on Varick being there, bringing his staff and his excessive luggage.

Bollocks, he thought. One week's disappearance, that's all he'd have to do. He'd be of age in a year and then he could leave his family behind forever. And maybe they wouldn't even be that angry. *It's not like they'll miss me.*

"Alright," he agreed. "I'll sneak out and go."

Tension eased out of the room as tangibly as if a heavy fog had hung all around them, suddenly obliterated by the sun emerging theatrically from behind a mountain.

Mercury's broad grin practically took up his entire face. "That's the spirit, lad! Good to see you being a team player. Now, let's focus on the next week going smoothly. From tonight until the morning we set off, you are going to be the best behaved little boy."

"I'm not a little boy," Varick snapped.

"Course not," Mercury agreed.

That quelled Varick's anger slightly. The man was, he had to admit, being awfully understanding about the disasters Varick had wrought.

Mercury went on. "But you're going to be as compliant as one. Just like when you were little, you're going to be helpful, respectful, and flexible. Put them at ease about you."

Varick decided it wouldn't be helpful to explain he hadn't been anything like those things when he'd been small. He'd learned from far too early an age that his family were meant to be avoided and distrusted at all costs. Whether that was what had made him mutinous or it if had come naturally was unknown, and neither here nor there at the moment. The proposed ploy made sense, though. He could pretend their starvation punishment had worked to trounce his rebellious spirit.

Varick agreed and remained at Mercury's Riffraff Inn until Coal and Marlowe returned with their report. Coal was all too happy to let them know that the Agate district was *not*, in fact, burning to the ground. The Restful Turnip was in pretty bad shape, but most of it was still standing and even still had some of its roof and walls.

"Looks like most of the destruction happened away from the kitchen," Marlowe said.

Varick knew how suspicious that looked. The kitchen was where fire lived, where, logically, it would have started. He wished he could hide the ledger now. Explaining it would mean explaining how the fire had started, how he'd failed to keep the world's most perfect tinder well away from the one, tiny flame in the entire building. And then doused it in something that turned out to have been the opposite of water. Carver and Fulcrum, he noticed—once he'd gathered enough scraps of self-respect to look at them anyway—kept sneaking glances at the mysterious volume. Varick kept it close, but tried to play things casual. He'd have a look at it soon, privately. Though not tonight. Fatigue was seeping into his muscles, and he still had to sneak back to the Dragon's Keep.

31

STRATEGIC LUGGAGE BUYING

The next morning, for the first time in years, Varick tried to stick close to his family. He'd snuck home under cover of darkness, quietly washed the worst of the grime off of himself, and then piece by piece, burned his smoky, grubby clothes. At breakfast, he kept an eye on his father, who read the newssheets over sausages, fried eggs, and toast everyday without fail. No image-still graced the front page of the morning editions, but that didn't mean The Restful Turnip fire hadn't made headlines. Varick still didn't think he was in any danger of his involvement being discovered, but he wanted to know how the event was being reported anyway. When a footman arrived bearing a silver tray with a missive addressed to Patricia, however, he had at least part of his answer.

"That wretched soup kitchen caught fire!" she exclaimed.

Constance, who'd been chatting about something to Victoria, whirled around. "Fire?" She sounded far too pleased by the idea. "Did it burn to the ground?"

Patricia's face pinched. "Sadly, no. Mostly the back office apparently."

"How'd that happen?" Magnus wanted to know.

Varick tried for an expression between innocent and horrified, but said nothing for the moment. He felt his cheeks grow warm at Magnus' question, but took a sip of tea to hide it.

"Probably some fool left a candle burning," Henry offered.

"Don't be absurd," Patricia shot. "The blasted placed is outfitted with petrolsene lights."

Varick raised his eyebrows, fighting a smile. His grandmother must really be in a pique if she was snapping at Henry like that.

"I was only suggesting—" Henry said defensively.

Patricia steamrolled right over him. "With the fuss Randolph made over the place, do you really think he wouldn't have installed all the most modern fixtures?"

"So how did it happen?" Victoria asked, clearly trying to steer the conversation.

Varick's ears perked. He too was keen to know what the leading theories were.

Patricia looked back to the letter. She glared at it like it had personally let her down. "They don't know. There's a lot of burned wood and paper, and the office was apparently where they stored the fuel for keeping food warm. The closed tins exploded and acted as an accelerant, so that's making things more complicated. That odious woman who runs the place says there's nothing left of the desk but charred splinters and book bindings."

So the letter was from Hannah. No surprise, considering how efficiently the information in it was laid out. That seemed to settle the matter for the rest of the family. All except Varick and Patricia returned to their juice and fruit and butter and cheese.

"At least you won't have to deal with that ruddy place any longer, Mother," Henry said. He'd already reopened his paper.

"You never did like it."

"Do none of you understand what this means?!" Patricia exploded.

Varick jumped, nearly dropping the fork he'd been holding in mock suspense.

"We now have to address this, *I* have to address it," Patricia railed. "I never wanted the wretched place, yet here I am saddled with it, no thanks to my useless, dead husband. I'm going to have to make a public statement and rebuild it and there will have to be a grand reopening. Stars, why must I be so put upon?"

As quickly as her anger came, it fled. Patricia pressed a hand to her forehead and leaned back in her seat, looking for all the world as if she'd just been asked to choose which one of two beloved children must die. Meanwhile, Varick squeezed his fork so hard he thought he might bend it.

Stay calm, he told himself. *Be a doormat for them.* Doormat was the replacement term he'd chosen over Mercury's little boy example. *Definitely don't throw your fork at her.*

"Oh, Grandmummy." Constance was the only one allowed to call Patricia that. She left her seat and knelt at Patricia's side. "Surely you don't have to do all that?"

Patricia waved Hannah's letter helplessly. "She says reporters are already clamoring, asking whether it'll be rebuilt. She assured them it would. The woman's a sour, horrid sort, but she knows about appearances. Besides, the bequeathment was announced in the papers. Everyone knows I'm the one in whose care the place was left."

Both of us, actually, Varick thought, but he wasn't about to say so out loud. Or should he?

"I'm so sorry this has happened, Grandmother," he said. He'd meant to add, "to you," onto the end, but couldn't bring himself to go that far. What he'd said, though, was true. He hated that he'd destroyed such a place, even with its problems. "What can I do to help?"

Patricia and Constance, and the rest of the family too, all looked at him like they'd only just realized he was there. Fair dues, he usually tried to wish himself invisible when he was around them.

Constance looked back to Patricia. "It would look very good in the newssheets for you both to make a statement together. And then Ricky can stand in for you in future you if necessary."

Patricia still looked unhappy. Probably because of whatever she'd been doing behind the scenes with The Turnip Network. If Varick was involved, she'd have to be extra careful about covering her tracks. But she'd been the one who'd taught Constance about optics, and her granddaughter had been absolutely correct about this situation.

Thus, later that morning, Varick found himself before a crowd of reporters and onlookers with a prepared statement in hand. They stood before the charred remains of the office. Blackened beams hung at jagged angles from what remained of the frame. The sign with the turnip had survived, and stood like a wounded survivor, a symbol of hope. Varick had written his own speech and was told to have Constance edit it.

"It's actually not bad," she'd said to him, looking over it at a writing desk in the library. "If only you put this much creative effort into dealing with Mother and Father, and Magnus too for that matter, you might have an easier time of things."

Varick swallowed his retort, that he hadn't been creative with it, but rather that he'd written from the heart. He repeated the word doormat to himself like a mantra. Just one week of this before he escaped to where none of them could follow, on an airship in the clouds. And then he had to *not* think about how much trouble he'd be coming back to.

"Will you need to make many changes?" he'd asked meekly instead.

"I really shouldn't." And she hadn't, only superficial ones, plus a line or two crafted to garner sympathy from the public.

Now, he waited as Patricia made her statement. It was mostly tinned expressions of grief for Randolph's memory and a list of statistics about the place since it had opened—how many pounds of food it had produced, how many people it had fed, how many days of providing for those who otherwise would have gone hungry. Every piece of data made Varick feel worse about his poor choices, and so the sadness and regret he carried with him to the amplification cone when it was his turn was entirely real.

"My grandfather, Randolph Pendragon, had a rare kindness about him. He saw a wound in our city and built a place to heal it. This loss is a blow to many, but as my grandmother said, we are already working to reverse the damage. The other Restful Turnip locations will continue to function as much as possible." That part worried him. Patricia had spoken of this during her speech too, and Varick was certain she'd publicized the uncertainty of the other locations' status in the hopes that she could shut them, at least for a time. He looked around at the gathered crowd, all sincerity and determination. "In the future, I mean to build on my grandfather's work, to make a place where people without recourse can come for what they need. For now, however, let us look to restoring what's been lost."

His voice wavered as he spoke, but he did not cry. He'd been told not to, that it was too theatrical, but Varick hadn't wanted to anyway. The crowd politely clapped, and Varick held his spot for a few extra moments to allow those with the expensive devices for capturing image-stills to do so. Afterward, he and Patricia went to meet with Hannah. It was strange being face-to-face with her again, especially in such a different guise. He might have worried she'd recognize him, but the circumstances today were so different. He was clean, wearing fine clothes, and talking sense. Nevertheless, she eyed him strangely as they shook hands.

He hadn't the foggiest as to why, while he did his best to broadcast how sane and well-fed he was in the strength of his grip, how tall and straight he held himself, and how seriously he spoke.

"We'll be in touch," he told her. "We meant what we said; we're going to get this place rebuilt as soon as possible."

Patricia let Varick do the talking and scowled at Hannah from the side. Hannah thanked them and said all the right things, but she very intentionally did not turn her gaze onto Patricia. Why was she looking at Varick like that?

Back in the privacy of their family coach, Patricia said, "Did you see the way that woman looked at me? Practically snarling. You'd think she might show a little more gratitude to the people keeping her in a job."

I can't blame her, Varick thought to himself. He'd decided the strange looks were because Hannah doubted their promises and intentions but had done a bad job of hiding it. He wouldn't let Patricia renege on this, though. He'd play nice and give her a chance to uphold her word, even if it was only for the wrong reasons, but by his blood and bones, he was going to make sure Randolph's Turnip Network came back bigger and better than ever.

The rest of the week continued in much the same way. Varick continued to avoid his family as usual, but when he did have to be in their company, he was as compliant as putty. Especially given that Carver's inquiries had indeed turned up that Varick was still very much on the airship's manifest, and they were ever so pleased to be hosting such a great young man—his name and image-still had appeared in the newssheets following his speech in front of the burned-out soup kitchen.

At the first opportunity, he investigated the ledger he'd stolen from that place. Varick read the letter on top first, the one from his grandmother. That turned out to be nothing more than a nasty little set of orders to Hannah to "Stop," as Patricia phrased it, "giving those selfless recruiters from Milgewort Workhouse an unfathomably hard time." It was much the same rhetoric that she'd given him when he'd approached her about the issue—it wasn't the recruiters' fault that people were so lazy and didn't want to work, but their mission was a good one and they certainly didn't need to be harassed by lowly spoon-feeders.

Most of the rest of the documents were in code, which Varick still failed to crack. He wasn't terribly good at puzzles to begin with. Or rather, he might have been if he had the patience for them. The only documents that weren't encoded were copies of Springhaven's various—and sometimes labyrinthine—regulations, standards, and bylaws regarding charity organizations, conservatorship, personal taxes, and a few other obscure subjects. Varick tried to read through these in order to glean some idea of why they interested whoever had pulled together this information, but without more context, there was really no way to know. He picked at the corner of the inside cover, where the last of the uncut sheets of the original ledger hadn't been glued down properly.

He thought back to seeing Patricia visit Mister Umpleby, about what she'd said to him: "…the poor lad won't need to hear of this until it's done." He couldn't convince himself that hadn't been about him. Looking at what little he had to go on, though, it was looking more and more like his grandmother was simply trying to cut him out of anything having to do with the Turnip Network. Though he wondered if that might have changed now with the fire and their public address. And maybe Hannah was just trying to bar the Milgewort people from being able to come in. Those explanations left some holes behind, he knew, but he didn't know where else to go from here. Preparations for the cruise, however, soon took over his thoughts.

First, there was the horse trials event he'd backed with Constance. In his effort to appear satisfactorily cowed, he'd agreed to join her. Varick knew Galineer likely wanted to try and wheedle yet more money from him, and Constance wasn't getting her precious horse from the chap until after the trials. She was clearly working to keep everyone happy until she had what she wanted. On the way there, in what was an obvious stratagem to keep Varick from asking awkward questions, Constance mentioned how very sorry she was that she hadn't been able to convince Galineer to give Varick a foal as well.

"You shouldn't mention it today," she said, her face a mask of regret. "He feels ever so badly about it, but he needs as many horses as possible for his breeding line, and he can't risk it becoming tainted."

She really must think Varick was a fool. He severely doubted Constance had even asked. And how could a horse be "tainted" anyway? Galineer had exclusive breeding rights. Ridiculous.

"Not to worry," Varick said easily. "I've been wanting to get in more riding time with Tallywags anyway."

Galineer's cob horses were magnificent, Varick had to admit. All of them white piebalds with either black, mahogany, or chestnut. He was working on bringing some greys into the line as well. After the event, Varick met the new foal that Galineer had at last gifted to Constance. The baby was nearly all black over its body with a mostly white mane and tail. Varick had to admit, it was quite striking, even with its scraggly little leg feathers.

"His name shall be Tuxedo," Constance informed her younger brother.

"That Tuxedo Which Would Clothe Heaven, to be exact," amended Galineer. He was a handsome enough young man, but like his horses had a tendency to speak in a very teeth-forward manner.

Varick couldn't help but think the awkward little foal must be deeply embarrassed by such a pretentious name, but he only smiled mildly and replied, "Stupendous."

Thank the stars Carver had been free soon after, as Varick had yet to sort the steamer trunk situation. He dashed off a quick note simply asking,

Fancy joining me for a shopping trip?

Carver had been more than game, and the two—with Carver dressed as Varick's secretary again—had a lovely afternoon engaging in some strategic luggage buying.

Carver seemed pleased it was just the two of them, because he wasted no time in saying, "I hope you don't mind my asking, but what was that book you were carrying the other night?"

Varick gave Carver a sidelong look. "Why?"

Carver returned a gentle but challenging eyebrow raise. "Because you never let it out of your sight, not once. Is everything okay? You seemed pretty shaken."

Varick sighed. He wasn't really certain. He'd looked through the documents a few more times and tried to puzzle out the code again, but he'd made no further progress.

Returning to Carver's question, Varick said, "I think my grandmother is up to something, something to do with The Restful Turnip. And maybe also me? And I think someone else thinks so too. I found their evidence, or something like it, but I can't make heads or tails of it."

"Want me to have a look at it?" Carver offered. "Two heads being better than one and all that?"

Varick shrugged. "Sure. I'll bring it with me on the trip."

A little pressure eased off of Varick's mind as he was pleasantly reminded that he was not alone, not anymore. It was a hard habit to quit, thinking he had no one now that Randolph was gone, but he was working on it. He had a crew, and they had each others' backs.

Another thing they had were measurements. Marlowe, Fulcrum, and Coal's, standing straight and scrunched up, to be precise. Varick had done a little browsing previously, so he had a good idea of where to find the styles of trunk they needed—those with domed lids. To Varick's irritation, however, Fulcrum's parameters resulted in him having to buy the most ornate, and therefore, the most expensive set. They'd needed something that would hide air holes, which would be drilled in after the fact. Decorative metal scrollwork overtop the wood beneath the slats was the answer to that.

After Varick had purchased the entire set, which even included an oversized wardrobe trunk that, once gutted, would just fit Marlowe's massive frame, Varick, Coal, and Fulcrum made a plan for sneaking into the shop's backroom and altering the pieces. Fulcrum had needed some help with the sneaking parts. He had said that wasn't his talent, and Varick couldn't help but feel more than a touch smug as he swarmed up the wall and through a back window in order to help lift the dour lad in after him. Coal took up the rear, keeping watch and telling his brother what to do. Inside, Varick's smugness evaporated as soon as Fulcrum took over. To speed their work, Varick had given Fulcrum funds to go buy a pneumatic drill, which Varick questioned was even a real thing. Through the power of pressurized air, which Varick provided by repeatedly stamping on a foot pump until he thought his leg would fall off, Fulcrum bored thin line after curling thin line around the scrollwork, which Coal backed with black muslin. It was hard, fussy work, and Coal swapped with Varick when he needed a break from working the foot pump.

By the end of the night, the steamer trunks, were altered,

disguised, and rigged with interior release mechanisms. Delivery to the airship docks had all been previously arranged, Carver having done most of that work, as he was meant to be Varick's secretary. This was it. No more jobs, except of course *the* job. It was happening. Varick couldn't quite believe it, and he suddenly found himself excited for the adventure.

32
STRAIGHT AS AN AIRRO

The morning of embarkation was crisp and clear. The air smelled clean and briny, and gulls wheeled overhead, looking for an easy bite, or for someone to target. Despite the cold, Varick stood under an awning, out of the sun, and slightly behind a pile of steamer trunks, all neatly tagged for their destination. He wasn't hiding per se, but being out in the open somehow felt like a mistake. It was early, half past eight in the morning, and yet the wharf teemed with people and activity. It reminded Varick of the bee boxes kept at strategic points within the orchards on his family's grounds. Porters hefted luggage here and there, holiday makers and their small dogs and/or children—the latter often being accompanied by a governess or other caretaker—complained and fretted while finding their way to their vessel, or to cabs and coaches to return home. Sailors dressed in wide, white trousers, blue jackets, and knotted neckties passed by in groups of two and three. They worked on the various steamships docked alongside the wharfs.

These were all pleasure cruises. Those which didn't have clearance to leave Springhaven would circle the expanse of Cobalt Bay. Briefly, Varick considered the possibility of Coal and Fulcrum, and possibly Carver or Marlowe too, escaping to Duskwood on one of the lifeboats attached to one of those smaller ships. Far more dangerous, Varick knew, one little rowboat trying to make it all that way, even if it never left sight of the coast. Those steamships that did have such rare clearances would hug Invarnis' coastline the entire journey—after the War of Light, Invarnis had lost the knowledge of how to build the great seafaring ships of the Old World, as well as how to navigate the boundless seas beyond the sight of land.

Other crewmen passed by and headed around to the back of the glittering, glass-walled station behind Varick. These were the airros, who served zeppelins in the same capacity that sailors served sea-bound ships. Though their uniforms differed slightly depending on the airship they crewed, all the airros wore white silk scarves, leather and wool hats with attached earmuffs and chinstraps, and thick moleskin trousers. They took the open-air lifts, operated by engineers working a complex system of pulleys and gears, up to the airship docks three stories above. A dizzyingly tall staircase, with an equally dizzying number of steps, were used only by the most hardcore of the airrocrew members, who likely sported legs like pistons, as well as adolescents trying to show off to their friends or siblings, and those poor soon-to-be knackered folks in too much of a hurry to wait for a lift.

Varick had arranged to meet Great Auntie Megaera down here on the water-side of the vast travel station. And, despite his various arrangements to cover his tracks, he couldn't help but think his parents or grandmother, or at the very least some unfortunate staff member, would come around a corner any minute and forcibly drag him back to the Dragon's Keep.

He'd ridden Tallywags here, having left even before sunrise, with his clothing and other travel needs packed into an extensive collection of bulging saddlebags, which he'd spent the last few nights gradually packing and squirreling away in a neglected corner of the carriage house. Once he'd arrived at the travel station and gotten Tallywags' boarded in the stables here, Varick had given over most of the bags to some porters to be taken to the airship.

In addition to his comment to Constance on the way to the horse trials about wanting to get more time with Tallywags, later that day, he'd mentioned vaguely in her presence a desire to take in a new exhibition at the Springhaven Museum of History and Nature. If there was one thing he could rely on his sister for, it was never keeping secrets for him unless he'd specifically brokered for her silence. Hopefully, that would keep his departure a secret for the day at least, perhaps even two if his family was especially wrapped up in their own affairs. Even so, his eyes kept scanning the crowds for unwelcome relations.

Carver appeared first, and Varick was pleased to no end that his character of Archibald Sweeney had decided to go clean shaven. It made him look considerably younger—he could get away with nineteen, or perhaps even a youthful twenty-something, but any older would be stretching the bounds of rational belief. Still, it would work, and would be a sight easier all round. Varick shuddered at the idea of Carver having to affect the dreadful false beard day and night.

"Everything in order?" Varick asked. He didn't want to come right out and ask, "Are our three stowaways all packed up in their trunks and en route to my stateroom, as per our nefarious plan?" That seemed like it might invite trouble.

"All set," Carver confirmed. "A couple of the union ladies are creating a distraction for us."

Varick had to wrack his brain to remember what union

Carver was talking about. Then he remembered the first time he'd gone to Viola Meadow. Carver had mentioned then that he was working to help the city's… well, sex workers seemed the most straightforward, collective term for the men and women doing that sort of job. In any case, Carver was helping them to unionize. Before Varick could respond, he heard a familiar voice calling his name.

"Varick! Yoohoo-ooo!"

He knew the voice, but he'd never been yoohoo'ed at in his entire life. He had to look to make sure it was really happening. Great Auntie Megaera had her arm lifted high into the air and was waving at him like a woman drowning. With a broad smile, she shimmied through the crowd toward the two boys with a well-practiced grace, accompanied by many a, "Pardon me," and "I'm a frail old woman, please make way." The crowd parted for the lady, who moved shockingly well for one so "frail," and she'd reached them in what felt like a blink.

Auntie Megaera breathed deep and exuberantly through her nose. "Ah! Smell that sea air. I'm always invigorated by the start of a trip."

While she surveyed the crowds and docked ships, Varick and Carver stared down at another reason she might have had such an easy time making her way through the crowd. Beside her, sitting placidly, was the largest dog either of them had ever seen.

Longish, grey, wiry fur covered its slender body, and its head rested against Megaera's ribcage. It's pointed ears flopped at the tips, and it somehow had both a wizened and cheerful expression —the former was likely down to the way its facial fur had conspired to look like a lush goatee.

Varick exchanged a nervous glance with Carver, who whispered out of the corner of his mouth.

"I thought you said her dog was tiny."

"He was," Varick replied in the same fashion. "This isn't the same one."

Megaera looked back to them. "Apologies, what was that?"

"Cute dog." The words left Varick's mouth before he had cleared them for exit. "I mean… where's Lionheart?" Was that suspicious to ask?

Whether it was or not, Megaera seemed not to have noticed. She crouched down to face the lanky beast—it was not a far trip—and gave it a good, double-handed scritching all around its ears.

"This is Harefoot," she cooed. "His breed originates in Duskwood, so I thought it would be nice for him to see his homeland. Isn't that right, my sweet princeling?"

Harefoot responded with a lolling tongue and a prolific effusion of warm doggy breath, which fogged in the cold morning air.

"Lionheart," Carver pondered aloud. "Harefoot. Are all your dogs named for an animal and a feature?"

Megaera looked at him and smiled again. "Well spotted. There's also Bat Ears, Bearhide, Piglet Tail—I call her Piggy for short—Robin Redbreast, and Skunkbreath. Halitosis, I'm afraid." Megaera blinked at Carver before adding, "Apologies, but who are you?"

"Ah! This is my secretary." Varick hurried to recover. "I should have introduced you. Apologies. Auntie Megaera, meet Mister Archibald Sweeney."

"I am absolutely delighted to make your acquaintance," Carver said, smooth as silk as he extended a hand. "Mister Pendragon's told me so much about you. It's an honor to meet such a legend."

Megaera chuckled. "The only thing legendary about me is my age, I assure you."

Carver gave her a smile that said all over, "nonsense," but before he could speak again, Harefoot booped his long, skinny head under Carver's outstretched hand as if to say, "My turn. Give me love. Now, please."

Megaera looked over Varick properly for the first time. "Is this it then?"

"Noooo." Varick looked meaningfully at Carver. "My valet should be coming too. Ca-ah-Archibald, where *is* my valet?"

He'd been so concerned with being discovered and then the gigantic dog, he'd rather forgotten about Mercury's role.

Panic momentarily flickered in Carver's eyes. His voice, however, rang with the determined tone of a man on a mission. "I… will find out for you."

With that, Carver zipped off.

Megaera's eyes roved over Varick again. "He didn't carry you bag for you?"

Varick remembered the one saddlebag hanging over his shoulder, the only one he'd declined to hand over to the porters earlier. He groaned internally. This whole bally trip was off to a great start, just fantastic. At least he could be honest when he answered her.

He made a face that said, "Strange, I know, but…" before actually saying, "I prefer to carry some things myself."

Megaera nodded approvingly. "I understand. I'm afraid I'm a bit of a clothes horse myself. Please don't judge me when you see how many trunks the porters deliver to my suite."

Varick nearly laughed as he replied, "Only if you promise the same. Must be a family trait."

"Your grandfather would approve." They shared a quiet moment of bittersweet silence, as if giving Randolph's spirit space to join them. Then, when it felt right, Megaera said, "Shall we then?"

She gestured toward the airship platforms high above them and the station. They rode a funicular to the platforms and soon found the *Angrec's Respite* amongst the other zeppelins docked beside long, raised jetties.

The airship was breathtaking, to be sure. The envelope shone a snowy white in the morning sun, and the huge steamboat-styled gondola beneath it had been painted a demure green between and around the panes of gleaming glass that encapsulated the passenger decks. The green flowed down and over the entire hull, within which, Varick assumed, much of the behind-the-scenes work happened. That, and more importantly, where the guests' most valuable possessions would be stored. Propellers stuck out off the backs of the envelope and the gondola, but they'd been cleverly fashioned to resemble the star-shaped nectar spurs of the Angrec orchid.

As soon as Varick and Auntie Megaera made themselves known as passengers of the great airship, airrocrew members began falling over themselves to assist with embarkation. More than once, someone offered to take Varick's bag, but he politely refused each time. Also more than once, people felt the need to tell him what great work he was doing with the Turnip Network. He wanted to confess that he hadn't done anything except neglect and then set the innocent place aflame, but he opted to try and keep things moving instead and simply thanked each person.

Beneath his greatcoat, Varick was sweating. Where had Carver gone? Where was Mercury? Were the trunks containing Coal and Fulcrum and Marlowe already aboard? What if they ran into problems or got left behind by accident? This was a terrible plan. And worst of all, it'd been *his*.

Harefoot tried to help by leaning against Varick. When one was the size of a pony, however, it rather came with a good deal of heft, and Varick had to push back on the well-meaning canine to prevent himself from being toppled.

Following directions provided by the keen gent who'd stamped their boarding paperwork, Varick and Megaera found their rooms with ease.

Everything was soft. The bed linens, the lines of the furniture, the subtly patterned wallpaper. No scratchy textures or sharp corners dared to threaten discomfort to any esteemed passenger. The colors too were bright as a jewel box, but not garish. The latest in heating technology—radiators—had been installed for when the airship ascended to the frigid climes of the troposphere. An enclosed glass balcony, replete with both heavy, light-blocking curtains and lacy sheers, and sporting the same wood-paneled floors as the cabin, jutted out from the wall, letting light pour in. Varick and Megaera had matching suites. Each of their sitting rooms, which were connected by a door that could be locked from Megaera's side, stretched large enough to comfortably host half a dozen. In the bedroom, which was closed off behind a door, at least three Varicks would have been able to fit in the splendid two-poster bed—only two because the headboard was built into the cabin wall. So too was all the other furniture. There was even a tub in the bathroom with two clawed outer feet, though that did make it look as if the wall was slowly enveloping the tub.

The staff quarters attached to each suite were considerably smaller. A set of bunk beds filled one wall, a door to a water closet plus a pair of sinks surrounded by efficient cabinetry took up the next, and a clever sofa-table-and-shelves combination comprised the third.

Varick looked around the magnificent cabin. Yes, this would do nicely. There would certainly be plenty of space for his entire crew. Well, *Mercury's* crew, he supposed, assuming the man ever showed up. And in Megaera's space, Harefoot would have plenty of room just for him. That made a nice replacement for the cupboard he'd been planning to store Lionheart in if it came to it. During their correspondences, Varick had learned, as he'd suspected, that Auntie Megaera, like her brother, did without staff as much as possible, so no unwanted nosiness from that angle either. Now there was nothing left to do but wait for his errant companions to arrive.

33

SAFE SPACES

he rest of the *Angrec's Respite* was every bit as grandiose and immaculate as the cabins. As their luggage had yet to arrive, Auntie Megaera suggested they go for a wander. They started at the top, on the Sun deck. Varick was pleased the ship's designers had gone in for practical, descriptive deck names. He could easily see some clodpole, convinced of his own genius, wanting to name them according to something arbitrary and florid, like gemstones or woodgrains or some such.

They'd looked in at the the pilot house up on the Sun deck, where they'd learned that various ship tours were available throughout the day. The gymnasiums—one for men and one for the ladies—were up here as well, stocked with exercise machines like the ones at the Dragon's Keep, as well as airrocrew members ready to assist passengers with their calisthenic routines. Varick might have to pop in for a workout or two. He was proud of the physique he'd built up over the last few months and wanted to keep it up. He also noticed quite a few officers up here, mostly standing around to answer questions and welcome passengers. Auntie Megaera struck up a lively conversation with one, at which point Varick learned that, once the airship took off, they'd all be busy, but for now, they were all too pleased to relax and enjoy the fine company of their passengers. Many an unattached young lady, judging by the lack of certain rings on their fingers, seemed to be enjoying the officers' company as well.

"Good on them," Megaera whispered to Varick. "One could do worse than bag a luxury cruise line officer." Together, they began to surreptitiously cheer the young ladies on in their quests, intermixed with an entertaining exchange of thoughts and predictions on the hopeful matches.

The Promenade deck was meant to be yet another place for passengers to get exercise, in this case by taking turns around the perimeter of the ship. It was a grand place for being seen and seeing what everyone else was wearing or to whom they'd attached themselves. Below that sat the Observation deck, which was taller than than the others and sported more windows. It also housed the main dining room, as well as a few lounges, again, some for men and others for women, but a few for mixed company as well.

Varick saw card rooms and smoking rooms, a long art gallery where passengers could purchase any piece that caught their eye, entertainment halls, a ballroom, and a library. All of which had been cleverly designed and arranged to slot neatly into spaces yet not undermine the spectacle of each place. The atrium, into which boarding passengers were strategically funneled, stretched three stories high. The roof of this was painted with scenes of airships floating over picturesque vistas of various sorts—the lush, verdant swath of jungle known as the Green Dragon in the south, just outside of Bone Port; Springhaven's polished Rose, Ivory, and Copper quarters, with the city gardens gloriously featured; the sharp, snowy peaks of the Bladed Mountains north of

Duskwood. At last, near the bottom of the ship, they began seeing more and more signs marked, AIRSHIP STAFF ONLY—these were signs to the boiler room, crew quarters decks, and other sundry places meant not meant for passengers.

"We ought to go back up," Megaera said. "We take off in about an hour, and I wouldn't mind watching with a drink in hand from that place with the constellations on the ceiling."

"Just a moment." Varick didn't look at her when he spoke. His eyes were on a particular sign: VAULT ROOM. A slender arrow painted beneath it indicated the direction. "I'd like to see what they offer in the way of safes."

"Alright, off we go then."

Varick cursed himself. He should have chosen his words more carefully. "You don't have to come. I can meet you up there if you'd like." When she hesitated, disappointment in her eyes— he couldn't imagine what she might be wondering given their family history—he gave her a bright smile and added, "Watching take off with you sounds marvelous. I'm excited for it. I'll be there, I promise."

Most of the disappointment eked back out of Megaera's eyes, and she smiled back. "Very well. I'll see you there."

Varick found the room easily. Within, a small, thickset man sat inside a glass-windowed booth. He had a counter on his side, neat as a pin, and a round grate had been set into the glass to allow for easy passage of speech between the two sides. Varick spied a plain wooden door at the back of the booth and a little placard attached to the booth's window that read, *This glass is alarmed; do not break.*

Varick smiled to himself at the obvious joke, something about the glass being frightened.

He suspected he was not lucky enough for the wooden door to lead to the vault, but it was good to think about possibilities. Walls stretched off on either side of the little office—austere, nothing more than more subtly patterned wallpaper, a bit of art, and a few tasteful petrolsene sconces decorated it. A door set into one of the walls. Not wood, but metal—thick and heavy and opened not by a handle but by a hatch wheel. Six miniature levers, all of which were currently set to the down position, sat above a keyhole shaped like a plus sign, all of which practically screamed that this must be the vault door.

The very door Varick and Carver were tasked with getting intel on.

Varick armed himself with his most charming smile. He said hello to the man and asked him his name and how he was doing, all things his grandfather had always done before making a request of anyone.

"Mister Dilley," the man said with the cool but practiced geniality of a man who often worked with wealthy, and therefore usually demanding, people. "How may I help you today?"

"I have some valuables I'd like stored, please," Varick told the man. "Could I perchance see my options?"

"Of course, Mister Pendragon," Mister Dilley replied.

Varick cringed internally. He'd not given his name, and the man was certainly keen to assist. He was already opening the door within his tiny office and summoning someone else from whatever space lay beyond—a Mister Eaddy. Peeking past the wooden door, Varick spied another small, spartan office space.

The man that emerged from that room, Mister Eaddy, was tall and lean, with a thin mustache and the sort of look of someone who made assessments all day, whether it be items or people. It was the work of a moment for him to open a door of glass and wood, seamlessly worked into the wall of the booth, and emerge next to the vault door. Varick heard a telltale click from the hidden booth door, and he suspected it locked automatically.

"Good day, Mister Pendragon," Mister Eaddy said. He applied the sort of affectation to his speech Varick had heard from toffiest of toffee-nosed men. He both lengthened certain syllables and added emphasis onto others, dragging the listener over verbal hurdles as they went. "I'll be very happy to guide you through our vault services. If you'll follow me."

Varick began to step forward when an idea struck him. He feigned a trip, allowing himself to fall to one knee before catching himself on the floor.

"I say," he blustered, "what is that? Why, there's a loose floorboard here. That's awfully dangerous, isn't it? Someone could really hurt themselves."

Mister Eaddy minced over and began to help Varick up. Varick resisted the urge to jerk away as the man gripped his elbow, apologizing profusely.

"We'll have the floor checked right away, Mister Pendragon, I assure you," Mister Eaddy said. To the man in the office, he called, "Dilley! Dilley, make it happen, if you please."

Dilley jumped to action, heading for a pneumatic tube receptacle attached to the side wall of his booth. Varick saw the option Maintenance get ticked under the Recipient section of a triplicate form Mister Dilley began filling out, while Mister Eaddy dusted nonexistent dirt from Varick's knee with a tiny brush he'd produced from somewhere.

While the maintenance request went zipping up and away through the pneumatic tube—with an impressive *shoop!* sound no less—Varick decided to stick with congeniality for now. He assured both men that he was fine and no harm done. Seemingly satisfied, Mister Eaddy asked for a moment, walked over to the vault door, and blocked sight of the small lever arrangement with his body.

Varick had no hope of unsuspiciously catching sight of it by simply peeking over the man's shoulder, so he pretended to be respecting the man's security measures by examining a bronze greyhound statuette sitting nearby. He'd write down everything he observed at his first opportunity, and he focused his senses. His ears pricked at the sound of the tiny levers clicking into place. More than six movements sounded, but he clocked a variance in the noise between the first he'd heard—when all the levers had been set to the down position—and the fifth noise. He suspected the first four levers had been clicked upward and that the fifth sound was a lever being returned to the down position. And, no, he certainly was *not* about to credit his grandmother and her years of forcing him to learn scales and to play by ear. Rather, he listened even harder and tried to pinpoint the location of each noise in order to puzzle out which lever might be in motion. It was no good now, but when he came back, he knew what to listen for.

At the end, after seven movements—four up, if he'd guessed correctly, and three down—the turn of cogs resounded, followed by a click as of some mechanism inside the door releasing. As Varick pretended to wind his watch, in his periphery he saw Mister Eaddy remove an X-shaped key from his pocket. A twist of the key one way, a quarter turn on the hatch wheel, the sound of more gears moving. Another twist of the key in the opposite direction, another turn on the wheel, then repeat once more before a final spin of the hatch. Varick heard a thump somewhere inside the wall—maybe a counterweight falling? He didn't know how these things worked—and the *clunk* of a heavy bar sliding back hard. Mister Eaddy pushed open the door, and for a split second Varick was able to partially catch sight of the levers. The first two were pointing up! Then Mister Eaddy's hand was pushing all six of them back down and gesturing Varick inside. On his way, he gave the arrangement a closer glance. It appeared the levers only had the two positions, up and down. He certainly hoped it was no more complicated than that.

The vault room was simple—walls lined in safes of various sizes, some as small as a letterbox opening and a few large enough to hold a person. The far wall was all windows and a pair of finely suited gents so tall and thickly shouldered that Varick suspected they had to watch themselves when going through doorways. One of the large window casements behind the men was open, allowing a window washer outside in a bosun's chair to buff the panes to an even sparklier shine than before. He held onto a thick canvas strap attached to the side of the ship.

"Is that safe?" Varick uttered the words without thinking. Thank goodness they were still docked. Anyone who'd try operating the bosun's chair while the airship was in flight must have a death wish.

Mister Eaddy smiled mildly at the man. "Not to worry, Mister Pendragon. All the cleaners are part of our staff and have had extensive background checks."

Varick had actually been referring to the window washer's safety, given that his rigging appeared as barely more than a couple strips of thick canvas, wooden rods, pulleys, and ropes suspended from somewhere above, but he didn't bother to correct Mister Eaddy. He couldn't imagine anyone trying anything with Hulk One and Hulk Two standing right there. Varick gulped as he thought of the plan. True, they were planning on using laudanum on these gents—or, if not them, some of their equally large cohorts—but each was quite a lot of person to take out with just a few little syringes and some sponges soaked in… whatever Fulcrum had planned. And true, Marlowe was a big lad, but if push came to shove, in a very literal way, these two were twice as many as Marlowe and three times as large when put together.

"He does tricks as well," Mister Eaddy was saying. To the window washer, he called, "You chappie, show us a trick or two."

The man tipped his flat cap obligingly and, with a great thrust of his legs, he pushed off from the casement. Cleaning tools still in hand, he spun in the air, twisting his ropes one way, swung back, and then repeated the move in the opposite direction to untwist them. Varick watched with his heart in his throat, terrified that the gent would at any moment suffer an accident just to entertain some puffed up, rich pillocks. The window washer ended the little routine by bowing at a forty-five degree angle from the window casement before returning to work. Varick was beyond impressed. He'd bounced up and down between buildings, but the cleaner was on the starboard side of the airship, opposite the jetty and hundreds of feet up in the air, yet he hadn't blinked or shown any sign of fear. Stars, the poor man must be asked to do this sort of thing all the time.

"Don't you find it nicer seeing the help, if they must be seen, providing a bit of entertainment while they're there?" Mister Eaddy asked. "Illustrious guests such as yourself often do."

I prefer to see people be allowed to work, with dignity and respect, and be paid fairly for it, Varick thought. He preferred to tell Mister Eaddy he was a great fathead. He preferred the idea of going over to the window washer, asking him his name, and shaking his hand for the incredible skill and bravery he'd just shown. All of these would draw attention and talk, though, two things Varick very much wanted less of, especially on this trip. So instead he settled for asking about the process for storing and safeguarding valuables.

While the window washer finished up and one of the security goliaths re-latched the window, Mister Eaddy fell into a well-practiced explanation. Two members of their rotating security detail were present at all times, and every safe had its own custom client key, just as Carver had said was likely the case. But, happy days, backup client keys were stored in a locked cabinet inside the back office. Varick smiled at that. Someone somewhere at Prism Line had anticipated the highly probable eventuality that client keys would be lost or forgotten, as well as the tantrums that would follow. That made Coal's workload much lighter indeed. And, also as Carver had said, a universal guard key was also needed to open the safes.

"So you see, Mister Pendragon," Mister Eaddy said, "Only with both keys working in tandem can your valuables be accessed. It's an extremely secure system."

Varick nodded approvingly, though his mind was unsettled. He needed to see where this guard key lived. He thought back to the adventure novels he'd read—always hidden from his family members because the Pendragons believed fiction rotted one's critical thinking skills. In a few of them, people had made key copies out of bars of soap. He suspected Coal had a similar idea for the vault key, but what if he needed to pinch the guard key off of Mister Eaddy and make a copy of it too? Coal was good, but getting two different key copies seemed too big a risk. And on top of that, how was he going to copy an X-shaped key?

Varick worried for Mercury's job, but at least Coal and Fulcrum were getting out of Springhaven. Even if this job failed, that was a victory in itself, wasn't it? He hoped it would be enough, but in the back of his mind, hard facts whispered that it wouldn't. That was assuming they'd made it aboard at all. He wanted to go back to his room and check, but Auntie Megaera was waiting for him.

Trust Carver, he told himself. *Carver was handling it.*

Varick found this difficult, given that he'd only ever trusted a select few people in his life—well, one really. This was real now. The game was on, and he felt the pressure of it on his shoulders, inside his head. The challenge of it felt good. He wanted to win, like he had at the casino night. At the same time, though, it also made him want to take control of all the pieces on the board. But no. He couldn't play all the parts. And, as Varick headed back up, deck after deck, past the one containing his cabin, he reminded himself of all that his crew had accomplished thus far. It was only that which allowed him to put one foot in front of the other and his faith in other people.

Varick wished the airship would just bloody well take off. It would be a welcome distraction from combing the jetty below for ominously familiar trunks which ought to have already been brought on board, or, possibly worse, family members. He kept reminding himself that he'd set things up well at home and that Carver and the rest of the crew had things in hand. They were all capable in their own ways. Well, maybe not Mercury, but if he hadn't made it on board, no great tragedy there. Varick knew the plan; he could easily step in for their so-called "mastermind." Which led Varick to thinking about what adjustments he'd have to make to his own part if it came to that. He had to leave off when Megaera asked him if everything was alright.

"Of course," he said, a tad too brightly. He only just stopped himself from unnecessarily adding, "Why wouldn't it be?"

They were tucked up in the lounge Megaera had mentioned and had managed to snag a table next to the windows. Here on the Observation deck, there was no walkway around the perimeter, which meant no pesky pedestrians to obstruct their view. As she'd observed, constellations decorated the deep blue ceiling with dashed white lines.

Megaera gave Varick a weak smile. "I don't mean to fuss. I hope you'll forgive me. Growing up in an environment like I did, well, like we both did, can make one a little…"

She let the words trail off and gave an elegant little half-shrug. She changed in that moment, right before Varick's eyes. It was like in the restaurant they'd gone to for lunch the day of Varick's visa interview. His great aunt had been wounded. She'd been a child denied even the most basic needs of love and security. And though she'd put herself back together—a thing worth celebrating all on its own, to be sure—scars remained. Varick turned away from thoughts of how that same treatment had affected him. He didn't like thinking the way he'd turned out was somehow incorrect or broken. But with Great Auntie Megaera, he could see what she was saying. She was extending vulnerability.

Which Varick hadn't the foggiest how to respond to.

As if she knew precisely how ill-equipped her great-nephew was for this moment, she tossed him a lifeline.

"I was beyond pleased when I received your invitation to join you on this trip. Thank you. I'm quite looking forward to spending this time together, and getting to know you better. Better than what Randolph wrote in his letters, I mean."

Her weak smile went lopsided, and Varick had another realization. *She feels awkward, but she's trying. Does that really never go away, even when you're her age?*

Something else tugged at his memory, though. "But you nearly said no. Rather, you sort of did, until I bullied you into it anyway."

Megaera chuckled and scratched Harefoot behind an ear. "I'd hardly call that bullying, but I was worried I'd ruin your fun."

"Why," Varick asked. "I wouldn't have been able to come if not for you. That would have been far worse."

She spread her hands. "I am an old woman, Varick. I won't be able to keep up with whatever shenanigans you mean to get into."

Varick laughed. If she only knew. Though he wasn't trying to flatter her either when he said, "You seem plenty spry." He hesitated a moment before adding in a sort of hopeful question, "For your age?"

Now it was Megaera's turn to laugh. "Thank you, dear. I do what I can."

He heard, however, what she wasn't saying in the downturn of her reply. She knew her time was coming. Having lived as long as she had, she was an anomaly, just as Randolph had been.

He gave her an encouraging smile. "I can only hope I'm as sprightly and sassy as you when I get there." A moment of thought and Varick added, "And half as tough until then. You are a paragon of resilience." He lifted his glass, offering a toast.

"To being sprightly and sassy and tough, all our days," Megaera agreed.

They clinked their glasses and fell into easier conversations. As airros below unmoored the ship in a complicated dance, Megaera shared what little she knew of the process and what to expect. Enforcers would have searched the cargo holds for stowaways just before they left, and the captain would be up in the pilot house right now, giving orders and ensuring a safe liftoff. Apparently this was as tricky as landing, what with the huge fireboxes in the airship's belly needing to be fed shovelfuls of coal very precisely to ensure a slow, controlled rise, but not so little that they didn't get enough pressure to power the engines, which allowed the humongous vessel to be steered.

With every foot they ascended, Varick felt his own spirits buoyed. He'd done it! He'd escaped his wretched family and was off on an adventure. He refused to think about the trouble of his return in just under a week. For now, he reveled in the feeling of being free. Springhaven gathered below them as they rose, laid out beneath them like jewels in a chest. The city's outlying farms began to appear next, those heavily-monitored spaces that ringed the vast city-state and ensured it had enough to eat. All up and down and along the sides of the ship, canvas straps like the one the window washer from earlier had held onto, fluttered in the wind, as if celebrating the launch and waving bon voyage to the world below. Varick didn't even realize he'd been leaning closer and closer to the window until his nose pressed against it. His breath fogged the glass, and he wiped it away with one deft swipe of his sleeve, not wanting to miss a moment.

He couldn't bring himself to turn away. The sight was too

fantastic, too precious. He'd seen artists' renderings of this, but nothing compared to really seeing it, in the moment and all happening right now, right below him.

"I did tell you travel was an invigorating experience," Great Auntie Megaera said from her seat. Just in his periphery, he could see her gazing down far more demurely. "If you don't mind me saying so."

Varick nodded, unable to find words, and watched on as the world opened before him.

34

SEX, MURDER, AND SNACK TIME

When Varick and Auntie Megaera finally headed back to their rooms, it was to dress for dinner. They'd ended up enjoying a casual lunch in the little lounge and then explored a few more places they'd missed on their first foray around the airship.

Varick's door was first on their path, and he opened it to a sight that gave him a deeply mixed collection of feelings. Bold as brass, the lot of them! Coal leaned against the radiator; Marlowe sat straddled on the arm of the sofa; and sprawled halfway to upside down on it, with his feet *along the top of it, right where people's heads went*—the git—was Fulcrum. They were chatting and eating something, though Varick couldn't see what, given how he immediately snapped the door shut again. It didn't quite slam, but nearly there.

"Everything alright?" Megaera asked.

"I'm great. Everything is great." Varick scrambled to recover. "I… thought I felt a sneeze coming on. Wait…" He lifted a finger

in the air, and then gave his best pretend sneeze. "Apologies. I'm sorted now."

Megaera gave him a funny sort of smile. "Alright then. I'll see you in a bit."

With that, she unlocked her cabin and went inside, Harefoot at her heels. Once the latch had clicked behind her, Varick practically threw himself into the room and leaned against the door.

"What are you all doing?!" he demanded in a strained shout-whisper combination.

"Wotcha!" Coal replied, with an especially cheeky salute.

"Shhh!" Varick shushed him. He walked over. "We have to be quiet. My aunt is in the next room over."

"Really?" Coal asked. "You'd think they'd take steps to keep sound from traveling. What if there was a honeymooning couple in here? You know, doing *stuff*."

"V's probably being paranoid," Fulcrum said. Then, he shouted toward the ceiling, completely deadpan. "Help. I'm being murdered. Knives. Knives everywhere."

They all waited, but nothing happened. If anyone had heard, they seemed to have decided to let someone else have the pleasure of facing a ubiquity of blades.

"Not a good test," Marlowe said, moving the thing he was chewing around to the inside of his cheek. "Again, but this time, add screaming."

Fulcrum opened his mouth, but Varick interjected before he could make a start.

"No! No screaming." Only then did he notice the package sitting on the sofa arm before Marlowe. That was some awfully fancy packaging. "What are you eating? Asphaug's Finest Reindeer… Jerky?"

"Hah! Ass fog," Coal snorted.

Fulcrum and Marlowe laughed, while Varick tried to figure

out what jerky was. He'd never heard of such a thing. The paper box was lined with butcher's paper and what lay within looked like strips of poorly tanned leather. He looked to Coal. He had a small tin of smoked herring sitting next to him on the radiator, and a slim jar of a pickles jutted out of his trouser pocket. Meanwhile, Fulcrum was eating small, doughy puffs of something out of a box that sat comfortably atop his stomach. Varick couldn't see the name of it, but that also wasn't his primary concern at the moment.

"Where…" Varick looked around and saw a brutally picked over gift basket sitting on a small occasional table attached to one wall. A card next to it read,

Enjoy these Duskwood specialties, with our compliments. Welcome aboard!

Sincerely,
Prism Line Air Cruises

Varick's first reaction was to complain, but he checked himself. He'd hardly spent the day stuffed inside a trunk and hauled about like a… well… a piece of luggage.

"Where are the trunks?" he asked, continuing aloud the conversation that had just been happening in his head.

"Bedroom," Marlowe said.

He was about to ask more questions when a frantic scrabbling noise started up from the other side of the door connecting his and Megaera's suites. Drawing close, he could just hear Megaera's voice trying to get Harefoot to settle. He thought he made out the words, "nothing there," and then, after a bit more one-sided discussion he couldn't quite make out, "Oh, very well." A second later came a sharp rapping.

Varick jumped and called, "Coming," but his voice cracked on the word. He spun, motioning wildly for his contraband crew members to get into the bedroom. They hoofed in inside and slid the pocket door closed behind them. It sounded like Harefoot was fairly destroying the connector door, which Varick opened, only to then be knocked aside by the huge animal loping inside.

Megaera's apologies followed in the dog's wake. "I'm so sorry, dear. I don't know what's gotten into him."

Varick watched the last half of Coal's smoked herring get into Harefoot, as he easily shoved his snout into the tin and half snorted, half inhaled the things, oil and all. By rote, Varick told her not to worry about it, even as he was extremely worried about it. Marlowe and Fulcrum had left with their snacks in hand, and Harefoot was already following the trail, snuffling his way toward the bedroom door. Varick trotted over, kicking the now-empty herring tin under the radiator as he went, and grabbed the giant dog by the shoulders. Is this how you moved a dog? Only then did he remember that Harefoot was big enough to bite off entire fingers. He lifted his hands, only for Harefoot to turn on him and shove his skull between Varick's palms. The dog had placed himself into the perfect position for ear stritchies, and Varick found himself automatically obliging.

How did I get here? he wondered vaguely to himself.

"Alright, you little cur," Megaera said affectionately. "You've made yourself enough of a nuisance for now. Let's go."

She gave a few more apologies and shut the connector door behind her and Harefoot. Varick then slipped into the bedroom to find everyone dropping crumbs, dried meat shrapnel, and pickle juice, respectively, onto the coverlet.

He gave the trio an incredulous look. "This is not hiding."

"Door's closed," Fulcrum informed him.

"I thought you were going to get back into your trunks." Varick motioned at the stand of variously-sized containers.

"Why?" Marlowe asked.

"I…" Varick trailed off with a sigh. It probably wasn't worth the argument. "Alright, well just stay in here then. Remember, we can't risk my aunt seeing you."

"She sounds nice," Coal observed. "I wanna meet her dog."

"Sorry," Varick said, absolutely not sorry.

"Aren't you supposed to be getting dressed?" Fulcrum asked. "You want us in here for that?"

Varick took a deep breath. How did the bloody tinkerer know just what buttons to push? "No," he said slowly. Then realization dawned. *Someone* was supposed to be here for that, on paper anyway. "Where's Mercury? And Carver?"

Coal lifted another pickle above his head, jaws wide like a shark. He asked, "Aren't they with you?" before lowering it with an enthusiastic, "Ar rawr rawr rawr!" and devouring it in one bite.

"Does it look like they're with me?" Varick asked.

The three just stared at him.

"Nevermind," he said. He opened his saddle bags and began to unpack his things. He'd brought the bare minimum but had chosen versatile items, most of which he'd made himself. Varick extracted a striped hatbox large enough for a top hat. He scrutinized it before carefully placing it safely at the back of his wardrobe. Meanwhile, an uncomfortable silence filled the space behind him.

At last, Fulcrum asked, "So you don't know where they are?"

"No." Varick's voice was low.

He knew what Fulcrum was getting at. Without Carver and Mercury, they didn't think they could pull off the job. Fulcrum and Coal would get out of Springhaven, but they'd be starting out with naught but the clothes on their backs. This was hardly the fresh start they'd wanted. Varick didn't know how much Marlowe cared about this job, but he must have been looking forward to the payout.

"Mercury didn't show up this morning," Varick explained.

"Carver went to go look for him and I haven't seen him since."

More silence. It grated on Varick. This was a good thing, wasn't it? They didn't need Mercury! Those hard facts that had whispered in the back of his head that morning woke back up, and they were no longer whispering. Well, Varick could give the crew, um, a little something. He hadn't brought oodles of valuables with him. Nor even much cash, not enough to start a new life anyway. Prism Line Air Cruises had a convenient credit system set up. Heaven forfend that guests didn't get to spend just because of a little thing like not having physical money with them.

No, they needed the money that would come from this job. The fear of what would happen if things went wrong returned to settle on Varick's shoulders. He grumbled inwardly. This didn't need to be his problem. He wasn't the one who had let their team down. He couldn't deny that he wanted to help Coal and Fulcrum and the rest of the crew, though. And that same feeling of challenge, of wanting to win, came back alongside the pressure of getting caught. The idea of taking on Mercury's role, which had germinated in his mind earlier, had begun to put out shoots, tendriling this way and that.

They could do this by themselves. What was Mercury even bringing to the table anyway? He might not actually be the scoundrel Varick had initially thought he was, before the gift of the mini-airship model and the night of the fire, but Mercury wasn't a good leader either. He didn't take care of his people the way he should, but Varick could. As he envisioned them succeeding, all on their own, he couldn't stop the little smirk that turned up in the corner of his mouth.

He turned slowly, lifted his eyes to meet their gazes. Marlowe's expression had closed off, but Fulcrum and Coal's brows pinched.

"Don't worry," Varick said slowly. "We'll stick to the plan.

I'll make sure it all works out."

Dinner that evening was a sumptuous affair. All the guests were dressed in their best finery, eager to make a grand first impression. Gowns and suits and jewels and ruffles and bows and rosettes and top hats filled the room, flashing their fabulosity like tropical fish in a coral reef. Prism Line Air Cruises, too, meant to put their best foot forward here on their first night.

Seven courses were served, each more delectable than the last. A plate of oysters with naught but a lemon to dress them, if the diner so desired. Then came beef bouillon, followed by some fish Varick wasn't at all interested in—he'd never liked fish and had spent his life perfecting the art of discretely disposing of it when it had been served to him at dinner. He'd even sewn special pockets into his clothes for secreting it into to discard later. It was all fine and good for Patricia, Victoria, and Henry to push away a dish, but the children weren't permitted. For the main, the airship's kitchen staff had prepared crown roasts of lamb, which were presented whole at table and then cut apart. Potatoes and autumnal vegetables sautéed in duck fat accompanied the roast. The salad that came next was cool and crisp and crunchy with a tangy dressing, the perfect follow-up to the rich courses that had preceded it. Dessert came next, which consisted of pears poached in red wine with a chocolate sauce artfully drizzled over them. At last, plates of cheese, nuts, and small, rich chocolates were laid out. Great Auntie Megaera had a sherry with the her after-meal nibbles and was explaining how some of her favorite sorts were aged on airships just like this one. They were called airsick sherries, which Varick might have found amusing if he'd been listening.

He'd split his attention that evening between chatting with

his aunt and searching for their mark—Spindle. He'd assumed he'd spot her quickly. Blonde hair, slight build, though no one knew how old she was now. No one had known when she'd stolen the Nightfall Crown twenty years ago either. But how hard could it be to spot one woman in a dining room? After all, he'd even seen a rendering. But that was before he'd gotten in here and saw what two-hundred people in one room looked like. Two-hundred was all the *Angrec's Respite* permitted, staff not included. And while obviously no staff supped with the guests— "Can you imagine?" Varick could hear his parents say—there suddenly seemed a preponderance of waiters crossing this way and that. One always seemed to be bringing a drink or answering a beckoning hand or clearing something away. And two were even flirting with each other from across the room when when they thought no one was looking.

"Are you alright, Varick?" Auntie Megaera asked at one point. "You seem rather distracted."

"Perfectly." He gave her a smile. He'd been prepared for this, keeping the explanation in his back pocket for just such an occasion. "I'm just observing the dinner service, to see how it all functions. Didn't I tell you I wanted to look into doing this myself?"

"Being a waiter?" Auntie Megaera asked this without a hint of judgement, only open curiosity, the same way Randolph used to do. On the floor next to her, Harefoot gave a little groan. "Or were you thinking of being a chef?"

Varick gestured vaguely at the dining room and beyond. "No, running one of these. A cruise line."

"Interesting. And would you be designing the ships?"

"Stars, no!" Varick and Megaera both shared a chuckle. "I have neither the passion nor the mechanical aptitude, but I like business. I like the strategy of it, looking for gaps that need filling, and I like the idea of placing good people in roles where they can shine and thrive."

Auntie Megaera leaned forward. She had more questions about the prospect, and Varick found he deeply enjoyed the discussion. He used the dinner they were currently enjoying as an example, pointing out things he thought worked well and ideas he suspected might make it even better. The exercise allowed him to keep searching the crowd for Spindle as well, though he failed to find her in the sea of diners.

"I'd want to run affordable voyages, though," he said. "Holidays like this shouldn't be limited to wealthy numpties like us."

Auntie Megaera laughed at that too, and Varick wondered if perhaps this ruse might actually be something he wanted to make a reality.

After dinner, a welcome reception was being held in the art gallery. Megaera had expressed interest in going, but Harefoot's little groans beneath the table had become smelly grunts, and she'd left with him after the cheese course before, as she put it, things got "unfortunate."

In the gallery, glasses of bubbly circulated the room and fizzed as much as the eager passengers. Alone now, Varick was free to wander and search for Spindle. He pretended to appreciate the various works of art on display as he slowly circled the room. He still didn't see her and was beginning to get worried. The plan could work even if they didn't know in which safe the Nightfall Crown had been stored, but it would take time to search each one.

Varick felt a little prickle of anxiety in the back of his mind. This was his job now; he couldn't muck it up. Coal, Fulcrum, and Marlowe were all off on their own missions. Coal was posing as a laundry boy in order to steal some uniforms. Fulcrum was back in the cabin doing some prep. Varick had told him what he'd learned and seen down in the vault room earlier that day, and

Fulcrum hadn't been worried about the X-shaped key. He had a plan for that. As for the rest, they all needed to gather what information they could about the levers and the guard key and all that. Marlowe was sitting tight until he got his hands on a staff uniform, at which point he'd find out where the vault security blokes liked to hang out in their off-hours time and start getting chummy with them—shift rotations, pain points, anything that might be helpful, Marlowe would be their new best mate, happy to lend a sympathetic ear.

And speaking of his various crew members, Varick spied a familiar figure in the arched entryway to an arcade of shops, all still open and eager to receive potential shoppers, especially those a little tipsy on bubbly.

Carver. At last!

He wasn't really trying to hide, but he was clearly trying to be inconspicuous. He was dressed in one of the suits they'd procured for him to play the part of secretary, and Varick gave a subtle nod to indicate he could come closer.

Carver sidled up to Varick and admitted in a whisper, "I didn't know the protocol about assistants here. Are these all guests?" What he didn't say, but Varick heard loud and clear was, "I *really* need to talk to you." Otherwise, why would he have been lingering in that doorway?

"Pretty much," Varick mumbled, hiding behind a flute of ginger beer. Prism Line Air Cruises seemed to have thought of everything, and this was one of several options for teetotalers and the like. In a more normal voice, he added, "Walk with me. There are some pieces I'm interested in buying."

And so Carver joined Varick on his slow, thoughtful circuit around the room. They fell into a sort of code as they went.

Pointing to a blonde woman depicted in one of the paintings, Carver asked, "Have you already seen this piece?" Translation: "Have you put eyes on Spindle yet?"

"No," Varick replied. He pointed to a portrait of a man next to it. "But I have questions about this one." Translation: "Do you have news on Mercury?"

"I'm familiar with it, if you'd like me to answer them."

And so the conversation went. Carver had seen Mercury and, yes, he was on board. "That's why I was so keen to find you this evening," Carver said. "It's an *exceptional* work."

Varick's eyebrows drew together in confusion before he could stop them. Carver had news, specifically about Mercury, news that couldn't wait until Varick had gotten back to his room.

"Tell me more," Varick said, giving Carver a meaningful look.

Carver motioned vaguely at the painting. "It appears the artist reconnected with an old friend shortly after setting off to create this piece, his greatest life's work."

"Actually, I believe you're thinking of the artist Charles Donegal," came a voice from beside them. A young man had joined them at the painting. He was possibly a few years older than them and held a glass of bubbly in one hand while using the other to push his spectacles up his nose. He went on, "An easy mistake to make, given how both this and Donegal's work are shamelessly derivative of Okorafor's. This one was—"

"Literally no one was asking you," Varick snapped.

The man huffed and muttered something about Pendragons and rudeness before wandering off.

"That's right, we're the worst. Tell all your friends," Varick called after him. He turned back to Carver. "I rather thought you might jump in there."

Carver gave him an incredulous look.

"Oh, right," Varick said sheepishly. "Rank and protocol and all that. Stars, it's so stupid. Where were we? Reconnecting with an old friend."

Varick reeled his mind back and parsed through what Carver

had said. Mercury had met with someone? When? Well, it had to had to have been today, right? And Carver had said, "shortly *after setting off…*" So Mercury met with someone here on board.

Varick asked, trying to keep his voice blithe, "Anyone I would have heard of?"

"A Mister Guthrie Cooper, I believe."

Varick forced himself to breathe slowly and think through the words. They hooked onto something in his brain, but he couldn't quite pull it all the way to the surface of his memory.

"We first learned of the gent while in the company of our most energetic of associates," Carver hinted.

Now it came rushing back to Varick. Guthrie Cooperage! Where he and Carver and Coal had seen Mercury shaking hands with that mean-looking chap. Varick nodded slowly, uncertain what to think. He'd decided Mercury wasn't so bad, but what else could this information signify?

"It's something to consider, certainly. Are you at all concerned about its value not lasting?" Translation: "Do you think Mercury is going to betray us?"

Carver hesitated. "It's uncertain." Varick couldn't tell if he was trying to be diplomatic or simply couldn't find the words to discreetly express whatever else he wanted to say. Though, knowing Carver, it was likely the former.

Varick nodded, mulling over on the facts. They were stuck on this airship together for the next three days. He couldn't risk turning Mercury into whatever authority existed here. He might rat them all out. But also, Mercury definitely seemed to be playing some game of his own, outside of the crew.

"Let's carry on. We'll need to consult with our associates."

35

SPINDLE AND SPITE

As Varick and Carver began to make their way back up to the room, they spied Great Auntie Megaera outside on a little enclosed veranda area. The space was designed for travelers like herself, or rather, it was designed for the canine companions of travelers like herself. A large swathe of grass had been planted here for animals to relieve themselves. A crew member stood discretely by to clean up when necessary. Despite the man's best efforts to keep his face relaxed and pleasant, he looked miserable. Nearly as miserable as Harefoot, who looked to be having regrets about scarfing down most of that tin of smoked herring.

Another woman came into view as the two lads headed through the door to join them. Spindle! Their mark. Varick couldn't believe his luck. He didn't dare look at Carver, for fear of letting his excitement show.

Spindle, for all her renown, did indeed cut a diminutive figure. She was short, plump, and spoke with a soft, tinkling sort of voice. Her blonde hair, which was swept into a tall updo of curls and loops, was shot through with streaks of white. Her rendering had made her look severe and commanding, but the woman before Varick looked more suited to the role of shepherdess or a fun teacher and less a master thief. Next to her roamed three small dogs, one black, one white, and one grey. All three had curly fur that had been styled in a way that was an affront to both nature and man. The cruel groomer had clipped close to the dogs' bodies around the face, waist, midpoints of the legs, and the tail, the rest having been impossibly poofed. Varick wasn't sure whether he felt worse for the dogs or the attendant tasked with cleaning up after them.

"…mix some pumpkin in with his food," Spindle was saying to Auntie Megaera. "Mine like it with a bit of honey, but they are spoiled little dears."

She looked down at her trio of dogs affectionately before clocking Varick and Carver's approach.

"Auntie Megaera," Varick said, showing he was not, in fact, the interloper Spindle probably thought he was. "Everything tickity boo?"

"I'm afraid not, but thank you for asking," Megaera said. "Ah, I see you found Mister Sweeney. Hello again. Gents, meet my new friend, Miss Delilah Mackillop. Delilah, this is my nephew, Varick Pendragon, and his personal secretary, Mister Archibald Sweeney."

Already on a first name basis, Varick observed. He knew Great Auntie Megaera was friendly, but that was some impressively quick work.

Carver and then Varick shook Spindle—also known as Delilah, apparently—by the hand. "I'm a great nephew," he joked.

Spindle gave a mild little laugh. "Delighted. Your aunt was just telling me about her collection of little ones. Do you have any dogs?"

"I'm afraid not," Varick confessed. "Still under the family roof, and my grandmother doesn't approve."

"That is a grand shame," Spindle said.

"I wholly agree," Varick replied.

The conversation progressed easily from there, and with only one stumble along the way.

"And what do you do, Miss Mackillop?" Varick asked.

"Oh, my background is terribly boring," she said with that same soft, mild tone. "The family business is in textiles."

Varick fully believed that textiles was her real life cover, but he quite liked the subject of textiles. When he tried to dig in, however, Spindle's eyes glazed and she grew visibly distant.

"And what is your dog's favorite fabric?" Carver asked.

Spindle came back to them like a moth to flame. "Velvet. They cannot sleep on anything else, sensitive little darlings."

As long as Varick kept dogs at the center of their chatter, Spindle was an open book. He had not missed the gemstone studded collars her dogs wore—Kissy, Prissy, and Lissy, he learned they were called—and he asked whether they had other accessories to show off.

"Of course," Spindle said. "These are their dinner collars. They have day collars as well, and satin capes for the banquet on our final night. And tiny crowns for each. Oh, you'll just die when you see them. They're so precious."

"And you?" Megaera asked. "Do you have a crown as well?"

Varick's skin went cold. Did Auntie Megaera somehow know?!

She went on, leaning toward Spindle with a coy smile. "Because I think you're an absolute queen, and you would look ravishing in one."

Varick struggled to keep his jaw from dropping, only just keeping his composure. No wonder Great Auntie Megaera was getting so familiar so fast. She fancied Spindle! The utter temerity of the woman! Granted, she didn't know anything about the job, so he supposed he couldn't be too upset. But Auntie Megaera, not now! Not while he was working!

Spindle colored prettily and smiled back at her. "I'm afraid not."

For a moment, Varick wondered if he had the wrong person. Then he remembered that people lie. Spindle wasn't about to admit that, oh yes, she did have a crown, and did you know it's the ultimate thief's prize?

"Aren't you worried, though?" he blurted.

Whatever magic was brewing between the two women evaporated, and they both looked at him. Spindle's eyes were wide and curious, while Auntie Megaera fairly scowled at him.

"Worried?" Spindle asked.

He pressed on, feeling the heat of Megaera's stare trying to sear his flesh. "About your dogs' accessories? Aren't you concerned they might be stolen?"

Spindle shook her head. "No, they're tucked safely away in the ship's vault."

Brilliant, he'd made it to the threshold, but now how to ask which safe her things were in? Varick dithered for a moment before Carver once again came to his rescue.

"Do you think we could see?" he asked. "Mister Pendragon and I discussed the idea of storing his valuables away—some important family treasures—but we weren't certain how secure they'd be. Could we..." he turned to Varick, feigning obsequiousness, "I apologize if I'm overstepping here, sir, but you were so worried. They are priceless pieces."

"I'd be happy to."

Spindle smiled at them, and Varick saw what Carver had done. He'd set out bait for the master thief in the form of fictitious Pendragon heirlooms.

"That sounds so lovely," Megaera put in. "We can all go together." She looked at Spindle, "And then perhaps a ladies' lunch? There's also a salon on Duskwooder flora and fauna tomorrow afternoon that sounds fascinating."

She looked at Spindle again, and Varick nearly cried out when Auntie Megaera batted, actually *batted her eyelashes*, at the master thief.

Great Auntie Megaera! his mind cried. *A cold shower is what you need.*

"Splendid," Spindle said, looking back at Megaera, eyes practically twinkling.

Prissy, or perhaps it was Kissy, started sniffing a pile of Harefoot's leavings, and Spindle's attention snapped to her dog. Before Varick could say anything more, Auntie Megaera fixed him with a gimlet eye.

"We should go," he said, not missing the unsaid words in that stare. "I have… work to do."

The gents tipped their hats to the ladies and made their escape. Spindle barely gave them a glance as they went, her focus entirely on… maybe it was Lissy.

In the stairwell up, Carver said in a low voice, "She is unhappy with you."

Varick didn't need him to specify that "she" referred to his great aunt. "I know." A moment later, he added, as if coming in from an entirely different conversation. "And anyway, she's supposed to be on holiday with *me*. Not trying to… to…" He couldn't think of a delicate way to phrase it.

"Get into Spindle's knickers," Carver suggested.

Varick groaned. "Don't phrase it like that. You're making my aunt sound tawdry."

"I think that might be how your aunt likes it."

"Gah! Can we not, please?"

Carver laughed, but left off tormenting Varick.

Back in his suite, Varick leaned against the wall, cogitating. Coal was parked against the radiator again, while Carver had settled on the couch and Marlowe and Fulcrum sat on a couple of the steamer trunks beside the small table where the gift basket of Duskwood goodies sat. It was even more picked over than it had been. All three stowaways had completed their various missions to some degree. There was time tomorrow too for any bits that still needed doing, but they'd need to work around Varick and Carver's visit to the ship's vault. And, there was still the question of what to do about Mercury.

Carver had related to the rest of the crew what he'd shared with Varick in code earlier. He was able to give full details this time, though. Failing to find Mercury on the docks and running out of time, Carver had been forced to board, but hoped that their communications had simply gotten crossed and he'd find Mercury on the airship. He had, after a fashion, seeing Mercury speaking to the chap from Guthrie Cooperage in one of the corridors of the airship's lower decks, near the cargo hold and boiler rooms.

"But you didn't speak to him?" Fulcrum asked.

"No, I stayed hidden," Carver explained. "I tried to make out what they were saying, but I was too far away." Fulcrum and Coal said nothing to this, and Carver added, a mite defensively, "I didn't know what he was doing. I still don't. I—"

"He's not up to anything," Fulcrum snapped. "It probably wasn't even him." When both Carver and Varick opened their mouths to object, Fulcrum steamrolled on. "You said yourself you were too far away to make out what they were saying. You were probably too far to see his face clearly too."

Carver looked away, and Varick saw doubt fill his expression.

"I believe him," he said. "We saw Mercury meeting with that

same chap back in Springhaven. Coal was there too!" Varick motioned at the smallest member of their crew, who looked smaller at the moment, hunched against the heat of the radiator. "That's too coincidental to be a coincidence."

Fulcrum gave him a scathing look.

"You know what I mean!" Varick said. "I mean, I don't think Carver's got it wrong. I think he saw exactly what he thinks he saw and that Mercury is up to something."

Fulcrum put his hands behind his head, threading his fingers together, and leaned back into them. "I don't agree."

Varick threw his hands up. "Why is it so hard for you to see, or at least admit that Mercury might be shady. I have dealt with unscrupulous people my whole life. We need to be on our guard."

"Aw, poor you," Fulcrum sneered. "Surrounded on all sides in that big house by horrible people. How sad that you didn't have a great big room and a great big bed with great big blankets to hide in and great big pillows to cry into. Oh, wait."

Varick's fists balled at his sides, and he forced himself to breathe in and out slowly through his nose. He wanted to say that none of that mattered when he'd borne his family's abuses, both large and small, day in and day out, that he'd only ever had one person who'd ever loved him and he was dead now. But it did matter. It mattered to someone who'd not had those things. It mattered because they too, Fulcrum and Coal and Carver, had all lost the people who'd loved them. And maybe Mercury was a sort of replacement for that. An unreliable, dodgy replacement, but it was something. He'd given them a place, at least to sleep and be, for a price anyway. Varick couldn't say that didn't count for anything. In truth, Varick couldn't say anything at the moment. He didn't trust himself not to speak destructive words he could never take back. He could feel his temper on a hair trigger.

"What does everyone else think?" Carver asked in a soft

voice. He looked to Coal and Marlowe.

Marlowe shrugged. "Not really worried about it, to be honest."

Varick looked over Marlowe's massive biceps. A bloke that big needn't worry about much, he supposed. Mercury wouldn't dare try going head to head with someone that big. Even two against one, Marlowe would be enough of a problem to ruin a plan, even if only for the time it took to take him out.

Coal shrugged too, but his was a squirmy, uncertain thing. "He may not even show up. We have Varick's plan. We can do that if Mercury's decided to abandon us. And if it's just some misunderstanding—"

"Form a proper opinion and stop prevaricating," Varick said. He regretted it as soon as the words were out of his mouth.

Fulcrum shot to his feet. "Don't talk to my brother that way! You're not our boss or our better. You're a—"

"Okay, okay," Carver broke in, stepping between them. "Let's all take some time. We're all tired, it's been a long day, and some of us haven't had dinner yet."

"No," Fulcrum spat, "because some of us were working while the other was stuffing his gob with the finest roast pheasant."

"I was working too!" Varick insisted. He only just stopped himself from adding, "And it was roast *lamb*!" That undoubtedly would only make things worse.

Even as Marlowe and Carver herded Fulcrum into the bedroom where they'd stored their food, Fulcrum turned back for one last parting shot. "Sure. I'll just go enjoy my tin of cold meat with some stale bread and cheese."

Don't, Varick told himself. *He's just trying to get under your skin.*

Instead, he turned to Coal, who was shuffling sadly behind the group. "Coal, I'm sorry. I shouldn't have snapped at you like that."

Coal gave him a weak smile in return. "It's s'okay."

"It isn't," Varick insisted, but no one responded to him.

They shut the door behind them. After a few minutes of waiting, it was clear the rest of the crew were all taking some time, as Carver had suggested, but all together. Without Varick. He felt the sharp pang of loneliness, of rejection, sink into him. It was like he'd always felt when he'd been excluded from playgroups as a child because of something Constance or Magnus had said or done, or after Varick had told off the snottiest of his fellow children, only for the rest of them to side with the bullies. That was back before he'd decided not to care about any of them or what they thought. Nevertheless, he felt an unwelcome heat behind his eyes, and then a prickle.

A knock sounded at the door just then, and Varick was relieved. It would be nice to have his aunt's company just now. Harefoot would probably be open to a cuddle too. When he opened the door, however, it was not Great Auntie Megaera who greeted him.

"M'lad," Mercury drawled.

He leaned against the doorframe with one arm above his head, looking for all the world like he was posing.

"What the blazes are you doing here?" Varick hadn't meant to say the words, but he didn't regret them either.

Mercury sauntered past him without answering. As he did, Varick's senses were assaulted by the smell of alcohol, something sweet and sharp.

"Stars!" he choked. "Have you been drinking? All day?"

He closed the door behind Mercury, who was looking over the room with a greedy glint in his eye.

"So this is how the other half lives, eh? Very nice."

"Where have you been?" Varick demanded. "You were supposed to meet us this morning."

The door to the bedroom cracked open, and the rest of the crew was suddenly spilling back into the suite's main living area. A garbled collection of similar questions filled the air, and Mercury motioned for quiet with the air of an indulgent schoolmaster.

"Relax, my little ducklings. I just got held up a bit, but here I am, hale and hearty."

"Held up doing what?" Varick asked. "You had a ticket. We had a plan."

"Don't fret, Little Lord Pendragon," Mercury said.

He definitely seemed drunk, Varick concluded. The plain black suit he wore to pose as Varick's valet was rumpled. One of the collar points was even bent!

Instead of explaining himself, Mercury went on consoling. "I would never abandon you all and leave you drifting in the wind." He grinned at his own cleverness.

Varick, on the other hand, rolled his eyes. "It's not about abandoning us. We're all competent and capable. We'd be fine without you. It's—"

Before Varick could finish, another knock sounded. This one from the door between his and Auntie Megaera's room.

"Bugger, everyone back inside," Varick said, motioning to the bedroom.

All but Carver and Mercury spilled back in and shut the door.

36

"GETTING READY TO DO CRIME!"

This time when Varick opened the door, it was Auntie Megaera who bowled him over. Unlike Harefoot, though, she did it with her words.

"Apologies for bothering you so late, Varick," she said, "but I was hoping you had something besides violet-scented hand cream. Delilah apparently doesn't like violets, so if you do, would you be willing to swap with me? Perhaps something in lavender or lemon?"

Varick blinked at her. "You're changing your hand cream just because De—I mean, Miss Mackillop doesn't like it? Is your burgeoning relationship worth it? You did *just* meet her."

"Oh, so you did notice that?" Auntie Megaera said, not unkindly. "I wasn't sure, given how you tromped all over our discussion."

"Tromped?" Varick objected.

She went on. "And don't look at me like that. I'm not some naive schoolgirl changing my entire personality for a pretty face.

I have the experience to know what's worth changing and what isn't, and I'm not so beholden to my violet hand cream that I can't swap it out to see how things go without it getting in the way." Only then did she seem to notice Carver and Mercury standing awkwardly in the background. "Oh, hello? Apologies. I didn't realize…"

Varick gave her a look, trying to be scolding, but he couldn't help the smirk that tugged at his mouth.

She returned a sassy eyebrow raise, but her expression mellowed when she looked back to the two other men.

Varick said, "Auntie Megaera, this is my valet, Mister Montgomery Preece. Mister Preece, my great aunt, Miss Megaera Pendragon."

She gave a genteel bob of her head. "How do you do, Mister Preece?"

Mercury smiled wide at her. "A pleasure, Miss Pendragon, I assure you."

He bowed in the way Varick had shown him to do, but Varick could tell by Auntie Megaera's gaze that she was taking in the rumpled suit and bent collar point.

"I have lemon and rosemary," Varick volunteered, to both distract her and get rid of her as fast as possible.

She turned back to him. "That would be grand, thank you."

Only then did Varick realize his toilet chest was in his bedroom. There was nothing for it; he'd have to slip in and out without letting the others be seen. He should be sending Mercury for it, he knew, but Mercury might have no idea where to look, and Varick couldn't have the man riffling through his things. It would also be suspicious to explain where to find it. After all, as his valet, Mercury would have been the one to unpack everything.

"Back in a tick," he said before rushing off.

"How's Harefoot doing?" Carver asked.

Bless Carver. He was always so good at seeing what a situation needed and filling the space appropriately.

"Empty, thankfully. At last," Megaera replied. "He's sleeping now, poor thing."

While Carver provided a distraction, Mercury began to mooch about the room again, inspecting the gift basket first. Varick subtly rapped the door to the bedroom once with his knuckles before opening it and slipping inside. Thankfully, the rest of the crew was nowhere to be seen.

The toilet chest sat upon a ladies' vanity table, which Varick surmised every room must have available for any women who might be staying there. Men didn't use them, though he didn't see why not. They were handy and convenient, and he'd already made use of the spot earlier that evening to ensure his hair looked just so.

A familiar head popped out through the closed bed curtains. It was Coal.

"Can we come out yet? Fulcrum spilled meat juice on your pillows and it smells weird." He paused a moment before adding, "It was an accident."

Varick narrowed his eyes. "I'll bet it was. And no, Auntie Megaera is still out there."

He grabbed the glass jar of hand cream from his toilet chest and nipped back out.

"—beautiful earrings," he heard Mercury saying.

Megaera's eyes were on Varick. She had to have noticed the strangeness of Varick getting his own hand cream. He didn't address it, though. That would only bring more attention to it.

"Here you go," he said, handing her the jar. "Keep it for as long as you like."

She thanked him, but hesitated. He didn't give her a chance to find a reason to stick around.

"Well, I'm very tired. Breakfast tomorrow?" He smiled at

her, hoping that would help somehow.

"Breakfast tomorrow," she agreed. "Sleep well."

Blazes, she knows something's up, Varick thought. He could see it in how taciturn she was being. As soon as the door had clicked closed behind her, he whirled on Mercury.

"You're doing a rubbish job. You need to get it together."

Carver, meanwhile, went to gather the rest of the crew.

Mercury held up his hands, "Well, well, look who's in big britches now?"

Varick bristled. "You look like you slept in your clothes and you stink of alcohol. You still haven't explained where you were all day. Are you even taking this job seriously?"

Mercury jabbed a finger into Varick's chest. "You seem to forget who's in charge here, Mister Pendragon." He pronounced the name like a curse. "This is my plan and my crew. If I say something needs to change, you hop to it."

Varick swatted the hand away. "You wouldn't be here if it weren't for me. You don't have a position here without me. Or have you forgotten that?"

"And what are you gonna do? Sack me?"

An unspoken threat hung in the air. Mercury could out all of them if he wanted to. Something tipped in Varick's mind. Mercury *would* do it too. Varick was suddenly certain of it. Mercury had too much to lose on this trip. He valued the crown and his chance at glory over the crew's safety. Varick had decided to give him the benefit of the doubt, because of a stupid airship model and a single show of compassion, to believe that perhaps Mercury was just a bad boss and a piss-poor planner, but no. They were all nothing more than pawns to him. Varick considered pressing the matter, bringing up what Carver had seen earlier that day, but decided against it. They were too entangled together and there weren't enough options to ensure the crew's safety, so Varick said nothing.

"That's what I thought," Mercury said.

Varick's anger burned white hot, and his eyes seared holes into Mercury's back as the man turned to face the rest of the crew. They stood at the doorway to the bedroom, watching the exchange with worried faces.

Varick thought back to his fight with Magnus, about the opportunity Varick'd had to break more than his brother's knee. Once again, he was aware of his mind coldly parsing out information. He marked the heartless choices at hand and admitted to himself the true capacity he had within him, like sitting back and letting the crew suffer whatever machinations Mercury had planned, just to be able to say, "I told you so." No, that wasn't who he wanted to be.

But what options did that leave Varick? Would it need to get… messy? He could not quite bring himself to think the word violent. He didn't want it to come to that, but it was just there, hiding behind the word messy.

"I think the difference," Carver had said, "is looking for other options and choosing them as often as you can."

Varick would keep his eyes open. He would look for other options, as many as existed, but he held in his mind too the knowledge that he might be left with no alternative, as well as all he was capable of.

♖

Breakfast went quietly. Harefoot was doing markedly better, but still a little subdued. Auntie Megaera scratched his ears while enjoying a Duskwood specialty known as cloudberry jam with her toast. Varick was tired, but trying to gather himself. He hadn't slept well the night before, knowing Mercury wasn't far off in the staff quarters. He'd allowed Coal and Fulcrum to share the bed with him, something he was wholly unused to, while Marlowe had taken what should have been Carver's bed and Carver opted to sleep on the couch. Carver was the easiest to explain should Great Auntie Megaera decide to forgo knocking and walk into Varick's living space. In case of such an event, he'd say he'd fallen asleep working on something. In between being kept awake by Coal's kicking and Fulcrum's snoring, Varick worried what poison Mercury might be pouring into Marlowe's ear. Varick liked Marlowe, but they'd been friends for so little time, and Varick had such little experience with friends. He didn't know how little it would take for Mercury to set the big lad against him, and then Marlowe might talk to the others and convince them to turn on Varick too.

"Varick?" came Megaera's voice through his reverie.

He looked up from his breakfast where he'd apparently been pushing food around his plate.

"Are you alright, dear?" she said. "I asked what you were planning on doing today while Delilah and I are having lunch and attending the salon?"

"Oh, uh…" He could hardly tell her the truth—"Getting ready to do crime!"—and his mind reeled back through their previous conversations, searching for something he'd said he was interested in. "I'm going to take that behind-the-scenes tour of the ship."

"Oh, that'll be lovely," Megaera said. Her expression turned sly. "You're not also going to try and bag yourself an officer? They're too old for you, you know."

Varick laughed tiredly. He was still underage; *of course* they were far too old for him. But also, he saw the ploy in play. She was asking about his own romantic interests. As a lead-in to discussing hers? He wasn't certain. Either way, he didn't mind. "No, Auntie, I wasn't thinking that. And before you ask, because I can see it written all across your face, chaps don't interest me. I like girls. And no, there's no one I fancy in my life right now."

Megaera raised appraising brows at him. "Very well, you sussed me out. I was only curious. You're a young man full of vim. I wouldn't be surprised if you did."

Varick shook his head. "I have no doubt I'll meet someone one day. That doesn't worry me."

"Ah, the privilege of a well-connected young man."

Varick couldn't really deny that. Even with all the horrible things his family said about him to others, as rich as he was, lots of ladies would eventually want to land him as a husband. It was finding one who loved him and not his wealth that would be tricky, but that was a problem for future Varick.

"To be honest," he said. "I don't know that I really want to get married."

"Oh?" Auntie Megaera sipped her tea thoughtfully.

"Why?" he asked with a shrug. "Most of the married people I've seen aren't really happy with the person they're tied to. And even if they were, why do you need to do a big public show for people to accept your commitment? The real work, figuring out what happiness looks like for the both of you and then making it happen, that seems like it'd come after the show. And it seems like a *lot* of work."

Megaera smiled around her teacup. Divorce was not a done thing in the upper echelons of Springhaven society. That was the purview of the middle and lower classes, as his family put it, whose poor moral fiber made it impossible for them to take their commitments seriously. Thus, secret—and sometimes not-so-secret—affairs were common amongst the upper class.

"That's a wiser observation than you may realize, o nephew mine," Auntie Megaera said.

Something warm bloomed in Varick at the praise.

"Who knows," she went on. "Perhaps you'll find someone you do want to tie yourself to, as you put it… one day."

Varick shrugged. His mind was firmly on the here and now.

"Speaking of, and I am making a loose link here, connections. Your valet, he's…" She swirled her hand in the air, looking for a good word.

"He's not the best," Varick allowed.

Megaera made a face that both said she completely agreed and also thought he could have chosen better words.

"He's… new. I've never had a valet before, so I thought maybe I would try it out." Varick gave a weak chuckle. "And I'm already thinking perhaps a valet is not for me."

Auntie Megaera tapped a fingernail against her teacup. He could tell she was debating saying more. "Something feels off."

Varick looked down to his plate, pretending to focus on his food. She didn't pursue the subject, for which he was grateful. He didn't know what else he could say in Mercury's defense. Thank the stars Great Auntie Megaera had plans. The less opportunity Mercury had to out himself through willful mediocrity, the better.

♜

The vault room was almost exactly as Varick had seen it the day prior. Mister Dilley sat in his little glass booth and the door to the vault was firmly shut, the tiny levers above the lock all pointing down again. Mister Eaddy was nowhere to be seen and therefore most likely in the back room beyond, just as before.

The only difference was that the two gargantuan security specialists on duty were out patrolling the corridors now instead of in the vault. Varick had seen one of the titanic, finely-suited men on his way here while Auntie Megaera and Spindle had been chatting, all four dogs taking up the rest of the corridor around them. Next to Varick, Carver walked with a small, locked case, which held the Pendragon "treasures" Varick had mentioned. In all, they consisted of a small, jade snail set on a leaf made of abalone and delicate gold inlay, which was meant to attach to a top hat's ribbon and provide a bit of extra decoration; a ruby and emerald encrusted fishing lure—some ludicrous gift once given to Magnus, which Varick had stolen and never given back—a sapphire cravat pin in the shape of a forget-me-not flower; and a few other bits and pieces Megaera had added to the collection, since they were coming down here anyway.

Almost as soon as they entered the lobby of the vault room, Mister Dilley assured Varick that a maintenance team was scheduled to have a look at the floor today.

Auntie Megaera and Spindle both looked at him curiously, but one of the smaller dogs—Prissy, Varick had learned—chose that moment to wrap her leash around Harefoot's extensive legs. The two older ladies worked to get their dogs disentangled, but Kissy and Lissy were trying to help now too, and somehow Spindle and Auntie Megaera ended up looped together, laughing as their dogs looked extremely pleased with themselves. This time, Varick gave them space and privacy, wandering over to a framed piece of art on the wall and pretending to examine it.

Carver followed to whisper, "They're really cute."

In the background, Varick could just see Mister Dilley summoning Mister Eaddy.

"I know," Varick said. He tried to smother it, intending to appear aloof and skeptical, but he couldn't completely quash the smile that crept up his face. "I can't stand it."

"You liar," Carver said, and Varick's smile fought harder to be seen. "You're happy for her."

"Of course I am. She deserves happiness." Carver was chuckling softly now too, which only made Varick want to do the same. His face was trembling with the effort to keep it straight. "Now shut up. You're making me laugh."

Carver faked a cough to cover his own chortle and then settled his expression. "Okay, serious faces."

"The most serious," Varick agreed.

They just managed it, helped by the appearance of one of the security specialists coming in, presumably to check on things. He said nothing, just circled the lobby area, exchanged a nod with Mister Dilley, and then left again. A moment later, Mister Eaddy opened the booth's door and greeted the group. He started in on the same spiel Varick had heard the day before, though this time for Spindle and Auntie Megaera's benefit. Previously, Varick had told Carver what they needed to listen for, and the scheme they'd put together for this moment went into play.

Carver produced a folder from his case and held it open in front of Varick. They murmured important businessy sounding things like, "As you can see from the figures here," and, "increases are predicted next quarter," just loud enough for anyone coming close to hear. From the corners of their eyes, they watched Mister Eaddy begin the vault opening process.

Varick had already noted that the first two levers would be set into the up position, and when he listened to the sounds of the first half of the unlocking process, sure enough, two identical sounding clicks resounded. His counted clicks with his fingers, ears straining to identify which levers in the sequence were being moved. It sounded to Varick as if the third and fourth were moved upward, but he couldn't tell which of them moved back down on the fifth click, which did indeed, as it had yesterday, sound ever so slightly different.

"Harefoot, darling, no thank you!"

Varick and Carver's eyes shot toward a scene of canine-induced serendipity. Harefoot was trying to bully Mister Eaddy into giving him some attention. The lanky creature leaned against the man and booped his long head against Mister Eaddy's hands. Harefoot's weight pushed Mister Eaddy over a step, and Varick caught sight of the last two levers. Yes! It was the third lever that had moved back down and four was still up. Mister Eaddy was already recovering, though, and Auntie Megaera was apologizing. By the end, just as before, Varick heard seven lever clicks in total, and now they'd seen the result of five. They just needed to figure out the last two. They had the rest of today and until tomorrow evening to do it. Varick felt the rush of the challenge rise up within him. Surely they could do it. Look how much progress they'd made since yesterday. They *would* figure it out.

As he'd done the day before, Mister Eaddy went on to explain how the vault worked and all the safety precautions in place. Carver asked a few thoughtful questions Varick had not thought of: "How often is the guard refreshed?"—Varick liked that wording—and, "What kind of training do they undergo in order to be ready for the requirements of this position?" He even clocked a set of locks set into the inside of the vault door. Varick had missed that on his first visit. A required safety precaution apparently, in case someone were to get locked inside. Mister Eaddy explained this with the air of a man who felt that some poor sap dying of hunger or thirst while trapped inside the vault was a small price to pay for security.

Working in tandem, Varick and Carver put on a good show, even taking a moment aside to discuss the decision as to whether or not to store the Pendragon treasures there. That was strategically done just as Spindle was putting away her trio's relatively more generic traveling collars and pulling out their day collars. She'd come back this afternoon and do the same with their evening collars. Varick and Carver snuck a glance inside the safe Spindle opened. No crown glittered inside. There wasn't even a container the crown could have sat in. Varick saw Carver's throat bob, and Varick felt the same apprehension as a new complication took shape before them.

36.5

High Caliber Peaches and Bad Tea

Later that day, after Auntie Megaera and Spindle had gone off for for their (hopefully romantic) lunch, and Varick and Carver had gone their separate ways—Varick off to his tour, which he hadn't been lying about, and Carver back to the room—Coal and Fulcrum, both wearing Maintenance uniforms and Coal in a false mustache, headed for the vault room. They knew exactly where to go, and even had a pinched work order to show in case anyone stopped them. But nevertheless, they kept a wary eye out for anyone who might give them trouble. Between them, they pushed an equipment barrow, which currently looked like a squat crate on wheels, but had the ability to fold out into myriad tools. Truly a marvel of technology! Or so Coal had decided. He could see Fulcrum was wholly covetous of the thing by the glint in his brother's eye.

Coal chewed the inside of his cheek as they walked. He'd been mulling over what Carver had said last night about seeing Mercury talking to the big bloke from Guthrie's Cooperage.

Fulcrum, he knew, was bound and determined to not believe—disbelieve? Was that a word?—any of it. Fulcrum didn't blame Carver. He'd told Coal so when they'd been hiding together last night, but he did blame Varick for being so insistent that it must be true. Coal wasn't certain what to think. He liked Varick, and Mercury had done a lot for them. Did it have to be either or? Was there more to that phrase? Either or what? Anyway, he didn't like the way everyone was fighting. Thus, he was determined to nail this. That, and he didn't want to get caught before they had a chance to set up their amazing new life in Duskwood.

They passed one of the vault guards in the corridor. Both Coal and Fulcrum tipped their matching flat caps to the man. He did not return the gesture, but his eyes followed them for a moment as they passed by one another.

I'm apprenticing, Coal thought to himself, rehearsing for if he was questioned. *Don't know why I'm so small. Always been the shortest in my family.* He thought the false mustache would help offset his size, though.

The guard did not stop them, and they made it to the vault room without incident. For effect, Coal popped a bit of chewing gum in his mouth and hooked his thumbs into the loaded tool belt hanging around his waist before following Fulcrum in.

Staring at his brother's back, Coal could tell Fulcrum was nervous. His shoulders were tight, but his brother was the most determined person Coal knew. They'd be fine.

Fulcrum tipped his cap to the gent sitting inside a large glass booth within the vault's lobby.

"We're here to fix the floor, sir," Fulcrum told the man. He held up the work order Coal had swiped from the Maintenance department after Varick had told them about his tripping ploy.

"Yes, yes," the glass box man said quickly. "Go ahead then, but move out of the way if any guests come in."

"Will do," Fulcrum said, with another tip of his hat.

"Will do," Coal repeated, trying to sound as serious as Fulcrum did. He tried to make his voice deeper too, which he thought added to his seriousness.

They began pretending to examine the floor, occasionally muttering softly between themselves.

"Could be a case of wood mites," Coal said.

"Wrong sort of wood," Fulcrum replied.

"Ah, you got a caliper grievance just here." Coal especially liked that one. He always liked using technical-sounding bosh.

Fulcrum nodded. "A deep one."

They went on like that for another minute or so, moving on to pretend ways to solve the problem. That was when the fake argument started.

"You can't get in there with a plug cutter," Fulcrum was saying, raising his voice. "On a ship like *this*? You trying to kill everyone here?"

"Well, I don't see you coming up with any better ideas," Coal shot back. "You overgrown moppet."

While they argued, Coal gleefully went about setting up a collapsible tripod drill. And not only that, but he was doing it as badly as possible. As he pulled parts from the equipment barrow, he threw tools here and there. Heavy ones that made a lot of noise when they hit the ground.

Fulcrum winced for what must have been the sixth time as Coal threw a weird, sproingy tool with lots of thin metal tubes attached. It made a pleasing *yeong-yeong-yeong-yeooooong!* sound when it landed.

"Don't you think you're being a bit reckless?" Fulcrum always hated to see tools misused.

"These people have things to get done!" Coal insisted. He grabbed a handful of metal files and dropped them all at once.

In the background, the booth man was shouting at them, but he wasn't coming out. Maybe he was trapped inside his glass box of anger. A second later, the moment they'd been waiting for came. Another chap, the key man Varick had described, emerged from the a backroom attached to the booth.

"Dilley! Dilley, Dilley, Dilley! What is going on?" he called over the arguing and tool abuse.

They waited for the key man to come out of the booth, which took nearly no time at all, and Coal made his move. He turned to the man and chomped hard on his chewing gum.

"Heyo, chum!" he said. "We see your floor problem right enough." He walked over, tromping atop the tools. Fulcrum would be cringing internally with each exaggerated footfall, and then Coal pretended to slip on an errant spanner, knocking into the key man.

"Flukes and flames!" Coal exclaimed, copying an interesting swear he'd read once in a book by a Bone Porti author. His arms pinwheeled before he caught himself on the man's jacket. His hand slipped his into one jacket pocket and then the other, finding the vault key and executing the lift. Fulcrum was suddenly there too, apologizing, brushing off the man's jacket and generally adding to the chaos. Except Fulcrum's head ended up where Coal hadn't expected it to be, and Coal's head smashed into his brother's nose.

"Cripes!" Fulcrum cried. "My blinking nose! It's bleeding!"

Coal couldn't believe his luck. This was great! Fulcrum's nose wasn't exactly gushing, but it was a steady flow and had already started dripping over his hands and onto the floor. The key man jumped back, eyes firmly on the blood and clearly thinking of potential stains. Coal used the situation at hand and pretended to faint before getting to work from his spot on the floor. In tandem, Fulcrum began a spectacular diversion.

He'd started off by swearing a bit more for real and then switched to feigned panic. Mostly incoherent screaming and fragmented questions like, "Is my brain partially crushed?" and

"Can you bleed out from your nose?" He was flailing a lot too and, best of all, swinging his head back and forth as he divided his madness between the key man and the one of glass box island. In his periphery, Coal could see that Fulcrum had successfully both flung and smeared blood onto the outside of the glass box. A bit had spattered across a funny sign that read, *This glass is alarmed; do not break.* The key man was simultaneously trying to avoid getting blood on him and calm Fulcrum down.

Meanwhile, Coal's hands worked fast, taking advantage of the distraction. From his own pocket, he pulled a small tin that had once held breath mints. Fulcrum had filled the insides, both top and bottom, with a sort of putty and dusted the surfaces of each with flour so that they wouldn't immediately seal together and trap the key inside. He'd also bored a small hole into the side to make room for the key's shaft. Coal pressed the strange four-sided key, into the putty and then closed the lid. It took a second as the putty slowly smooshed around and into the key's various notches and grooves. At last, when the tin clicked closed between Coal's palms, he called it good. It stuck a bit when he opened it again, and the key needed a bit of futzing to extract it without ruining the fine details, but Fulcrum's nose was still going. No one had even glanced at Coal.

Satisfied, Coal slowly and quietly got to his feet and putpocketed the key the back into the key man's jacket pocket.

"What happened?" he moaned. "Oh, Johnny, you having another one of your moments?" He patted the key man's arm. "Not to worry, guv, it takes him like this sometimes. Lemme just calm him down." And then Coal began to warble in an off-key, high-pitched voice an undulating repetition of, "Loooo loooooo looo looloolooolooloooooooooo."

Fulcrum's hysterics abated, and a far-off look of serenity overtook his face. He looked to Coal. "Cheers, mate."

"Right-o!" Coal gave an excited little arm pump and looked

to the key man again. "Give us two ticks and a tock and we'll be out of your shiny, well-coiffed hair."

The key man pressed his lips into a thin line and exchanged a look with his partner in the glass box, who looked ready to faint himself despite having been fully shielded from the blood spray.

While Coal and Fulcrum went back to shamming maintenance work, the key man said, "Remind me of your supervisor's name. So that I might tell him what a grand job you two are doing."

"That'd be Mike," Coal said. "You know Mike, with the hair and all that skin. 'Course you do; everybody does."

Coal could tell when they'd worn out their welcome in a place. He grabbed a basic hand plane from the barrow and mimed swiping it across the pretend problem area while Fulcrum made quick work of re-packing all the tools strewn about.

"Apologies again. You're some real understanding peaches," Fulcrum said as he went. "True gents of the highest caliber. Must've had your own share of troubles to be so patient."

"The highest caliber peaches," Coal agreed.

Within minutes, the place was clean again, and Coal had pronounced the issue, "tidy as a cat." The brothers wished the two men a good afternoon and smoothly made off with the barrow and their new key mold.

♖

Carver went back to the cabin after visiting the vault. He'd hit a bit of a lull in his part of the heist. That was rather the cost of having such a public presence in the plan. Coal and Fulcrum and Marlowe were all unknowns; they could pose as anyone, so long as none of them crossed paths as one character with someone they'd previously met in a different guise. Carver didn't come back into play until tomorrow night, when he would help clean out the safes. Varick'd asked for help with his strange ledger, so Carver had decided to sit down with that for a spell. Varick had told him how to open it, and Carver started by reading over the letter from Varick's grandmother to Hannah, the manager at The Restful Turnip. He couldn't help but agree with Varick, the older woman certainly seemed like she had something to hide.

After that, he skimmed over the pages written in code. They were all written in the same hand, but the cipher would take time to break. He let his eyes rove over those pieces, not thinking about anything in particular, just seeing if he picked up on any patterns or other clues. Idly, he picked at a peeling corner of paper on the inside of the ledger cover. Nothing jumped out at him in the code, so he moved onto the little booklet, which also told him nothing, and then the copies of Springhavian bylaws and whatnot.

Carver wished he'd paid more attention to his grandfather's work when he'd had the chance. Then again, he might be being a touch harsh on his younger self. Who could really blame a child for not being interested in the minutiae of legal documents? But it might have helped him now. Even though his grandfather's area of expertise had been labor laws and workers' rights, and these regulation documents all seemed to pertain to other subjects—running charity organizations, conservatorship, personal taxes—maybe understanding the language, even vaguely, could have given him a clue.

Beneath his finger, Carver felt something new. He looked to where he'd been picking and discovered he'd pulled back the peeling corner almost an inch from where it had been. Familiar handwriting peeked out from underneath. There was more hidden inside the ledger's front cover!

Carefully, Carver peeled away the paper that had disguised this second hiding spot. None of the papers here were in code. Carver's heart beat fast as he skimmed the text. They were letters, sent from Hannah to Varick, all stamped *Return To Sender*. Carver didn't want to pry into Varick's personal affairs—trust had been hard-won in that corner—but it didn't take more than a few accidentally caught lines to realize that Hannah had been trying to contact Varick for some time, and that her efforts had all been thwarted.

At the bottom of the stack was also a typewritten form. It was a document entitled *Petition for Conservatorship*, which meant precisely nothing to Carver, save for the fact that someone was asking for something. That someone appeared to be Patricia Pendragon, but she was working through her solicitor, a man called John Umpleby. The name pinged in Carver's mind. Why did he know that name? Varick's name was on the form too, as well as his signature, but the legalese, as Carver's grandfather had jokingly called it, was thick all throughout. Carver couldn't make heads or tails of any of it. What even was a Conservator? Someone who… conserves something? It sounded like jam. Stars, some jam on toast sounded good right about now. He hadn't had lunch yet.

Carver got up and plucked the cloudberry preserves from the ransacked gift basket. Then he nabbed a slice of bread from the food stash his stowaway companions had brought. It really was stale; Fulcrum hadn't been being overly dramatic about that part, though Varick hadn't really deserved the blame for it. Either Coal or Marlowe had left the bag open, and neither of them could agree on how it happened. Carver had forestalled any further argument about that by saying they could simply ask Varick to order some room service. Fulcrum had scoffed at that but hadn't said no. In any case, for now, stale bread was a bit like toast, or so Carver told himself. Thus, armed with cloudberry jam on subpar toast, Carver returned to Varick's pilfered collection of mystery documents.

"Everything good?"

Carver looked up. It was Mercury, and he was holding a tray of full teacups. The older man must have entered from the staff quarters. He looked better today, though that wasn't saying much. His clothes weren't rumpled anyway, but if Carver was playing a valet, he'd never go anywhere without the requisite jacket. As it was, it looked as if Mercury thought he was the one on holiday.

"Yeah," Carver said, puzzled as to why any one person needed so much tea, at least in the same moment. "All good. What's…"

He let the words trail off as Mercury gave a chuckle. "I was practicing. Never really made tea before."

"Because you hate tea," Carver said.

He took the opportunity to casually tuck all the papers back inside the ledger and close it up. Varick wouldn't want Mercury privy to any of this.

"I know," Mercury said, "but I figured I ought to be able to brew a decent cup in case Varick or the crone asks."

Carver's eyebrows cinched together. He debated how to respond. He understood Mercury's bitterness toward the upper class. If they all pooled just a tiny, little bit of all their money and put it toward providing for those without basic human needs, the world would be far better off, sure, but like all people, there was good mixed in with the bad. Varick's grandfather sounded like he'd been a good man, and his sister seemed to have been cut from the same cloth. He tried to give Mercury the benefit of the doubt, though; he'd not spent much time with her to know that. The reason as to why made worry cloud over that thought. Who was that man he'd seen Mercury talking to yesterday? And why had it taken him so long to show up?

At last Carver simply said, "Miss Pendragon is a decent woman." Mercury was still his boss, and the man who provided him with a place to sleep at night. He wanted to stay on his good side, but his conscience would have nagged at him if he'd let the insult go without a word.

Mercury made a dismissive noise in his throat and carried his tray of teacups around to place it on a small table. He then handed Carver one of the many cups.

"Have a cuppa," Mercury said. "That's the last one I made, so it's still warm. I think I've gotten the knack for it."

Carver gratefully took the cup and sipped… and fought the urge to make a face. Mercury decidedly had *not* gotten the knack for it. The tea was bitter, over-brewed, but it was hot anyway. The flavor of the cloudberry jam also might have been clashing with the tea. In either case, Carver wasn't about to complain. It wasn't often that Mercury did favors, and with all the tension between him and Varick lately, Carver didn't want to add to that. He added a little cream and sugar to cover the taste while Mercury placed a cozy over the teapot to keep the rest of the batch warm.

"What's all this then?" Mercury asked, gesturing at the ledger.

Carver gave a shrug. "Just a little side project. Nothing to do with the job. And nothing that'll distract me from it either."

Mercury nodded. He began to wander about the cabin, investigating cupboards and poking at gleaming fixtures.

A knock sounded at the adjoining door to Megaera's suite. Carver and Mercury looked at one another, the former then motioning uncertainly to the latter. A traveling valet was a bit like a butler, right? So for appearances' sake, shouldn't Mercury answer it? The man rolled his eyes and went to open the door.

"Oh, hello," Megaera greeted as Mercury stepped aside for her to enter. "Mister Preece, Mister Sweeney. She looked around as Harefoot nudged Mercury's hand for scritchies, pretty please.

Carver winced as he realized Mercury still hadn't bothered to don a jacket to complete his valet uniform, and now Varick's sharp-eyed aunt was here. Thankfully, Megaera was busy looking around the cabin, while Harefoot unabashedly padded over to try his luck with Carver after Mercury had refused the scritchie request.

"Mister Pendragon is still out on his tour," Carver offered, seeing the question on Megaera's face. He obliged Harefoot with a good rub inside the dog's soft ears. "He should be back in about an hour, I believe."

"Tea?" Mercury offered.

"Thank you," Megaera said.

While Mercury fixed a fresh cup, Carver asked how her doggy date lunch had gone. He didn't mind mentioning Miss MacKillop's name, given that Mercury didn't know it. Apparently, the two ladies were already planning trips to visit one another's homes. Mercury excused himself after handing over the teacup and disappeared back into his own room, closing the door behind him. Carver had a feeling the man had little desire to return while Megaera was here. With tea in hand, Megaera sat down next to Carver on the sofa and took a small, delicate sip.

"So what does my dear nephew have you working on?" She set her cup down and picked up the ledger. It didn't take but a moment for her to realize it wasn't what it seemed. "Oh, is it a puzzle box?" She immediately began trying to figure it out.

Carver hesitated. This was Varick's business, but his great aunt clearly cared for him and might even be able to help. Carver stalled for time by drinking more of his tea, trying to ignore the bitter, over-brewed taste.

Megaera tapped Carver's tea saucer. "You don't have to drink that. It's vile." He'd already drank nearly half the cup, and it seemed rude to turn up his nose at the gift. When she saw Carver dither, as if reading his thoughts, she added, "I'm sure he knows you appreciate his labor, but life's too short to drink bad tea."

Carver smiled sheepishly and set his cup down, feeling a little relieved. Megaera took their cups and the rest of the tea things and placed them outside the cabin door to be taken away.

He, meanwhile, took a bite of his toast before realizing how rude it was for him to be eating here, in front of her. He started to apologize, but she gave him a gentle wave.

"Not at all. Varick isn't working you too hard, is he? He's giving you proper time for all your own activities?"

Carver smiled. "Of course."

"Good, good." She sat back down and returned to the false ledger. "Now, what is this thing? I do love a good puzzle."

Carver still wasn't certain how to answer. The opportunity disappeared as Megaera pulled on the ledger's little ribbon bookmark and the hidden clasp clicked open.

"Aha!" she declared victoriously.

The ledger fell open, and the *Petition for Conservatorship* greeted them. Megaera's eyebrows knitted together in concern. Harefoot stopped staring at Carver's half eaten not-toast and went to his mistress to lay his slender head in her lap.

"Archibald, where did you get this?" Her voice was soft and serious. And the sudden familiarity she used with him made the question feel all the more urgent.

"I… V, I mean, Mister Pendragon, he…"

Stole it from your late brother's soup kitchen, he finished in his head. He had no idea what to tell her.

Megaera took command of the ledger. In short order, she'd laid out the encoded papers, looked through the little booklet as well as the bylaw copies, and begun furiously working through the code. Carver fell into assisting her. What else could he do? Not that he would have made any other choice anyway. Whatever had alarmed the woman seemed dire indeed, and he would help Varick if he could, even if he didn't understand exactly what the risk was yet. Now and again, Megaera would occasionally mutter under her breath. Carver couldn't make out much, but what he could involved several severe insults directed at Varick's grandmother. The help came at just the right time too, because over the next hour or so, Carver felt his focus on the task begin to slip.

37

SUSPICIONS CONFIRMED

When Varick returned to his room, he was feeling rather spry. His tour had gone extremely well, and plans tumbled about in his head like freshly born butterflies, each one bright and energetic and full of possibilities. He'd even managed to nab an extra tour brochure for Coal, which included illustrations of some of the ship's modern innovations. Coal would enjoy reading about the architectural features, and it was a good apology gift after last night's nastiness.

Thus, it was a rather cold splash of water when Varick walked into his cabin to find Great Auntie Megaera poring over the various documents he'd asked Carver to help him decipher. Why Carver had thought to involve her, Varick couldn't guess, but he suspected Carver rather regretted it, given how pale he looked when he met Varick's eyes.

Then his vision was filled up by Megaera, shaking a sheaf of papers at him. He hadn't seen her move. One moment, she had been sitting on the couch next to Carver, the next there she was.

Rather impressive for a woman of her age.

"How long has this been going on?" she was asking.

Varick's mind reeled. How did she know about the job? Still, he wasn't about to betray his crew. "How long has what been going on?"

She shook at the papers as if sprinkling answers from them. "This! What do you know about it? Why didn't you tell me?"

"Auntie Megaera, what are we even talking about?"

He took the papers from her, still wondering what written evidence existed to out him and the team. Oh, it was the contents of the false ledger. He still had no idea what most of it meant. He looked at her, blankly.

Realization dawned across her face. "You really don't know, do you?" She turned away, and pressed a hand to her forehead. "That… That…" And then a phrase fell from Great Auntie's Megaera's lips that made Varick blanch. That was a term of abuse he'd not heard before, but it was plenty descriptive. How did a body even swivel one of those? She fixed him with a hard look. "Not to worry, Varick. It won't stand. She has no real grounds. She only got this far because no one was fighting her, but that's about to change. As soon as we land in Duskwood, I'll send a letter to my solicitor."

Now Varick was really worried. What had happened that Auntie Megaera needed to involve solicitors? He skimmed the papers, stopping when he saw the *Petition for Conservatorship* form. When he saw his name and signature on it.

"What's conservatorship?" he asked.

Megaera's lips pulled into a thin line. "She's appealing to the city to deem you unfit."

"Unfit to what?" Varick asked.

"To be independent. To control your own finances. It's easier for minors, especially if there's no one to advocate in their favor."

She meant no adults, Varick realized. Stars, he wished he was of age. "Can't I advocate for myself?"

Auntie Megaera gave him a slow, sad shake of the head. "I'm afraid not." She pointed to his signature on the page, dated the day of the will reading. "This has granted her permission—or rather, her Mister Umpleby—to open the case."

As the gravity of the situation began to press down on Varick, a growing anger pressed back. "Why do they always do this?!" He began to pace. "They can't let me have anything, not even my own life now!"

"I know," Megaera said softly.

He looked to her. "You really think you can stop my grandmother from having me… " He didn't know the right term. "Conservatored?"

"You have my word. Right now, there's only her claim."

"Hers and the rest of the family. You know they'll back her if they think they can benefit."

"I know," Megaera said again. "There are tests, though, that can be done to prove you're of sound mind. And when you state your objections, that'll help too."

Varick nodded, but said nothing. He didn't trust that. He didn't trust that his family wouldn't buy off someone, everyone they could, to get their way. And anyway, he shouldn't have to go through any stupid tests to fight them off.

"Do you know how she got your signature?" Auntie Megaera asked. "Do you think it's a forgery?"

Varick studied the large loops, the scrawled middle bits. "If it is, it's a very good one. I haven't signed anything since…" He looked at the date again, and fresh horror dawned on him. "The will reading."

Megaera's gaze was hard and sharp enough to cut glass as she nodded.

"There were so many forms," Varick said, his voice so quiet now. "I just wanted to get through it."

His great aunt warmed and softened. She looked like she wanted to take Varick into her arms and hug him, but he'd wrapped his own arms around himself, fortressing himself off. She took in a steadying breath and instead said, "This is not your fault, Varick. She has been a savage intrigante her entire life. You are not the one to blame here. Do you hear me?" When he didn't reply, she repeated his name.

"I hear you," he muttered.

"Good, because this is important, more important that any of their villainy. You, my great-in-every-way nephew, are bright and strong and clever. You deserve love and care and security. And what they do does not need to define you. You do not need to be tied to them."

Varick swallowed a lump that had been forming in his throat. Great Auntie Megaera's words had been what he needed to hear in that moment. The light that Randolph had always kindled in him, that the rest of his family were always trying to snuff out, had dimmed with the grim news. Each heartfelt kindness of Megaera's, though, was a bit of kindling, and Varick suspected they were what she too had needed once upon a time. Stars, had she had anyone to gift them to her then?

He reached one hand out, which she took in her own, her wrinkled skin papery and warm, and he leaned gently into her. The only other person he'd shown such a gesture had been her brother.

Only after they broke apart again, Auntie Megaera giving Varick's hand a squeeze before letting go, did Carver delicately interrupt.

With a little cough, he said, "There's more, I'm afraid." His head was down, looking at the papers still left on the table, and Harefoot had his head in Carver's lap.

His voice sounded shaky, and Varick's stomach dropped. What fresh hell was this now?

"Patricia is breaking anti-kickback laws," Megaera said, sounding strangely triumphant now.

"I knew it!" Varick said. "Wait, what are those? I thought she was just trying to shut down the Turnip Network."

"Oh, she's trying to do that as well," Megaera explained. "She can't close it outright, not with it being left to you once you come of age. But she can make it so difficult for the people who work there that they'll eventually leave. Once it no longer has the staff to function, they'll have no choice but to shutter the place." Auntie Megaera's mouth curled up into a wicked grin. "Thankfully, however, your friend Hannah has been collecting evidence. That's what this puzzle box was, all her findings, where the proof lives, the people involved. Patricia is in league with the folks running Milgewort Workhouse. Hannah even obtained copies of what she could. I don't know how she got her hands on that conservatorship application—it had to have been stored at this Mister Umpleby's office—but I'd like to meet her, shake her hand, and buy her drink. Several, actually. There's more than enough evidence to make Patricia's life a living hell."

Varick grinned now too. "I can help there. Newssheet reporters *love me*." He felt renewed strength flowing through him. Or maybe that was just the power of spite. In any case, he promised, "She won't kill grandfather's legacy. We won't let her."

Carver stood then, a weak smile on his face. Harefoot circled him, staying out from underfoot, but only just. It was then that Varick realized his friend was sweating. Profusely. A sheen across his cheeks caught the light as he moved, a bit unsteadily.

"Hannah's been trying to contact you and warn you. We think she tried sending you letters in the usual way first, and when you never responded, she started sending certified letters. She has several here that were returned to her. They'll…" Carver's voice faltered as his feet failed him.

Harefoot was right there, breaking the lad's fall as he went down.

"Carver!" Varick cried. He rushed over, suddenly realizing he had no idea what he was supposed to do.

It was all action for a while after that. Megaera sent Varick to flag down a steward in the corridor, who was apprised of the emergency and flew into action himself. Within the hour, Carver had been transported down to the airship's sick bay and was being attended to by the staff doctors. He was stable, but his blood pressure was alarmingly low and his breathing shallow. Varick and Auntie Megaera were questioned as to Carver's activities and diet that day, and signs of illness leading up to the collapse.

When Megaera mentioned "some poorly prepared tea," alarms went off in Varick's head. Mercury must have done something. Carver had apparently not finished his cup, but what if he had? Would he be dead now? Varick suddenly had a hundred questions for Carver, but couldn't ask a one.

"I'd like to request that no one be permitted to visit my secretary but myself and my aunt," Varick told the medical staff. He didn't summon his superior, you'd-best-do-what-I-say-or-I'll-have-you-sacked voice, but rather his this-is-too-important-to-be-up-for-debate voice, which he'd not even realized he possessed before that moment. "He needs rest if he's to recover from this affliction."

Someone agreed—Varick had failed to catch any names amidst the flurry of activity—and they made a note of the request. After that, it was all over. Carver was in the hands of the airship's doctors. Varick and Auntie Megaera left, their footsteps quiet as they went. He felt as if he were walking through a bad dream, and he chewed the inside of his cheek. Was Carver going to die? Only that night, when Varick had been threatened by those two thugs and Coal had saved him, had he been this frightened, but this was somehow worse. Carver didn't deserve this, and there was nothing Varick could do to help. He worried over plenty of ways of making it worse, though. He sorely wanted to ask Megaera to keep what had happened to herself, not to mention it to "Mister Preece." He wanted to see how Mercury would react if he thought Carver was perfectly fine, but then his aunt would know something was up. He also wanted to accuse Mercury outright, but he had no proof, just his own gut feeling. Could he tell the rest of the crew his suspicions? Maybe not all of them…

"Varick," Auntie Megaera asked, interrupting his thoughts, "Why did you call Mister Sweeney Carver?"

"Huh?" Varick said automatically. Internally, he winced. His parents hated that word, and it had gotten him a smack a few times.

But Auntie Megaera's gaze was filled only with concern. "When he fell, you called him Carver."

Varick made certain to look Megaera right in the eyes. Lies worked better that way. "Did I? I barely remember anything I said." Working a thread of truth into the lie helped too.

"Ah, strange," was all she said in reply. Varick was fairly certain she didn't believe him. Being a fellow black sheep of the family likely meant they'd learned similar tactics, but he didn't say anything. He didn't want to keep attention on the issue.

They walked on for a while longer, silence like a specter walking with them.

"I really hope he'll be alright," Varick admitted.

"I do too." A pause, and then she asked, "Would you like a hug? It's alright to say no."

Varick nodded. He didn't cry, though the hug rather made him want to, for reasons that he didn't want to think about. He suspected Megaera needed a bit of comfort herself, and he did feel a bit better afterward. Not that he was about to start hugging people all the time, but just now, in this situation, with this person who'd proven herself an ally, he was glad for the support.

They automatically threw themselves back into the deciphering work once they got back to the room. It only seemed right, given that Carver had been trying to help. Varick took on the work of transcription while Megaera continued to chip away at the last of the code. It turned out not all the documents used the same one. Clever. While he filled sheet after sheet with words, he cogitated on the problems.

What had Mercury done to Carver? *Why* had he done it? Carver didn't have a huge role to play in the job, but he'd been tasked to help clean out the vault. Just that thought very nearly convinced Varick that he'd gotten it wrong, that Mercury couldn't be behind whatever was wrong with Carver. But Varick couldn't let it go. Maybe he was being too stubborn or proud, but Varick guessed that Mercury must have known, somehow, that Carver had seen him talking to the man from the cooperage. Had Carver confronted Mercury about it while they'd been alone? If Mercury suspected that Carver had told the rest of them, then Coal and Marlowe and Fulcrum might be in danger too. Varick decided he'd stop antagonizing Mercury for now and use Carver's situation as a cover for changing his tune. Maybe that way, he could protect the others from ending up in Mercury's sights.

38

RED IN THE MORNING

The morning of the day of the heist dawned red. Varick hadn't wanted to be awake this early, but Coal was up and was being about as quiet as if New Year's had come early. He was practicing his tasks for the heist that night, going through the motions and reciting to himself the steps for his part. Fulcrum was still asleep in the bed—drat him, the jammy heavy sleeper. Or perhaps he was just immune to his younger brother.

Varick hadn't had a chance to catch up with the rest of the crew last night. He and Auntie Megaera had worked on the documents until it was time to get ready for dinner. She'd immediately glommed onto the idea of keeping them safe and hidden, for which Varick was grateful. He was also grateful that she hadn't asked how they'd come into his possession. She knew about the fire at the Turnip Network's main hub, of course, as well as Patricia and Varick's public statements about bringing it back, but none of that came up as they'd worked. After dinner, they'd gone to check on Carver, but his condition was unchanged from before.

They'd decoded and transcribed all but a few of the pages by the time Megaera retired for the night. Varick didn't understand a lot of what the documents said, just that it outlined and cited sources for the various ways Patricia and the Milgewort Workhouse people were colluding to break those anti-kickback laws Great Auntie Megaera had mentioned.

Before Varick had slipped into his bedroom to change and sleep—very late indeed by that time—he'd checked the staff quarters. Both Marlowe and Mercury had been snoring away. Varick had been tempted to sucker punch Mercury just for spite, but that would accomplish nothing except make him look like the prick. Varick didn't know what, if anything, the man had said about Carver's absence. Fulcrum and Coal had also already been asleep when Varick came to bed and neither had stirred while Varick crept about his business.

That morning, with the red dawn peeking through thin slits in the bed curtains, and as Coal failed every attempt to be quiet, Varick tried to roll over and ignore the lad. He felt bruised all over, and definitely hadn't gotten enough sleep. His brain, however, was up now and wouldn't shut up about the previous day's events. Crumbs hiding within the fine sheets prickled his skin too, and he mentally scowled at Fulcrum. Thus, begrudgingly, Varick got up and put on a dressing gown, motioning for Coal to be quiet. The two tiptoed out to the sitting room, and Varick checked outside his door for breakfast. He'd ordered extra for everyone, despite knowing how suspicious it would look if Auntie Megaera saw the piles of toast and scones, pots of jam and butter and clotted cream, small mountains of eggs and blood pudding and bacon, and a vat each of stewed mushrooms and roasted tomatoes.

There had been talk of Marlowe using his time spent working in the kitchen to steal food for his stowaway comrades. That was apparently tricky. It turned out all kitchen staff members had to show the contents of any bags before they left to ensure no one was stealing.

Tell me you don't trust your team without telling me you don't trust your team, Varick had thought. So much for those thorough background checks.

Breakfast was already there and covered with a large, silver dome to keep the heat in. After doling out plates for Coal and himself, Varick put the tray aside and covered it for anyone else who wanted some.

"Whatcha doing?" Coal asked between mouthfuls.

Varick was just placing a bandage over a bit of honey on the palm of his hand. Not looking up from his work, he replied, "I burned myself during my tour yesterday. Didn't listen to the safety instructions. How's your breakfast?"

"Resplendent. I just learned that from a book I found in the library about Duskwood. I figured I should give it a look, you know, since I'm about to be living there and all." Coal barreled happily onward about other things the book had taught him. Did Varick know that Duskwood's main industry, logging, was in fact, *not* their main industry at all? Well, it was *a* main industry, but they also had bustling fur and agriculture trades.

"And they don't have a tram system like we do. Not on the ground anyway. It's up in the *air*, suspended between the trees!" He said it with the same awe as if the Duskwooders had figured out how to fly like birds. "They call it a monorail, a bit like that thing at the docks. It hangs off a cable at the top and gets pulled around, and you can look down over the city as you go!"

Varick nodded, not really thinking about Coal's words. What should he tell him about Carver? Coal probably assumed their grifter had been with Varick and Megaera all evening and night, but might Mercury have told the team some other tale? Of everyone in the crew, Varick had the best rapport with Coal. If anyone was likely to believe Varick, it was him.

"Coal…" Varick began, and then realized he wasn't certain how to proceed. He didn't even know if Carver was going to make it, and as much as he didn't want to distract Coal from the job, Coal was his friend. He needed to know the danger. "I need your help with something."

Coal's attention zeroed in on Varick with a focused torch level of intensity. "What's up?"

For a moment, Varick felt a high of being in charge, of someone looking to him with utter trust. And then the weight of what he was about to say came crashing back down. He took a deep breath.

"Last night, did Mercury say anything about Carver?"

"No, why?"

"Did he say anything at all? Was he acting strange in any way?"

Coal shrugged. "No. We only saw him while you and your aunt were at dinner, while we were sneaking back in. He asked to speak to Marlowe and then Marlowe didn't come back out."

Varick nodded. That was concerning, to be sure.

"That's kinda normal, though," Coal went on. "Mercury's never been much of a talker. Even at The Riffraff Inn, he never talked to us much. Just left us to us and kept himself to himself. I used to try now and again to be chatty with him. I like chatting, you know? Getting to know people as people."

"I've noticed," Varick said, and he couldn't help but smirk.

"Yeah, he never really went for it. I think he thinks I'm a little annoying." Coal admitted this last part with a touch of shame, beginning to fidget, and Varick felt a flare of protectiveness blaze bright. "After a while, he'd usually say something like, 'Don't you have your keep to be earning?'"

Coal's impression of Mercury was not ridiculing, but neatly captured the thing that always rubbed Varick the wrong way. That superiority so many adults held over young people's heads, that children were not real people with desires and feelings and, therefore, could be talked down to and dismissed, like a pesky cat or even a servant who, if they were not serving the adult in question in some way, had no reason to be present.

"Maybe after this job he'll warm up, though," Coal said.

Varick suppressed a groan of sympathy. *Oh, Coal, no…*

"I'm gonna start writing him letters after we get settled in Duskwood. Maybe he'd like being pen pals better. Some people converse better in writing than in person, you know?"

Varick nodded, feeling like the world's biggest heel as he gathered his courage to tell Coal what had happened with Carver.

"You should know," he began, "Carver's in the medical bay."

There had probably been a better way to segue into that, but Varick hadn't a clue as to how it might have been done. Coal paled.

"Is he okay? What happened?"

"He's… sick, or something. I don't really know. He fainted yesterday afternoon. He's not breathing well and his pulse is weak, but the doctors are doing what they can to help him, and he wasn't any worse when we checked on him after dinner. They said that's a good thing. I'm going to check on him again in a bit."

Coal nodded, features pinched. Varick could tell he was trying to put on a brave face when he asked, "Can I go with you?"

It broke Varick's heart when he shook his head. *Just let him,* a little voice in his head urged. Coal and Carver had been friends far longer than Varick had known either of them. At least, he assumed so. He suddenly realized he didn't know how they'd met.

"Only Auntie Megaera and I are allowed." He decided it would be better if he didn't mention that part was at his request.

Coal nodded, presumably making his own assumptions about the reason.

"How long have you known each other?" Varick asked gently.

"Carver's granddad was running some kinda group litigation against the factory where Fulcrum and I had worked. I dunno how he tracked us down, but he did, and he asked Fulcrum if he'd give testimony about the accident. Too bad it didn't go anywhere. That was a few years ago, and I don't really understand what happened, but the factory owners won. Carver's granddad died a few months later. Carver came back to us, and we eventually teamed up with Mercury and Marlowe."

Varick sifted through Coal's words. He wondered if Carver's grandfather had been killed for meddling in the affairs of men with too much money and too few scruples. "I didn't know you and Fulcrum worked in a factory."

"Yeah." Coal motioned at the side of his head, where Fulcrum's bore bald spots and scars. "It's how his scalp got all messed up. We made cloth. There were these huge spinning machines with giant spools of wool and cotton. You had to walk around on these metal walkways to get to some of the pieces. They usually had us smaller kids do that sort of thing, because the paths wove all around the machines and sometimes the spaces between got really small, but there weren't safety railings or anything. A kid fell off the side one day trying to hurry. They were always after us about not moving fast enough. He barely caught himself on the edge. Fulcrum ran over and pulled him up, but the spools caught some of his hair and… well, he's not dead anyway."

Varick could only imagine the horrific event. He put a hand to his own head. Poor Fulcrum.

"What happened to the kid?"

Coal, unbelievably, smiled. A soft, sad smile, but full of

pride. "Saved him. Fulcrum stayed put, even with the blood running down into his eyes and the pain. And he pulled the kid back up."

That kid was Coal, Varick realized. That smile told him so. Fulcrum had risked his life and been maimed for his brother. As many times as they'd quarreled, Varick wasn't surprised to learn it. Fulcrum had no love for Varick, but he was loyal to those he counted as his. Varick couldn't help but respect it.

"I'm so sorry that happened," he said. "That's really awful."

Coal took a big bite out of his toast, which drooped under the weight of all the butter and jam he'd slathered atop it. "S'kay. Wer bet'r off no," he said, mouth full.

Varick opened his mouth to say that, no, in fact, they weren't, that Mercury had it out for all of them. But the words died on his tongue. Did Varick know that for sure? Mercury was a ratbag of the highest order, without a doubt, but did that make him a *murderer*? As soon as Varick thought the word, all his certainty from before shriveled inside of him. No, Varick only had his gut. No actual evidence. Well, bullocks. He didn't want to cause problems, especially not problems as big as, "Oh, you know the man who's given you a place and who you're holding a candle for as a maybe-or-maybe-not father figure? Yeah? Well, if he thinks you're in his way, he might try to kill you! Or not. Could be I'm wrong. Guess we'll all find out together." Alright, he wouldn't tell Coal about his suspicions now. But Varick would remain vigilant.

"You excited for tonight?" he asked instead.

Coal grinned, nodding so hard he nearly spilled jam off his toast.

Varick suppressed a sigh. "Just be really careful, alright? After Carver… got sick… I'm worried about you all."

Coal did a little full-body bobble. A highly technical and precise medical examination it turned out, because he pronounced with certainty, "I feel fine."

Fulcrum eventually appeared, as did Marlowe, who thanked Varick for ordering them breakfast.

With a jerk of his head toward Varick, he said to Fulcrum, "See, Carver said it'd be okay."

Varick had no idea what Marlowe was on about, but he didn't say so.

"I'm happy to order extra food." He pointedly did *not* look at Fulcrum when he said this, not wanting to bring up their argument from the other night.

Fulcrum, however, had no such qualms. "You coulda said so the other night."

Varick narrowed his eyes. He shouldn't rise to the bait. He knew he ought not to, especially knowing what Fulcrum had sacrificed for his brother, but he just... *couldn't.* "I wouldn't dare endanger that death grip you've got on your pride."

Before they could get into it again, Coal piped up. "It doesn't matter. Carver's sick. Proper sick, in the med bay."

That thoroughly shoved any burgeoning arguments out the door and locked it. Marlowe and Fulcrum looked at the smallest member of their crew. He relayed what Varick had told him, and Varick nodded in confirmation.

"Does Mercury know?" Fulcrum asked.

Varick looked to the crew's hitter, but Marlowe, in his usual taciturn way, only shrugged. "Didn't say anything to me."

"Is he up?" Varick asked.

"Must be. He wasn't in his bed just now."

When did he leave?! Varick's mind demanded. He suddenly wondered if the breakfast they were all enjoying had been tampered with. Sod everything. Varick was suddenly so tired. He wanted to put his head in his hands. He wanted to pull at his hair. He couldn't wait to be done with this job and off this blasted airship. He had to keep his composure, though, lest he start gabbling about tainted scones like a madman. He took a deep breath, and then another. He didn't feel any better.

"And no one has any idea where he is?" Varick couldn't keep the frustration from his voice. How did no one else see how suspicious this was? And a bloody good job he was doing being vigilant on top of it.

"Are you really starting in on that again?" Fulcrum asked, his tone dry.

"Are *you*?" Varick snapped. So much for keeping his composure. "Why don't you go put more crumbs in my bed while you wait for Mercury to stab the rest of us in the back like he did Carver?"

Fulcrum gave him a nasty smile. "Gladly." He grabbed a few extra slices of toast on his way out.

Bugger. Varick had made a right meal of this. Not much for it but to go in for another bite. He looked to Marlowe. "Are you going to keep being ambivalent?"

Marlowe gave him a casual head bob of assent.

"Bloody brilliant," Varick sneered. "Thank you so much for looking out for the rest of your crew."

He didn't need this. He didn't need to be here or a part of this group, who couldn't see a wolf in their midst even after one of their own had gone down. He didn't need to do Mercury's job. And why should he? When Mercury, in his infinite wisdom, had disappeared on them on them at every opportunity. What kind of leader did that? Varick, still in his dressing gown and slippers, headed for the door. Coal called after him, but Varick ignored him. Varick knew he was about to look like a younger version of one of those eccentric, old, rich men who took glasses of cognac and cigars first thing in the morning, but he didn't care. What he really wanted was a good strop, some hot chocolate, and a heavy dose of petty revenge to soothe his soul.

39

MORAL ARITHMETIC

A tantrum in lush bed slippers and thick dressing gown around a luxury airship was far less fun than Varick had hoped. For one thing, it was very hard to be stroppy when everyone was being so bloody accommodating. The first steward to lay eyes on him had politely asked him if he needed anything. It was, after all, highly indecorous for one to be out and about in such attire. But that's where privilege raised its ugly head once again. It would have been one thing if Varick had been poor or a woman. As he'd imagined, a man of his station and current attire quickly shifted from indecorous to eccentric, and the steward helpfully offered to lead him to a private men's lounge where other early risers like himself could enjoy their morning in leisurely comfort. No such thing existed for women, as a woman in the same situation and garments would be tantamount to exposing herself, as if uncoiffed hair and literally the same clothing as a man made her essentially naked. Varick thanked the man—being wantonly unkind to staff wasn't stroppy, it just made you an entitled prick—and headed, not for the promised lounge, but for a secluded little lookout at the prow of the Observation deck. There, he ordered his hot chocolate and proceeded to stew.

He thought about everything, the arguments he'd had with the crew, his conversations with them, not just here on the airship but since they'd met. He thought about what they'd learned from one another and the time they'd spent together. He thought about the conservatorship paperwork and wondered how he'd ever face his family again. True, so far it appeared that only his grandmother had been working against him in that way. For all Varick knew, though, his father and mother and possibly even siblings were involved too, but had kept their noses clean so far. That was the worst part, the uncertainty of it all. It wasn't even a question of *whether* his family members were capable of such a thing, ostensibly trapping Varick within his own life for their own means. They absolutely could and would. And just when he'd thought he'd finally found some friends, people he could call his, they'd all chosen someone else. Everyone always chose someone else, never him.

Varick had felt alone many times in his life, but never had he felt quite this alone. He nursed his hot chocolate as he sat in the plush, wingback chair, looking out over rolling, green forests and meadows. A river wended its way below them, though Varick didn't really see any of it.

"Hello, nephew."

He didn't know how long he had been sitting there when Great Auntie Megaera found him, though the collection of six hot chocolate cups told him it must have been a few hours. At least, he hoped it'd been a few hours. Otherwise, he might start feeling really rather ill soon, and not because of anything Mercury had done.

Blazes, he hadn't checked on Carver. He'd been too mired in self-pity to even think of it. That was the first thing he asked

Auntie Megaera about when she took the wingback chair next to his.

"He's doing better," she said, clearly pleased. "Not really coherent, though. He keeps muttering in his sleep. The doctors don't know why, but his pulse and breathing are both stronger, and they tell me that's a far better sign than what any mild ravings might signify."

Varick nodded, but said nothing. He wasn't as comforted. What if whatever Mercury did had damaged Carver somehow? Permanently?

"He'll be alright," Auntie Megaera soothed.

Varick nodded again. He couldn't bring himself to say more. He found keeping his composure in front of his aunt was just as much of a challenge as it had been in front of the crew, just in a very different way. And he absolutely was *not* about to start crying in front of her. Stars! He was fifteen, after all. Far too old for any of that sort of nonsense.

She ordered a fruited bun and a hot chocolate for herself from a nearby server and waited. Only after it arrived, along with another hot chocolate for Varick, did she speak.

"So to what are we drowning our sorrows?"

Varick began to play dumb, but she pointed a single, well-manicured nail toward his phalanx of empty cups, and he deflated.

"Everything," he muttered.

"Everything?" she replied. "My, I can see why you needed six, well, now seven rounds. That's a lot to drown." The unspoken question hung in the air as loudly as if she'd shouted it.

Would you like to tell me about it?

Varick, in a particularly petulant move, pulled his feet up onto the cushion and his knees up to his chin. He rested his nose atop them and mumbled into his legs.

"Everything is terrible."

"Hmm." Just that little noise said volumes. It said, "You are young, and everything is huge when you are young," but also, "I was young once too, and I remember everything being terrible. It's alright to feel that way." The noise said, "You're rich, and that can make many problems simply go away," as well as, "Your family, who are also rich, as well as united, have every intention of using you." "You're fortunate, because you're far away, on a luxury airship," and, "You have the utter misfortune of having to eventually return home."

All of these things were true. Varick imagined he could see them, all listed out on the broad windows before him. It helped a little, pulling apart the various pieces like this, but it did nothing for the fact that they were still there.

"None of the family… None of them know I'm here," he admitted.

"Is that so?"

How did hid great aunt do it? She was so good at leaving space for him without pushing. He told her about the argument with Magnus and breaking his knee, about losing his grandfather's watch and the four days of starvation and being disallowed from coming on this trip and the family's failure to do anything to actually make good on their pronounced punishment. Auntie Megaera's face took on a complicated expression of wry approval and concern.

"Well…" she said at last. "I know what it's like. That shouldn't have happened, any of it, but I don't know that I can blame you either. You poke a bear long enough, you can't exactly expect the bear to never poke back."

"I'm not a bear, though," Varick said, though he said it more out of petulant misery than any actual conviction or pedantry.

Megaera canted her head to the side. "It's not a perfect analogy, I'll grant you, but I suspect you understand my point."

He wanted to argue some more, just for argument's sake, but

he couldn't find the energy.

"Did you only sneak off for spite then?" she asked.

"No."

A pause ensued. "I'm afraid I won't be able to protect you for long once we're back. I don't have the legal grounds, but you're welcome to come stay at my house for as long as possible."

Varick nodded and thanked her. He'd not allowed himself to think about what would happen once he returned to Springhaven. It wasn't going to be pretty, whatever came.

"I made a commitment." He said this in response to her question earlier, but didn't bother to explain that.

Megaera tore a piece from her fruited bun and offered it to Varick, who turned it down. He was starting to feel a little jittery from all the sugar and chocolate.

She popped the morsel into her mouth. "And are you breaking that commitment?"

"…I'm thinking about it."

"Will people be hurt if you do?"

Varick didn't know in what context she meant, whether emotionally, physically, financially, or otherwise, but it didn't matter. "Yes."

"Will you be hurt if you don't break it?"

Ah, moral arithmetic. He hated it, but only because it was a sort of illogical logic he couldn't argue. "No, at least probably not." Probably not because there was still a non-zero chance Mercury was going to try and pull something.

"Hmm. Well, if I can help, you know I'm here." And again, she said so much in so little. He knew what the right thing to do was, even if he didn't like it.

Varick caught a glimpse of himself in one of the broad, brass panels that made up so much of the airship's decor. They reflected light and broke up the detailed, hand-painted murals that stretched across various swathes of corridors around the airship. His tailcoat was black as midnight, his gloves white as starlight, and the lining of his cape a deep ultramarine, like a pre-dawn sky. No one had been in Varick's cabin when he'd returned that afternoon. The crew were scattered to the winds of the ship, readying the last few details for tonight's heist job. A note, however, had been waiting for him.

We need a diversion tonight, or the job fails. Meet me by muster station eight during the art auction.

☿

Mercury had used the symbol for the planet of that same name as his signature, which Varick begrudgingly admitted was both clever and even a little bit classy. He rather liked the idea of a using an emblem over a written name for clandestine activities. What he didn't like was being bossed around with guilt trips. If he didn't show up, the whole crew was in danger.

Varick checked his fob watch. It was nearly time for his cue.

The art auction, the final one of the trip, was being held before dinner. Varick had come down with Auntie Megaera on his arm, but she'd spied one Miss Delilah MacKillop and begged off. Varick had smiled indulgently when he told her he didn't mind. He really didn't; he wished his great aunt all the happiness in the world, and besides, now he wouldn't need to invent an excuse for leaving. He sat in the back of the auction crowd, only half listening as the auctioneer introduced the next item up for bid, a Duskwood crystal decanter set commissioned by Prism Line Air Cruises specifically for this voyage.

"A real memento of this grand tour, and the only one of its kind," the auctioneer said.

As bidding began, Varick lifted a finger.

"A generous bid by Mister Pendragon!" the auctioneer said. "Thank you, sir. Do I have any others?"

He'd done this a few times now, never really meaning it. As soon as he attached his name to an item—and the auctioneer never missed an opportunity to name him—the bidding got heated. This was the sort of petty revenge he'd wanted earlier but hadn't been able to enact. Putting more money into artists' pockets and parting rich twits from it was always a balm to his nerves. He actually wanted the decanter set, though. The craftsmanship was of equal quality to the pieces created by his favorite glasssmith back in Springhaven. It'd be nice to have a souvenir from this mad voyage, and he spent the next few minutes squaring off against a fan-raiser, a mustache-twirler, and an ear-tugger. The ear-tugger lasted the longest, but Varick's finger lifts won out in the end. As the auctioneer had the crystal decanter set carried away, the next item, a taxidermied creation, was brought in. The artist in question was famous for building fantastical combinations of creations nature had never thought to make. This one was called a Wolpertinger, a rabbit with wings, antlers, and even tiny fangs, and Varick was glad that all eyes were on the strangely adorable beastie as he stood and walked to the appointed meeting place.

Mercury was there, as expected, next to an emergency exit window, out of sight from the art gallery and auction. He was dressed in a steward's uniform and smiled that smarmy smile when he saw Varick coming.

"I wasn't sure you'd show," he simpered. "I've been hearing some upsetting talk from the rest of the urchins."

"I've got my crew's back," Varick said coldly, ignoring Mercury's gibe. And because he was who he was, he couldn't help but add, "Unlike you."

Mercury's insincere smile grew. "I don't know what you

could mean by that."

Varick wanted to question him about Carver—who he'd suspiciously made no mention of—to call Mercury out on all the ways he'd failed the crew, about all his suspicions, but now wasn't the time. They were too close to showtime. When this night was done, Coal and Fulcrum would have their ticket to their new life and Varick could cut ties with Mercury.

"Why did you ask me here?" Varick said.

Mercury, however, seemed to feel the need to address their issues. "You know what the difference is between you and me, Varick? You're an idealist. You think there's a certain way everything should be and everyone should act, and everything else will just fall into place. And then there's me, a pragmatist. I take things as they are and I work with what I have. And pragmatism looks evil to an idealist like you. That's why you think, off in your little fantasy land, that I'm this big, bad villain, when really, my only offense is living in reality."

Varick's jaw clenched. Mercury was so wrong about him, so wrong about himself. "Laziness isn't pragmatism."

Mercury leaned against the wall, resting his head against the space between the emergency exit and the window next to it. "Do tell."

Varick took a deep breath and shook his head. This wasn't the plan. They shouldn't be getting distracted.

"What? Scared? Or is that your whole argument? You're nothing but a bored, little, rich boy with a big mouth and an empty head."

Something inside Varick snapped. As if the weather knew his mood, thunder rumbled in the clouds outside. "Settling for quick, easy scores and siphoning off of kids isn't pragmatism. You're a user and a taker. You could have been doing so much more." Mercury tipped his head, inviting more, and Varick took the bait. "Your whole team is so talented. You could have comfortably set

yourself up and the rest of them ten times over by now, but you fail to support them and cooperate and put in the bloody work. And you're bitter that you don't have more? Only now, when a shortcut to becoming King Thief comes up do you go for a big job. It's pure luck that the others will get anything out of this, not by your generous design. Because you don't give a toss about any of them. Or are you planning on taking all the loot for yourself and leaving them w—"

Varick saw his mistake only a second before Mercury acted. He saw the man's fist come for him, and Varick dodged, but just barely. The fist made a glancing blow, not enough to knock Varick off of his feet, but enough to buy Mercury an extra second or two. The man yanked his arm back, driving his elbow into a glass case on the wall. In his periphery, Varick could only just catch the words, *Case of Emergency*. An alarm bell started to ring from the top of the case. Mercury was already reaching for the lever within. Varick's brain scrambled for options.

The horrifying *shoop* noise of air pressure releasing along the seam of the emergency exit sounded, and Varick made a wild grab for Mercury. His fingers brushed the man's arm as the window opened. The entire pane slid sideways. Varick heard the *ka-chonk* sound of it catching on the rollers, as wind and changing pressure pulled him backward. Mercury's other hand was hanging onto on iron and brass bench bolted to the floor behind him. He grinned as Varick failed to grab onto his sleeve. In slow motion, Varick felt himself pulled out through the window. His grasping fingernails raked down Mercury's hand. Then, the icy fingers of the wind yanked Varick across the threshold and out into nothingness.

40

PEELING PUNCHY

alf a second after Varick was ripped out of the airship, a juddering yank rocked his shoulders, threatening to rip them from their sockets. He looked to find his hands clenched around one of the canvas straps dotted all up and down and along the airship. The others fluttered wildly, as if either panicked for his predicament or cheering for the lucky save. That same innate survival instinct that had likely helped him to catch it in the first place made him hold on for dear life. As the wind tossed Varick up and down like a paper decoration in a rained-out-garden party, he thanked every star in the sky for whoever or whatever had caused these small, tightly woven saviors to exist. Lightning flashed somewhere nearby, lighting up the side of the airship into sharp relief. It was so cold. Bitter, painfully cold. Varick let out a hysterical sort of laugh as he thought back to his behind-the-scenes tour, to the part where the airro guiding it had pointed the safety straps out. At the time, Varick had innocently puzzled at how anyone might "accidentally fall overboard," as the airro had phrased it.

When there's a murderous ratbag out to get you, Varick now knew. *That's how.*

Varick couldn't hear anything but the wind in his ears and the snapping of his cape flying straight out behind him. He tried to remember what the airro had said about how someone who'd fallen overboard got back in. Oh right, someone else had to rescue you.

Seems like there's a wee hole in the strategy, Varick thought. Definitely something for the *How Can We Improve* comment cards.

Thankfully, people were already gathering from the nearby auction. That alarm bell was awfully bloody loud, thank these capricious heavens in which Varick was currently suspended. As the wind buffeted him upwards again, he could just see airrocrew members urging guests to stay back. The pressure in the airship had equalized, so no one else was in danger of being sucked out. Rather, it would have been like walking toward a hurricane. The people beyond screamed and pointed, while three more airros had gathered near the gaping hole, hustling to strap on safety lines. For a split second, Varick actually felt as if he could relax. He had a good grip on the safety strap, his muscles were straining, but nothing too bad yet, and help was on the way. He was going to be alright.

Then he saw her. Great Auntie Megaera.

She was practically thrashing a pair of airrocrew members with her handbag as she fought to push through. Spindle was there too, doing the same, and the dogs were enthusiastically adding to the chaos. It might have been funny if Varick wasn't terrified of his great aunt having a heart attack.

Eventually, though, and with the efficiency of well-trained professionals, the airros hauled Varick inside to solid flooring and light and warmth and safety.

Varick's legs gave out beneath him as the door was, with great effort, shut again. People were speaking to him, but he couldn't process what they were saying. Somehow, his head both buzzed and rang empty. He was *alive*. Mercury had tried to murder him.

Mercury.

Had tried.

To murder him.

But failed. And his failure was going to come back with a vengeance so sharp and swift he'd never see it coming.

Varick's head began to clear then. He had to find Mercury before he could hurt any of the rest of the crew.

"Varick, for heaven's sake, say *something*," came a familiar voice next to him.

He looked up from where he'd been crouched on the floor and saw Auntie Megaera there. Her hands were on his cheek and shoulder, and her expression was so drawn, he imagined he could see all the bones of her face just then.

"Please don't have a heart attack." The fear from earlier fell from his mouth without him meaning for it to.

"Oh, thank the stars!" She hugged him, and Varick felt wetness on his face. She was crying. Shock tried to take hold of him again, but he pushed it back. There would be time for that later, after he'd dealt with Mercury.

"I should go back to my room and change," Varick said.

He politely declined the various offers of help several airros made, including an offer for an escort down to the medical bay, and broke away from the group. Megaera insisted on joining him, but he mumbled an apology, assured her that he was fine, and hurried off faster than she or anyone else could follow. Thoughts of what might have been fueled Varick. He'd been mere inches from plummeting to the unforgiving earth below. It was possible she'd never know what had become of him. Mercury had very nearly done that to one of the kindest people Varick had ever known, and the only family left that he cared about. Hot, precise anger bubbled in Varick as he went. He wondered if perhaps Mercury had planned to off him the entire time.

Varick made a beeline for the vault several decks below them. Anyone with questions about how the "accident" with the emergency exit had happened would go looking for him in his cabin. And with the ship's guests at the auction and dinner to follow, his journey was quiet. Stewards and other airrocrew members were thin on the ground lower down too, with guest rooms needing to be refreshed before bed and the final night's activities to attend to. A grand show in the atrium was scheduled for later that evening, with musical numbers, acrobats swinging from silk trapezes, and dancers swirling around the floor. Or so said the scuttlebutt that Marlowe, Fulcrum, and Coal had gathered.

Thinking of Marlowe, Varick wondered if he was in cahoots with Mercury. After all, the big lad had never really been much fussed about their leader's strange behavior.

Varick slowed a few corridors from the vault. He didn't know how the guard-incapacitation part of the plan was going, and if Marlowe too was a traitor and feeling punchy, Varick didn't want to come across him by surprise. Marlowe had done his reconnaissance well. He'd buddied up to the vault guards, bonding over their shared travails in finding clothing that fit—the shoulders were always the hardest—favorite publications, and, to everyone's surprise, forays into vegetarianism. And thus, Marlowe had learned both who was scheduled to be on duty and how their rotations worked. The crew had hours to complete the job, nearly until dawn, before the next guard shift began.

Thank the heavens for small mercies.

Marlowe would have to be quick, though, and unseen. Two alarms, one inside the vault itself and one without, could be sounded, which would alert airrocrew members elsewhere in the ship. Varick held onto the idea of setting one off if things got really, horribly ugly, but that was the lastest of last-ditch options.

He peeked around corners, using the inside of his pocket watch's cover as a mirror, before flitting from one spot to the next, ears always pricked for the sound of shoes plodding down the hall or the wet meat noises of someone having the snot beat out of them. True, Marlowe was armed with laudanum syringes in order to avoid violence, but there was always a chance that part of the plan went pear-shaped. Varick came upon an auspicious sight as he peeked around a corner just a few hallways from the vault. There, making surprisingly little noise, was Marlowe. He wore a vault guard's uniform—helpfully stolen by Cole—and was dragging one of the real vault guards toward a supply closet where they'd planned to leave the unconscious bodies. Varick didn't know whether this was the first or the second guard, given that he couldn't see inside the closet, and, as before, he kept out a weather eye, worried the other might still come up behind him.

Soft grunting emanated from the closet as Marlowe presumably positioned the man inside. He'd also be administering the soporific sponges to keep the guards insensate. The crew planned on removing these once their work was done, but the effects would take a bit to wear off, and when the guards awoke, they should feel as if they'd indulged in a night of heavy drinking and shouldn't remember anything.

Varick turned his head to check again that no second guard was sneaking up behind him. The coast was still clear, but when he looked back in Marlowe's direction, he saw the man from the cooperage, also dressed in a guard's uniform, loping on near-silent feet toward the closet with fists clenched and ready for a fight.

And Marlowe would have his back turned. He'd be caught by

surprise.

Without thinking, Varick called out Marlowe's name. Varick's legs tensed, ready to run but in which direction? If a second guard was still stalking about, he'd have heard the cry for certain. The cooperage man looked in Varick's direction, but disappeared behind the open door of the supply closet. A second later, the dull, heavy sound of someone being hit squelched through the silent hallway. The cooperage man staggered back out of the closet, throwing punches but avoiding them too. Thank the stars! And Varick finally moved.

He ran forward to help Marlowe fight off the man. Varick still wasn't a great fighter, but two against one were much better odds. He remembered what Coal had taught him about using what he had. He leaned into his quickness and bounced off the wall of the corridor before driving his knee into the man's back and bounding away again. As he went, he saw that two guards lay prone within the closet. The cooperage man didn't buckle under Varick's strike, but Marlowe landed a clean punch to his stomach. Varick turned and came back for another shot, but the cooperage man saw him coming and drove his elbow back, making Varick need to dodge, before aiming a blow at Marlowe's face. It landed, and Marlowe staggered back a step.

The two hitters were evenly matched muscle-wise, and Marlowe was taller, but the cooperage man was older by probably ten years, and he had experience on his side. He exploited his opportunity and drove his other fist into Marlowe's face as well. The big lad's lip split, and Varick took a second to flick out the small blade Fulcrum had installed into the sole of his evening shoe. Marlowe threw a weak punch at the cooperage man, but he blocked it easily. Varick's own attack was minor but vicious, kicking hard at their opponent's leg. It slid easily into the man's ankle, stuck for a moment, making Varick stumble, and then snapped off of Varick's shoe. The cooperage man flinched and grunted in pain, but he put all of his focus into incapacitating Marlowe. He struck again, twice, and Varick could see Marlowe was going down. There was nothing he could do to stop it. The little boot knife was the only weapon he'd had on him, and anything else he might use waited beyond, inside the closet. Varick could use his tie as a garrote, if the cooperage man wouldn't simply rip Varick off his back. He couldn't even call for help since both vault guards were unconscious within the closet, the soporific sponges already in place over their faces.

Varick had some choices, though. He could stick around to get pummeled; the cooperage man would squash him flat in minutes. He could abandon everyone and wash his hands of the entire job. Or, if he couldn't help Marlowe, maybe he could still save Coal and Fulcrum. Varick didn't even have to think. He spun and headed for the vault.

Varick ran pell mell through the door to the vault's reception area, nearly crashing into it in his haste to get the sodding thing open. He slammed it shut again, not caring if anyone heard. Though that was the beauty of this plan. No one was supposed to be down here right now besides the guards. Coal, who was kneeling down at the vault door and dressed in a housekeeping uniform, and Fulcrum, dressed similarly and standing just beyond, looked at him with expressions of curious surprise and annoyed indignation, respectively. A housekeeping cart waited nearby, and Varick knew it contained the rest of their supplies for the heist. Mercury stood there too, wearing a set of knuckle dusters on each hand and leaning against the wall like someone trying too hard to appear languid. He was still dressed in the steward's uniform, and only the barest hint of surprise flashed in his eyes before it disappeared again.

"Get out," Varick panted. "Mercury's double-crossed us."

The man in question chuckled. "What are you on about? You indulge in too many drinks upstairs?"

"Oh, come off it!" Varick cried. "You're out to kill us all." Stars, he knew he sounded like a lunatic, but what else could he do? The cooperage man might come through the door any second. He looked to Coal and Fulcrum. "You have to believe me! He pushed me out of a window. I still have the blood on my hands." Varick displayed his fingertips. Blood stained beneath his fingernails. When the two brothers squinted at the sight, Varick exclaimed, "I know it's not much, but Mercury just had Marlowe beat up too, if not murdered, and he tried to poison Carver. Please!"

The *please* was what seemed to snag Fulcrum's attention. He tipped his head to the side as he scrutinized first the wreck of Varick's hair, the state of his clothes, and then Mercury. His eyes focused on the angry red scratches down Mercury's hand, but it was too late. The door behind Varick opened, and the cooperage man looked huge as he filled up the doorway. The door made no click behind him as it closed, no squeak on its well-oiled hinges, but Varick imagined he could hear air leaving the room. No way out.

"Bollocks," Varick cursed under his breath.

Fulcrum's eyes narrowed as his younger brother's widened.

"What's this about, Mercury?" Fulcrum demanded. "Where's Marlowe?"

The facade fell off of Mercury like a brick through clouds. "There's been a change of plans. Marlowe's no longer trustworthy." He looked to his goon standing before the now-closed door. "Thumper, get rid of the toff."

"You don't want to do that." Varick spoke the threat before Thumper, as the man was apparently called, had even taken a step. His voice had gone low and dangerous. Impressive, considering how watery his insides felt. He didn't wait for Mercury to ask why. He wasn't ever going to give that man the benefit of the doubt again.

Thumper didn't stop advancing, but at least he limped a little from the tiny stab wound in his ankle. The reception area wasn't large, which was a blessing and curse. The bronze greyhound statuette Varick had pretended to examine just two days ago took only a split second to grab, but that was enough time for Thumper to get within arm's reach of Varick. His big, beefy hand was just touching the lapels of Varick's dinner jacket when Mercury raised a hand to stop his crony.

Varick had raised the sculpture toward the glass box where Mister Dilley worked. He couldn't help but smirk when he saw Mercury's eyes rest on the little, now-slightly-bloodstained placard that read, *This glass is alarmed; do not break.*

"You're down two men," Varick said. "You won't get as much loot without my help. You might even risk being caught if Thumper here is too rough with me."

The more exact words in Varick's head were, *If Thumper here does a bad job of hiding my body,* but he didn't want to give Mercury any ideas.

He went on. "People will notice if I'm gone, and you've been seen with me. You're part of my staff. Misfortune befalling two members of our party? Very suspicious indeed. Why don't we have a truce instead?"

A long moment passed, wherein Mercury rubbed his chin thoughtfully. Beneath his fine, though disheveled clothing, Varick sweated like he'd never sweated before. Really, only Great Auntie Megaera had seen Mercury with Varick, and maybe that's how the man had planned it. Maybe he'd been so absent, not just because he had a side-goon to manage, but because he hadn't wanted people to be able to connect him with Varick. He could send Thumper after Auntie Megaera to dispose of her too, but that would be harder, considering she tended toward public areas, instead of skulking about in secret like Varick. And she had a great, massive dog to guard her too, but Mercury could still try.

Varick pressed harder, tapping the corner of the statuette ever so slightly against the glass. That was harder to do than Varick had imagined, given the weight of the thing, and instead of a little tap-tap, the piece made a single, solid thump against the thick glass. Coal and Fulcrum jumped, and everything inside Varick clenched as he waited for the sound of cracking glass, but he didn't blink. And the glass remained unmarred, thank heaven.

"This doesn't need to get ugly," he said, pouring the energy of his anxiety into lowering his voice into a controlled rasp.

Another moment, and Mercury at last nodded. "Alright then, truce. But one hint of trickery from any of you, and the pipsqueak suffers." He put one heavy hand on Coal's shoulder, knuckle dusters gleaming in the low, petrolsene light.

Coal paled, and Fulcrum swallowed hard, but neither said a word. Varick hated to relinquish his one weapon, but he replaced the statuette and raised his hands in a peaceful gesture. He didn't for a second believe Mercury wasn't still planning on stitching them up, but for Coal's sake, Varick needed to play nice for now. He sidled up to Fulcrum, while Mercury had Thumper take up the rear, guarding the only path out.

"Get to it," Mercury snapped at Coal. "Time is money."

Coal's hand shook as he held the slip of paper with the lever arrangement written on it.

They hadn't figured out the last piece of this particular puzzle, but Fulcrum had calculated that, if indeed there were four movements up and three down, and the first two levers pointed up by the end, and if Varick was correct in having heard levers one through four all move upwards in the initial sequence, taking into account that Carver and Varick had both seen lever number three in the down position after Harefoot's mischief, that that left two downward moves to figure out. But, assuming all of this was correct, that left only lever number four available to be moved down, leaving one orphan downward click. Fulcrum had been convinced that Varick had gotten things wrong. Varick had unhelpfully snarked that Fulcrum was welcome to go down to the vault and have a look for himself. And they'd all meant to try and come up with more solutions, but that had never come to pass.

No one mentioned any of this now as Coal clicked the first four levers upward, and then the third down again. He paused and looked at Fulcrum, who looked at Varick. The two taller boys were united now; they needed to take care of one another.

"The next one should be the fourth lever going back down again," Varick said as confidently as he could. His eyes, locked with Fulcrum's, added a silent, "That's right, right?"

Fulcrum nodded and said in his usual flat tone, "Yeah, that's correct."

Coal did so, and a small metal plate silently sprang upward to reveal a seventh tiny lever. The plate, like the outer door to Mister Dilley's booth, had fit so seamlessly when closed that it disappeared into the rest of the vault door. The new lever sat dead in the center of its channel, both up and down options for movement. That was why there was an orphan downward noise in the sequence.

"Down?" Coal asked.

"Down," Varick and Fulcrum agreed together.

Coal did so and the sound of cogs turning resounded, followed by a mechanical click inside the door. Then it was time for the key. Coal drew his copy, made of glue and crushed eggshells, from the mold and began to sing to himself, as he often did during a bit of mischief. It seemed to center him.

"Breaking in the vault, I'm breaking in the vault, breaking in the vault, I'm breaking in the vault."

Coal turned the key one way, then the hatch wheel, following the pattern Varick and Carver had observed. The key stuck now and again, and Coal jiggled the fragile-looking thing in an effort to complete his rotation. His voice grew quiet as it became clear they'd not created a perfect copy.

"Talk to it," Fulcrum said softly, and Varick had a feeling this was some sort of encouragement technique, or perhaps an inside joke, known only between them. "Maybe it needs a bit of encouragement."

"Legally," Coal said, as if assuring the lock. "I'm legally allowed to be here. I'm legally breaking into the vault."

Whatever the lock might have thought about that claim, Varick and the crew would never find out because a moment later, a quiet snap resounded, and Coal froze in his spot.

"What?" Mercury demanded. "What's happened?" Coal didn't reply, and Mercury grabbed the boy's shoulder to shove him away from the door.

Barely sticking out from the keyhole was a short, jagged sliver of pulverized eggshells suspended in dried glue. Coal held the broken end of the shaft in his hand.

"What the blazes is that?" Mercury asked. A second later, he answered his own question. "Is that the key? *Is that the sodding key*?! What did you do, Coal?"

"He didn't do anything," Fulcrum said. "*I* made the key. It's my fault it broke."

"Did you think to make more than one?"

Mercury's tone dripped with condescension. It made Varick want to kick him right in the tallywags, but he forced himself to stay still and silent as his mind raced.

"You said to only make one," Fulcrum said. "I told you I wanted to make two, but you said no, that it'd be a waste of time and resources."

Varick had not been privy to this conversation, and he saw paranoia written all over it. Mercury hadn't trusted one of his own team not to use a spare key to do their own heist.

"We have time." Coal interjected. "We can make another. We can make one right now. Right now. Right now?"

"*Not* now, Coal," his brother snapped.

Varick's ears pricked up at that. To someone who didn't know Coal, they might have just thought he was babbling out of fear, but there was something beneath the words, some hidden message passing between the brothers.

"Shut up!" Mercury snarled. "Both of you, always like a couple of buzzing, little gnats." He shoved his hands in their faces and mimed tiny, annoying bugs flying around. "Fulcrum, since you stupidly only made one key, you'd better fix the one we have. Or your little brother will pay."

Behind them all, Thumper cracked his knuckles menacingly. Fulcrum paled.

"I…" he began.

Then he knelt down and starting trying to work what was left of the key in the lock, but there wasn't enough of it left to grab onto, much less manipulate. He drew a set of pilers from a pouch on his belt and grasped the end. Even after much wriggling and a few swears, Fulcrum still failed to turn the key. Fear pinched his face, and Varick saw the lad struggling with what to tell Mercury.

"It's not going to work," he whispered.

"Sorry?" Mercury snipped.

"It's… stuck."

Mercury rubbed his fingertips across his brow. Through gritted teeth, he said, "Is that it then? You're telling me there's no other way?" No one spoke. Anger rolled off of Mercury like heat from a smelter. At last, he said, "What a shame," and reached out to grab Coal.

41

THE DISGRUNTLED CATERPILLAR OF ROT-HOG LANE

"**W**hat about the window?" Varick said. His voice came out dead and flat. He envisioned Mercury outside the airship being buffeted by the wind, freezing air stinging his skin. Just as it had Varick.

Mercury yanked Coal toward him and snapped, "What?"

"You can go in through the window," Varick said. "The cleaners open it up from the outside, so it must be possible. And the vault's easy to unlock from within. It's a safety precaution."

"*You* can go in through the window," Mercury growled. "And make it quick. I'm running out of patience."

Varick opened his mouth to object. He hadn't really thought through the suggestion. He'd just wanted to protect Coal. There were a million reasons not to do it, but Mercury wouldn't listen to a one of them. The realization that *this* might well be

Mercury's new plan for getting rid of him splashed cold water over Varick's brain. For spite, he refused to show any fear.

"Get ready for the next step in the plan. I'll won't be long, so don't waste time." And he strode out of the vault's reception area.

Rain ran in livid streaks down the window, liquid darts waiting to sink into Varick. He glared back at them as he checked his rigging again. The helpful map he'd received on his ship tour had given him vital information. Just a few decks directly below him was the window he needed. Other windows stood between him and his target, and while guests would still be at dinner, there was always a chance a member of staff or an airro might spot him while attending to their duties.

Varick had wanted a better rig than the stolen bosun's chair, but he was no tinkerer like Fulcrum, even if he'd had the luxury of time. At least he'd been able to make a second fortuitous find in a supply closet on his way here.

The window he would exit through was not an emergency one like that which Mercury had sent Varick through earlier that evening. It was small, in the backroom of one of the many expensive shops, and didn't have an alarm. The shop's doors were locked, but the ventilation system was wide open. Varick's suit was looking especially bedraggled now, given how dusty the shafts were, to say nothing of his hair, which had been further mussed, if that was even possible, by the huge but thankfully slow-moving fans, which constantly moved warm air—collected from the great boilers down in the belly of the vessel and from hot, metal tubes that ran from taps and radiators—all over the airship. This was the great, beating heart of the heating system used to keep all the guests comfortable, just like the sort Coal had described to Varick the night they'd broken into the offices of

Pendragon, Umpleby, and Johnson.

Now, before the window, Varick forced himself to take a deep, slow breath. And ignore the worsening storm outside. Lightning flashed constantly now, and thunder kept growling like a huge, hungry sky-dwelling beast.

"There's nothing for it, mate," he told himself. "You just just have to do it."

Or Coal, and Fulcrum too, he had no doubt, would pay for his delay.

With his heart in his throat and his body tethered firmly to avoid being sucked out again, Varick slid the window open. The air that blew inside howled and yanked at him, but his tether held. Then, when the air pressure stopped pulling and had started to push, he untethered himself and trudged forward through the riotous wind. Varick started his journey by clipping the bosun's chair rigging to a couple of the safety straps outside the window, slipping a handheld cleat into a groove beneath it made for this sort of maneuvering, and then forced himself into the night.

The rain wasted no time in needling into his skin, and Varick was very nearly blown completely helter-skelter as he fought to hold onto the cleat, which had instantly grown slick and cold as ice. From within the attached bosun's tool bag, Varick pulled a second metal cleat, which also neatly slotted into the same groove as its twin. Thank the stars someone had through to attach leather straps to the cleats, so even when Varick's grip slipped— which took all of about three seconds—the straps caught him.

Slip, reach, groove, secure. This was the mantra that repeated over and over in Varick's head as he went. He never removed both cleats at once, bosun's chair or no. That had the potential to send him spiraling back even farther than where he'd started.

"Come on, you little git," Varick growled at the one in his hand, which had slipped while he'd been trying to insert it into its next place.

Even secured as he was, relatively speaking, the wind still regularly picked him up and dropped him back down. The short lead the leather straps gave him made it so his knees took the worst of each fall. Varick swore more on that journey than he ever had in his life, and he made up quite a few creative new insults. Thus, slowly and colorfully, soaking wet and shivering, he inched his way like a disgruntled caterpillar down the side of the ship, lightning seeming ready to reach out and strike him at any moment. When he finally made it down to the vault window, where rot-hog lane crossed wank-stank way, his fingers were nearly numb and his exposed skin felt as if it'd been stung by thousands of bees. Varick braced himself against some black marks on the window frame, and fumbled with the lock until he gave up and stuck his freezing fingers into his mouth to get some life back into them. Only then was he able to manipulate things again and unlatch the window. The escaping air blew his sodden hair straight back and up, but it was done at last. He half fell into the vault room and stumbled toward the door, worried he'd taken too long. He didn't know how much time had passed, but Mercury was no doubt furious by now. The inside locks clicked cheerily from Varick's side, each one sliding easily from their bolts, save for one. He had to force the last one, and it opened with a crunch. That must have been what was left of the eggshell key.

Well, here's hoping that's made it harder to get in come morning, Varick thought.

Once the door was open, Mercury practically shoved Varick out of the way to get inside, but at least that left him, Fulcrum, and Coal out of Mercury's sights. Varick couldn't tell if the brothers had suffered in his absence, but it seemed Fulcrum had used his time well. He was already dressed in his final disguise— a lovely aqua-colored evening gown with a floral print and a chocolate brown swath of velvet at the waist, which was gathered and draped over the bustle. Fulcrum had even done a rather nice updo, replete with coils and braids that cascaded over the scarred side of his scalp. Varick couldn't help but wonder if he'd protected his brother by insisting Coal help him dress.

"You look nice," Varick said sincerely.

Fulcrum took in his dirty, soaked clothes; windblown hair; and splotchy, reddened skin. "You don't." With that, he swept past Varick with all the pomp and poise of a princess. He turned back then, with a soft smile and whispered, "Thank you."

Varick smirked back, and then sniped loud enough for Mercury to hear. "I can always rely on those terrible manners of yours." He gave a little wink.

"Children," Mercury warned dangerously. "Coal, over here with me."

Thumper came forward and filled the vault doorway, while Varick and Fulcrum were tasked with getting the guard key and various client keys from the backroom. The daren't say anything while Varick went to work on the hidden door of the booth, and they wasted no time once they were in the backroom to get into the locked cabinet of client keys. It was during these few stolen minutes, while Thumper still guarded the door to the vault, that Varick risked one, quick comment to Fulcrum.

"If anything happens to me, you can trust my gams."

Varick wasn't even certain Fulcrum had heard him. He didn't respond, and Varick wasn't willing to risk trying again, given how Thumper kept his eyes rotating between them and Coal.

The guard key was trickier to find, and Varick worried he and Coal would have to pick each guard lock individually. It'd be easier once they'd done one since they'd all be the same, but it would take a lot more time. Mister Eaddy had simply had the key on him when Varick had stored his valuables in his safe; it was possible the man took it with him when he left for the night. Thankfully, however, Fulcrum found a small, locked drawer in the backroom's only desk, which, after Varick had broken in, yielded the guard key. Then, with access to all the keys, the real looting began.

Mercury had Varick show him Spindle's safe. And, even though he and Carver hadn't seen any crown, they opened it first.

Mercury emptied out the jeweled doggy crowns and collars and swore when he saw no other treasures waited within to be plucked. Varick peered inside and, after a moment, canted his head in thought.

"Something looks off," he said.

"What?" Mercury asked.

Varick held out his hands. "May I?"

Mercury nodded, and Varick reached his arm inside the safe. When he stroked the side wall, it was smooth and, even in shadow, dimly reflected the light of the petrolsene sconces dotted around the room. The back, however, was dull, unreflective, and had a slightly textured feel about it. He looked up at Mercury with a grin.

"She's hidden it in the back, disguised as part of the safe."

Mercury, however, was scowling. "How'd you spot that?"

What Varick really wanted to say was, *Because I pay attention to, you dolt.* What he actually said was, "The shadows looked strange."

It took some shimmying, but they managed to extract a small, pasteboard box, which appeared to have been crafted to perfectly match and fit inside this particular safe.

"Clever," Fulcrum said, taking in the details.

With the greatest of care, Mercury opened the lid. Even with the petrolsene just barely turned up, the Nightfall Crown exploded into brilliance as soon as the lid was lifted. Everyone there let out little gasps of wonder as light and color shattered through the gemstones and delicate loops of glass and splattered over the inside of the box and up onto their awestruck faces.

"I've done it," Mercury breathed. "I've actually done it."

Varick bristled, but didn't address it. Instead, he suggested, "We ought to put it away and get pillaging."

Mercury nodded slowly, as if afraid that any sudden movement might cause the crown to fall to pieces. Unlikely, given the padding strategically placed around it, but even so, he closed the lid with the utmost care. Fulcrum was already adjusting his skirts to reveal the bustle beneath. Varick had custom ordered the bustle, choosing one of the newest models, which were tending toward a larger extension in the back. Varick's design was practically avant garde, given the extra few inches he'd had added to ensure the crown would have plenty of room. It was a good thing he had, because they hadn't accounted for it to be inside of a box. Fulcrum had built a small platform and securing straps of braided fabric scraps inside the fullest part of the form. It was onto this rig that they placed the Nightfall Crown's box, tying it securely in place.

Once Fulcrum's skirts were back in order over the undergarment, they went to work, focusing on the smaller safes first. Even Thumper got in on the action, leaving the door propped open with the greyhound statuette, and they dumped their ill-gotten goods into the housekeeping cart that Coal had nicked. Most of them anyway. Varick spied a few of the smaller but highly valuable pieces make their way into secret pockets he'd sewn into Fulcrum's skirt, only when Thumper and Mercury weren't looking, though.

Varick, for his part, wanted them all to just get out, but Coal and Fulcrum seemed to still have their fresh start in mind. Varick wondered if the brothers thought there remained a chance that Mercury was going to uphold his end of the bargain, but he certainly didn't. The only reason Mercury wasn't trying to kill them was that they were useful. As Varick pillaged, he kept an eye out for opportunities, though it didn't seem likely one would appear with Thumper there. That is, until a figure bolted through the doorway, one big fist ready to strike.

Varick watched in elation and fear as Marlowe, face bloodied and bruises blooming all over, shot into the room just as Thumper was passing by the doorway. Marlowe landed a solid hook into the side of the goon's jaw. Thumper dropped almost instantly to the floor. Marlowe really did know how to knock someone out with just one hit. It took only a moment before Mercury sized up the situation and grabbed Coal.

"Don't try anything or the kid gets it," Mercury growled, though a higher note of fear threaded into his words.

Varick grinned nastily. Marlowe might have been in cahoots with Mercury before, but after that backstabbing, no longer. On his way up to the shop's backroom, Varick had nipped into the supply closet where Thumper had left Marlowe with the guards. There, Varick had found Marlowe unconscious, but still alive. Thumper had placed a soporific sponge over Marlowe's damaged face, just as had been done for the drugged guards. Varick had removed it, hoping Marlowe would wake up soon and, with luck, provide some much-needed help. Things could not have turned out better if Varick had planned them like this. Now, he was in control. They just needed to—

"Now, Coal," Fulcrum said.

Quick as a flash, Coal stamped his foot down, drove his elbow back, and then turned to knee Mercury in right in the groin. The sight of Mercury crumpling filled Varick with a twisted sense of joy, but it was short-lived.

"Scarper!" Coal cried, and he took off like a loosed crossbow bolt, grabbing the cart of stolen goods and driving it out at breakneck speed.

Fulcrum was right behind, and Varick saw Marlowe hesitate.

"Leave him," Varick told Marlowe. "We're still on the job."

Marlowe glared at Mercury, who was getting to his feet

again, face contorted in rage. Light glinted off the brass knuckles. Marlowe might have figured that, battered as he was, Mercury actually stood a chance against him. Or maybe he did have some loyalty to the crew. Either way, Marlowe turned and ran as fast as his injured body would let him. Varick pulled the vault door shut behind him and spun the hatch wheel. Mercury would just flip the inside bolts back and follow, but at least it would give them a few seconds.

"Cover our tracks," Varick told Marlowe. "Get the sponges we left on the guards."

Varick was fast, and after giving this command, he pulled ahead of the big lad in moments. The hallways down on this deck didn't branch off much, at least to places where any of them could access, so it was pretty direct path until the stairs. That was where Varick caught up with Fulcrum. He was doing a good job managing both his dress and the high heels he wore, but it was still slower than Varick, who could take two and three steps at a time. And Mercury, no doubt with his longer legs, would be on them soon.

"Where's Coal?"

"Service lift. It's how we got down here. We split up so Mercury couldn't get us both."

"He's going to come after you first," Varick said.

"I know," Fulcrum panted.

Bugger all, Fulcrum had done it again. He'd put himself in harm's way trying to protect his little brother. Behind and below them, they could hear the sound of fast footsteps coming down the corridor toward the stairs. Fulcrum swore and hiked his skirts higher.

Varick turned and started back down. "I'll try to slow him down. Remember what I said." He gave nothing more away, in case Mercury could hear them.

Varick didn't know what exactly he planned to do, but he was going to do it as hard as he could. Mercury appeared at the bottom of the stairway, which was, unfortunately for Varick, wide enough for several people and bisected by a railing. Mercury saw Varick pounding back down the stairs toward him and took the section opposite. As Varick had suspected, the man's long legs ate up multiple steps at a time. Not knowing what else to do and time to do it whooshing away, Varick pushed himself up onto the railing that divided him and Mercury and leapt.

Varick's feet cycled through the air, fruitlessly trying to steer. His arms reached, but Mercury was too fast and easily ducked under the would-be tackle. At least Varick's foot managed to clip the man's head, causing him to stumble. The corner of the small blade, broken off of Varick's shoe earlier that evening, left a shallow slice where it connected, and blood leaked out to run down the side of Mercury's face. Varick would have smiled had the wall not abruptly and pitilessly stopped his descending arc. He landed hard on his wrist. Pain burst inside the joint. Varick let out a grunt as he tried to push himself up to chase Mercury, who was just nearing the top of the stairs. He faltered and knew then he had no chance of catching up with the man.

41.5
DAMSEL IN DISTRESS

Thank the stars for people. Fulcrum had made it to a passenger lift on the next deck up. Ideally, he would have liked to flee to Varick's cabin, but he didn't have the key. Only Coal did. And Fulcrum was pretty sure Mercury had already figured that's the first place they'd both go. Thus, Fulcrum headed for the Observation deck where most of the airship guests were still having dinner, or if they'd been really speedy, having after dinner drinks before the night's entertainment began. Mercury might have even seen him get into the lift, and Fulcrum hoped he had. If Mercury was chasing him, he wasn't chasing Coal. Fulcrum entered into the art gallery area, searching for safety. He didn't know what would happen if he tried to head for the dining room; he didn't know the protocol. Would they turn him away if he, oh, he didn't know, failed to tell them some secret rich person passphrase to get in. Rich people were like that.

Fulcrum hated that he'd had to slow down up here. Someone

might start trouble if they saw a damsel in distress such as himself running. He wanted safety, not attention. He pulled a fan from the chatelaine hanging from his waist and fanned himself. Blazes, this disguise was heavier than he'd imagined it would be. Then again, he hadn't thought he'd have to run in it.

The plan had originally been to find Spindle and present the crown as a group. The idea had made Fulcrum feel good when Mercury had said it. Now Fulcrum wondered how much of the entire scheme had been a lie. How far would Mercury have led them before doing away with them? Or did Varick only have it half-right? Maybe Carver was just regular sick. Maybe Marlowe had planned to double-cross Mercury and Mercury had found out? Fulcrum wanted so badly to believe that, but no. It didn't add up. Mercury had brought in that Thumper bloke. And he hadn't hesitated to threaten Coal. Maybe Mercury had only pretended to go along with Varick's plan—which Fulcrum felt had been a tad overwrought; the ponce clearly just liked dramatics—in order to keep Varick happy.

Fulcrum's heart stopped as he saw Mercury's tall form making his way into the art gallery. He tried to hide behind his fan, but it was too late. Mercury was making a beeline for him. The man was bleeding, not badly, but it was down his face. Someone was going to notice and start asking questions. Fulcrum swept his gaze about the area. Where could he go that Mercury couldn't follow? Then he saw it. The sign was small, very nearly hidden—because *propriety* and all that blarney—but it was exactly what Fulcrum needed. And throwing appearances to the wind, he dashed for the ladies' room.

Inside, he stopped short. A woman was in here!

Well, of course a woman might be in here, twit, Fulcrum thought to himself. *It's the* ladies' *loos.*

She was older, with snowy white hair and a single, elegantly designed moonstone ring on one hand. She stood at the long mirror that overlooked the sinks, checking her hairstyle. The woman caught sight of Fulcrum standing there, and she paused, looking concerned.

He spun before she could get a good look at him, headed for a stall, and locked the door behind him.

Moments later, he heard the sounds of outside flow in as someone opened the door. It closed again almost immediately, and Fulcrum wondered if that had been Mercury. Had he spied the old woman and turned tail? Would Mercury really be so brazen as to come into the *women's* restroom? Here? In such a public setting?

He waited, listening for the other woman to leave. Instead, a tentative knock sounded on his door. "Apologies, my dear. This is very forward of me, but are you alright?"

Fulcrum knew that voice! He wasn't certain what to do. Another moment passed, and the voice came again.

"Do you need help?"

42

A Lotta Fights and No Prizes

When Varick finally made it back to his suite, his wrist was still sore, but doing better, just so long as he didn't bend it a certain way. He'd searched for Mercury and any members of his crew, but had come up empty. He'd even swung by the medical bay to check on Carver, who was doing better. He'd woken up for a bit, but he was weak and sleeping again and the doctor on duty had recommended that he not be disturbed. Only when the doctor raked his eyes over the state of Varick's hair and clothes did Varick recall that he looked as if he'd been dragged through a river. He'd gotten out of there in case the doctor decided to insist Varick stay for a medical examination or some other rot. Back in his cabin, Varick found Marlowe sitting on the sofa and trying to patch up his wounds. Coal was there too. He'd transferred all the stolen goods to the largest of the steamer trunks, ditched the housekeeping cart in the hallway, and was doing his best to assist Marlowe.

"Where's Fulcrum?" Varick asked without preamble.

Marlowe shook his head and winced. His bruises looked even worse now. Coal's brows pinched as he did the same, sans the wince.

"I looked for him," Varick assured Coal. "Everywhere I could think of, but Fulcrum is smart. He'll have tried to get somewhere safe as soon as possible."

Coal said nothing, and Varick understood.

"Keep your chin up," Varick said. "I'm going to keep looking, as soon as we regroup."

Coal set his jaw and nodded.

Varick looked to Marlowe, fixing the big lad with a hard glare. "Did you know that Mercury was planning to kill me?"

Marlowe only glowered in reply, dabbing at a cut on his face with a cloth.

"Well?" Varick pressed. "You've been blasé about him this whole time."

Marlowe's voice was low as he spoke, and Varick didn't know if it was from anger or guilt or embarrassment from falling prey to Mercury's machinations. "He told me plans had changed. That we needed to cut you out 'cause you posed a danger to the job. I didn't think he was gonna try and bump you off, though."

"Funny," Varick said, not amused at all. "That's like what he said about you when Thumper showed up, after he bashed in your face." Marlowe's expression darkened, and Varick added, "Mercury sent me through a window. We can start a club together."

"So were you siding with him or weren't you?" Coal wanted to know.

Varick's eyebrows bobbed in agreement. He'd been getting to that, but he liked Coal's directness too. Marlowe's expression, on the other hand, closed off, and Varick also saw the trouble with such an approach.

"You need to be honest with us," Varick said, softer now.

"Mercury stabbed you in the back, so I understand if you're hesitant to trust anyone, but we're a team." He gestured between Coal and himself. "We look out for each other, and I think you see that. I think that's why you came to the vault."

"I wanted to punch that puff guts Mercury brought in," Marlowe explained succinctly.

"Fair dues," Varick granted, "but you could have run. You didn't, though, because you're not a bloody coward."

Marlowe nodded, and Coal, impatient as ever, asked, "So? Did you know Mercury was gonna do the rest of us dirty?"

Varick had to fight not to visibly cringe. *Come on, Coal,* he thought. *I'm working on him here.*

Thankfully, Marlowe relented this time, in as much as Marlowe probably ever would. "I could tell Mercury was being slippery. I'm not stupid."

Varick had a feeling lots of people in Marlowe's life had called him stupid.

"But no," Marlowe continued. "I didn't know. I didn't think he actually cared enough to stitch us up."

"I think he was going to pin everything on you all," Varick said. "He couldn't do that with me, though, so he needed to kill me."

"Do you think he'll kill Fulcrum?" Coal asked.

Varick shook his head. "Not if Mercury can't find him."

"I need to get back out there," Coal said.

"You can't," Varick replied. "If you go out alone and Mercury finds you, he'll try to use you against us again."

"You're not the boss of me," Coal snapped, but he stayed put too.

"Not technically," Varick admitted, "but we're not done yet, not until everyone is back together and we're all off this ship with our plunder intact. And someone needs to call the shots when we can't agree."

Coal opened his mouth to argue, but the door to Megaera's suite opened just then. Harefoot bounded through, ecstatic at all the new friends for him to meet. Auntie Megaera, however, paused in the doorway.

"Here you are then," she looked surprised as she took in the dumbstruck faces of Marlowe and Coal. "Fulcrum hasn't gotten back yet?"

"Uuuuh, what?" Coal asked. "Did you see my brother somewhere?" He'd already begun petting Harefoot, who was eating up the attention.

"Is it brother?" Megaera asked. "I wasn't certain and I didn't want to assume. But yes, he and I met in the ladies' room. I offered to walk with him, but he didn't want to put me in danger, so he left before me, he said, to draw off that odious man of yours."

"He's not ours," the crew said in unison.

"Why would you have been in danger?" Varick asked, coming forward.

Auntie Megaera smiled indulgently. "I think he was concerned for the helpless old woman he thinks I am. And because he gave me this for safekeeping."

She disappeared back into her room for a moment before retuning with the pasteboard box that held the Nightfall Crown. Varick's eyebrows bobbed. This was an impressive bit of maneuvering on Fulcrum's part that Varick had not expected. Coal gasped, while Marlowe gave a little smile.

"Good to know we got the bleedin' thing instead of that ratfink," he said. Then he seemed to realize the sort of language he'd used and muttered, "Apologies, ma'am."

She looked around at the collected crew again. "I did think Fulcrum would back by now. Perhaps he's taken the long way."

Coal stood. "I need to go find him. He'd do the same for me."

"You can't go alone," Varick said. "And Marlowe can't go with you because…"

Varick gestured, and Marlowe nodded. "I look like a prize fighter with a lotta fights and no prizes."

"Precisely. But I wonder. Coal, did Fulcrum bring that suit I gave you?"

Coal nodded, and Varick told him to go get changed. Meanwhile, Auntie Megaera took over helping Marlowe get cleaned and bandaged up. When Coal returned wearing the suit, Varick fixed his hair and made them both look presentable. While each went about their tasks, Marlowe asked the question Varick knew was coming.

"How'd you know who we were, ma'am?" He directed this at Megaera, who was using the inside films of that morning's leftover hardboiled eggs as makeshift plasters.

"Varick," she said simply, inviting him to explain.

He was currently looking far less dredged than before and applying some last minute adjustments to his clothes. Specifically, making sure the few, small blades he'd secretly tucked into his sleeves weren't showing or anything. The throwing knives Fulcrum had made weighed the cuffs a bit, but that could be blamed on bad seam ironing, assuming Mercury even noticed things like that. Varick didn't like the idea of carrying weapons. That meant he needed to be prepared to use them. When he thought of his broken crew, however, some gathered here in the sitting room, some suffering because of Mercury, he knew he didn't have a choice. Mercury hadn't left them with any other options. He'd proved he couldn't be trusted, that he had no qualms about killing members of his own team. Varick would have to stab Mercury in the back before Mercury did the same to them again.

He didn't look away from his work as he spoke. "I didn't know what else to do. I thought all of you might have been against me, and I knew Auntie Megaera could be trusted not to rat us out."

A pause ensued. Marlowe and Coal waited, exchanged a glance, and looked back at Megaera.

"Isn't this the part where you tell us you don't approve or whatever?" Marlowe asked. A hint of obstinacy colored his voice.

Auntie Megaera gave a noncommittal head wobble. "I was concerned, of course, about you getting caught. Your lives would be over, and what a waste that would be, promising young things like you. But who am I to judge? I was born with a silver spoon in my mouth." Coal looked *very* confused at that, but he didn't interrupt. "The peacocks will be fine without their trinkets. I must ask that you to return Delilah's pieces, however."

"Soooo you know about her too then?" Coal asked. "About her… other profession."

Megaera nodded. "I do. And I shall be addressing that with her, but only after you all have completed this mission of yours." She smiled. "I know you've all worked hard to earn this crowning achievement."

Varick sighed so hard he deflated, bending at the waist and resting his chin against his chest. "Auntie Megaera," he groaned. "That was painful."

Coal and Marlowe, meanwhile, were laughing, though Marlowe with some difficulty.

When Coal and Varick were ready to head out, Auntie Megaera told them to look out for one another. They brought Harefoot with them, just in case. And before they left, Varick's aunt had a private word with him.

"Be careful out there," she said, eyes glistening. "I nearly lost you tonight."

Varick reached out and squeezed her hand with his uninjured one. "I will, I promise." His opposite wrist was wrapped in a bandage, though he'd insisted he didn't need it.

He'd only just turned away when Megaera said, "And thank you."

"For what?"

"For trusting me. I know that doesn't come easy."

Varick smiled. "Thank you for for giving me reasons to trust you."

With that, he and Coal and Harefoot headed out. They heard the lock click behind them. It was quiet this time of night, just past midnight. Lots of people were still out, but the night's main entertainment had ended. Guests would now be in the various lounges and card rooms and whatnot. The trio padded quietly along the corridors, speaking softly. If Fulcrum was hiding somewhere within earshot, they wanted him to hear them, but they didn't want to attract attention. Coal had asked if Harefoot could sniff Fulcrum out, but Auntie Megaera had explained that he wasn't trained for that kind of work and wouldn't know what they were asking of him. Coal then suggested they scope out the lounges.

"Fulcrum might have thought it was safer to stay near people if he thought Mercury was still tailing him. And he wouldn't want to play cards or other parlor games."

That sounded plausible to Varick, and so they went to the women's lounges and those that permitted mixed company. He knew they wouldn't be permitted into the ladies-only areas, though they could ask for a message to be delivered. He worried they wouldn't be allowed into the mixed company ones either, given the late hour and that they were minors. Though Varick could pass for someone who was of age—that, and who was going to turn down Pendragon money?—but Coal, though he looked respectable now, still looked several years shy of his majority. They struck out a few times before entering one establishment where they did not find Fulcrum, but rather Mercury.

All the patrons were deep in their cups, and the bartenders only gave the trio slightly sideways looks. Mercury grinned when Varick's eyes landed on him, and he beckoned them over. Varick cut his eyes to Coal, who scowled openly at the man, but he gave Varick a nod. With a beastie as big as Harefoot with them and surrounded by people as they were, it seemed safe enough.

"Wotcha," Coal said coolly when he sat.

Varick had his face set into an impassive mask. "Mercury."

"Good to see you too," Mercury simpered. "Where is it?"

As if they'd rehearsed it, Varick and Coal exchanged a clueless look.

Mercury jabbed a finger at them and hissed, "Don't mess me about. Fulcrum doesn't have it on him. I have waited too long and come too far to play games with a couple of brats."

All deceit fell away from Coal's face at the mention of his brother, replaced by naked fear.

"Here's what's gonna happen," Mercury said. He pointed at Varick. "In one hour, you're gonna bring the crown down to cargo hold two for me." He pointed at Coal. "You won't join him, nor will Marlowe, nor will that mongrel."

He started to stab the finger in Harefoot's direction, but the dog bared his teeth, and a soft, deep growl emanated from his big chest.

Mercury snatched the hand back and glared at the two boys. "Don't think about involving that crone of yours either, Varick. If you don't follow my instructions *to the letter*, if I see the merest *hint* of trickery, I'll kill Fulcrum. Do I make myself clear?"

Varick fought to keep his mask in place, but he couldn't help the hard swallow that came when Mercury threatened Fulcrum's life. Varick wanted to ask if Mercury planned on letting him live once he handed over the crown, but the mad gleam in Mercury's eyes answered that for him.

"The crown in exchange for Fulcrum's safe return," Varick

said. "In one hour. Those are the terms?"

"Those are the terms," Mercury agreed.

Varick wasn't about to shake on it, not trusting Mercury with even that. He didn't trust the man to stick to any agreement, no matter what it was. Instead, Varick simply replied, "See you in an hour then," and got up and left.

43

INEVITABLE BETRAYAL

The airship's cargo holds were actually one massive space, accessible from inside the craft through numbered elephant doors, which had normal-sized, easier-to-manage doors set within them. When Varick pulled the handle of the door marked with the bottom corner piece of a gigantic, painted number two, he found it, as expected, unlocked. Inside was dim, and he fully expected Thumper to be waiting, ready to ambush Varick.

He wasn't going to let that happen without giving Thumper a hard time, so, using one hand to secure his top hat in place, Varick sprinted inside the cargo hold, listening for footsteps.

The main entry area was empty, but not far from there, walls of crates and barrels and other cargo rose up. Low petrolsene lights from above barely illuminated the area just ahead, but it was enough to see that ropes secured most of the cargo. As he ran, Varick decided he'd leap and climb them if necessary. He ran to the center of the entry area, his evening cape flowing behind him, but no footsteps pursued. He stopped and turned to look.

Light from the corridor outside spilled across the path he'd taken. No one had followed him.

"You look like an idiot," came a voice from above.

Varick craned his neck back and saw Mercury's backlit form up on a grated metal walkway above. It had to be a story and a half up there, and Varick took in the network of other catwalks that criss-crossed the space above them. Metal piping suspended them from the walls and ceiling. Climbable, he supposed, if you were a spider.

"You can't blame me for taking precautions," he called up.

"You still look stupid."

Varick gave an amenable shrug. "Is Fulcrum with you?"

Mercury gestured, and Fulcrum's voice called down. "I'm here."

"You alright, mate?" Varick asked.

"As good as can be expected."

Varick didn't know what that meant exactly. All the more reason to get this done and dusted. "Shall I come join you up there then? Or would you all like to come down here?"

Mercury bobbed his head. "Up here."

Varick found the ladder that led up to that level easily enough. It was a dizzying climb, even with the metal safety cage that started a little ways up, like a ribcage for catching anyone who fell. He tried not to think about what might happen to a body if they did, especially as he got higher and higher. The ladder continued upward, but its caging opened up at the catwalk for people to get on and off there if they wished. Varick was grateful there were no tricky walls or anything to hide behind. Nothing but metal poles for handrails and and gridded flooring. He still didn't see Thumper, and that made him nervous.

"Where's your large friend?" Varick stepped off of the ladder and onto the metal walkway. He held up his hands making a show of how very unarmed he definitely was.

"Thumper's around," Mercury said.

Behind him, Fulcrum gave an almost imperceptible shake of his head. Mercury's eyes, meanwhile, were busy raking over Varick, clearly looking for where he'd stashed the box holding the crown.

Varick's eyes went to the form of Fulcrum, standing beyond with his hands bound behind him, tied to the handrail, and his dress torn and mussed around the bustle area. Mercury had clearly not respected the fine fabric or the painstaking craftsmanship when he'd been searching in vain for the crown. That by itself was bad enough, to say nothing of what Fulcrum had endured.

A sharp *schnict* noise yanked Varick's attention back to Mercury. The man held a switchblade in his hand, the stabby bit deployed.

"Where is it, son?" Mercury demanded. "I said no tricks." He pointed the knife back toward Fulcrum. "Do you want him to die, because I'm about to—"

"Keep. Your hair. On," Varick said slowly. As he spoke, he lifted his top hat straight up and off his head, revealing the crown nestled luminously atop his hair. He couldn't help but beam.

Mercury glowered and shook his head. "You're such a poncey little prick."

"I can't deny that," Varick agreed.

"Set it on the floor, there, *carefully*. I won't have you risking it with any more of your antics."

Varick removed the crown from his head and did as Mercury said, setting it on the floor of the catwalk midway between them.

"Now back up," Mercury said.

"Send Fulcrum over," Varick replied, not backing up.

"Don't be stupid," Mercury snapped. "He might step on it. Now back *up*."

"*I* might step on it." Varick lifted a foot. "Fulcrum first."

Mercury's voice took on a new, manic edge as he gesticulated with the switchblade. "Is this really the game you wanna play? How much patience do you think I have left after tonight? Is your friend's life worth the gamble?"

Tension stretched between them, taut as a violin string. Varick scowled, but took a step back.

"Go on," Mercury said. "Farther."

Varick took one more. "This is as far as I go without Fulcrum."

Mercury stalked toward the crown and carefully picked it up. He looked lost for a moment as to how to deal with it.

"You just had to make things difficult, didn't you?" he sneered.

"For you, yes. Now set Fulcrum free."

Mercury gave a nasty smile and spun his switchblade around his fingers once, then gripped it hard, ready for attack. He turned, back toward Fulcrum. This, *this* had been the betrayal Varick had been waiting for.

The small, pewter blade was between his fingertips before Mercury had even completed his turn. It slid out from the little slot Varick had sewn for it in his sleeve, and when he released it, it flew straight and true. The small blade bit deep and hard into Mercury's shoulder blade. Varick was already firing off another one as he started to run forward. That one went wide, flying over the side of the catwalk and disappearing into the gloom.

"Thumper!" Mercury shouted.

Varick leaned his shoulder forward as he picked up speed over the last few strides separating him and Mercury. Mercury arched his body, cradling the Nightfall Crown protectively. Blazes, but he was solid when Varick slammed into him, and they both let out heavy grunts of pain. Mercury grabbed for the railing with the hand holding his switchblade, sending it clattering across the grate and then down over the edge. Varick reeled as

Mercury swung a wide, backhanded strike toward him. It missed, and Mercury ran down the catwalk. Varick pounded after him, pulling another blade from his sleeve. He had to slow down to aim and sent this one sailing at Mercury's midsection. It missed, but landed in the man's thigh instead. Mercury stumbled, and Varick was after him again like a hound after a fox. This time, Mercury turned to face him, ready to start punching with his free hand. Varick rolled with the blow, which glanced off his ribs, sending a dull, thudding pain radiating from the spot. He pulled the tie on his cape loose and and sent it sailing over Mercury's head.

It gave him only a moment, but Varick seized that moment with everything he had. He snatched the Nightfall Crown from Mercury's grasp. Now that he was between Mercury and Fulcrum, this was going to be their ticket out of here. He'd hold it hostage until they were safe and…

One of Mercury's flailing elbows caught Varick in the chin with a wild uppercut, sending his head snapping back, his feet stumbling. His teeth cracked against one another, and pain sparked all along his jaw. In his periphery, Varick could just see Mercury fling the cape away. He tried to leap back, out of the man's reach, but he'd gotten turned around with that last hit.

Varick's inertia slammed him against the handrail, his top half cartwheeling while his feet left the ground. Mercury's body shot forward as Varick tipped. The man was leaping forward to grab the crown. Too far forward. As Varick released it to reach for whatever pieces of the walkway he could, Mercury pressed a hand to Varick's chest to push him away. The Nightfall Crown, loosed from Varick's grip, spun end over end through empty air for a few seconds. Then Mercury's hand reached it again, but he'd launched himself clear off of the catwalk. Gravity well and truly had him in her grasp. As Varick's body spun under the force of Mercury's push, he watched in slow-motion horror as

Mercury's wild dive took him down.

Varick's legs swam through the air, arms flailing for anything to save him from the deadly fall. He was fully upside down when his hand touched the catwalk's grated floor, and he wrapped his hand around the edge. It was the wrong angle. His legs were still coming around in an arc and their trajectory would rip his tenuous grasp right off of the thin ledge of metal. Still, instinct drove Varick's other hand to reach for the only bit of safety left to him. It found one of the handrail's vertical support pipes. As his legs came down, his elbows twisted painfully. Where he'd fallen on his wrist earlier that night flared sharp and searing. That was the hand holding the pipe, and Varick cried out as pain rocketed from his wrist all the way up into his shoulder. Adding insult to injury, that was also the hand bearing the burn that he'd treated with honey that morning. It all melded into one, great mass of agony. He fought against his whole body not to let go as he swung by one hand back and forth beneath the catwalk. He saw Mercury's body fall next to him, keep falling past him, down and down, still holding the crown. Stars, Varick didn't want that to be him, and he let out a howl of pain and frustration as his agonized wrist trembled with the excruciating effort of not letting go.

Something grabbed the fabric of his sleeve and yanked upward.

"Give me your sodding hand!" The straining voice came from above Varick.

He looked up and saw Fulcrum there, gripping Varick's sleeve in one hand, the other reaching down. Coal appeared a second later, and Varick pinwheeled his other arm up and around, just barely catching Fulcrum's outstretched fingers. Coal joined in, and they shifted their grips, each holding onto one of Varick's wrists. Varick yelped and let fly a blue streak of swears as the pain in his injured wrist flared anew. The brothers ignored this and began to inch backward.

442

"Don't fall off too!" Varick shouted, seeing Fulcrum and Coal edging toward the other side of the walkway.

"Don't be stupid, we won't," Fulcrum snapped back.

Fulcrum and Coal pulled together until they managed to get Varick to where he could swing a leg up and hook it onto the next vertical support pipe along the line. Fulcrum grabbed Varick around the middle and helped haul him back up onto the catwalk, while Coal continued with one wrist. All three laid there for several moments, panting and, in Varick's case, marveling at the fact that he was still alive. That made him think.

"Did you see Mercury?" he began.

"Yeah," Coal replied, gulping in air between words. "He's… he's gone."

"Right," Varick said. That was, after all, an eventuality he'd known might come to pass when he'd brought weapons, but the fact that a life had been snuffed out because of Varick weighed heavily.

"Don't," Fulcrum said.

"Don't what?"

As if he could read Varick's mind, Fulcrum said, "Don't blame yourself. Mercury made his choices. If he'd just let the crown go…"

Varick nodded, though he didn't know if Fulcrum or Coal could see it. That helped a little, but it was something Varick was going to have to come to terms with later.

"Coal, did it go how we planned?" Varick asked. "I couldn't really see any of it."

"Just like we said." Varick could see Coal's hands illustrating aloft as he spoke. "Came in through the ventilation shafts, climbed down here when Mercury was distracted, cut Fulcrum loose, saved your life."

"Great, great." Varick nearly had his breath back now. "Do I… owe you something now? For saving me?"

"Huh?" Fulcrum asked.

"You know, like those Old World stories about debts and stuff."

A moment of thoughtful silence passed before either of them replied. It was Coal who said, "I think we'd have to, uh, call in the debt or something."

"We'd have to care to hold you to it, and I cannot be bothered," Fulcrum added. "Besides, I don't really believe in any of that stuff."

"Yeah, and anyway, we've been debting into each other all over the place. Who's even keeping track?"

"Fair," Varick said.

The conversation died briefly before Coal asked, "Hey, where's Thumper? Shouldn't he have been here to cave in our faces by now?"

"I don't know," Varick confessed. Remembering Fulcrum's little head shake, he added, "Was Mercury shamming about him being around?"

"I haven't seen or heard from him since the vault," Fulcrum explained.

Coal asked, "Think maybe Thumper decided to cut his losses and go solo?"

"I don't think he has losses to cut," Fulcrum said. "A few of those open safes hadn't been emptied yet." Varick could practically hear the dour lad's eyes widen. "Oh. And we left all the keys there. He might have finished cleaning out the place." Another pause. "Yeah, he really didn't need Mercury after that."

Varick sucked at his teeth. "Huh. You're probably right. We should make a move, though, just in case."

"Agreed," said the brothers together.

With groans and a curses, they hauled themselves up and made their way toward the closest ladder down.

"Thanks, by the way," Fulcrum said as they went. "For

coming for me. I mean, you're still a toffee-nosed pillock, but thanks."

Varick grinned. "You're welcome. And thanks for not letting me fall."

Fulcrum shrugged, but he was smiling too.

"'Course," Coal said with an obvious head bobble.

The conversation lapsed while they kept an eye out for, well, anyone, but they passed out of the cargo hold undetected. Once they were back in the relative safety of the airship's corridors, Varick picked the thread back up.

"My family wants me declared inept, and probably locked away."

Coal scowled, the meanest look Varick had ever seen on the boy's face.

"That's really awful," Fulcrum said in that usual flat tone of his. In his periphery, Varick saw Fulcrum turn his head to face him. "I'm sorry that's happening."

Varick nodded. "Thanks. That really means a lot."

44

"We Didn't Die!"

Back in his suite, Varick found Marlowe asleep on the sofa. Varick wanted to sleep too. By now, it was the wee hours of the morning, and the day had felt like years. Marlowe awoke at their entrance and grumbled a welcome back to Fulcrum.

"So you didn't die," he said.

"We didn't die!" Coal cheered.

"You're being bloody loud," Marlowe griped.

"Where's Auntie Megaera?" Varick asked.

"Asleep," Marlowe replied. He shot a reproachful glare at Coal, who'd struck up a rousing rendition of his new favorite song, *We Didn't Die*. He then went on to explain, "She wanted to stay up, but I told her to go when she started nodding off out here. Figured her body wouldn't thank her if she didn't use a proper bed."

Varick smiled at the consideration. Meanwhile, Coal started bickering with Marlowe.

As Coal said, "…can't blame me. I'm excited! My brother isn't dead. V isn't dead. I'm not dead," Fulcrum went to go change out of his badly abused dress.

"Exactly!" Marlowe shot back. "He ain't dead, so you can shut up and be happy." He was already settling back down as he spoke.

A knock on the cabin door, however, had them all on their feet. Varick shooed the stowaways into his bedroom, Fulcrum complaining about the lack of privacy and Marlowe muttering as they went.

It can't be Mercury, Varick thought. *He fell. He's gone.*

Could it be Thumper, though? Had Mercury told him where to find Varick's suite? It didn't make sense, especially if Thumper really had made out, well, like a bandit. It wasn't Thumper at the door, though, but Carver, looking a little peaky, but standing on his own power. A nurse stood beside him, an apologetic smile on her face.

"I'm sorry to bother you so late, sir, but he kept insisting."

Varick's face split into a huge grin. "Archie!"

He ushered his "secretary" into the room, thanking the nurse and agreeing wholeheartedly as she lauded what a dedicated employee he had in Mister Sweeney. She left after fussing over him only a little, leaving pointed instructions for Varick that he shouldn't work Mister Sweeney too hard and that the sweet man needed rest.

After she was gone, the crew came out again, all congratulating Carver on also not being dead. Auntie Megaera, woken by all the noise, came out as well and cupped Carver's face in her hands at seeing him alive and well. Harefoot was beside himself at Carver's return, and stretched his long body across the sofa in order to have his head in Carver's lap, and he utterly refused to be moved.They scrounged up what food they could for a late night/early morning snack, and caught Carver up on everything he'd missed.

"Shame about the crown," Carver said at the end of it. "Did you three not go collect the pieces?"

Fulcrum looked bashful and rubbed the back of his neck. "To be honest, I just wanted to get out of there. And we've got plenty of other loot." He exchanged a happy look with his brother. "We're gonna have a great start in Duskwood."

Varick had to agree. He hadn't wanted to go see Mercury's body, much less take anything from the corpse. Though he had another reason for not having bothered, one only he knew about.

"It's not… quite the shame it appears to be," he said.

Quizzical stares zeroed in on him from all around, and he went into his bedroom, returning a moment later with the striped hatbox his top hat had travelled on board in.

Carefully, and with a bit of dramatic flourish and timing—he couldn't help himself—he lifted off the lid and revealed the Nightfall Crown sitting safe and whole within. Sparkles of color flashed all around the room as everyone stared in bewilderment.

"But… how?" Fulcrum asked.

45
CROWNING GLORY

THE NIGHT BEFORE...

After bidding Auntie Megaera good night, or as good a night as was possible after their late-night decoding, Varick checked his top hat and crept out into the deserted corridor. He'd intentionally not changed out of his dinner clothing. The tour earlier that day really had been extremely enlightening. He'd learned about the safety straps all over the outside of the airship, as well as the clever cleats-and-groove system used by cleaners, engineers, and anyone else needing to traverse the sheer wall of glass and wood and metal. Of course, that was usually when the *Angrec's Respite* was docked and immobile, not airborne and full steam ahead. He'd also learned about the rather ingenious and state-of-the-art ventilation system on board, which kept all the guests nice and cozy warm even while traveling through the coldest climes of the upper atmosphere. Truly a marvel of modern technology!

While picking the lock to an unattended supply closet and nicking a bosun's chair had been easy, finding an out-of-the-way spot to carry out his clandestine activities had been a much stickier wicket. The brochure Varick had been provided on the tour had included front elevation diagrams and deck layouts of the *Angrec's Respite*, and Varick had used these to pinpoint the slim segment of the airship that would best serve his purposes. He'd spent a little time that afternoon after the tour pretending to browse the various shops that fell within the designated area. He'd had to summon his sharpest sneaking skills, scuttling about and avoiding the eyes of eager-to-please shop clerks and fellow "shoppers." Fortunately for him, the arcade was bustling, and the clerks were all run off their feet helping more enthusiastic—and in several cases, demanding—guests. Within the sixth shop he explored, Varick found the little back storeroom with a nearly-straight shot down to the vault's windows.

That night, getting into the ventilation shaft had been easy. Openings disguised with decorative grates dotted the airship's interior walls everywhere. He need only find a deserted area, unscrew one of the grates, crawl inside, pull it back into place, and he was on his way. He was able to go slow tonight, unlike his foray the following night would be, when he was concerned for Coal's safety. He took time to check his map, peeking out through grates he passed to ensure he was still on the right path. He did lightly burn his palm by accident on a hot copper pipe, not realizing that's what it was in the low light of the small oil lamp he'd brought from home. When he came upon the slow-moving fans scattered throughout the ventilation system, his top hat had nearly blown off, and Varick had taken a moment to pull down from inside of it a set of chin straps he'd sewn into it. It would be windy outside the airship too. How much more windy? Varick wasn't sure, so he'd used thick, quality leather and his finest silk thread, doubled up for even more strength. He'd broken a couple of good needles making the thing, but it moved not a jot when he strapped it on in the ventilation shaft.

Thus, when he dropped down into the little backroom, Varick was feeling pleased as punch. This was going to be a cakewalk. He didn't know why Mercury had made such a fuss. As to why he was pulling his own heist, Mercury was at the center of that too.

Initially, Varick had planned to do it for spite. Then, when he'd started believing Mercury might not be as bad as he'd thought, Varick had nearly abandoned the idea, but something in his gut had convinced him to come prepared, just in case. What was the harm in being prepared? And now, with what had happened to Carver, it was personal.

The ratbag talked such a big game about how clever he was, but where was he in life? Some two-bit criminal using kids to pad his pockets. Just like his grandmother and parents did with other people, Mercury saw Varick and the rest of the crew as nothing more than tools to be used. There wasn't anything outright that Varick could do about his own family—they were all too firmly positioned. That was why he pulled all his little tricks at the Dragon's Keep, but he could show Mercury. Really show him. Varick could prove he was so much more than Mercury thought. And it would feel so good to hold the secret of who actually stole the Nightfall Crown over the scumbag's head. That would be protection too, protection for Coal and Fulcrum and the rest of the crew, in case Mercury decided to take revenge after the fact. Even just the idea of that sort of power over such a complete prick was intoxicating, and the desire burned inside of Varick like a focused torch.

As for his own family, well, Varick wasn't sure about that yet. He'd always known they would be furious when he returned. But now that he knew what they were doing, that Patricia wanted this conservatorship enacted… he wasn't certain what he could do. They might even use him running off on this trip as ammunition, some kind of false proof of his unfitness. Auntie Megaera was going to help him, and he had faith that she could certainly make it hard for them, but to actually stop it from happening?

Varick shook his head as he rigged up the bosun's chair harness around himself. One problem at a time. He'd have to figure out how to deal with his family later. When he opened the window, he made sure to only open it a crack, remembering what the tour guide had said about air pressure and all that. Then, when air had stopped sucking out and was instead blowing in, he opened the window the rest of the way. The wind blew at his face so hard, Varick thought it might permanently stretch his skin. That couldn't actually happen, right? And it was cold too! The hat was still staying put, though, and that was what was important. He could deal with a bit of cold.

After groping around a bit outside the window, Varick found the nearest safety strap and grabbed a hold. Then, with one last look at the instruction manual for using the bosun's chair, Varick clipped the various cables and whatnot to the safety straps as the instructions showed, and climbed out.

Blazing bullocks it was windy out here! Like being-caught-in-a-typhoon windy. And so much colder. The wind knived through his fine clothes, right to the bone, and this was his good wool dinner jacket!

As soon as he was halfway out the window, the gusts flying down the sides of the airship snatched at Varick and half-dragged him the rest of the way. He yelped as his body dropped the few feet of slack he'd given himself before the bosun's chair cabling caught him. Then wind batted him around like a cat with a toy mouse, and Varick swore and spun in the rigging. The tails of his tailcoat flapped straight out in a ninety-degree panic. No one ever talked about the aether as a mad, screaming entity. They always described it as gentle and serene, tickling wispy clouds with feather-soft breezes. But scream it did. Rather an odd soundtrack to such a lovely, clear night, unlike the next one would be.

Varick managed to catch the edge of the open casement with one hand and get his bearings. He looked down to where his target window gleamed dark in the bright light of the moon. He did this while trying *not* to glimpse the night-shrouded landscape sliding slowly by, far, *far* below.

I could turn back, he thought to himself. But no. Not when he was so close, not when he thought back to the things that had been said to him, the *way* they'd been said. Those memories scorched his insides. The anger sizzled against some of the cold, turning it to steam, and it propelled him.

He. Was Varick. Sodding. Pendragon!

And while he didn't buy into all that noble blood rot, he knew what he'd endured as he'd run the race of his life. He'd come through bruised and scarred, in every way, but come through he had. And he wasn't done yet. This opportunity to show that he was capable of so much more than Mercury thought, to *win*, it was too good to pass up.

It's just a little ways down. You can see it, he told himself. *Just a few measly decks down.*

And so, Varick began the slow, arduous job of what he'd initially imagined as rappelling down the side of a blustery airship. Given the reality of the situation, however, there was far less rappelling and far more flailing about in the screaming wind, and gripping the safety straps for dear life. Where were those sodding cleats supposed to be, the ones for the grooves running back and forth and up and down all around him? He didn't see a single cleat anywhere. So instead, Varick eventually developed a system of, when he was between safety straps, leaning against the airship's hull and shoving his toes and fingers into the grooves, using them as holds, and pulling himself along. Thus, when he was occasionally bashed against the airship's side, his legs, hips, and shoulders took the brunt of the impact. Varick did everything he could to keep his feet under him, but the soles of his dress shoes were smooth and unsuited for such athletics.

At least I never have to do this again, he thought to himself, as he took a short rest with a safety strap clutched to his chest.

He spun away and lost progress a few times, but at least there were always more safety straps nearby to grab a hold of when it happened. Varick's gloved hands soon got to know the feel of brushing against one and automatically closing around it. Nevertheless, each instance was accompanied by a stream of verbal abuse at the wind, which Varick decided would be his lifelong nemesis.

After what felt like hours, drenched in sweat that froze on his skin wherever the wind got under his clothes—which was to say *everywhere*—he reached the vault window and grabbed a hold of the adjacent safety straps. There was no way in this stars-forsaken sky that he was going backward now. And then, as Varick tried planting himself against the window frame, his impractical shoes slipped, leaving the black marks he'd put his feet onto the very next next night.

Thankfully, he fell away only a foot or so before catching himself, and he resisted the urge to punch the airship—somewhere, distantly, where his rational side was shrieking itself silly, he knew that would only hurt him. Once he'd pulled himself back into position, being careful not to slip again, Varick produced a thin, metal file from within the hem of his waistcoat. He slipped it between the window sashes and began to work the latch. His dinner glove, however, slipped on the frosty metal. Having pulled it off with his teeth, Varick looked around for a good place to stash it. That was when he noticed the bosun's chair came with a handy little attached pouch. Varick opened it to store his glove, only to find a couple of the groove cleats meant to facilitate the sort of journey he'd just completed. He glowered at the cleats as if they'd hidden from him on purpose.

"Never again," Varick grumbled to himself.

Then, he blew hot breath onto his fingertips and at last managed to unlock the window. The blowback from the air pressure equalizing in the vault sent him careening into the hull one last time, but finally! He was there!

Once inside the vault—after he'd taken a couple of minutes to lie on the floor and be grateful for its presence—Varick unclipped the bosun's chair rigging from himself, allowing the rest to flap freely around in the breeze, waiting for when he returned to the shop's backroom and retrieved it in order to cover his tracks. Now, time to get down to business.

He picked the guard and client locks open on Spindle's safe and, in a small travel notebook with a compact pen, he drew a sketch of each piece and where exactly it had been laid inside the safe. It was during this intricate examination that Varick first noticed the lack of shine at the back of the safe. It simply didn't match the rest. He didn't dare move anything until he was finished recording the recreation information, but after that, it was fair game. He wondered if Mercury would take time to examine things like this. Varick actually worried the man would fail to find it and tried to think up a way to hint at the solution beforehand, given that Varick wasn't meant to actually be present at the heist. He'd look for opportunities tomorrow and try to slip something in if he could. This was, of course, before everything went so pear-shaped the next morning.

When Varick extracted the pasteboard box, his breath caught. He was doing it. He was actually doing it! The shattered light refracted through the Nightfall Crown lit up Varick's grin like a beacon from heaven. He worked so carefully as he set the box down, unstrapped his top hat from his head, and extracted an exact replica of the crown from within a safety harness built within the hat.

Back in Springhaven, after seeing Coal's meticulous drawings in his self-made lock picking guide, Varick had asked him to do some depicting the Nightfall Crown in highly detailed glory. Thanks to these, Varick had been able to commission his favorite glasssmith to create a perfect copy of the crown. The gemstones were expertly crafted, but nothing more than paste, and he'd paid well for the piece, as well for discretion. Then, the replica had come aboard with him, hidden all this time either inside his top hat or the top hat's hatbox, both with ample padding and support, similar to what they'd created for Fulcrum's bustle, to keep the delicate piece safe.

Once the false crown was settled inside its box, just as the original had been, Varick tucked it back where it belonged, reset everything exactly the way it had been, and shut the safe. He straightened his hair and clothes, all while the real crown sat secured inside the little safety harness within his top hat, which he donned once he was presentable again. Varick listened for the guards and, knowing their schedule and how they operated, avoided them without any trouble. As he made his way back up to the higher decks to finish covering his tracks, Varick felt on top of the world as he sauntered off with the crown atop his head.

46
WHAT MAKES A WHOLE LIFE

The crew stared at Varick as he finished his tale. Great Auntie Megaera had an eyebrow raised at him, and he was fairly certain he was going to get an earful later about pulling, what he imagined she would term, "such a bally foolish stunt." Harefoot didn't care; he was softly snoring away with his head in Carver's lap.

"Bosh," Marlowe said. His expression was like when someone witnessed a really spectacular bit of prestidigitation, wherein they didn't want to let themselves believe, but couldn't even begin to explain how the trick had been done.

"Oh, *now* you'd like to be a skeptic?" Varick asked incredulously, though a chuckle burbled up inside of him.

He looked around at the rest of the crew. "Believe me or don't, but why would I make this up? And besides, I'm not keeping it." With that, he reverently set the Nightfall Crown before the rest of the crew. "It's all of ours. We all worked on this plan. I wouldn't even be on this stupid airship if it hadn't been for you all."

"But…" Coal began, "but you know what this means. You did the thing. You're King Thief."

Varick's smile melted into a smirk. "You know I'm *actually* descended from royalty, right? But a single big thing, like being born a Pendragon, doesn't define me. I think all the things I have done and will do are what make me anything. Mercury had it wrong. Pulling off the ultimate score is great, but it doesn't make a whole life." Everyone was quiet at that, and he shrugged off the awkward silence. "At least, that's my philosophical takeaway."

Fulcrum was staring at the Nightfall Crown, eyebrows tugging together. Rather suddenly, he declared, "I don't want it." Everyone looked at him. "I mean, I kind of agree with Varick." Coal's expression turned to one of overly theatrical, heart-stopping shock, and Fulcrum pulled a face at his brother. "Don't get your knickers in a twist. We're not about to become bosom buddies."

"Thank heaven for that," Varick put in, but he was still smirking.

"All I'm saying," Fulcrum went on, "is that this competition is stupid. And I for one have zero desire to keep it going. Marlowe?"

"Nah," he replied definitively.

"Carver?" Fulcrum asked.

Carver shook his head. "No. I've had my fill, thanks."

Fulcrum looked to Coal, who shrugged. "I don't want to be criminals anymore. I wanna go to school and have options outside of that world."

Finally, Fulcrum looked back to Varick. "That's it then. What do you say? Do we stop this barmy tradition once and for all?"

Varick looked around him. "Shall I do the honors?"

Fulcrum motioned for him to have at it. Varick picked the Nightfall Crown back up, gripped it at the apex, and snapped off

the topmost sunburst of jewels.

Coal and Megaera gasped, Carver and Marlowe's eyebrows shot up, and Fulcrum's face remained impassive.

The latter said flatly, "That'll do it."

"It was so pretty," Megaera whispered.

"So shiny," Coal agreed.

Varick began to break off another piece. "Fair is fair, everyone gets a share."

47

FAREWELLS AND INTRODUCTIONS

The *Angrec's Respite*, jewel of Prism Line Air Cruises' luxury airship fleet, docked in Duskwood about a half hour before the sun even deigned to start previewing the first of her glorious pink and golden rays. Varick, his Great Auntie Megaera, and the rest of the crew, disembarked as early as possible. They'd covered over bruises and cuts with makeup and dressed Marlowe, Fulcrum, and Coal as nondescript members of Varick and Megaera's staff. Varick checked out himself, Carver, Auntie Megaera, and his "valet"—that is, Marlowe dressed in a role-appropriate suit and staying away from anyone who might look too closely. It was as easy as leaving any ordinary hotel. Meanwhile, Fulcrum and Coal blended into the furniture and luggage, as staff were expected to do. Varick had kept an ear out for signs of panic, but as it was barely sunup now, he suspected Mister Dilley and Mister Eaddy probably hadn't even clocked into work yet. If Mercury's body had been discovered, airrocrew members were likely trying to keep it quiet until they could

gather more information as to who he was and what he'd been doing in the cargo hold.

Airros tipped their hats in passing as all six of them, plus Harefoot, walked off the ship and made their way to the heart of Duskwood via monorail. Gliding above the treetops on a cable, just as Coal had read about, the group was able to take in great swaths of the vast northern city-state all at once. Coal pressed his face so hard against the glass of their little travel pod that his nose squashed against it, while Harefoot's doggy breath fogged right next to him.

Instead of clearcutting, the city of Duskwood had grown up and around the great conifers, working in tandem with the trees and designing municipal infrastructure around them. Lifts of various design were prevalent in the city, as many eateries and hotels and shops were built out of enormous, interconnected networks of tree houses. As Varick watched Coal, the smaller boy's eyes wide and trying to take in everything at once, he imagined he could see his friend fitting right in here. This city was an architect's dream, and Coal had all the determination and cleverness to make it, or anything he wanted really, happen for himself. It made Varick a little sad he wouldn't be here to see it, but more than that, he was happy for Coal. For both him and Fulcrum, for the new life and freedom that lay before them. Varick wanted that sort of freedom too, so badly he could taste it. He'd finally figured out a way to get it, too. Now that he'd seen what he was capable of.

Auntie Megaera took the crew to a chic little cafe she'd been frequenting for years, and the owner greeted her as the old friend she was. There, they had a traditional Duskwooder breakfast with all the bells and whistles—potato scones and blood pudding, fried mushrooms and savory porridge—and watched the city awaken. They'd all crash at the hotel later, where Varick rented extra rooms for the other crew members. He made sure to charge it to his family's line of credit. He went out by himself later in the day in order to withdraw an impressive sum of cash from a local bank, and then more at another location, and again and so on.

Varick wasn't worried about anyone coming around and asking questions about the airship robbery today—they'd be too busy cataloguing the missing items, talking to the airship staff and airrocrew, and taking statements from irate men and women who'd lost their valuables in the heist, valuables that were likely insured to the hilt. But even so, he booked himself passage on the next train going back to Springhaven rather than taking the one the cruise fee had paid for. Carver and Marlowe and Auntie Megaera could enjoy that together. The latter's enjoyment, however, might depend on how her "chat" with Spindle aka Delilah MacKillop went. They were scheduled to have dinner together that evening, and Varick really did hope it went well. His train-related change of plans had been discussed as they were all packing earlier that morning. One of several reasons for it was because Varick wouldn't at all be surprised if his family, or some representatives thereof, would be waiting for him to arrive on the scheduled train tomorrow. He was also looking forward to enacting some decisions he'd made, which he'd very intentionally discussed with everyone *except* his great aunt. But the earlier departure left Varick little time to say goodbye to Coal and Fulcrum. So, just as evening was drawing a curtain across the sky, he gathered with the brothers and bid them farewell.

"You sure you know what you're doing?" Coal asked. "It's not really something you can come back from."

Varick nodded. "I don't want to go back. There's nothing there for me. Are you two going to be alright?"

Coal flapped a hand at Varick, "Of course. We take care of each other. Plus, your aunt's friend from this morning already gave us some recommendations for places to stay until we get on our feet. He even offered me a job! Busy boy."

"Bus boy," Fulcrum corrected. He wore the faintest of smiles and extended his hand. "Best of luck, Varick. You're gonna do fine."

Varick's eyebrows bobbed as he returned the handshake. "My, my, what high praise."

"Don't get all soppy," Fulcrum replied.

Varick laughed at that, and they finished their goodbyes. He didn't like losing them so soon after he'd met them, but this was the start of a better life, for all of them. Afterward, Varick headed over to where Great Auntie Megaera was waiting while Varick'd had his private word with Coal and Fulcrum. Carver and Marlowe had said goodbye earlier at the hotel, given that they already had plans to get together with Varick not long after they arrived back. The discussions Varick'd had with them, out of Megaera's hearing, had solidified both their decisions to return to Springhaven.

"Despite all the misadventures," Megaera told Varick, "I have enjoyed getting to spend this time with you more than I can say. Thank you again for inviting me."

"I've really enjoyed this too," Varick said. He fought back an annoying burning in his eyes. Different words wanted to burst out of his chest, but he couldn't let them. It was safer for her not to know what he planned to do next. He did allow himself, however, to admit, "I wish I'd had the chance to get to know you sooner."

"Oh darling, so do I. But let us cherish what we do have." She opened her arms to him. "How do we feel about a hug?"

Varick didn't hesitate. He squeezed his great aunt, doing just as she'd said, cherishing what little time they had together.

♜

Days later, well after Varick had arrived back in Springhaven, the local newssheets reported the story of the massive robbery aboard the *Angrec's Respite* luxury cruise airship. Enforcers in both Springhaven and Duskwood were working hard to solve the case, but a few of the newssheets reported some difficulties in the two organizations working together. A few others made mention that a crew member or passenger—reports couldn't seem to agree on that point—had suffered an accident on board and died. Whether or not the death was related to the theft was also a point in contention. And anyone with any information that might assist in bringing the dastardly thieves to justice was asked to come forward.

Varick was reading one particularly salacious rag by the light of the waning gibbous moon when Carver showed up to join him at the offices of Pendragon, Umpleby, and Johnson, Fiduciary Advisors and Probate Solicitors. Or rather, in a little alleyway nearby. It was late, far later than any member of polite society should be out, but these two were far from polite society.

"You ready?" Carver asked.

"Absolutely," Varick replied.

They pulled dark cowls over their faces—not Varick's favorite, but acquiring better clothing for illicit activities was lower down on his to-do-list—and made their way inside through nontraditional methods. After climbing around the outside of an in-flight airship, breaking into a building on the ground was a breeze. Varick caught the pun in his own internal monologue and grimaced. *That* was certainly not a habit he was about to develop.

Now that they knew what they were looking for, they found the paperwork Patricia had filed to begin proceedings for Varick's conservatorship with ease. He wasn't surprised to find she'd added to it since he'd been gone. He dearly wanted to confront her about it, but he'd learned with Mercury that some people were so dangerous, so toxic, like weeds, they required extra finesse to deal with. You couldn't let yourself be entangled. You had to fight them by other means. Fire worked well, as Varick had also previously learned. It was fast becoming a favorite method of his, burning any documentation that could be used against him.

He didn't fear being suspected. His last recorded activity, the hotel rooms charged to the Pendragon credit line and the cash withdrawals large enough to buy a couple of houses outright, had occurred in Duskwood. With luck, anyone looking for Varick would think he was still there. He wished he could have closed his accounts entirely, but that would have required an in-person visit back in Springhaven. Once he'd been missing for long enough, his family would scrabble for what remained. Far, *far* less than what Randolph had initially left to him, but they wouldn't learn that for some year's time. In any case, Patricia could, of course, always try to start up the conservatorship process again, but Varick could always set more fires too. He could even sneak into his old home if he needed to and destroy things there at the root, though he'd vowed to himself to never go back. He'd grown beyond them; he didn't need to endure that garden of thorns any longer.

Later that night, after he'd watched his grandmother's machinations against him go up in smoke, Varick swung by the old food pantry he'd accidentally done the same thing to. Rebuilding efforts had begun, but they were mostly for show. Much more could have been accomplished in the fortnight or so that had passed since he and Patricia had made their pledges to bring the place back. Typical.

Finding Hannah's details had been harder, but with the help of Carver's network, Varick had managed it. She lived in a flat in an older building on the edge of the Sand district. The thick envelope flopped far too loudly when he shimmied it through the mail slot in her front door. He'd left the note inside sparse, including only the most necessary information.

Dear Hannah,

You've been doing great work. This is so you can keep it up, on your own terms. Thank you for caring for those in need.

The envelope contained the documents from the false ledger he'd stolen, sans those that pertained to him, as well as enough money for Hannah to open multiple new soup kitchens. Varick planned on keeping an eye on things, though he suspected he had nothing to worry about in that quarter.

This wasn't how he would have arranged things if he'd had more choices, better choices. But he was proud nevertheless. He was, in a way, keeping his grandfather's legacy alive. He wasn't able to see Hannah's reaction, of course, when she opened the envelope, but over the coming weeks, he saw the moves she made in the community and was pleased his trust had not been misplaced.

Varick sauntered around the basement of the old warehouse with Marlowe and Carver. He'd dressed in a new suit, with some alterations of his own. He'd also darkened around his eyes with makeup and gotten a haircut in an effort to appear different from the depictions of him in the newssheets. As he walked with his comrades, Varick imagined what was to come. The setup was rather like the one Mercury'd had, with a large office area overhanging what would become the sales floor. It seemed loads of abandoned buildings out here in haunted old Char, or at least the former high-end shops, shared this sort of design. Carver had helped with the logistics. The landlord, thankfully, was crooked as a weathervane that had lost a fight with a tornado. And his lack of curiosity about his tenants made him very popular.

"It won't be anything too fancy," Varick explained. "Tables

all along here. Merchants will rent the space on a monthly fee. Flat rates, so no one can try and stiff me by fudging their numbers. It'll be a bit pricier than a usual stall, but they get to keep all their own profits." To Carver he added, "You'd be proud of me, I've been talking with loads of people in Viola Meadow, getting the inside scoop on the system there."

"I am proud," Carver said with a grin. "So what are you thinking for staff?"

"I'm going to need security, obviously, of which Marlowe will be the head." He looked back to the big lad with a cheeky grin.

Marlowe gave him an affirmative nod, which was great given how non-effusive the chap usually was.

"And I'd like an intelligence network of my own. I'll share, of course, and it'll have to start small, but I want it to grow with the business. Like any good kingdom, the bigger, more successful it gets, the more eyes and ears it'll need."

Despite his word choice, Varick did not think of himself as a king. Kings, at least in chess, were limited. That's why they'd never been his favorite piece.

Carver nodded. "That shouldn't be a problem. Is it going to have a name?"

"Not officially. I'm just referring to it as the underground market. I'm open to offering some specialty goods, but mostly I want to make it a place where people without recourse can come for what they need."

Carver nodded again. There was a pause before he said, "Have you reconsidered seeing her?"

Varick mentally pulled a shell over himself. He was getting better at it. "No. I told you, I can't. She'd be in danger if I did."

"You can trust her," Marlowe said. "She won't snitch on you."

"I know," Varick said. "And that's why I won't risk it. Auntie

Megaera deserves a nice, quiet, safe retirement."

Varick seriously doubted that any of his illicit activities thus far would come back to haunt him. He'd covered his tracks well, but he'd been with Great Auntie Megaera while he'd carried out most of them. He needed her to be ignorant of his location. He knew it would hurt her to lose him. Deeply. It hurt him too, more than he knew how to express. That was why he'd only risked a single letter, delivered in person by Carver. He had quite the rapport with her, after all. And Carver had never been cursed with either celebrity or infamy, so Varick hadn't seen any risk in having him deliver the bad news. At least it came with a friendly face.

Dear Auntie Megaera,

You are the best aunt anyone could ever ask for. I love you. I don't think I've ever said that to anyone before, besides Grandfather. That's why I hate to have to tell you this, but you won't see me again. I have things to do, but I have to disappear to do them. I'm sorry. I know that's not enough, especially when we just found one another, but it's all I have. That, and my love. Please don't try to find me. And please burn this letter after you've read it. I will miss you forever.

Your great nephew,
Varick

PS: I've boarded Tallywags privately through the end of the month. He's yours if you want him.

Carver had looked sad about the assignment, and though he'd said there might be ways for the two to stay in touch, Varick also knew he understood. He'd lived in this world far longer than Varick had. Even so, the next time he'd seen Carver, Varick hadn't been able to help but ask how she'd taken it.

"With a stiff upper lip," Carver had said. "But she's upset. She didn't try to hide it. She said if you want the jewel back, though, you'll have to come get it yourself."

The jewel in question had been the top of the Nightfall Crown, that which he'd broken off first. Auntie Megaera had shown it to Spindle as proof of the crew having been the ones to steal it. Now that he was in this world for good, he was relying on codenames only. Varick had smiled at the ultimatum his great aunt had given to Carver, and thought his own strategic mind must have come predominately from her.

"How'd their chat together go then?" Varick had asked next.

"Really well actually. Spindle was impressed you got the crown, but she said you failed because it got broken. She swore to your aunt, though, that she's done with that life. And she's glad she is. They're already planning another trip together. Just as soon as your aunt… how did she put it? 'Nails that shriveled scorpion to the wall.'" Carver had smiled at that. "Megaera's already got her solicitors looking over the documents you found. And she wants to see if law school is an option for me. The gap in my, well, whole life is a problem, but I was never a *known* criminal, and we're proceeding carefully, so who knows?"

Varick had been pleased to hear all of that too. He'd not wanted to leave Auntie Megaera alone.

Back in the here and now, in the newly acquired warehouse, he could look forward.

"And your new name?" Carver asked. "People might still recognize you from your pictures, but you should make it difficult for them to connect you to your old life."

Varick smiled again. "Marlowe and I were discussing that earlier actually." He jerked a thumb back at his new head of security. "He didn't even laugh."

"S'a good name," Marlowe admitted.

Now Carver looked really impressed. "Oh yeah? What's it

gonna be then?"

Pulling on the new business persona Varick had been developing for himself, he marched over to Carver, put on his most winning smile, and extended his hand to shake. "The name's Rook. Pleased to meet you."

If you enjoyed this book, please consider leaving a review on StoryGraph, Fable, Goodreads and/or Amazon, etc. Even a single line is massively helpful. Thank you in advance for taking the time to share your thoughts.

To get more goodies from Dana, consider joining her Patreon at https://www.patreon.com/wordsbydana

You can also sign up for early updates, cover reveals, and exclusive content by joining her VIP newsletter. You can sign up for that on her website: https://www.wordsbydana.com/

An Excerpt from Out of the Shadows

She wasn't going down without a fight. Maybe by some miracle she'd catch a break and get free again. Lenore drove both elbows back as hard as she could, which may have just worked if it weren't for the fact that she and her captor were already falling backwards. She landed on something soft in complete darkness and was on her feet again in less than a second. There was that complete darkness thing, though. When she had been running a moment ago, her path had been lit by the soft glow of petrolsene lights and the moon. Where was she now? Lenore backed up until she hit a wall and remained ready to fight. She began inching her way to the side, thinking there might be a door somewhere. The sound of heavy boots running approached and then faded, followed a few moments later by a single match light. The match light became an oil lamp, and the area all around Lenore was suddenly bathed in a warm, yellow glow. She saw the man first, gingerly holding his arm across his abdomen. She was about to cry out, "You!" but a delicate hand clamped itself over her mouth with a determination that belied its delicacy.

"Shhhh!" a female voice hissed in her ear. "Do you want to get us all caught?"

Lenore did not try to speak, but shook her head earnestly. Of

course she didn't, but what did her would-be accusers have to worry about?

"I'm going to let go of you now, but you must stay silent. Understand?" the woman said firmly.

Lenore nodded this time and was released. The woman joined the man and began to poke and prod him in a way that looked more like a medical examination than anything else. The man made no move to stop her, and Lenore watched them both warily. Finally, when the woman seemed satisfied, she kissed the man on the cheek and turned her attention back to Lenore. She glanced at what Lenore could now see as a cellar door and motioned for her to follow. Lenore had no desire to do any such thing, but couldn't think of a better idea. There were Enforcers outside looking for her, but these two could just be planning to turn her in later. That logic didn't really make sense, though. If they had any kind of sense, they wouldn't waste time that the Enforcers could use to accuse them of helping Lenore. Besides, there were no Enforcers inside…as far as Lenore knew, anyway. That being the case, she followed, but at a distance that kept her safe from the couple's reaching arms in case they tried to grab her again.

The three walked up a narrow staircase and up into a large kitchen replete with a potbelly stove large enough to cook an entire lamb in. From the kitchen they walked through a butler's closet—*closet my eye,* Lenore thought—and into a grand dining room. The woman motioned for Lenore to sit, which she refused to do with a defiant glare.

"Suit yourself," said the woman with a very unladylike shrug.

She then sat while the man stood behind her and put his hands on her shoulders.

"First of all," the man said kindly, "let me apologize. I am deeply, deeply sorry for drawing attention to you. We did not mean for you to be discovered."

Lenore was very confused and intrigued by this, but still said nothing.

"Allow me to make the introductions," the man continued. "I am Sir Gwenael Allen and this is my lovely wife, Philomena."

"Mina will do just fine," the woman interjected suddenly, giving her husband's hand a squeeze.

He smiled and added, "You may call me Neal."

Lenore didn't call either of them anything. She simply remained silent, wondering whether or not she could make it out the cellar without being caught.

"We're not going to turn you in," Mina said after several moments.

"Why not?" were the first words Lenore said to the couple.

The two shared a smile that seemed to hold a great meaning for them and then turned back to Lenore.

"We do not…agree with the severity with which criminal punishment is exacted," Neal explained.

"Don't think that means we condone criminal behavior either, however," Mina added firmly, giving Lenore a hard glare.

"Well, I appreciate you hiding me and all. Trust me, I really do," Lenore said defensively, "but, seeing as how my criminal behavior is going to continue, I'll just be on my way."

Lenore turned to leave, but Mina spoke again with such force that Lenore stopped in her tracks.

"And just what is so important for you to get back to?"

Lenore narrowed her eyes at the woman there who was now standing tall and ramrod straight. She didn't like the woman. Who was this stuck up peacock to think she had any business asking Lenore such personal questions?

"Thank you both again," Lenore snipped. "Good night." With that she turned on her heel and left the way she came.

❖

Bitsy was waiting for Lenore back at the attic when she arrived just before dawn. It wasn't really an attic so much as dead space between the attics of her parent's old house and the one attached next door. It grew almost unbearably hot in the summer and bone achingly cold in the winter, as simple wooden walls were all that separated Lenore from the outside. She'd discovered the space when she was little, having accidentally found the hidden latch to the small door and crawling through. She'd found a similar entrance on the neighbor's side and jammed the handle with some scrap metal. Thankfully, no one on the other side seemed to know about the space. At least, Lenore had never heard anyone try to get in. If they did, she didn't know what she'd do or where she would go.

Lenore had to move in her cramped little space carefully, always being as silent and stealthy as fog creeping over the earth, lest the neighbors or new occupants of her parent's old house heard her. She only ever came and went when it was properly dark outside, sneaking out via a window in the attic and the large tree growing just outside.

As for Bitsy, Lenore never worried about her little companion; it was easy for him to disappear when necessary. He was sitting on a rafter when she came in and leapt down to greet her ecstatically. The little creature nuzzled her neck and wrapped his long bushy tail around it as he chattered happily.

"I'm glad to see you too," Lenore sighed. "That was a close one tonight. Glad I caught a break for once…"

Lenore's mind drifted back to the couple that had saved her from certain torture. They were certainly different, odd maybe, but they had been kind, and Lenore had not experienced real kindness in a long time. Oh well, it was done now. Lenore took just enough time to fill her stomach with some stale bread and dodgy-looking cheese before falling asleep to the sounds of a waking city.

✣

<u>*Ninth Year of the New Age, Second Day of the Earth*</u>
Official report submitted by Fifths Campbell and Ellis:

We were alerted and gave chase to a thief this evening. The thief was preying on citizens visiting the gardens. Cries from the latest victims—a Mister Malachite Nichols and Miss Temperance Hester—alerted us to the trouble just after a quarter past twelve as we patrolled our usual route. Mister Nichols reported a prized piece of Old World Jade as stolen. See the end of this report for a record of the eyewitnesses' descriptions of the thief. As we began pursuit, the perpetrator made for the Rose quarter of the city. Visual contact was difficult to maintain through the alleys she took between the manors. She disappeared completely somewhere between the Chicory Lane and Anemone Green. We recommend working with local shopkeepers and residents to put up barriers and fences to block these types of escape paths.*

Eyewitness Description Report: Female, small, probably about fourteen years of age. Most likely a vagrant, judging by the clothing, which was black, made for a boy, and very shabby. Very dark eyes and long, dark hair. Light skin.

**We understand there were two other eyewitnesses, but they disappeared before we arrived, and neither Mister Nichols nor Miss Hester could name them or remember anything about them.*

~*~

To find out what happens next, you can purchase *Out of the Shadows* from anywhere that sells books. Available in ebook, print, and audio.

Enjoy More of the Broken Gears World

Out of the Shadows

Pride and Prejudice* meets HG Wells with a dash of *The Hunger Games

- The beginning of Lenore's trilogy
- Adventure | Light Romance | Some Fantasy Elements
- Chronology: followed by *Into the Fire* and then *Across the Ice*

Raven's Cry

A dark retelling of *Swan Lake*

- Standalone
- Dark Fantasy | No Romance | Fairytale Retelling
- Chronology: precedes all other Broken Gears books

Rook's Gambit

***Ocean's 11* style steampunk heist**

- Standalone
- Heist | Light Background Romance | No Fantasy Elements
- Chronology: precedes *Out of the Shadows*

Falcon's Favor

A queer, cozy mystery romance full of food, cravings, tea, and found family

- Standalone
- Cozy Mystery | Sweet Romance | No Fantasy Elements
- Chronology: follows the events of *Across the Ice*

Death Cults and Taxes

For those who want more from the Broken Gears world

- Assumes you've read Lenore's trilogy, but any spoilers are mentioned at the beginning of each story
- Chronology: stories take place during various points in history

ACKNOWLEDGEMENTS

This is hands down the most challenging book I have ever written! First off, a huge shout-out to my husband Mike, who sat down with me when I'd hit a plotting wall and talked with me until I was able to climb over that wall.

Thank you to Scout Underhill for providing Coal's break-in soundtrack. Sorry my house screamed at you.

Shannon Lee gets all credit for the term, "putpocketing."

Sally, thank you for saying things were utter sh!t when they were. That meant more than I can say during the worst week of my life.

To Rachel Oestreich of The Wallflower Editing, you are every bit the editor this book needed. Thru cuts and new chapters, you have been a vital part of making this book as awesome as it is.

High fives to all my Patreon patrons for their support: Jenn Dunigan, Zack Jones, Shannon Lee, Doug Peterson, Rebecca Williams, as well as Ace Torpedo, Nancy Schwarzkopf Jarmin, Diane, Rachel Ahrens, Daniel Seymour, Jeff Platt, Kerry Gisler, Jeff Zakrevsky, Arabels, Karen P, Nam Sohanta, Anke Wehner, Murky Master, and DJ Gray.

Thank you to my brilliant sister, Heather, who makes me sharper and is one of my favorite coworkers. Speaking of coworkers, thank you, Engineer Zack, for coworking with me so often after I lost my regular writing buddy. So much coffee, yet so many unexplored cafes in Nashville.

My late father deserves recognition for the title of chapter thirteen. He raised me right, on lots and lots of Pink Floyd music. Feel free, dear reader, to sing along if that song's in your head now.

And thank you to my mom for setting up my dad's old desk so I could work there during my visits. You're totally right; he'd love that one of my books got made in his old space. Thank you as well for going on that cruise with me and being patient while I took notes for research. And thanks to all the crew on that trip who took such great care of us.

Dear reader, thank you for taking a chance on this book. Book people are without a doubt the best people! And thank you to anyone I forgot. I take notes for these, but I forget sometimes. Thank you, everyone.

ABOUT THE AUTHOR

Dana Fraedrich is a three-time Kirkus Star recipient, dog lover, self-professed geek, and author of the steampunk fantasy series Broken Gears, which includes the Amazon bestseller, *Out of the Shadows*. Dana's books are full of secrets and colorful characters that examine the many shades of grey that paint the world. When she isn't busy writing or attending conventions and book festivals, she can be found co-hosting the podcast *Steam-Powered Movies*, playing D&D and video games, and exploring new interests.

Even from a young age, she enjoyed writing down the stories that she imagined in her mind. Born and raised in Virginia, she earned her BFA from Roanoke College and is now carving out her own happily ever after in Nashville, TN with her husband. Dana is always writing; more books are on the way!

If you enjoyed reading this book, please leave a review. Even it's just one line, that really helps authors.

⚙ Find Dana online at www.wordsbydana.com and sign up for her VIP Newsletter, where you can read new short stories as they're released and keep up with her adventures

⚙ Facebook: https://www.facebook.com/wordsbydana/

⚙ @danafraedrich on Bluesky, Threads, and Instagram

⚙ Follow Dana on Goodreads, BookBub, or her Amazon Author page

⚙ Or you can get goodies and support her on Patreon - https://www.patreon.com/wordsbydana - Thanks!